Each
watched a
emptied the second magazine, he pulled a loose round from his shirt pocket, laid it on the magazine follower, and closed the bolt. Letting the rifle rest on a large limb, he slid the safety on and replaced the spent magazine with a fresh one. He didn't bother to look at the color coded bullet tips as he reloaded; he knew they would all kill. He slid the fresh magazine in his pocket and returned the weapon to his shoulder, looking for more men willing to die. His breathing was slow and easy, one breath about every seven or eight seconds. The crosshairs of the scope never wavered after they locked on a man almost a mile away. One shot, one kill. Even with the recoil-reducing features of the custom rifle, his right shoulder started to ache after the second clip. *I'm going to have to get some more modifications made in this thing when I get home,* he thought, squeezing off another round and ejecting the case to hear it fall through the branches below.

The Long Way Home

by
Ray Davies

Commonwealth
Publications

A Commonwealth Publications Paperback
THE LONG WAY HOME

*This edition published 1995
by Commonwealth Publications
9764 - 45th Avenue
Edmonton, AB, CANADA T6E 5C5
All rights reserved
Copyright © 1994*

ISBN: 1-896329-20-9

No part of this book may be reproduced or utilized in any form or by any means, electronic or mechanical, including photocopying, recording, or by any information storage and retrieval system, without permission in writing from the publisher.

Printed in Canada

*Cover Illustration by:
Scott Taylor*

To Linda, Melissa & Marty
and
For those who must take
The Long Way Home

Prologue

The direct hits by the North Vietnamese mortars imploded and collapsed the command bunker seconds after the helicopter carrying Lieutenant Frank Wilson, Sergeant Don James, and the body of Sergeant Stacy Marshall lifted off into the rain filled clouds. *Well that takes care of the last of the Americans,* Vinh Ngu thought, running toward a breach in the back defensive wall. *It would be nice if my next assignment is an air-conditioned headquarters building. This is too dangerous.*
The air was acrid with the smell of smokeless powder, the burning village, and burning flesh. The packed clay embankment was slick with mud, blood, and tissue juices. Vinh slipped and slid as he attempted to scramble through the breached earth and bamboo wall. Ngu's hand touched a large chunk of fatty flesh, all that was left of the hapless defender of that firing position. He looked at the grease, blood, and fat globules sticking to his hand and tried to wipe it on his pants while he scurried through the wire and sharpened spikes and into the cover of the underbrush.

Mi Ling watched the chopper disappear into the clouds before she returned to the front wall. "Don't worry about your man," the man, about ten years older than her eighteen years, said gently. "You will both live to be together again." The tiny woman didn't answer as she carefully picked her targets and fired her .30 caliber carbine with deadly accuracy, each round felling one of the enemy the way she was taught by the American Special Forces team.

The gun and mortar fire dwindled to a few random shots while the NVA pulled back, leaving their dead and wounded. Mi Ling noticed the smell for the first time, like a slaughterhouse in the summertime. Falling to her knees, she started to retch and then cry, the mud felt cool to her forehead as it touched the ground. She felt a comforting hand on her shoulder. Turning, she looked into the confident, compassionate face of the man beside her. "You will both live long," he said, kneeling and holding her close. "You both have many battles to fight before you sleep with Buddha."

Chapter One

Da Nang, Vietnam - 1992

"Morning, Colonel Ngu," said the fat general with beady, pig eyes, sitting behind the massive, carved, mahogany desk. The battle flag of The Peoples Republic of Vietnam was draped on the office wall behind him. "I have just been informed that a group of Americans will be coming, sometime in the next few weeks, to look for their war dead. They want to use Cam An as a base of operations. We can't have that, can we? We have two choices, suspend operations... or kill them all."

Colonel Vinh Ngu was aware it was not going to be a normal day when General Xuan addressed him by rank and not by his first name. The colonel pulled himself up to his full height of five feet four inches and stood ramrod straight, staring directly ahead. *Just what I need*, he thought. *This idiot has a problem and he's going to want me to solve it for him. I'm the one who should be sitting behind that desk, not him. One of these days... who knows, maybe the Americans will be of use to me.*

"Relax, Vinh. Sit down," the general continued. "Have a cigarette." He removed a Kool from an ivory box on the desk and lit it with a Zippo. "We can't afford to have this operation compromised. You and I have too many years invested in those plantations to quit or to tolerate any interference of any kind."

The colonel sat silent for a moment, formulating a plan while he glanced at the wall covered with captured French and American weapons. "We can tell everyone the area is high in outlaw activity, and we do not have the manpower to protect this group. Then, when they are killed, we're not responsible. I believe our Mr. Howard can be considered an outlaw by any definition," Ngu said, twisting his mouth into an evil grin.

"Good idea, Vinh. We still have a few weeks before we have to make it so." The general smiled, stroking all four of his chins with his pudgy fingers. *Vinh is smart*, he thought. *Perhaps too smart. I just wonder how much longer he's going to be content with being number two around here. When this is over I'll have to see about removing him.*

Steamboat Iowa USA 1992

Frank Wilson laid *The Sunday News* on the kitchen table and stepped to the counter to refill his ancient coffee cup. He looked at the company motto, 'Chromatography is a gas', stenciled on the side of the mug. *So some of our junior senators have just returned from a fact-finding tour of Vietnam,* he thought, returning to the national news section. *Those hypocritical bastards hid behind their deferments and demonstrated against the war while the rest of us were getting our asses shot off and sleeping in the mud. Now they expect us to believe their junkets to South East Asia, with stops in vacation spots along the way, are all for the MIAs. Bullshit. They're just having a good time and trying to buy votes. It'll be interesting to see what happens when something is really done about the MIA issue.* He left the paper lying open on the table and walked down the hall to the first room on the right; the room contained his biochemical library and the family computer system. Pushing the master switch on the surge suppresser, he turned to the door and paused. He looked carefully at the pictures of himself and his men in Vietnam, thirty years ago. *I'm not too bad off for a man of fifty-seven,* he thought. *Hell, I'm only twenty pounds heavier, and I can still see my toes. Not as much hair, though.* His eyes were drawn to the picture of his wife, dressed in ill-fitting fatigues and holding a .30 caliber carbine. *My God, she's even more beautiful now than she was then,* he thought as he continued down the hall and stepped through the door of the bedroom she had converted into her private space and office. Frank watched Mi Ling sit at her drafting table, every inch covered with large maps of Vietnam that were in turn covered with a large sheet of acetate marked with gridlines and circles. Stacks of folders, notes, and data books were piled on every shelf and scattered around the room. Frank recognized French, English, Vietnamese and Cambodian language labels. From where he stood, it appeared the small woman was literally up to her neck in paperwork.

"Well this is the last of the data I have on the grid area around the village," she said, looking up. "I've come up with thirty-seven probable sites where we can find the remains of missing GIs within a fifty kilometer radius of Cam An. This isn't counting Doc and Sparks – we know where they are. I don't believe I can get any more data for this area. Some of these files go back to the first American occupation, before you were there. So what do you think? Mi Ling used her finger to trace from point to point on her grease pencil-marked map. "Any point with four or less separate sightings is in black. The ones with five or more are in red. I consider the red to be one hundred percent correct. We will find something, some evidence that a body was there."

"Great, now all we have to do is to find someone to do the digging," he mumbled under his breath.

"Let me log these into the computer and get them off to Frank Junior. Why not call the Bosworth kids and we'll go out for breakfast?"

"Good idea, it's been a couple of months since I got Dr. and Mrs. Bosworth out of bed. These young kids think they can stay in bed and screw their weekends away."

"Well, dear, we must still be young. We do a pretty good job of it ourselves at times," Mi Ling replied with a smile.

Frank returned to the kitchen, poured another cup of strong, black coffee and picked up the phone. *I'll bet Tom's already been up for hours working on something, probably another grant proposal. Somehow I don't think he's as happy being a professor as he thought. I need to get him out away from everyone and everything and have a talk with him. It would be good if he's asleep.* Frank grinned, thinking of Mi Ling's remark. He dialed. "Good morning, Karen. I hope I didn't pull you away from anything important."

"No, Frank, I could only wish. Do you want to speak to Tom?"

"No, no, not at all. Mi Ling just finished her MIA charts and we decided to invite you two out for brunch. How about The Old Mill, say ten o'clock?"

"Sounds good, that is if I can pull Tom away from that damned grant he's been working on."

"Tell him he's taking academic life too seriously and needs to mellow out a bit. We'll see you later. Bye now."

Tom Bosworth sat in front of his home computer with a cigarette burning down in the ashtray on his left and a cup of cold coffee on his right. *No. Jesus, how the hell can I write this so it makes sense to a committee?* he thought, taking a drag from his cigarette before crushing out the butt with a vengeance. His left hand moved back to the key-board while his right hand picked up the coffee cup. *Damn, cold coffee. Let's try this: Wilson and Bosworth (1991) have shown the growth and repair of cultured neuronal cells in vitro using techniques developed by Wilson, et. al. (1985). Yeah, now you're on the right track.* As Tom typed the thought, he vaguely heard Karen's conversation on the bedroom phone.

"Bye, Frank," he heard Karen reply as she hung up. "That was Frank, he's buying us brunch," she called as she walked out of the bedroom and into Tom's study.

"Karen, I can't. I've got to get this grant done and there's still a lot to do on it." Tom gently removed his wife's arms from around his neck.

"Frank said you're taking this too seriously. You've still got more than three months before the deadline, so there's plenty of time. Besides, it's not like you really need this." *Damn it, Tom, wake up and see that I need you. Not the department of biochemistry or the university. Me,* Karen thought, taking a step back from the desk chair.

"It's the principal of the thing. I'm the newest faculty member, and we're still living on grants Frank and I got years ago," he mumbled as his eyes went back to the legal pad of notes beside the keyboard.

"Bullshit. You know as well as I do there are some people in the department who have never had a grant. It's just that damned ego of yours." Karen raised her voice in frustration while she reached around his neck and hit the 'escape/save' keys on the computer. "You, my dear, are finished for now," she said as her left hand moved to the power switch. "Come on, time to get cleaned up and dressed."

"I thought your nagging was bad before we got married, but it's worse now," Tom said, moving the chair away from the computer table and standing, then wrapping his arms around her tiny waist and pulling her close. He could feel his warm erection starting as her chest meets his and he started to playfully nibble on the side of her neck.

"You should have thought of that earlier. Now hit the shower while I try to find something to wear."

"Did Frank give any reason for this, or is he getting tired of Mi Ling's cooking?" Tom called from the bathroom.

"Mi Ling just finished the MIA data she's been working on, and Frank thought it's time to celebrate," Karen called back. "I almost think we should swap mates. You're always working, and so is Mi Ling. You two would never miss each other."

"What were you saying, dear? I couldn't hear you with the shower on."

"Nothing, just nothing," she answered, wiping a tear from her cheek. "I was wondering what you were going to wear."

"Well that's off," Mi Ling said, shutting down the computer and turning back to her husband. "I wonder how long it will take Frank Jr. to process it."

"When you consider all the stuff the State Department has him doing and all the stuff you've sent him the past few weeks, I think he's doing a fine job," Frank answered as he started rubbing the back of his wife's neck. "So, what's the next step?" he asked, stepping back and letting Mi Ling stand.

"Don said we have a good program, and he's sure he can get us financial backing."

"Money's not the entire problem. We'll need someone to do the work, and more than that, we've got to get permission to do the digging. I'll be damned if you're going without me. I'll never let you get away from me again. Being separated from you for twenty-five years was long enough."

Mi Ling passed Frank and started walking toward the kitchen door. She stopped for a second and looked back. "Well, it's still something we have to think about. We need someone we can trust and who's young enough to get the job done."

"You mean someone like Tom," Frank replied as he

picked up the car keys from the table. "I'm not sure Karen would let him go, but I think he's getting fed up with academic life now that he's in it for real and not just doing research with me. Come on, we'll be late," he said as they walked out of their small, ranch-style house and to their older model Ford station wagon.

Tom walked dripping from the bathroom, toweling himself as he moved into the bedroom. "Karen, you know I need to get my own grant based on my own merits. I'm beginning to wonder why I ever let Frank talk me into getting a Ph.D. and joining the faculty in the first place. Hell, I'm not even doing my own work anymore. The research assistants know more about what's going on in the lab than I do. I'm turning into a damned politician like most of the rest of the department. I don't have time to do anything else." He picked up the shirt Karen had laid out for him.

"Now you've hit the nail on the head," Karen replied loudly enough to get his attention, looking directly into Tom's dark brown eyes. "I don't know whether you understand what this is doing to our relationship or not. It stinks. Tom, I want to have kids but I want them to have a father who has time for them. Sometimes we find time to make love on the weekends, but only sometimes. It's almost like I have to make an appointment to touch you. Damn it, Tom, we've been married less than two years and already you have to find the time to fit me in. What happened to the excitement we used to have in our lives?" Karen wiped away a tear and followed Tom out the front door to the car sitting in the driveway.

"I don't know. Maybe I got lost somewhere along the way. We'll make the magic again, I promise. Trust me," Tom said. They drove the rest of the way across town in a tense silence. *What the hell am I trying to prove and who am I trying to prove it to? Christ, I'm one of the luckiest men in the world. I've got a wife who loves me. We've got all the money we need. Everything's paid for. Bosworth, you'd better get your shit together or you're going to lose everything.*

Tom pulled the black Dodge Shadow into the parking lot of The Old Mill restaurant and shut off the engine. "There's Frank and Mi Ling. We'll continue this conversation later," he said, breaking the silence that had lasted most of the ten-minute drive across town.

"Tom, I really do still love you. You know that," Karen murmured as she opened the car door and stepped into the warm, mid-west sun.

"Yeah, I know. I love you too. You've given me a lot of things to think about. Let's go," he answered as they walked across the parking lot by the river to meet their best friends.

"Hi, kids. You two don't look too happy. Fighting again?" Frank asked, holding the door of the restaurant open and allowing the women to enter first.

"No, Frank, just discussing. We're alright," Tom interjected before the subject could get started. "Now that you've finished your MIA data, when do you think Frank Jr. will finish the map work?"

They walked into the restaurant foyer and were greeted by a young hostess. "Four for our buffet? This way please." She led them to a window table in the smoking section, overlooking the river. "Go ahead and help yourselves and I'll be back with your coffee in a moment. Enjoy your meal," she said, turning away while the four took their seats.

"I hope Frank Junior can finish the data soon so we can pass it to Don James, then he can try to get us some government help." Mi Ling passed the ashtray to Frank and Tom when she saw Tom reach for his shirt pocket. "If we can get everything done in the next six months we can get in there before the next rainy season in the mountains." *If we go into the coastal plains we'll have monsoons. It's going to be hot, humid and wet, even without the rains. I wonder if I can ever get used to that kind of world again? Frank's not in bad shape, but even still, he's not young like he was when he was there thirty years ago. Tom can make it, he's only about forty. But if he goes, what will happen to Karen and their marriage? I would hate to see anything happen to them.*

"It's Mi Ling's system, so she has to go, and I'm not going to let her go without me." Frank handed Tom his old, battered Zippo lighter without thinking. "So, it looks like you're going to be running the lab for a few months."

"Like hell I am. That was part of what Karen and I were arguing about on the way over. I'm already putting in too much time. Karen was kind enough to kick me in the head with that thought this morning." *Man, did she kick me in the head. I'm going to get my priorities straight, and home and family are going to have to come first.*

"Good job, Karen, you're doing what my first wife didn't – talking about it," Frank said, taking a sip of his coffee.

"Good morning, folks, everything okay?" the waitress asked while she refilled the cups, putting an end to the conversation.

"Let's get something to eat and we'll wait until we get back to the table to continue this," Mi Ling said quietly as she stood and started walking toward the long buffet table. Mi Ling and Karen started along one side of the buffet while Frank and Tom moved down the other, picking and choosing from the breakfast and lunch entrees offered on the long steam table. Each filled a plate to a socially acceptable limit with a combination of the offerings and returned to the table.

"Now, let's see, where were we?" Frank said, returning to the conversation left moments before. "Oh yes, options. As I see it, you have some choices. Continue the way you are and get a divorce in a couple of years or less. Or you could make a choice between teaching and research. Third – and this one I think would be the best for you – is to tell the department to go to hell and get a job in industry. You two don't need the hassles of academic life, and the money is better on the outside. Yes, yes I know, the money doesn't make any difference."

"Tom has an open offer to work for my father in the Kodak R and D labs," Karen said in passing as she spread grape jelly on her toasted English muffin.

"You know I can't work for your dad. Herb's a nice guy and all that, but if we worked together we'd probably kill each other. We're too much alike in too many ways."

Mi Ling looked silently across the table at Tom for a few seconds, as if trying to think of the correct words. "Tom, I've barely known you as long as Karen. I love you both greatly. But I think you have to make a choice between your work and your family. Having lost Frank during the war, I know the choice I would make."

"If we had kids they would call him 'Uncle Daddy'," Karen sarcastically remarked, her voice sounding cynical as her blue eyes stared coldly into Tom's.

"Okay, okay, I get the message. I'll see what I can do about the situation. Karen and I will continue this conversation later. Now, let's table this discussion," Tom said, trying to maintain his composure and put an end to the portion of conversation making him uncomfortable.

"I never really understood what Frank Jr. was doing with your data. Can you give me a better explanation than Tom has?" Karen asked, starting on a short stack of blueberry pancakes, finishing the question with a bite in her mouth.

"Well, with the data I've collected in years of interviews, Frank Jr. is plugging the coordinates into a program in his computer," Mi Ling explained. "Some of the maps go back to the French occupation of the fifties. He's putting all my data in and then processing it into a grid system that a satellite tracking system can use. So with luck, we will be within a few yards of where we want to be when we start."

"The problem, as I see it, will be getting governments to go along with the plan. Then, of course, there's always the money," Frank said, motioning to the waitress walking by with a full coffee pot.

"There are a lot of people who say they will donate, but will they? We don't know yet," the tiny Vietnamese woman replied, looking around the table.

"If you and Frank are going, I want to go too. I've got to keep you old folks out of trouble. What do you think dear?" Tom asked as he laid down his fork and picked up his coffee cup. *This could just be what I need to get me out of this rut. It seems like forever since I did anything besides research. I wonder what Karen thinks about this. Maybe if we could get the hell out of Iowa for a while we could see things differently.*

"I'm going too. It all sounds so exciting. Besides, I've heard Vietnam is a beautiful country," Karen added with the first hint of excitement in her voice that Tom had heard in months.

"Well, now there are four of us on this expedition. Not much, but at least it's a start. I'll call the good senator, Don James, when we get home. If anybody can grease some wheels, he can," Frank said, signaling for more coffee. "I have my doubts if even he can get everything done in time to go this year."

"We'll have to wait and see. After all, they've lain there this long, so a few more months won't make any difference to the dead," Mi Ling answered. "Now what do you two have planned for the rest of the day?"

"Well, I had planned to work on that grant proposal, but I think I've had my mind changed for me. Honey, what would you like to do the rest of the day?" Tom asked as he lit a cigarette and started to take a sip of his coffee. *In for a penny, in for a pound. I guess I can try to rebuild something that I didn't even realize I almost lost. To hell with the grant, Karen's more important. Bosworth, how could you be so blind?*

"Well, just spending the day together will be a start. From there, there's no telling what can happen," Karen looked into his brown eyes with the first hint of a smile he'd seen in a month. "Who knows, I might even make a little dessert like I used to."

"I don't have a problem with that. I'll even work off the extra calories."

"I'm not sure what the hell you two are talking about, but somehow I don't believe it has anything to do with food," Frank said with a grin over his coffee cup. "Tom, I see you turning out to be what I used to be. There are a hell of a lot of things more important than the lab, department, or even the university. A day like today is one of them," he added.

"Well, dear, do you have any idea how to waste the rest of the day?" Karen asked with a mischievous glint in her deep blue eyes.

"I think I can figure some way to get into trouble. That is your middle name this week, isn't it?" Tom replied with a lecherous grin.

The rest of the meal was filled with the general chit chat of everyday life. The subjects of work and university business were tabled for another time. Tom and

Karen stared at each other like lovesick adolescents. Mi Ling watched with her knowing, serene smile and Frank chuckled under his breath at his friends' antics.

"Hello," Carolynn James answered the phone in the family room of their modest Washington home.

"Hi, Carolynn. It's Frank Wilson. May I speak with the senator if he's around and not busy?"

"Sure, Frank, let me yell for him. How are your mom and dad doing? It's been at least a month or so since we talked to them," the senator's wife said, laying the Sunday paper on the oak and marble coffee table. Covering the mouthpiece, she called, "Don!"

"Fine, the last time I talked to them," Frank answered, hearing the click of another receiver. "Hi, Don. Look, I just got the last of Mom's data this morning on the area around Cam An. I'd like you to look it over, if you have time. Maybe some of this stuff will mean more to you than it does to me."

"Sure, son, what's the problem?" the senator from Texas answered in his long, slow drawl.

"I'll let you two talk now, Frank. Come on over when you get a chance. We miss you," Carolynn said, hanging up her extension.

"I'll do that Carolynn, thanks," Frank answered before he heard the click of her extension. "Well, I've got all these maps I've been using for reference and plotting, and some of the stuff doesn't jive. What I'd like for you to do is to look over the landmarks on the topographicals before I make the final drafts. I've got everything on acetate overlays, all supposedly brought to the same scale, and it still doesn't look right."

"I'm not sure how much help I'll be but I can at least look. Would you like to come over now?" the senator asked, picking up a pencil from the desk tray and tapping on the stack of papers covering his desk.

"That would be great. I can be there in about an hour, if it's no trouble."

"None at all. I'm just working on a speech to baffle my colleages with bullshit, and I'll be happy to have a break. We'll see you when you get here. So long, son." The senator hung up and called, "Carolynn, it looks like

Mi Ling has finished her work on the area around Cam An." *God it's hard to believe she's pinpointed bodies down to a few yards,* he thought as he walked toward the family room.

"What, dear? I can't hear you from in there," his wife replied.

Don James walked into the room where his wife was engrossed in the Sunday edition of *The Washington Post.* "I said that it's hard to believe that Mi Ling has finished her work on our old AO. If we can get someone over there, we can at least bring back Doc and Sparks."

"What's an AO, dear?" she asked, looking over her half-frame reading glasses.

"Area of operations. That's where Frank and I were when we got our ticket into your heart. Frank Jr. is having some trouble fitting the different maps together, so he's on his way over to pick my brains on what I remember about the place."

"Do you think it's wise to dredge old memories up again? You know how hard it is on you when you talk about old times with Frank and Mi Ling. The nightmares return and it's weeks before you get a good night's sleep," she replied, her concern showing when she remembered the uncounted times she'd been awakened by her husband's screams.

"Memories of battles won and lost are one thing, but now I have a chance to do something good with what I can remember," the tall Texas senator replied in a forceful voice, his eyes holding the faraway look of remembrance.

"Thank God we've got some Valium around, I'm sure you're going to need it," Carolynn answered, laying the paper aside and turning her full attention to her husband.

"I'm not sure which hits me first when I remember – the sights or the smells. You know, when I visit the Vietnamese shrimpers down in Galveston it's almost like being in country again. God, if I could only be that young and as full of piss and vinegar again," he said with a hint of sadness.

"What are you going to do when Frank Jr. and Mi Ling get this stuff together?"

The senator hesitated before answering, thinking of all the political steps which must be taken before the expedition could even get into the planning stage. "Well first I'm going to try and get permission for a search team to go in. The real problem will be in getting an official American group into Vietnam, and also in getting the right people to go." The senator's eyes changed from a blank stare to a shiny glint as he started to smile.

"Donald Henry James, if you're thinking what I think you're thinking..." Carolynn stood and took a step toward her husband, "forget it. There is no way in hell I'm going to let you go running off to Viet-fucking-Nam. You try that and I'll not only divorce you but I'll tie you up and throw you in the basement with the rest of your God damned relics. You're not the twenty-five-year-old kid that was there thirty years ago." Carolynn's anger was apparent by the swear words she seldom used, and the fact she had barely taken a breath during her tirade. She ran her fingers through her short salt-and-pepper hair and breathed a heavy sigh. "Don't even think about it."

"Whoa, hold your horses, little lady. I know I'm not going. There's no way Doc Martin would let me go after that last heart attack. This old warhorse has been put out to pasture, and he knows it. Besides, there's plenty of work that needs to be done on the political side of things for me to feel like I've gotten something accomplished. But even still..." he let his voice trail off, thinking of what might have been if he were younger or in better shape.

"I'm glad you're finally getting it through that thick Texas skull of yours. Even if it wasn't for the heart attack I'm still not sure I'd let you go. You're too old for this stuff. That leg of yours keeps you from doing very much. Not only that, you haven't gotten any exercise in years. You're out of shape. There's no way in the world you can come back at your age."

"Look, damn it, Carolynn! I'm well aware of my physical limitations. For Christ sake, stop rubbing my nose in them."

"I'm sorry, Don. I didn't mean it that way. Come on, let's see what we can throw together for lunch."

Don couldn't maintain his anger for more than a few seconds whenever she turned on the charm that attracted him when he was a patient in the navy hospital in 1963. "Yeah, what do we have that we can throw together this morning?" he asked as she reached for his hand and led him into the kitchen.

Chapter Two

The old dream weaver sat on his heels staring into the night fire, his pipe smoke rising as tendrils toward the bright stars. The half moon cast its cold, pale, ghostly light on the village of Cam An. The inhabitants were many hours asleep. The old man watched faces form in the flickering flames. "They will come," he said in a whisper to the pyre, "but will they be in time. We have waited so long." He closed his eyes and rested his chin on his chest. Without opening them, he dropped another handful of wet herbs on the glowing coals. Inhaling deeply, he visualized the smoke as it rose and was carried to the east by the gentle night breezes.

"Do you think Tom and Karen will make it through this trouble?" Mi Ling asked as they left the restaurant.

"I think so, if we can get Tom to slack off and act like someone who has a life apart from academics. They have a chance. If he keeps going, she's going to divorce him, sure as hell."

"They're nice kids, I would hate to see that happen. Karen is almost like a daughter, and you treat Tom like you do our son."

"Tom was like a son for a lot of years until you came back into my life. If he doesn't change fast I know what's going to happen. I went through it. I don't want that for these kids."

"What would have happened if you had still been married when I found you?"

"I honestly don't know. I know I never stopped loving you. I'm glad it worked out like it did," Frank replied, opening the car door.

"Do you think Tom is serious about wanting to go to Vietnam?"

"Oh, he's serious all right, and I think it might be the best for him." Frank got into the driver's seat and started the engine. "He's the kind of man who has to be in on the doing. Now he's more or less just forced to watch. You should have seen him when we were out to destroy Timmonds and Olson! Once he started, he never let go. I think when he came back to school he was just looking for the time and the place to rest. I'm surprised we've kept him this long. I think he'd be back with the CIA if it weren't for Karen."

Mi Ling looked across the front seat and asked, "What about you, dear? Do you also miss the action?"

"I believe I do. When we went after the corruption in the department I think I was the most alive I've been since I was in the army. Hell yes, I miss it. I'm looking forward to going back and maybe remembering what it's like to be young again. I've been hiding behind a desk and in a lab too long."

"Dear, I hate to bring this up, but you aren't a young man like you were when we first met, although you aren't dead yet either. It just takes time for you to recover!" Mi Ling smiled as she reached over and caressed the inside of Frank's thigh.

"Even after all these years you still know how to make my day."

"Look, I promise not to put in more than ten hours a day, five days a week for the rest of the semester," Tom said, looking into the deep blue eyes of his wife.

"Yeah, that sounds nice, but will you do it?" Karen replied, her voice louder than normal.

"With this trip to Vietnam coming up I've got to get into at least halfway decent physical condition."

"You're not just doing this for Mi Ling and Frank, are you? There's a lot more to it than that, isn't there?"

"Yeah, there is. What would you think of living somewhere around Washington?" Tom replied, turning onto the block where they lived.

"You're thinking about going back to work with the CIA, aren't you?"

"Yeah, I guess I am, if you'll go along with the move."

"Janet and the guys are there, but there are a lot of people here in the Midwest I'd miss too. I'll do what ever it takes to keep us together. Do you have any idea what you'd be doing if you went to work for them?" Karen asked, the sound of defeat in her voice.

"The last time I talked to the Sergeant Major he wanted me to do some research on some toxins that have been showing up in the Middle East. When you develop anti-toxins, you have to develop new toxins. It's a vicious circle," Tom replied, watching out for the kids playing on the sidewalk.

"Do you think that kind of work would make you happy?"

"Well, I was happy working there part-time before. We can come back to academic life if things don't work out," he answered, gently tapping the brakes to slow the car even more.

"Tell you what, we'll think about it. Talk to Frank and Ted Mason; see what they think of the idea. I'd be happy just to have a husband who keeps normal hours. Well, if we're going to Vietnam we have to get into shape. Let's start you running today. Come on, let me give you a taste of what you're going to be missing for a while," Karen opened the car door and sprinted toward the house.

What the hell are you going to do now? Tom thought. *You know how she feels about the company. Bosworth, you've got a problem. That damned ego of yours. Which do you want to keep, the family or the attitude?* He unfastened the seatbelt and climbed slowly out of the car, watching Karen bound onto the front steps. She stopped and smiled in his direction. *You know what you have to do,* he thought as he ran the few yards to the house and his waiting wife.

"Here's the problem I'm running into, Don," young Frank Wilson said, unrolling a stack of maps. "I'm using maps from the fifties, sixties and seventies, and trying to line everything up on the same grid system and match them up to the landforms and landscapes. Now I'm finding that some of these are as far as two or three miles off from one map to the next," he said pointing to the marks and overlays.

"So what do you think I can do to help?" senator Don James gruffly replied. "Okay, let me see the earliest one first." Frank unrolled the large photograph and Don used books to hold down the edges. "Carolynn," he called, "where's your needle point magnifier? We need to borrow it for awhile. How long do you think it'll take you to put this together once you get the map problems figured out?"

"I've already got everything entered into the computer. Now all I have to do is get the maps to jive so the points mean something. After I have a correction for the maps, I would guess maybe, oh, another twenty-four hours of computer time."

"Any idea what your mom and dad's plans for this operation are?" the senator asked. *They had damned well better include me. Back to where it all started. It's not just refighting the war. It's something more.* He looked from the maps to the photographs.

"I think Mom was planning on leading the search team. After all, it's her work, and I know dad wouldn't let her go without him," the Amerasian man of about thirty answered.

"Don," Carolynn called from the kitchen, "Frank and Mi Ling are on the phone."

"Well, now we get to find out what their plans are. You want to get on one of the other phones?" Don picked up the phone, "Hi, Frank, Mi Ling. Congratulations on getting the data done."

"How did you know it was finished? I just sent it out this morning," Mi Ling answered sounding surprised.

"Frank Jr. is over here. He needed some help with some of–" there was a click of an extension being picked up, "the landmarks."

"Hi, Mom, Dad. I tried to call earlier."

"Hi, son," Frank replied, "we just went out for Sunday breakfast. What's the problem with the landmarks?"

Frank Jr. explained some of the problems he had been running into, and then summarized, "The printed maps are all a bit different from the aerial maps, plus the fact the aerial mapping was done on a pattern that doesn't mesh with anything else. I need to get everything together before I can remake my system."

"He seems to think that it'll only take about another twenty-four hours of computer time. Where do you want to go after that?" the senator asked.

"I know it's not likely, but I would like to lead a recovery team in over there before the rains start," Mi Ling replied, "or the monsoons hit the lowlands."

"Do you have any idea how much trouble and work it'll be just to get permission for a search expedition, much less get outfitted and over there?"

"Yes, Don, we are aware of this. Even if we can't get it put together for this year we can have plenty of planning and supply time for next year," Mi Ling answered defensively.

"Those bodies have been there this long, another year won't make any difference," Frank replied. "Even if we only bring back Doc and Sparks, the trip will have been worthwhile."

He would have to bring them up, Don thought. "Perhaps so, but we still have the problem of getting the permission to go. Not only from their government, but from ours as well. You know how much they like civilians getting into these things."

"Remember those ambushes we used to pull off? Hell, we buried most of them. We should be able to find some of those spots and dig 'em up. Tell the Vietnamese government we'll make 'em a trade. Their bodies for ours," Frank replied, offering the thought of more enticement.

As if I could ever forget the shit we went through. "Look, I said I'd help out but I'm not God. I'll see what I can do. I'm not sure it'll work, but I'll toss it out. The Vietnamese government is trying to get back in our good graces, so who knows? I'll try to talk to their UN ambassador sometime this week," Don replied with a trace of frustration in his voice.

"Do you think it would help if we could put a written proposal in front of them? You know, outlining everything from how we planned the search pattern to how we're going to handle the bodies?" Mi Ling asked, sounding a bit more confident now that there was more of an agreement from Don.

"Mom and I could get together on a computer link and turn out something in a day or so." Frank Jr. added.

"I'll give it a shot. That's all I can say. Put together a proposal and put down that you have up to a half million in financial backing for the whole thing. I know where you can get at least that much. What do you have as far as a party size goes?"

"We haven't really gotten that far. Now it's just Mi

Ling, me, Tom and Karen. I would guess we can get by with ten or twelve of us. I hope we can get some help from the Vietnamese government as far as transportation and labor goes," Frank answered.

"I'll see what I can do in the next few days. Get that proposal written up as soon as you can and I'll take it from there. I'm not going to make any promises about how good I'll do. I'll get off and let you talk to Frank Jr. for a while. I'll call you when I know something. Later." Don James hung up the extension thinking, *Jesus, why am I being such an asshole about this? Could it be I'm jealous that I can't go? Christ, I wish I were young again. I'm going to have to call back and apologize. Why the hell did I let that damned woman upset me like that? Fuck it, time for a drink. God, if I could just get one night's sleep without the dreams.*

"Son, what's wrong with Don? I've never heard him like this before," Frank asked, knowing the senator wasn't listening.

"I don't know, Dad, he was upset when I got over here. He's always been eager to help out before. I think we have this problem ironed out now, I'll call you tonight."

"Sure, son, we'll talk later. Bye now."

"Frank, if you talk to your folks before I do apologize for me. Are there any more suggestions I can make for the maps or any other way I can help out?" the senator asked when young Frank returned to the paneled office.

"This should about do it for now, Don. Thanks a lot. I want to get back to the computer. I'll let you know what I come up with in a couple of days. If nothing else, Mom and I will have that proposal ready to go and I can drop it off at your office."

"No problem, son. Hey look, I'm sorry I was such an asshole. I've had a lot of things on my mind recently. I'll try to get hold of the ambassador tomorrow. If there's anything else I can do, just give me a call."

"Sure, Don, no problem," Frank Jr. replied as he started rolling the collection of maps, charts and photographs, securing them with large rubber bands. "One of us will get hold of the other in the next day or so."

"Don't forget, you've got a budget of at least a half mil when we get this off the ground. I have a solid commitment for at least that much."

"We'll do that, Don. Carolynn, I'm out of here," Frank called when he reached the foyer.

"Stay and have some lunch with us, it won't take but a second to throw something together. You know you're more than welcome," the senator's wife replied, walking out of the family room.

"No thanks. I'm this close, so I want to get back at it. I'll take a rain check."

"We'll hold you to it. Be careful going home." Don walked Frank out of the white ranch-style house toward his late model Chevrolet. "We'll see how fast we can get moving on this. Who knows, we might make it this year." *The sooner the better. I've got to go with them. I've got to find what I left behind. I'm going. Come hell or high water, I'm going.* He watched the red Chevrolet drive off. Don James turned back to the house, walking a bit straighter than he had moments before.

Chapter Three

The morning stillness was broken by the sound of rifle fire coming from inside the jungle. The villagers stopped their after breakfast chores and started forming a ragged line toward the wooded trail leading north, away from the collection of huts. The only people who were allowed to remain in Cam An were those too young or too old to work in the fields. The three white mercenaries were dressed in black cotton work clothes and looked a lot like the peasants they forced into a single file. With shouts and curses they marched the people up the trail and away from home.

The old dream weaver watched as the guards enforced their orders with rifle butts while they hurried the villagers up the path towards a long day's work in the hot Southeast Asian sun. *I wonder if these men would be so brash if they knew they were going to die,* he thought as he watched the last of his people disappear into the bush. *Buddha, protect them and give them strength,* he silently prayed, continuing to clean the bowls and chopsticks from the morning meal.

"Yes, good morning, Miss, this is Senator James. Could I please speak with the ambassador?" Don asked as he leaned back in his chair and propped one leg on his office desk.

"One moment please, sir. I will see if he is available. Could I please inquire what this is in reference to?" the cultured female voice came over the phone line.

"Yes, a possible expedition into Vietnam in search of MIA remains – both ours and his," Don answered.

"Thank you, sir. Will you hold a moment, please?"

Don James sat in his senate office with his good leg propped on the corner of his polished walnut desk. He patiently listened to the on hold music while sipping his third cup of decaffeinated coffee. Christ, he thought, nothing but decaffeinated coffee, no fat or cholesterol meals, no alcohol and no cigars. Hell, Carolynn's even afraid to have sex with me anymore because she's afraid it'll kill me. Shit, I may as well be dead. I wonder about that secretary down in Kennedy's office.

"Yes, I'm still holding, thank you. Good morning, Mr. Ambassador. I'm calling on the behalf of some friends, and also because I believe I have some information which may be helpful to all parties concerned. Yes. My friends have a plan to find and recover the remains of soldiers on both sides of our past conflict. Yes sir, I believe their plan is sound. No, I'm contacting you before I attempt to take it through the channels. I believe if we work something out between us first it would not only help the project's chances, but it could be a feather in our political caps. We can always improve our political standings, no matter what government we work for. Of course, I would be happy to help you and your government work to re-establish diplomatic relations. No, I believe this expedition will most probably be strictly civilian. I can't promise, but that's the way these folks are looking at it now. Yes, I can understand why your people would be concerned to have American military people there. I believe we both can understand how the military from either side could foul things up. I have already asked them for a written proposal and it should be ready later this week. Yes, I understand you can't give any answer now, I was just thinking, if you and I can get the ball rolling before we get our governments involved, we have a better chance of getting something accomplished. Yes, thank you. Friday? I believe I can make that. I'll fly up in the morning and we'll meet for lunch. I should have their proposal in hand by then. Thank you, Mr. Ambassador, I looked forward to seeing you Friday for lunch. Good bye," he said, hanging up the phone. *Well, so much for that. Now we'll just have to wait and see what he can do.* The senator pushed the button on the intercom. "Cindy, could you get hold of Frank Wilson over at State, and Frank or Mi Ling Wilson in Steamboat, Iowa? The numbers are in your file. Oh yeah, get me some real coffee, this decaffeinated stuff tastes like shit."

"Right away, sir," came the reply.

"Yes, Harriet?" Frank addressed the dour-looking secretary who walked into the lecture room.

"Dr. Wilson there is a call for you from Washington,

some senator's office. I thought it might be important so I came after you instead of taking a message."

"Thanks, I'll be right there." Frank turned back to the class and continued, "Okay class, we only have about another ten minutes, so for tomorrow I want you all to know how to find what we put together and what our final compound is. I'll see you tomorrow; class dismissed."

Frank and the older woman walked down the hall of the chemistry building, past the display cases filled with raw elements and the everyday finished products they became. Neither noticed the DNA display falling apart; sections of the chain lay on the bottom of the case. For the most part, no one noticed the displays, except for how the large oak cases made the halls more congested.

"Here you go, Dr. Wilson, you can take it in here," the tall grey-haired woman announced, pointing to an office door. "I'll transfer the call."

"Thank you." Frank walked into the empty teacher's assistant office. The phone rang a few seconds after he sat at the old, battered, wooden desk. "Frank Wilson."

"Just one moment, sir, I'll transfer you to Senator James." Frank could hear the hint of anger in the secretary's voice from her time spent holding.

"Hello, Frank," the Texas drawl of the senator came over the line. "First, let me apologize for yesterday, and second, I just got off the phone to the Vietnamese ambassador."

"No problem, Don. We just figured you were a bit out of sorts or had something more important on your mind."

"Well, that's part of it," the senator answered. "No, hell, I'll tell you the truth. Carolynn and I had a fight. I've had a couple of small heart attacks and she's afraid I might do something stupid. Like running off to Vietnam with you all. Well, she's right. Count me in."

"I don't know, Don. What does your doctor have to say about it?" Frank asked, letting the words sink in while he looked at the various posters tacked to the walls.

"Oh, I'll get clearance from the doc, but hell, the way I've been living the past six months I might as well be dead. Carolynn's cut me off from all the good things in life, even real coffee," Don replied, his voice dropping to a conspiratorial level.

"Well, I hate to say it's your funeral, but I guess I'm glad to have you aboard."

"Thanks, buddy. I told the ambassador that we would have a proposal in front of him by the end of the week. I'm flying up to New York to have lunch with him on Friday. Can Mi Ling and Frank have it here before then? He wants to feel out some members of his government before we proceed."

"I think we can have it in your hands by mid-week," Frank answered.

"When they write it up, have them say that to the best of their knowledge the group will be civilians, and that they plan to hire locals to do a lot of the work for American cash. The way their economy is, they'll eat that shit up."

"That was pretty much what we were thinking of saying. I think it would be a good idea to have someone who knows something about graves registration along, though."

"Good idea. I put a bug in the guy's brain that a trip like this could help the relations between his country and ours. Who knows? It may help. If nothing else, the trip would help us both politically." Don let the last sentence slip accidentally.

"Is that the only reason you want to go? Politics?"

"Hell no, but you can't say it won't help. I just want to feel alive one more time before I die. Hell, I'm dead already. All I have to do is to lay down. Look, buddy, I've got to run. I'm going down to the dining room to have a good steak and bread with real butter. You'll probably hear Carolynn yell all the way out there when she hears about it. But that's the way it is. I'll see the doc this week. Don't worry, I'll have clearance."

"Okay, Don, we'll get this end of things done and I'll talk to you in a day or so." Frank hung up and left the office. *Well, may as well go up and see if Tom's in his office; let him in on the news.* Frank ran up the three flights of stairs to the office area, only to be gasping for air on the third landing.

"Hi, Frank, come on in. Throw that shit off the chair

and sit down. Coffee?" Tom asked, reaching for the pot on the only uncluttered spot on the desk. "Sounds like you're a little out of breath."

"Yeah, I tried to run up the steps. Didn't work," Frank answered between gasps. "I just talked with Don and he wants to go. The problem is, he's got a bum ticker."

"Have him clear it with a doc. If the doc thinks he can make it, good, it's not your problem anymore. I know, he's a friend and you'd hate to have him kill himself, but if you don't let him go it could damage your friendship. You're damned if you do and damned if you don't." Tom handed Frank a cup of strong, black coffee. "Thanks for yesterday. Not only did I enjoy myself for the first time in a long time, I got laid. I gave Azwan the grant stuff I've been working on; he needs it more than I do anyway." Tom shuffles some files together and tossed them onto a half-empty shelf in the grey metal bookcase.

"'Yeah, he does. If he doesn't get promoted this year he's out of here. I must say you're looking better than you usually do. I'm not sure whether it's our good advice or Karen screwing your brains out."

"Combination of both," Tom answered, refilling his cup. "So what else did Don have to say?"

"Just that the ambassador and he talked and that they want a written proposal when Don goes up to see him Friday. You weren't bullshitting when you said you wanted to go with us, were you?" Frank asked, watching the expression on Tom's face.

"You know better than that. I'd never bullshit about something as important as this. What do you think of inviting Miles and Hayes along?" Tom replied in a hopeful tone.

"It'd be great to have those two crazies along, for the comic relief if nothing else. Think their women will let them go, even if Ted Mason said yes?"

"Hell, Mi Ling and Karen are going. You know Janet will go. I don't know about Liz; she keeps a tight rein on Miles. I found out how out of shape I was last night. Karen and I hit the five-mile trail and she ran away from me. I pooped out at two miles. Have you thought much about your shape, besides running up the stairs?" Tom asked while he moved copies of reprints off the typewriter shelf of the desk so he could open the drawer.

"Not really, but I'm going to have to. I'm too old for this shit. I need something like basic training where I can go in like this and come out in shape."

"You're out of your ever-lovin' mind! There's no way in hell we could survive something like that again. But I think you've got the right idea. Let me call Ted Mason and pick his brains. We've got to clear Miles and Hayes through him anyway." Tom set his coffee cup down and started rummaging through his top left desk drawer for his address book.

"How long has it been since you talked to any of these people? The way you've been lately, you've barely spoken to me," Frank said in a mildly accusing tone.

"I talked to Hayes last month when Karen called Janet, and remember, we were out there five months ago. The Sergeant Major wanted me to find a way to stabilize the cyanide in tapioca so it wouldn't decay when heated." Tom continued digging in the drawer until he found the battered, black book buried amid the junk. "I'm not sure who owes who anymore. It's been a good relationship the last ten or twelve years. I don't care for the company, but I love the Sergeant Major," Tom said, thumbing through the pages.

"We sure would have had a hard time getting that stuff on Timmonds and Olson if it hadn't been for him and the guys. Even with good behavior, Timmonds won't get out for another five years. I wonder if Jimmy Baker has converted him to 'The Power Of God' and the PTL yet," Frank said with a wry smile, making a mental picture of the possibilities.

"That would be the closest thing to hell I could think of; sharing a cell with those two for the next few years." Tom laughed as he started dialing the main CIA switchboard at Langley, Virginia. "Yes, I'd like to speak to Ted Mason, please. Yes I do. He's in weapons, chemicals and biologics. Yes, Tom Bosworth. Thank you. She's transferring the call now. Interesting music they have on the line - Mozart's Requiem Mass. Good afternoon, Sergeant Major. Are you starting or stopping revolutions in the third world today?" Tom asked with a grin as he reached over, switched on the speaker phone and motioned for

Frank to shut the door.

The booming voice of the Sergeant Major came over the speaker. "Monday? I always start a war on Monday, loot the treasury on Thursday, and I'm home for supper on Friday night. You still owe me sucker. Now, what can I do for you?"

"Bullshit, you owe me! I did the last job for you. Besides, I donated five dollars to your favorite charity when you moved up to that Caddy. Did you ever get your official certificate from the NAALCP?"

"So you're the asshole who did that! I've been blaming everyone around here for it. It wouldn't be so bad but I hear from them every week now. So what do you need this time?"

"I've got Frank Wilson in here. He and Mi Ling have finished their plan to locate some of our MIAs in Vietnam. First, we'd like to invite Miles and Hayes along, and second, we're wondering if you have some kind of training camp for a bunch of old farts like us."

"We do have a camp for agents who need to get back into shape, and we have courses for new field agents. Anybody got any physical problems?" the disembodied voice asked.

"Just Senator James. He's got a wooden leg and a bum ticker. The rest of us have just been sitting on our asses too long," Frank answered.

"I think we might be able to swing it if we listed everyone as contract employees. We'll get a medical on the senator. I think we can get everyone else through with just a checkup. When do you plan to start?"

"Well, Don is working on securing permission by going through some back doors first. There's still about six months until the monsoon season, and we'd like to get in there before then if possible. If we don't make it this time, it's next year," Frank answered with a short pause before the last sentence.

"Top, let us get together and figure out some logistics and get back to you on that. What about Miles and Hayes?" Tom asked.

"Hell, they might as well go. I can't get any work out of them anyway. Miles is always on the golf course and Hayes is still trying to screw his brains out. Sometimes

I wonder why I ever let Miles marry my daughter."

"Yeah, I know how it is. They were both lazy bastards way back when, but you got to love them anyway," Tom replied, remembering the long association with his two army buddies.

"Frank, you probably know better than anyone else around there what kind of shape you old folks are in. Do you think all of you could handle an intensive training course?"

"Well, Mi Ling, Karen and I can, but I'm afraid it'd kill Tom," Frank replied, grinning across the desk at Tom.

"Okay. Get things together and let me know when. I'll send out the applications and contracts this afternoon."

"Thanks, Top. We'll let you know when we get all our shit in one sack."

"Sounds good, Tom. Just don't send me a blivett," the voice said before the click of the phone hanging up.

"What say we get together over at our house tonight and set up a conference call to everyone?" Tom said, replacing the telephone receiver in its cradle.

"After we get it together we can hit the boss up for a leave of absence. Do you think Biology will let Karen get away?" Frank asked. He took a swallow of warm coffee and grimaced.

"If they don't, they'll just have to find someone else to do the job. It'll be the same way if Isaacs doesn't let me have the time off," Tom replied, crushing out his cigarette into the overflowing ashtray.

"Jesus, Tom, it looks like we really got to you yesterday. I'm glad we convinced you of what's important. Come on, let's get the hell out of here and have some lunch."

"Let's drop by the lab for a bit and see how the kids are doing. Then let's get the hell away from this place. I think I'm going to take the rest of the day off. I didn't sleep very well last night, I was dreaming about two women plowing a rice paddy with a water buffalo – damned strange."

"Yeah it is. Go home and take a nap. I wish I could. I've been having some strange dreams recently too," Frank said as they stood. Tom reached for his jacket on the back of the chair and followed Frank into the hall. "Go ahead down to the lab. I'll meet you there. Stop off and see if Karen can join us and I'll call Mi Ling."

"How about we go to The Terminal for pizza?" Karen asked as they walked into the bright sun from inside the Basic Sciences Building.

"The rest of you can have pizza," Tom answered with a trace of regret, "I'm on a diet of rabbit food."

"Good boy, Tom. What are you going to do with the rest of the afternoon?" Frank asked as they crossed the grass in front of the English Building.

"Join a health club. Karen's got me working on my legs and cardiovascular system, so I guess I may as well get the rest of the body in shape as well. I need all the help I can get."

They entered the bar and took the last booth under the mural of Main Street, circa 1930. The waitress appeared within seconds with their silverware, water and menus. "Can I get your usual drinks while you looked at the menu, or do you already know what you want?"

"We'll have a medium deep-dish special," Karen replied, "and I'll have a 7 Up."

"I'll have a draw of Bud," Frank added.

"Kim, I'll have the garden salad with blue cheese dressing and an iced tea. I'm on a diet," Tom answered without thinking.

"Oh, Dr. Bosworth, you don't look like you need to be on a diet, but if you say so," her voice trailed off. "I'll be right back with your drinks," the slim, light brown-haired waitress said as she walked away, followed by the eyes of both men.

"Alright, you two, get your minds out of the gutter and your eyes back in your heads. You're both married. Besides, she's too young," Karen remarked, watching her companions. "How come she's so familiar with you, Tom?"

"She's in one of my classes and in lust with me like you used to be." Tom changed the subject to the upcoming trip. "We talked to the Sergeant Major this morning. I know how much you hate the CIA, but he's sending contracts so we can go through one of their training courses, plus the fact I'm sure we can put to use some of the intelligence files they have. He said he'd cut Hayes and Miles loose to go with us. Do you want to talk to Janet and Liz about going too?"

"Liz is pregnant. If Bill goes, you know Janet will. She still can't keep her hands off him. What's he got that you don't?"

"Nothing," Tom quickly answered. "Ted has a training class for agents we can use to get into shape," Tom continued. "Some of us need it more than others, but it will do us all good."

"Here's your drinks, folks." The young woman handed the drinks around. "Your order will be ready in another five minutes. Dr. Bosworth, can you give me an idea on what I should spend the most time studying for your mid-term? I'm a journalism major, not a science major."

"You'll need to know the basic elements and what reactions you get if you mix them together. There will be a number of questions on bonding and structure, and a couple of basic molar concentration questions. I'm not only looking for what you know, but also for your thinking processes for the correct answers," Tom answered, watching the waitress start to frown.

"Sounds rough. Maybe I should just drop out and audit the rest of the semester." Her grey-green eyes seemed to loose their luster and her smile disappeared when she heard of what the upcoming test entailed.

"Kim, I'll tell you what he told me a few years ago. Go home and study your ass off. I've seen the test, and if you know the basics, you'll do alright," Karen said with a comforting smile.

"Thanks, I'll follow your advice. I'll be back with your lunch as soon as I can," she said, dashing off to take care of another table in her section.

Frank removed a cigarette and his aging Zippo from his shirt pocket. "I just wonder what they have for a training course for people like Don, Mi Ling and me. I have my doubts it would be the same as for you kids."

"I guess we'll have to wait and see. Karen, you need to tell the folks in Biology about this now, even though we don't know when we'll be going. Frank and I need to see Isaacs too."

"If Don can swing it for this season, we'll have to leave shortly after midterms. If we tell everyone now it'll make their lives easier," Frank said, lighting a Winston.

"Frank and I should have no trouble taking a leave of absence. They'll bitch, but they'll almost have to let us go. If they give you any problems, just give them their two weeks notice."

"Tom, you know I have to be working. We went over that before we got married," Karen replied with a frown, looking from man to man.

"Honey, you will be working as this thing gets put together. Mi Ling is going to have a lot of last minute things to do. The success or failure falls on her, and I'm sure she's going to need help rechecking everything."

"That's right Karen, the reason she's not having lunch with us today is that she's breaking her butt on a written proposal outlining every step we plan to make." Frank was interrupted by Kim and the arrival of their meals.

"Here you go, a medium special and a salad? Dr. Bosworth, you're going to need more than that salad, so I brought you a plate too," Kim said, the smile and the sparkle returning to her grey-green eyes as she set the plates on the table. "Here, let me refill these drinks for you," she added, taking the glasses without asking.

"Let me talk to Mi Ling and see if she wants the help. If she does, I'll just give them my notice. What we're doing really doesn't interest me anyway. This is good. Sean must be in the kitchen today."

How do I want to say this? Mi Ling thought, staring at the computer screen. *Okay, let's try this. To the governments of The Republic of Vietnam and The United States. Re: Recovery of war dead remains from the area surrounding Cam An, Vietnam. Dear sirs... No, that's not right.* She backspaced. *Honorable Gentlemen... That's better. For the past fifteen years, my son and I have been collecting data and interviews of combat... No, not right. Erase combat... incidents where it is known the bodies of some combatants were forced to be abandoned. Good. Through these interviews and records, we have been able to map, with reasonable certainty, the locations of the resting places of these heroes. The war is now long over, and it is up to historians to decide which side was right or wrong, or who won, or who fought with the most honor. The families of these brave soldiers must still fight the war and deal with its effects until their loved ones can be recovered and laid to rest in their own religious – no, not right – rest as their religion dictates. The families' war will end, and the heroes will be with their gods as it should be.*

Enclosed, please examine a simplified version of how we arrived at our data and conclusions, and how we wish to undertake the search and recovery of the officers and men who died fighting for what they believed was right. Sincerely... Well, that looks good in English. I'll have to have Frank check it, Mi Ling thought. *Now, let's see how it looks in Vietnamese.* She moved away from the computer and picked up a pen and paper, pausing for a moment while she switched her thinking from English to her native language.

"Ah, Senator James, I'm glad to meet you at last. I've heard much about you since we talked. Please come in." The short Vietnamese ambassador welcomed Don and young Frank Wilson into his UN office.

"Thank you, Mr. Ambassador. This is Frank Wilson, one of the people who put this project together. He has a sound plan for recovering our war dead. I think he can better explain it than I."

"Of course. Please, make yourself comfortable. I see you are half Vietnamese, do you remember our language?"

"I'm sorry, sir, no. I did as a child, but I'm afraid I've forgotten most of it. I'm sure I'd remember if I had to but, I'm an American now," Frank replied, making his point. "If I may use your desk to roll out these charts, I believe I can better explain our plans."

"Yes, of course. I have been making inquiries of my government since we talked on Monday, Senator. They believe it would be a fine way to show our people can work together again. Proceed Mr. Wilson, please." The ambassador stood aside and let Frank Jr. begin.

"Thank you sir," Frank started, unrolling the charts and maps on the desk top. "As you can see, this is the area from Da Nang through what used to be called the DMZ. I have more detailed maps, but I thought this would give the best overview. My mother and I have interviewed literally thousands of our countrymen about combat engagements they witnessed or were a part of during the war. With this overlay – could you hold that corner down please? – we have marked red for US soldiers and yellow for Vietnamese who had to be left behind by their comrades for one reason or another. We consider these red and yellow marks almost one hundred percent accurate, since each of these sightings was confirmed by five separate people. The blue and white marks are those sites that we are less certain of. As you can see by this large map, there are a number of places to search. We have decided to concentrate our search in the area around Cam An. This was my mother's village and also where my father and Senator James were stationed. If the search around Cam An is successful, then we can turn the data and maps over to others for future searches, when we find out if our plan is sound. We have marked in the area approximately a hundred and fifty remains of the dead on both sides. We know of a cemetery where villagers buried a number of Viet Cong soldiers in a mass grave," Frank explained, pointing out various marks with the aid of the tip of his ball-point pen.

"Yes, yes, this is all very interesting. As I have said, many people in my government support this idea as a way to help the relationship between our two countries. You have brought your written proposal?"

Don James opened his briefcase and pulled out the file Frank and Mi Ling had prepared. He removed the paper clamp and handed it to the ambassador as Frank started rolling up the charts and maps.

"You understand that since the war my country has become one of the poorest countries in the world. My government is in dire need of hard currency, so it has been proposed that we charge you two hundred and fifty thousand dollars for our assistance in this operation. Wait, please, before you say anything. The proposal is also that we pay you one thousand dollars' equivalent in our currency for each of our war dead you recover. This way we have a currency exchange to show the world bank there are people who believe in us. Agreed, this is a small amount as far as nations go, but it is a start for us."

"If we can clear this with the people who are financing this, how long do you believe it would take to get clearance from your people?" the senator asked.

"I believe with what you and Mr. Wilson have shown me today, and your proposal, I would say we can get everything cleared and your visas approved within a very few weeks." The ambassador opened his desk drawer and pulled out a sheaf of papers. "I have taken the liberty of drafting our own proposal as far as the costs and the services my country can provide. It also explains what we wish to do as to the currency exchange situation. I'm sure we still have a lot of negotiating to do, but I believe we are on the right track. Please looked these over and let your financiers decide. Now, shall we go to lunch? There is a very good Vietnamese restaurant just a few blocks away."

"Dr. Boatman, could I speak to you for a moment please?" Karen asked, looking up as her boss walked by the lab door.

"It'll have to wait. I just thought of an idea for a new set of experiments and I have to make some notes before I forget them. Come to my office at three thirty and I'll see if I can fit you in," the tall, thin biologist dismissed Karen without a thought.

"Well it looks like another hare-brained scheme that won't work. Haven't you learned the only time you can talk to 'his royal high-ass' is when he wants to talk to you?" Scott, the other research assistant in the biology lab, said. "If I didn't have a wife and kids, I'd have told him to fuck off when I started three years ago. I'm still not sure putting up with his shit is worth it."

"Well, I wouldn't be here if I could work in biochem. You know how this place is about having relatives working in the same department. What causes Boatman to be such an asshole anyway?" Karen asked as she continued staring through the microscope.

"I've got three possible reasons: One, he was born that way; two, he went to Stanford; three, he has no sex life. I mean, after all, could you see yourself going to bed with someone like him?" Scott poured some pink nutrient fluid into the plastic petri dishes. "Okay, looks like that son-of-a-bitch has been messing around in here again without telling us. He probably opened the incubator again when these cultures were just starting to grow and upset the gas and temperature balance. Wait and see, it's going to be our fault. He can never do anything wrong. Boatman has gotten to be such a perfect asshole I'll bet he doesn't even have hemorrhoids. So you're really going to quit? You going to tell anyone who counts why?"

"I don't know, I think I'll just play it by ear and see how he acts when I tell him. If he's half-way civil about it, I'll just let it slide. If he's his normal self I'll probably make some noise. Well, that's the last of them. Now if he'll leave them alone, these cultures might recover, but I doubt it." Karen slid the last petri dish from the stage of the microscope and carefully passed it to her associate. She stood and bent backward, flexing her stiff back before picking up the finished culture trays and returning them to the incubator. "Did you notice the temperature setting on this thing? That idiot raised it up to a hundred and five! No wonder the cells are dying. Time to go give him my two weeks. We'll have to wait and see how that goes." Karen closed the carbon dioxide incubator and reset the temperature. "I'll see you when it's over." She walked out of the lab and down the pale green hallway toward the faculty office area.

"Dr. Boatman," Karen said as she walked into the immaculately clean office, "I wanted to tell you I'm planning to leave and to give you my two weeks notice."

"No. You can't quit. I need you here. I won't let you get away with leaving. If you do, I'll make sure you never work for this or any other university again. Your husband may be the golden boy of the biochemistry department. That doesn't mean anything in this department or anywhere else. Say goodbye to academic work, ever again," he replied loudly in a deep, growling, threatening voice.

"Look, you pompous asshole, I was being nice and giving you notice so you could try and find a replacement. I quit," Karen replied, her voice rising with her anger. "Go ahead, don't give me a recommendation, or even give me a bad one. I don't care. You may have your lips so far up our chairman's ass that he doesn't see how you teach, do research, and treat your staff. I think the administration would like to know. That's who I'm talking to next." Karen's voice was loud enough to be heard down the hall at the secretaries office.

"You can't talk to me that way. I won't stand for it," Bruce Boatman replied, almost shouting in rage.

"Yes I can, and will. You're just another spoiled brat who's gotten an education. Your mother should have spanked you and taught you to respect others. People with an attitude like yours don't deserve to be in any society, much less a university one," Karen yelled back at the man sitting behind the clean, freshly polished desk. Turning slowly, she walked out the open office door. As she walked down the hall she was greeted by the smiles and silent clapping motions of the half dozen secretaries who shared the main office. Scott leaned against the wall beside the office, waiting until she walked up. Karen could feel her former boss's eyes bore into her back.

"Karen, wait a second," Scott said as she stopped. "I think you might be interested in this." He walked up to Boatman's office and looked him in the eye, their faces less than a foot apart. "Fuck you, Boatman. I quit too." Scott turned on his heel and returned to where Karen stood smiling. "Come on, Karen, let's get the hell away from here. I'll buy you a beer," he said as they left through the fire-door.

Chapter Four

The morning sun was starting to burn off the ground fog that covered the field of six-inch-tall opium poppy plants. The captive peasants formed a line at the ends of the long rows nearest the river. Milling around like cattle, they waited for the guards to order them to work.

"Get those irrigation ditches open," one white guard yelled in broken Vietnamese. "Make sure all the rows have adequate water before you start pulling grass." The other guards positioned themselves around the growing field, making sure nothing was done which could harm their profitable crop. One guard watched the women as they used their feet to drive the water wheel. His thoughts turned to sex while he watched the two young woman putting one foot in front of the other, rolling the teak log. Their narrow hips swayed with each step, and their legs were exposed almost to the hip. He licked his lips in anticipation of what would be his when the work day was over.

"I talked with Miles and Hayes this afternoon," Tom said, handing beers to the people gathered in his living room. "Hayes is up for going if Janet can come. I told him yes. Miles wants to sit this one out. He doesn't want to leave a pregnant wife. I can understand his point."

"I've still got my worries about Don. I don't know how bad his heart is, and that artificial leg of his is going to put a damper on things," Frank commented as he sat in the green, overstuffed armchair sipping his beer.

"How long did the operator say it would take to get this together?" Karen asked, walking to the tape deck and pushing the play button. They listened to the soft sounds of Vivaldi beginning to fill the room.

"She said she'd make the final connection at seven-thirty. Tell Frank and Mi Ling about what happened with Boatman today," Tom encouraged his wife with a smile.

"Boatman? He's that asshole who went to Stanford, isn't he?" Frank asked. "That guy is about the biggest laughing stock of any faculty member of any of the science departments. The grape vine has it that he'll be out of a job at the end of the semester. What'd you do, tell him off?"

"Among other things! I quit on the spot, so did Scott. It's going to be interesting to see how he goes about explaining my comments to the department. All the office doors were open and the secretaries were standing around listening to the fireworks. Did you know Tom's the golden boy of biochem? That's what Boatman called him," Karen said with a grin at her husband as she crossed the room and sat on his lap.

The telephone rang as Tom started to reply. "Hello, yes operator, thank you. Frank, want to grab the kitchen extension? Mi Ling, you and Karen can get on the speaker phone in the office. Hayes, old buddy, glad you could join us. Hang on, let's get everyone hooked up."

There was another click on the line, followed by the Texas drawl of Don James. "Hello, Don, you're number two. Let's wait for Ted Mason," Frank said before the senator could say any more.

"Mason," was the next answer to the clicking on the line.

"Hello Top, looks like you're the last of us, so why don't we get this show on the road?" Tom was heard to say over the line.

"Don, you've got the latest news from the ambassador. What's he have to say?" Frank asked.

"Unofficially, it's a go. He believes he can have official word within a couple of weeks. We should be able to make it this year. There is a small problem. They want a quarter of a mil up front for their services. Our bankers might balk, but I doubt it. The people behind the money want us to take one of their people along. Since they're putting up the cash, I guess that's their right."

"Don, it's Mi Ling. Who's financing this? You told us we had a half million to work with but you didn't say where it came from."

"I'm sorry, I'm not supposed to say anything. Let's just say these people aren't claiming a tax deduction or keeping receipts," the senator replied.

"Okay, so we have to assume the money is laundered. What the hell, it's going for a good cause," Frank replied to Don's last comment.

"Senator, are you sure you want to go along with this bunch?" the voice of Ted Mason asked. "From what I hear you're not in the best of health, and that leg of yours could be a hindrance."

"I can still hunt all day back in Texas, and if I can get away from this rat race, I think the rest of my health problems will improve. Don't worry, Ted, I'll have medical clearance before we start. Speaking of training what have you got for us?"

"You folks aren't going to like this. I've got a Marine Gunnery Sergeant out of Force Recon. From what I've seen of his 201 file, he's a real son of a bitch. He started out in Nam and has been in every action since. I'm not sure I'd want him working on me, but you folks are the ones who want to get into shape."

"You don't have to go, senator, you can back out and no one would blame you," commented the voice of Bill Hayes.

"Not on your life, boy. Just remember what they say about age and treachery. I was an NCO too. I think I can handle him and me," Don James answered defensively.

"Janet," Karen asked, "what do you think of this trip?"

"If you're going, I'm going. I let you out of my sight once and you got messed up with this bunch. I've got to keep an eye on Bill, or at least keep a hand on something of his to keep him out of trouble," Janet answered in her musical laughing alto voice. "Who knows, we might have a real adventure."

"Okay, whenever you folks want to start I can get a place within a week. I need those contract forms and physicals back as soon as possible. I've got to cover my ass on this, you know," the boom of Ted Mason came over the lines. "I've picked up some intelligence data on the area of operations you folks are going into. I'll ship it out tomorrow. Hayes, I'll put a copy in your mailbox. Senator, I'll send yours over with the courier. It looked like you folks might be dropping into a hot LZ."

"Why so, Sergeant Major?" Frank asked with a new interest.

"Well, somebody's growing a lot of poppies up that way, and I don't think they're for Veterans day decorations. I've got an idea whoever it is wouldn't want anybody snooping around, even if it is for a good cause."

"But we'll have the permission of the government to be there," Karen piped in.

"Karen, the government can't or won't do anything. The dope dealers will do as they damned well please, just like here," Tom replied.

"Mr. Mason," Mi Ling started, "do you think we will be in danger if we go now?"

"I think you'll be in danger anytime you go, but that's up to you," Sergeant Major Mason answered.

"I have no idea what kind of person our backers will send, but I'm also going to try and get the Army to give us someone from graves registration, just so we can do this right," Don James added.

"After we get this other guy, I'll find out who he is for you," Ted Mason boomed. "I'll even know the type of underwear he likes."

"Nada, Top, this one stays strictly confidential unless he chooses to tell us," the senator replied.

"I'm not sure I like it, but I guess we can learn to live with it," Hayes announced after a few seconds of silence on the phone lines.

"Enough of this happy horse shit. Don, keep us informed on the negotiations and try to get us an undertaker. Top, we'll plan on starting in about thirty days if we can get the clearance from both governments. Anybody got a problem with that?" Frank took control of the conference call and became the de facto leader. "We'll just have to take care of any new problems as they come up. I think we've accomplished about all we set out to do with this call, and we all have something new to think about. If anyone wants out, now's the time to say so."

There was silence on the phone lines for a few seconds, followed by voices reaffirming their decision.

"Okay, I'll get a training schedule set up and you can start when we get the final word from Don. I'm sure glad I'm not going with you. I'm too old for this shit," the Sergeant Major said. "I'll talk to you folks later."

"I'll get back with you later. Time for me to give Carolynn the news and catch hell until it's over," Don said, hanging up.

"Karen, I'll talk to you later when it's not so expensive." Janet said before her and Hayes's line went dead.

Tom and Frank heard the click of the office phone as they hung up their extensions. Karen and Mi Ling returned to the living room while Frank grabbed four more cans of beer from the refrigerator and returned to the small living room.

"I knew we could do it," Mi Ling said as she displayed a winning smile. "I just wonder who is financing us and why they're being so secretive about it."

"Here," Frank handed the beer around, "I don't like working with someone we don't know anything about, but it doesn't look like we have much choice at this point."

"After we get into training, we'll learn something about him, and I think the Sergeant Major can check on him without Don finding out," Tom added, popping the ring on his can of PBR.

"That's awful sneaky, but I have to agree. The money's not important, but I hate this secret agent stuff someone's trying to pull on us. When we get this thing rolling, Frank and Mi Ling can work on Don, and the rest of us will see what we can get out of our mysterious stranger." Karen walked back across the room and turned on the tape deck that was turned off when the phone rang.

"We're going to have to be a unit on this thing or it's not going to work. This odd man shit is liable to foul up everything. One way or another, we'll know who he is before we leave the States," Frank replied, downing half his beer and covering his mouth to stifle a small belch.

Chapter Five

"Well, Colonel, the field looks good," the fat General said, looking out over the large field of ten-inch-high poppy plants. "I believe we can expect a good harvest this season if the Americans don't interfere. They are expected some time in late July or the first of August," he continued, his black, beady eyes staring down the rows. "Do you think you can convince them to stay away?" he asked, making the question sound more like a statement.

"I believe their government has been warned about the outlaw activity going on in this part of our country. If they insist on coming to restricted areas... well, they have been warned. I believe our security force can handle the problem." Colonel Vinh Ngu reached down and nicked a poppy stem with his thumbnail and watched the white sap collect into a droplet.

The General waited a moment before he squatted and collected the drop of opium latex on his fingertip. The sticky sap remained in a drop as he examined it closely before touching it to the tip of his tongue. "Very good. It will bring a good price on the Hong Kong market. Let nothing or no one get in the way of harvesting. Lives and fortunes depend on us." The General turned and walked toward the waiting helicopter, with Vinh close behind. "Where is the leader of this bunch of animals? I'd like to talk with him."

"He and his men have their camp at another field a few kilometers from here. We can be there in about five minutes," Vinh yelled over the sound of the helicopter as he slid the door closed on the converted Huey UH-1 helicopter. Tapping the pilot on the shoulder, he gave the thumbs up signal before he put on the radio headphones and issued further orders.

The stillness of the South Carolina pine forest was broken by the cries of crows and blue jays. An occasional squirrel jumped from a tree to the needle-carpeted floor, then ran to a more suitable place to play. The rising sun started to chase the morning shadows from the camp hidden deep in the pine woods.

"All right you lazy-assed civilians, time to get your butts out of the sack! You've got five minutes. Get out here or it's going to cost you a mile for every minute you're late! Come on, damn it! Move out," the tall dark-haired man wearing camouflage fatigues bellowed through a bullhorn.

Karen rolled over and saw Tom already almost half dressed. "Holy shit, what's that? I can't be out there in five minutes, it takes me at least a half hour to get going. I look terrible," she said as she slid out of bed with only a thin, nylon teddy covering her petite body.

"If that's what I think it is, you'd best forget about your hair and a shower and get a move on. I have an idea this is why Ted Mason doesn't envy us. Come on." Tom pulled on his tee shirt and sat on the side of the bed, tying his running shoes.

"Come on you people! What the hell do you think this is? Sunday in the suburbs? Now get the hell out here and stop wasting my day," the amplified voice boomed.

"I think we had best get out there now." Tom rolled off the hotel-style double bed. "Remember, we asked for this."

"All right, you people took long enough, the day's half gone already. From now on, I want you people out here and standing tall at 0500 every morning," the tall, dark man with an almost shaven head bellowed. "Now, on the line. Move it. You asked for me, I didn't ask for you. You got that, civilians?" he yelled, making the term sound like a dirty name. "My name is Gunnery Sergeant Sherlock, and God doesn't like me anymore. He caused me to be pulled out of my recon platoon for you people." Sherlock walked up and down the line, looking each person in the eyes. His back was ramrod straight, his shoulders were back and his head erect. "Since God doesn't like me, I don't like you. If you're religious people, you'd better give your hearts to your maker, because your asses are going to belong to me." The gunnery sergeant took a few steps backward so he could view the entire line without moving his head. He took a deep breath and slowly let it out with a heavy sigh. He closely examined the people on the white-painted line, then continued in a more normal tone. "I recognize you, senator, and I'd like to thank you for your help on the military appropriations the last few years." Then even quieter, "Now, I don't give a rat's ass who you were, you're mine now." His voice started at a whisper and continued to a roar. "Besides, I don't like politicians! You're always where you don't belong. Like now. The sooner you drop out, the sooner I can get back to my Marine Corps. They've given me six weeks to get you people in shape the best way I see fit, so let's get started with some calisthenics. Spread out, fingertip to fingertip. Come on, we've got a lot of things to do today. Okay, good, start arms straight out from your sides, now rotate forward," the unsmiling Marine yelled. "Reverse. You. I said reverse. Are you hard of hearing or something?" he yelled at Tom, who was a bit slower to shift directions than the others. "Stop. Now hold those arms straight out from the shoulders until I tell you to let them down. Before this week is out, you people are going to question my parentage. Let me assure you that my mother and father were married. And my mother does not sleep under the porch or chase cars. Okay, arms down. Relax a second. You know who I am, now who in the hell are you? Start at this end."

"Frank Wilson."

"Well, Frank Wilson, it looks like you and the senator have a long way to go." Sherlock shook his head, made a parade ground left face, took two steps and turned to face Mi Ling.

"Mi Ling Wilson."

"Mi Ling, you're Vietnamese, aren't you? I've got some good and some bad memories from that place. How old are you? Early forties?"

"Early fifties, Sergeant," Mi Ling replied with a smile.

He repeated the parade ground movements to the left and faced Janet. "Beautiful long red hair. Cut it off, braid it, or do something with it. You're not going to want it dangling. It'll get in your face, or worse, get caught in something. Now, what's your name?"

"Janet Morgan, and I'm with him," she answered, glancing at Hayes with the corners of her eyes.

"All right, Him. What the hell is the rest of your

name?" the big man snarled, stepping in front of Bill Hayes.

"Hayes, William B."

"I don't give a shit, Hayes, William B. And you just made my list. So you're an ex-GI, big deal! You're mine now." He turned and took two more steps to the left. "Well, well, what do we have here?" he said, moving in front of a tall woman with short brown hair; not beautiful in a cosmetic sense, but having sleek, powerful muscles and the intense look of a gazelle.

"Spec. four Kimberly J. Matthews, graves registration, Gunnery Sergeant," the woman called out, loud and strong. She only had to raise her eyes a little to return the cold, hard stare.

"Very good," Sherlock answered. "This is how I want you all to look this time tomorrow morning. Your clothing will be issued later on this morning. Next," he said, side stepping in front of Karen.

"Karen Bosworth."

"How tall are you Karen?"

"Five feet, Sergeant."

"Don't you think you're a bit small to be getting messed up with something like this?" Sherlock asked, trying to sound intimidating.

"Tri-nitro-toluene comes in small ampoules, Sergeant. I'll hold my own," Karen replied as she tilted her head back so she could see Sherlock's face.

"Tom Bosworth."

"Tom Bosworth, you don't look like you're in too bad a shape. Nothing that a little fresh air and exercise won't cure. Soon I'll see what kind of shape you really are in. All right, Senator, you're next."

"Don James."

"Don, you're in the same boat as everybody else. Don't expect any privileges." Gunnery Sergeant Sherlock stepped to the next person on the line, a sandy haired man of about thirty, smooth muscled, and about six inches shorter than Sherlock's six-foot-four-inch frame. "Name!"

"Sagretti, David Segretti."

"David Spaghetti, are you an ex-GI?"

"Not unless Brooklyn has an army."

"Well, I guess it's all in how you look at it. Alright, let's see how fast you people can move before breakfast. This trail is marked with white flags. When you come to a blue one, turn around and run back. This is a nice easy mile. My grandma can run this in nine minutes and she's eighty-five, I expect all of you to get back here in less than eight. Ready, take off." Sherlock hit the button on the stopwatch in his pocket. *Jesus Christ!* he walked over and sat on a log. *I just wonder if these old men can get through this without one of them having a heart attack.* He pulled a pack of cigarettes and a lighter from his pocket and lit up. He shook his head as he returned the cigarettes and pulled out the stopwatch. *Jesus, and me getting close to retirement. I should have told the old man to shove this assignment. Two tours of Nam was enough for any man.*

Gunnery Sergeant Sherlock just finished spreading the tobacco from his field-stripped cigarette into the pine needles when Kim and Janet broke into the clearing, followed closely by Karen and Mi Ling. He looked at his stopwatch and called out, "Six oh nine, six ten, six twelve and six fifteen. Nice job, ladies. Take a breather and cool down." He continued watching the trail for any sign of the men.

"Hi Kim. I'm Karen, this is Janet and this is Mi Ling." Karen made the introductions to the almost masculine-looking woman. "Sorry we didn't get to meet when they brought us in last night."

"No sweat, I'm sure we'll get to know each other before this is over," Kim replied in a husky voice. "By the way, what is this?" she asked, waving her hand, indicating the training camp.

"They thought we civilians should get into shape before we go to Vietnam." Janet replied in a casual manner.

"Vietnam? I agreed to go on temporary duty, but nobody said nothin' about fucking Vietnam," Kim replied in disbelief.

"Here comes Tom, Bill and the other guy," Mi Ling said as she stood for a better view. "I still don't see Frank or Don."

"Seven ten, seven fourteen, seven seventeen. Not

good enough. Do it again. You men should be ashamed of yourselves, letting the women run away from you like that. Now move your lazy asses," the gunnery sergeant bellowed as the three men broke from the trail.

"I get the idea this is not going to be a fun six weeks at camp," Karen said as she started walking and stretching.

"At times like this I'm glad I've been working out. I feel sorry for the guys, though, but not much. It couldn't happen to a nicer species," Janet replied with a wry grin.

"Do any of you know anything about David? I tried to talk to him on the way in, but the only thing I could find out is that he's from New York and he's thirty-two," Kim said as she followed Karen's lead and started stretching her long, lithe arms and legs .

"All we know is he's here to represent the financial backers for this trip. Beyond that, nothing," Mi Ling explained as she leaned against a pine tree. "We don't even know who the backers are. They've given a half million for this project, but only Don knows who they are, and he's not saying."

"What's the project, and why is graves registration involved? Nobody told me anything except that I was on TDY until further notice. I got that at Fort Dix last week and then I got dropped off here three days ago."

"We're going after the bodies of soldiers who never made it home. Here come Frank and Don, and they don't look well." Mi Ling continued, "Over the years I've been collecting information on unrecovered bodies and now we get to see if I was correct. I'll go through all the details later. I have an idea this sergeant would be very hard on us if he caught us talking like school girls." Mi Ling stood away from the tree and looked closely at Frank and Don as they staggered into the clearing. *Don is white as a sheet. I wonder if he's okay,* she thought.

"You old men jog in place until the young turks get back. Nine and a half minutes just ain't gonna cut it in this outfit," the drill sergeant bellowed.

Don and Frank were noticeably short of breath and sweating. It was evident to all that Don's artificial leg was causing pain, but he continued to run in place. No words escape his clenched teeth and drawn lips as his tee shirt dripped sweat, forming a circle of mud at his feet. Frank's breathing sounded more like whistling than exhaling, showing the years of lack of exercise and heavy smoking. Neither man showed any sign of quitting. Dropping, maybe, but not giving up.

"Frank and Don were in Vietnam in the early sixties. That's where they met Mi Ling. They both got wounded and sent home, and Mi Ling found them again almost thirty years later. Mi Ling and Frank were married in their village, but that was over when they thought the other was killed. There's a lot more to it than that, but we've got six weeks to talk," Karen added to the conversation, talking like a school girl gossiping in the restroom .

The tall woman from graves registration watched the two older men jogging in place and wondered if she would have to put her training to use within the next few minutes. "Yeah, that's nice, but I still don't know what I'm doing here. You folks are all friends, and Segretti and I are outsiders. I'm not sure where we're supposed to fit in. I know about taking care of fresh bodies, but the other kind I've only studied about."

"All right, Spaghetti, cool down. You old farts rest before you drop. Bosworth, Hayes, as of now you two are on my list, and you can bet your asses it's not for Christmas cards. I'll give you five minutes to catch your breath. Then we take a nice easy double time to the mess hall."

Frank and Don staggered to the nearest log and almost collapsed as the younger men walked around, stretching to help eliminate the lactic acid from their muscles.

The time was more like three minutes than five before Sherlock started yelling again. "We've got a few obstacles to go over, under, around and through before we get to the mess hall. By this time next week you should be able to make it from here to there in five minutes. This one time we're going to be taking it slow. Now follow me." They moved down the marked trail at an easy trot-for all but Don and Frank. The obstacles were mainly dodging and long jumping, with a few barriers they had to crawl under or over. They broke from the woods into another clearing with a smaller building like the barracks they left a short while ago, a long set of parallel bars along the side, painted the same shade of forest green as everything else. "There are twenty-five bars here. Today I just want you to make it across. The number will increase every other day, and next week there will be mud in this pit. The mess sergeant don't let nobody in his mess hall with muddy feet. Is that clear? I don't care how you make it across, as long as you make it. Who's first?"

"I'll go first. I have this in PT all the time," Kim volunteered and jumped to the bars.

"Okay, Karen, show us how it's supposed to be done," Sherlock said with a growl.

"I'm Kim, that's Karen," she pointed to the tiny blond, while hanging with one hand before starting across.

Kim started across, hanging straight down, grasping each bar as it came into reach. Tom whispered to Karen, "Swing your body, you should be able to skip a couple of bars with each reach. Now go for it."

"Nice job, Kim. Okay, Karen, you're next. Take off," the drill sergeant said, a bit softer than a yell.

Karen climbed the steps, jumped to the forth rung, and let her momentum swing her forward, allowing her to miss every other bar. As Karen reached the halfway point, Mi Ling followed in the same manner.

"That's using your head, Karen. I only said you had to make it across, I didn't say how." Sherlock almost broke a smile watching the women. The others followed, with Frank and Don each dropping off once then returning to the first bar and trying again. David Segretti brought up the rear, hanging straight down, grasping each bar with three fingers. "What the hell are you trying to prove now, Spaghetti?" Sherlock bellowed as David dropped at the end of the bars. "You're trying to be different, boy, and I don't like different people."

Once inside the mess hall, they picked up trays and proceeded through a buffet line filled with a breakfast of eggs, bacon, toast and fruit. The food was barely warm and didn't have the most appetizing appearance. "Just like we had in basic training," Hayes remarked, filling his coffee cup with a vile-looking, thick black liquid.

"Looks like we're going to be losing some weight."

A voice came from the kitchen area. "Shut up, eat up, get up, and get out. This is my house, and if you don't like the food you can damn well starve." The cook stepped around the corner. "You will scrape and rinse those trays on your way out. You will not come into my house with dirty boots. Most of all, you will not bitch about my food. Is that clear? The more you bitch the worse it gets." No one answered as they took seats at the large table. Gunnery Sergeant Sherlock took a small table for himself, and sat down and started to eat as the cook brought a cup of coffee and joined him. The group quietly ate breakfast, the only sounds being that of utensils on trays.

Sherlock spoke to the group for the first time since they entered the mess hall. "After you finish eating, we're going to get you people issued clothing and equipment. When you get that squared away, I'll take you for your physicals and shots. When the medics are finished with you, this afternoon you're on your own time. I don't think you're going to feel like doing much of anything after that." He lit a cigarette and continued, "Tomorrow is going to start the same as today. At 0500 I'm going to be standing in front of the billet and you all had damn well better be there."

"But we just had physicals, why do we need to have another one?" Janet asked, looking up from her tray.

"Because the people who run this place said so. The clothing they're going to issue us is something new the military wants us to try out. It's not supposed to rot as much as other uniforms, and it's supposed to be almost indestructible. It's mostly cotton, so it breathes, and every third thread is kevlar. Among other things, that makes it almost a body armour. That's what we're going to be wearing in country, so they want us to get used to it now."

Frank lit a cigarette and leaned back in his chair. "You've mentioned we and us a couple of times. Does that mean you're going with us?"

"That's the word I got. They want someone from active duty to go along and help you people out. My job is to get you into shape and working as a team, then we ship out."

"According to the restrictions they've placed on us, the only active duty person is supposed to be from graves registration. That's Kim," Mi Ling said in a worried voice as she looked at the man sitting apart from the group. "If you are going, that could destroy the whole mission."

"I've heard the rules. My enlistment is up before we ship out. I won't be a Marine when we leave. They mention no offensive weapons in the deal, so we're all going to be armed with handguns. Issue and practice starts the day after tomorrow. Tomorrow will be briefing and more conditioning. Now let's get the hell out of here and get busy. It's only a mile to supply-just an easy jog in the park," Sherlock said, walking over to the counter beside the back door, spraying water on his tray and setting it in the drain rack.

Chapter Six

The converted US helicopter landed about fifty feet from another large field of opium poppies. Vinh Ngu and General Xuan unstrapped their seatbelts as the guard slid the door open. Jumping down and bending low, they moved quickly out from under the spinning blades. Once out of the blade wash, they straightened and the General brushed dust and bits of debris from his clean, starched, tailored, olive drab uniform. Looking up, they watched three men leave the protective jungle undergrowth. The leader was a tall black man with the sleeves cut from his black, silk shirt. His arms had biceps as large around as the colonel's thighs. He carried an M-16 rifle with a casual, relaxed manner of long familiarity. The two men beside him were tall, well-muscled caucasians, each armed with an M-16, held in a ready position. The two white men stopped about ten paces from the two Viet officers. They stood back to back, watching the surrounding area for any possible signs of a threat. The black man continued his advance, stopping a couple of steps in front the officers, and saluted with a sloppy wave of his right hand toward his forehead.

"Comrade Howard, what do you have to report?" the General asked, returning the salute in much the same manner.

"De fields, dey be growin' fine and we ain't had no problem wid de locals yet. There be five o' six weeks afoe we kin start cuttin'. Everythin' be quiet and borin'. I've got ten dudes on each o' de ten fields, an de reports fum dem be 'bout the same as it be here; nothin' happenin'."

"Comrade, in about six weeks a group of American civilians may be arriving in Cam An. I don't want you to use any of the people from there in the harvesting. Do you understand?" the General ordered quietly but forcefully.

"Let me git mah main dude on dis. Bush, git yo' honkey ass up here," the black man yelled back to one of his bodyguards, "da general wants ya' t' leave Cam An alone."

Bush stepped away from his defensive position and closed the distance before replying, "Just where in the hell are we supposed to get the work force we need to harvest that field then?"

"Comrade, this group of Americans may be arriving in Cam An at harvest time. They seem to think they're going to retrieve the remains of war dead. I want that village left alone this year. Do you understand?" the General asked in perfect English. "The Americans have been warned about hostile activity in this part of the country, so if they come close to the fields, I want you to discourage them from persuing the matter any further. You men maintain security the best way you see fit, but try not to kill them." General Xuan and Colonel Ngu turned away without another word and returned to the waiting chopper, bending low beneath the spinning blades.

"Where de damn fuck we goin' t' git mo' suckas t' work de fields if we can't use Cam An?" Howard asked as they watched the helicopter lift off.

"If we try to shift workers from other fields we'll never get done. There's got to be some place we can come up with more people. If nothing else, we'll have to get another village and truck them in. Then we'd have to take care of 'em. I think we're fucked," the white man said as they watched the helicopter disappear over the tall trees.

The group rose and followed Sherlock outside. The gunnery sergeant waited next to the horizontal bars with his hands on his hips and his feet planted shoulder-width apart. "It's just a nice easy jog through the woods to supply. They will issue your field equipment and measure you for clothing. If anybody has to puke, do it off the trail so the rest of us don't have to step in it. When we get finished in supply, we'll jog back to the barracks and I'll give you some time to get your shit squared away. Let's move out!" Sherlock yelled as he took the lead across the clearing away from the mess hall.

The trail was like the others they'd seen meandering through the pine woods; covered with mulch and pine needles. The birds and small animals payed little attention to the humans running past in single file, disturbing the quiet. Gunny Sherlock set a slow, even, mile-eating pace, followed closely by Kim and Janet, with Frank and Don bringing up the rear. Within minutes they arrived at another building, the design and boring color as the barracks and the mess hall had been.

"Jesus, this place is getting boring already," Janet remarked as they stepped into the clearing. "They could at least use some color for the trim."

"Yeah," Kim replied, "the only thing not green around here is us. Speaking of green, here come the old men. I wonder if they'll live through this." The tall brunette made a mental list of the items she would need to embalm Frank or Don.

"Frank'll make it. I'm worried about Don. Tom, you and Bill are going to have to stop smoking. I can hear your breathing from here," Karen said as she looked at the younger two men.

"Damn, I've been at a desk too long," Tom gasped as they joined the two women and he tried to regain control of his breathing. "Dave, you haven't even broken a sweat, much less started breathing hard."

"Please call me David. I notice the women aren't hurting either. You two are just going to have to work harder. Here come the others." Frank and Don ran into the clearing with Mi Ling running beside them giving encouragement. "I really think these old men should drop out before they kill themselves. Nothing is worth what they're going through."

"Give them a couple of weeks to get used to this, I think they'll surprise you. They're both tough old buzzards," Tom replied as the group assembled beside the building.

"So nice you all decided to get here," Sherlock bellowed sarcastically. "Line up and let's get this show on the road, we don't have all day. They're going to measure you for your BDU's and boots. They'll be delivered to the barracks later on today. Then move along and pick up your field equipment. When you come out the other side, take a break. Ladies first." Sherlock almost yelled the command as he entered the building, letting the screen door slam behind him, ignoring the rest of the group.

Karen started the line inside the small building. She was pounced on by one man with a tape measure and another with a clipboard.

"Name?"

"Karen Bosworth."

The man with the tape called off the numbers. "Chest, 32; waist, 20; inseam, 22; boots, 5. Move on. Next," the man said in a bored voice, like he did this job every day. The measuring took no more than five minutes as the group moved along one at a time.

"Name?"

"Kimberly J. Matthews."

The measuring process started all over. "Chest, 35; waist, 25; inseam, 28; boots, 8. Move on. Next." Janet followed Kim in the line as Karen moved to the next station.

"This is your field equipment; belt, harness, pack and frame, sleeping bag, and everything else you're going to need while you're here. You don't need to check it," the army man with one stripe on his sleeve said. "Sign at the bottom of the sheet." Karen signed her name on the marked line and struggled to pick up the large box. Leaving through the back door, she heard the bored voice. "Next. This is your field equipment..."

In less than a half hour, Gunnery Sergeant Sherlock exited, carrying the same type of cardboard equipment box as everyone else. "Take everything out of the box and stuff it in your packs for now. I'll show you how to put everything together correctly later. For now, just get it together." The gunnery sergeant wasted no time or motion removing the pack, and placing each item inside the pack or on the belt. Finishing, he lifted the ALICE pack and slid his arms through the straps while everyone else was still digging in the boxes. "Come on, people, I haven't got all day," he growled.

Tom and Hayes were the first finished and looked to see who was behind. Tom moved to help Mi Ling as Hayes moved beside Don. Kim finished and gave Karen a hand stuffing the bulky sleeping bag into the top of the pack and tugging the flap down. David Segretti started picking up the empty boxes and stacking them beside the door next to the building.

"Let's go! Back to the barracks," Sherlock yelled, almost breaking a smile. "This is what I want to see more of, you people working together. Before this six weeks is up, I want everybody to be acutely aware of everybody else. I think I may be able to make a team out of you people yet." Sherlock lowered his voice to an almost normal level. "Come on, let's hump this shit back to the barracks and get squared away. There's only about twenty-five pounds in these packs now, and they're going to get a lot heavier before it's all said and done."

"Okay, you've had chow and time to get your stuff squared way. Follow the red-flagged trail until you come to the second building. Kim, you lead off, set a pace that everybody can keep. I'll bring up the rear. Move out," the gunnery sergeant yelled, watching them form a ragged line in the direction of the path.

Kim turned and started an easy trot up the small incline through the woods. She glanced back every few yards to see how Don and Frank were doing. She watched Sherlock as he ran beside Frank and Don giving encouragement or harassment, she couldn't hear which. She jogged into the clearing of the first building and shortened her long stride to ease the pace.

"Come on, men," the gunnery sergeant said under his breath to Frank and Don. "I know you want to lay down and die, but not today. One foot in front of the other. Pick 'em up and put 'em down. This time next week this will be a walk in the park."

"The only way I'd move like this through a park was if somebody was chasing me," Don managed to say through panting breaths.

"You men aren't that much older than me. You'll make it. We've got six weeks. You'll make it. Just keep telling yourselves that." They entered the clearing as Kim started back into the woods on the far side. "You've got to admit you've got a good view of the women from back here. Let your fantasies take over, block the pain. One foot in front of the other." The gunnery sergeant kept talking as he ran beside the two older men. "Don't even think about running," he whispered.

"Fuck it! This is going to kill me anyway, might as

well make somebody work for the body. Let's go," Don said, lengthening his stride a bit and picking up the pace. They closed the gap between themselves and Tom and Hayes, passed on either side, and now had Karen directly in front of them. "You're right, Gunny, it's a lot nicer following a world class ass than it is staying out of sight," Don grunted through exhalations. Karen turned and smiled as she heard the comment.

Kim jogged into the second clearing and saw another building like the rest they'd seen, the only difference was the red cross painted on the green roof. She continued up to the building and stopped, waiting for the rest of the group to break out of the woods. She noticed Frank and Don ahead of Tom and Hayes. "Good going, guys," she yelled as she gave them a thumbs up.

"Take a break. Frank and Don, come with me." Sherlock slowed to a walk outside the dispensary door. "This is James and Wilson, they're expected over at the hospital. The rest of the bunch is outside," he told the medic sitting at the desk filling out reports.

"Right, Sarge, I'll take care of them and alert the docs. You might as well bring them inside where it's cool. You can wait in the break room over there. Let's go, sirs. Follow me." Frank and Don followed the young medic down the hall to the door marked 'Driver'. "Joe, these two are supposed to go to the hospital. Can you run them over?" the medic asked.

"I reckon so," the man in whites answered in a slow, southern drawl. "Come on out the back door, we'll take the jeep," he said as he walked out of the room and led them down the narrow hallway.

The medic returned to the break room where the group had gathered, each trying to catch as much of the breeze from the window air conditioner as possible. "We'll take you two at a time, the first door on the left and the right. After the doc finishes with you come on down the hall to the lab. We'll need blood and urine samples from each of you. The latrine is just across the hall from the lab. After you finish in the lab, go to the last door on the left - that's the shot room. Be prepared to have sore arms for the next couple of days because we're going to inoculate you for everything there's a shot for. First two, let's go," he said, handing out brown manila folders to each person in the room.

"That's all folks," Sherlock said when he walked out the back door of the green dispensary building, buttoning the last buttons on his BDU's. "Now we take a nice easy stroll back to the barracks and the rest of the afternoon is yours. Chow is at 1730. Let's move out." The gunnery sergeant led them down a trail which looked to be more in a straight line to the barracks than the one they had run up.

As they entered the barracks clearing, they noticed a large, open tent had been erected under the trees, under which were two sets of free weights along with a Universal weight machine. "This is just a little something to help keep you busy during your free time," Sherlock said as they moved into the shade of the tent. "I highly recommend you use it this afternoon; it'll help keep those shoulders from tightening up. Use your heads and start off easy, you can't afford an injury this early in the game. The afternoon is yours till chow call."

Gunnery Sergeant James Sherlock left the group standing around the weight equipment as he walked into the olive green barracks building. Turning right, he walked to the last room at the end of the light green hall. Opening the door, he threw his sweat-drenched hat on the tightly made bed. He unbuttoned his shirt before he reached over and opened the locker, removing a bottle of vodka. He looked at it carefully before unscrewing the cap, debating his needs. Upending the bottle, he downed about four ounces before taking it away from his lips. He replaced the cap and returned it to the shelf. His eyes were drawn to his dress blue Marine Corps uniform with badges and ribbons covering the left breast from the pocket to the shoulder. He reached out and ran his finger over the yellow ribbon with red and green stripes – The Vietnam Service Ribbon. *After all these years, I'm going back to where it all started. I wonder if I can leave the ghosts there this time... or will they follow me the rest of my life? God, so many faces and names. Too many friends. That little briefing you had; well, Jim old son, looks like you're in the shit again. Jesus, what a bunch I've got to work with – old people, women, and a couple of smart asses. Then there's Segretti, the wild card. What the fuck is he doing in this?* Jim Sherlock removed his shirt and tee shirt and hung them on the back of the folding chair to dry. Walking over, he picked up his hat and tossed it onto the small writing desk before stretching out on the bed with his boots hanging over the end. An old habit held over from boot camp almost twenty-five years ago. *That Kim Matthews is one fine looking woman. I wonder if she'd have anything to do with an old, beat up Marine?* He drifted off to sleep, and to the all-to-commonly recurring dream of walking point with his M-16 down a trail in the jungles of Vietnam. The men following him were torn and bloody, their lifeless eyes boring accusingly into the back of his head. He recognized each man as they call him by name, every voice blaming him, every one of them beckoning him to join their never-ending march into Hell.

Chapter Seven

The camouflaged, woodland green pickup truck raced up the sandy, dusty road leading to the barracks. The young driver hit the brakes and slid to a stop at the front door. The truck, and everything else in the area, was enveloped in a cloud of light brown dust. "We're here," he said casually as Don and Frank climbed out of the passenger door. "Could you guys give me a hand unloading this stuff?" he asked as he grabbed two of the bundles and carried them inside the building. Frank and Don each grabbed two bundles as Kim and David walked around the corner from the new outdoor gym.

"Hi guys, we were wondering what happened to you," Kim said as she and David each grabbed a bundle.

"It's a long story," Frank replied. Then he asked, "Do you have any nail polish remover?" while scratching the glue in his hair.

The driver grabed the last two bundles, rushed them inside and dropped them, not bothering to close the door. "Thanks for the help. I'm on my own time now," he said. He waved and climbed back into the truck, then sped off the way they came.

Tom and Karen walked around the corner and saw Frank and Don talking with Kim and David. Karen turned and yelled to the rest of the group still under the canvas, "They're back! Come on, let's see what's up." She and Tom walked to the door where Frank and Don had started to explain their afternoon. "What's so special about you two? We've been finished for almost three hours," Karen said as she pulled at some of the glue-like substance in Frank's hair.

Frank stopped his explanation of their ordeal at the main dispensary until everyone was gathered around. "Let's go inside where it's cool and we'll tell you all about it," he said. "If anybody's interested, we got our new clothes."

"Let's go to the TV room, they've got cold soda in there," Janet said, walking into the building and turning to the big room at the end of the light green hallway.

"What did they do to you at the hospital?" Hayes

asked as he started handing around cans of cold 7 Up.

"Among other things, I got an EEG, and they proved once again I don't have a brain. No, really, they were looking for the seizure activity caused by that NVA bullet I stopped thirty years ago. Besides that, they ran us through the mill; X-rays, stress EKGs, lab work and about a dozen different shots. I doubt that there's anything we can catch now," Frank answered, popping the top on the can of soda.

"They gave me a new leg," Don interjected. "It has a knee joint and a built-in shock absorber. Something real interesting is that from my stump up, it's lined with some kind of silicone mixed with something else. Not only does it feel good and work well, it stays cool. The way it works, it's almost like I've got my foot and leg back. Hell, it doesn't even hurt to run anymore." Don started kicking his right leg in the air, then switched to deep knee bends. Next he started to run in place to demonstrate his new bio-mechanical marvel.

Sherlock walked unnoticed into the day room. "Well, I see they let you two come back to us. They must think you're healthy enough not to die on me."

"Gunny, we're tough old buzzards, we won't die on you. Besides, we like to see you disappointed," Don replied with a grin as he started to jump up and down.

"Just when I was starting to think about being nice to you old men. Well, let's get these new uniforms on and get ready for chow. One thing I have to suggest for those of you who wear nylon underwear, get rid of it and change to cotton. It'll be a lot cooler and more comfortable." Sherlock started to paw his way through the bundles of clothing until he found the one with his name on it. Without another word he turned and started down the hall to his room.

"Gunny, just where in the hell are we supposed to get cotton underwear out here in the middle of God knows where?" Janet asked.

"We'll get you to the PX tomorrow night after chow," he stopped, turned, and answered. "Now, ladies and gentlemen, shall we dress for dinner?" Sherlock growled sarcastically.

"Yes sir, but of course, sir. We can be ready to join

you for dinner in a few minutes," Karen replied as if she were a slave answering a master.

"Damn it, don't call me sir. My father is sir. You call officers sir, and I'm sure as hell not an officer. Now move out and get in the uniform of the day. Chow call in fifteen minutes," he growled as he disappeared behind his door.

They walked quickly down the trail to the mess hall. Sherlock led the group down a trail free of obstacles. Don stopped, climbed the three steps on the horizontal bars and jumped to the sixth one. He swung his body and grabbed every other bar. He made seven.

"You didn't have to do that. I told you, you were finished for the day. If one goes, you all go. Take off Frank, let's see you beat that."

Frank started off and made it across with little problem but lost his grip when he made the turn. Hayes followed and made three complete trips across and back before he droped. Mi Ling, Janet and Karen each make two trips across. "How many, Gunnery Sergeant?" Kim asked as she took her place on the ladder.

"Give me a hundred."

Kim took each bar hanging straight down. Close to the end of her forth turn she dropped. "Close?" she asked.

"Close enough," the gunnery sergeant answered with a smile. "Go for it, David," he said when Segretti took his place on the bars. Segretti made one hundred and fifty rungs before he dropped. The gunnery sergeant jumped to the first bar and hung. "How many?" he asked nonchalantly.

"Two hundred," Kim replied, while she and the rest of the group rubbed their sore, aching biceps.

"Two hundred? Okay, be done in two minutes." Sherlock took the bars one at a time. His hands moved so fast it was almost as if he barely touched each bar. At each turn he stopped, did five chin-ups, and continued. "That's two hundred. Let's eat," he said, swinging his body through the uprights and landing on the balls of his feet.

The evening meal of the first day was well-done roast beef, mashed potatoes, gravy and corn. The portions were generous, and as with most military food if was a well balanced but not too flavorful meal. Finishing supper quickly with little conversation, the group took their trays to the dishwasher in twos and threes and left through the back door.

Jim Sherlock finished the last bite of his meal as Kim stood. Walking up behind her, he asked, "Well Kim, what do you think of the people you'll be spending the next few months with?"

"Well, they seem nice enough, but I've only had a chance to talk with the women. I worry about the old men though. Bosworth and Hayes will be okay as soon as they get into shape. Segretti... I don't know, he seems to be on the outside of everything. It's as if he doesn't want to get involved," Kim replied as she dumped the remains of her meal and stacked her tray with the others.

"I'll see what I can do about getting people to talk more about themselves," Sherlock said, holding the screen door open for the tall army specialist. Tom, Frank and Bill stood outside having an after-meal cigarette as Sherlock and Kim walked over. Sherlock pulled a cigarette from his pocket. "Got a light?" he asked no one in particular.

Frank handed his aging Zippo to the big marine.

"Lieutenant Frank Wilson. Special Forces, huh? What years?" Sherlock asked, closely examining the lighter's crest and engraving after he lit his cigarette.

"1962 through part of '63. Don and I were stationed in Mi Ling's village. That is until he got blown all to hell and I stopped a bullet with my head," Frank answered as if it were an everyday question and part of every conversation.

"I was around Quang Tri about ten years later. Sure was a hell of a time," Sherlock replied, handing the lighter back. "You know we're going to have a hell of a time getting enough cigarettes in country to last us through this thing," he commented in an attempt to draw any of them into a general conversation.

"Well, according to what their ambassador said, we won't have any trouble with customs. He told Don we would be traveling under diplomatic status. To the best of my knowledge, the only thing we have to worry about is the activity around Cam An," Frank replied, returning the lighter to his shirt pocket and buttoning the flap.

"Yeah, if the help we get is anything like the ARVN's I had dealings with, we're better off without them. We have an intelligence briefing tomorrow morning on the mission and the area." Jim Sherlock took another drag on the cigarette, crushed it out on the heel of his boot, stripped the paper and scattered the tobacco with his foot. He put the paper and filter in his pocket and continued, "Get everybody together in the TV room at 1900 hours. We'll start putting together the field equipment. Kim, I'll race you back to the barracks."

"You're on," she replied as she took off in a sprint.

The group gathered in the large room with chairs, card tables and a TV. Each had their pack crammed full of their All-purpose, Lightweight, Individual Carrying Equipment (ALICE). Jim Sherlock walked into the room with his pack slung on one shoulder and a large cooler in his hands. "There are four beers apiece in here. Enjoy while we work," he said, setting the plastic cooler on the floor. "Go ahead and grab one and we'll get started putting this shit together." Reaching in and pulling out four cans, he handed one each to Janet, Mi Ling and Kim, popped the top on his own and took a long swallow before he set it on a table. "Go ahead and dump everything on the floor in front of you and find the belt," he ordered in a friendly voice, swinging off his pack and upending it on the floor. "So, Frank, you, Don and Mi Ling were together in Nam in the early sixties? This long after the war it's probably about like it was then. Why don't you tell us about it?" he asked as he dug through his pile. "The trick of this equipment is to balance the load, those of you who have used this before, help the others." Sherlock instructed before Frank could get started with his story.

"Don and I were part of an A-Team in '62. Our job was to win the hearts and minds of the people in and around Cam An and use it for our base of operations." Frank talked with frequent hesitations while he remembered, or attempted to forget.

"They had ARVNs dressed like VC make a raid on the village. Then Frank, Don and the rest of the team came in and chased them off. Needless to say we were grateful. I didn't find out about the trick until after they were wounded and evacuated. By that time, it didn't make any difference," Mi Ling added to the tale. "I was young and in love. Then I got pregnant and next thing I knew Frank was gone."

Don continued the story where Frank left off. "When we got there, there were perhaps seventy-five people in the village. By the time we got hit, the population inside the wall was up to around a thousand. The NVA hit us with everything they had, probably a couple of battalions of hard-core regular troops. We beat off that attack. Frank and I got hit and evacuated. Then they came back and wasted the place." Don stopped, his face grimaced with the pain of remembering his last minutes in Vietnam.

"The combination hospital/radio shack sustained a number of direct hits and collapsed. Doc and Sparks are still buried there. I went to Da Nang before the NVA made their final assault and started working for MAC-V, and a few months later Frank Jr. was born." Mi Ling placed a comforting hand on Frank's thigh, knowing how the memories hurt.

"Karen, slide the canteens more to the sides so you have room for your butt pack," Sherlock said. "What's the terrain like around where we're going?" he asked, while helping Karen with her canteen pouches.

"Cam An is on the east side of the highlands at the base of the mountains and beside a branch of the Cam Lo river. We'll be working in everything from triple canopy jungle to swamps. As far as working goes, I guess most of the time we'll have to make our own trails," Mi Ling answered deftly assembling her equipment as if she did it every day.

"Tom, you and Bill are both ex-army. Want to tell us your stories? Janet make those suspenders longer, you can tighten them up after you do everything else." Sherlock continued his instruction in between the stories.

"Tom and I were part of a Delta Team that tried to

rescue the hostages at the American embassy in Iran in 1980. Operation Eagle Claw, they called it," Hayes started. "Tom, me, and Bill Miles were detached from the main group at Fort Bragg and sent in, supposedly for recon work." Bill stood and adjusted the harness on his LBE.

"What really happened," Tom interrupted and continued, "was that we were supposed to be a trade item. There was supposed to be little resistance at the embassy if we were captured. The CIA hung us out to dry. After the mission was aborted we had to fight our way out of Iran. With the help of a lot of people we made it back to the States." Tom walked to the cooler and passed more beer around. "Then we got even with the two bastards in The Company who sold us down the river."

Bill Hayes jumped in and continued where Tom had left off. "When we healed from our various injuries, we went to work with The Company. Tom got smart and got out; Miles and I are still working there. Frank and Tom had some trouble with the university where they work a couple of years ago, so Miles and I came out to give them a hand. That's where I met Janet and she hasn't let me out of her sight since."

"All these guys are just being modest," Karen said as she opened her second can of beer. "Frank has a Medal of Honor and a bunch of other stuff. Don, I know, has a bunch of medals; Hayes has a bunch; and Tom has all kinds of stuff, including a Silver Star," Karen said with pride as she smiled at her man. "So, Sergeant, you can see that you're not dealing with just run-of-the-mill ex-GIs. You're working with some genuine heroes. Janet and I are old roommates and when Tom and Frank got involved with getting even with the biochem department, we got involved with them. That's basically our story."

"Here, Kim, have another beer." Sherlock handed another Budweiser over, opening it first. "Let's get you drunk enough to talk about yourself."

"My uncle is a mortician. When I joined the army I thought I could get all the free training I needed to work with him when I got out. I've got two years left to go in my second hitch, and I've passed all the tests needed to be a real live funeral director. The C.O. asked if anyone wanted to go on a temporary duty assignment, so here I am. Nobody told me the TDY would be Vietnam. If they had I'd probably told them to shove it. That's all about me. What about you, David? Why are you here?" All eyes turned to Segretti in hopes they would learn more than what was obvious about the cold-eyed man.

"I'm here because the people who are paying for this trip want me here. I'm sorry, all I can say is, I'm David Segretti and I'm from New York, and what I'm supposed to do is tied to your mission. I'm to be a part of your team until it comes time to do what I'm supposed to do and then I'm yours again, or out of there – my choice." The sandy-haired man popped the top on his second beer and returned to adjusting his equipment. He ignored the questioning looks from everyone else in the room. *Just another job*, he thought. *Life would be easier if I didn't have to deal with all these people. One of these days maybe I'll draw a simple assignment.*

"Could you hand me another beer, please?" Mi Ling asked. "How will we know when you do whatever it is that you're supposed to do?" Mi Ling's tone of voice showed her worry and concern as she asked the question that was on everyone's mind.

"Don't worry, you'll know. Let's change the subject from me, I've told you all I can," Segretti replied apologetically. "Gunny, why don't you tell us something about yourself?" *I wonder how many of these people are going to survive this trip? God, I hate it when innocents have to die for the greater good. Pater Noster que est in terrum.*

"I joined the Corps when I was eighteen. I started out in Vietnam after boot camp, close to where we're going. I spent two tours there and I've been in every action since. I've never played politics. I've caused a bit of trouble now and then; so I'm still a Gunnery Sergeant. Besides, I'm the type of guy who likes to get in and do the job, get my hands dirty, not give the orders. My platoons have always been the best, and if I have anything to do with it, that's what you're going to be when we leave here – the best," Sherlock answered with pride. "I'm not going to say when we get to Vietnam it's going to be a walk in the park – it isn't. But with all the training and experience we have in this room, it's going to be a lot easier. My job is to get everybody in the best physical condition possible and to keep us on track. When we leave here we're supposed to be a team. Teams work together, so if anybody has any ideas on how to do a job better or easier, let everyone else know about it. At least for this six weeks I have the final say. Now, let's see how this stuff fits then let's drink up and hit the rack. The alarm goes off at 0430." *So this is who everybody is. I sure would never have guessed these guys were that well decorated. Made my Bronze Star look like nothing. That Segretti is a real spook. I wish to hell we knew something about him. Well, there's still time.*

The large camp of thatched bamboo huts was well illuminated by the light of gas lanterns. Twenty men sprawled amid the remnants of a large meal of pork, rice and fish. The Vietnamese women quickly passed among the revelers with their heads bowed, gathering the dirty dishes, utensils, and most important, the leftovers. Scraps left from this meal could feed their families for days. The women in the cook tent carefully divided the remnants into the woven baskets each had brought from Cam An.

The muscular black man stood, belched, and scratched his ass before he addressed the men. "De general say we goin' t' get company about de time we start de harvest. He don't know anythin' 'bout dem 'sept dey're a bunch o' civilians and dey be stayin' at Cam An. He tol' me dat we're supposed t' leave the village alone dis year, so der'll be some place fo' dese fuckin' do-gooders t' see. Now de way Ah sees it, we ain't gots no choice buts t' use dem gooks. We barely gots 'nough people to take care o' de other fields. So whut de fuck is we supposed to do now?"

"Howard, God damn it, you speak English as well as anybody else. How come you're always talking this jive shit? There ain't no need for it," a voice from the crowd called out.

"A 'cause Ah wants t' talk like dis, ya' cracka' son o' bitch. Anytime ya' tink ya kin change it ya can come on down here. Ah'll tear ya' a new asshole. Now shut the fuck up and listen. If we don'ts git a full harvest, everybody is goin' t' be losin' bread. Ifin we duzn't use Cam An people we kin kiss off dat field. What it is, me and de boys dun decided de only thin' we kin do be t' take ova'

Cam An. Ifin we gots t' waste us some US civilians den dat's jest too damn bad. Anybody gots any betta' suggestions, lets hear 'em."

"We could try a peaceful approach first – just tell these people we're taking the villagers out for a work detail and there's not a damned thing they can do about it," a voice called from the back of the large hut.

"OK, duPage, ya' gits t' try it. Don't blame nobody ifin ya' gits yo' honkey ass blown away. You had better come up with a full harvest out of that field, or I'm going to hang your lily white ass out for the buzzards." Howard had switched to standard American English to make sure his threat was understood.

"I have to agree with duPage," another voice said. "We deserted from the military, but I still consider myself an American. I'd hate to have to fight against our own people."

"Sheeeit, hand me dat bottle. You dumb shit, you ain't no fuckin' 'merican no more! How many o' de rest o' ya' sentimental idjits wants t' leave dese damn people alone? Show me yo' handed. Okay, ya' fuckers git de field by Cam An, an ifin it duzn't git harvested, it's yo ass. Drink up, it's goin' t' be a long trip home fo' some o' ya. I wants a list o' names o' ya' assholes who wants t' be peacenicks fust thin' in de mornin' so's Ah kin do some shiftin' around." The large black leader grabbed one of the younger Vietnamese women, pulled her to his lap, ripped off the buttons on the front of her thin blouse, then take a tiny, firm breast in his mouth.

"Howard," the man called duPage said, "Washington and me will move our bunch down from camp three. We'll find some way to get that field taken care of."

Howard dumped the woman off his lap and stood. He took a drunken step forward and was stopped by the long table. "I'm warning you, you son of a bitch. You just keep trying to move up and take over, don't you." All traces of the inner city jive talk disappeared when he faced duPage. "White boy, after this crop gets in, you and me are going to tango." It was difficult to determine which turned Howard's eyes from white to red, the alcohol or the rage of having someone, especially a white man, challenge him. *I'm going to kill that honkey son of a bitch,* he thought, watching the two men leave.

Chapter Eight

The group was jarred awake by the fire alarm bell when it started ringing at 4:30. The women had the first chance at the one gang shower in the barracks building. The men started their morning by shaving in the small sinks in the rooms. Even in the air-conditioned building it was apparent that the day was going to be hot and humid.

After the first day, each member of the group had developed the mindset of a basic trainee. They would follow Sherlock anywhere. Not because of fear or intimidation, like in the military basic, but because each realized they knew their job. Even the strongest of the group recognized the tough gunnery sergeant would be in command during the next weeks of training.

"Everybody looks bright-eyed and bushy-tailed this morning," Sherlock yelled as the group assembled outside the barracks. "Okay, let's start getting limbered up with some windmills. We've got a long day ahead. Let's get moving." After about five minutes, "Now," he barked, "let's see how many push-ups you out-of-shape people can do. Hit the dirt and count off." Sherlock put his feet together and fell forward, catching himself with his nose less than an inch from the ground. Sherlock pushed himself off the ground and stretched his arms above his head. His push-ups used the power of his lower arms and fingers as opposed to the upper arms and shoulders of everyone else. "Frank, keep that belly off the ground," he yelled between numbers twenty-eight and thirty. "Come on, I can't hear you. Sound off like you got a pair." He heard Karen and Kim each call off thirty as Don struggled to get the word 'sixteen' out. Sherlock finished fifty and called a halt. "Who got less than twenty?" Frank and Don raised their hands. "Okay, gentlemen, we'll work you up gradually, ten at a time, a number of times a day. When I tell you to drop, give me ten. Let's move over here for some chin-ups." They walked to the end of the building to the three sets of bars. "There's room for two on each bar. Go for it, give me ten."

The chin-ups continued with the usual chorus of grunts and groans. Frank and Don were the last to finish, after having been the first to start. Kim and David rushed through with one a second. Karen, Mi Ling and Janet weren't far behind. Tom and Bill each took at least ten seconds for each pull-up; a five count up and another five down.

"Very good. Now for the same mile run we did yesterday. I hope you're wearing heavy socks; new boots can cause blisters in a hurry. The thing you have to remember above all else is to take care of your feet." Jim Sherlock removed the stopwatch from his pocket. "Everybody ready? Let's move out!" Pushing the start button, he took off across the compound at a seemingly easy trot. Kim followed close on his heels and drew alongside before they were out of the clearing.

"Race?" Kim asked with a smile as she pulled alongside and started increasing her pace.

"Yeah, may as well see what you're made of," he grunted as he started to sprint. They reached the turn point. Sherlock reached out and grabbed the trunk of a small hickory, using his hold and his momentum to make the turn. Neither had a clear lead when they started back. When they met the rest of the group, Kim dropped back in to single file to make room for them to pass. When they broke into the clearing, Kim was about three paces behind.

"Five four five. Damn fine time," Sherlock said between gasps. "You had me working there."

"Yeah, I would have beat you too if I hadn't dropped back. I want a rematch," Kim panted.

"Six oh oh," he called out as Janet, Karen, and Mi Ling entered the clearing. "Six oh seven," when David Segretti broke out of the woods with Tom and Hayes close behind. "Six twenty, good time." Frank and Don came into the clearing running side by side, sounding like a couple of horses after a race. "Seven forty. Good show, under eight minutes. How's the leg doing Don?" the gunnery sergeant asked, showing the first genuine concern any of them had seen.

"The leg's doing fine, I'm not doing worth a shit. Can I lay down somewhere and die?" the senator asked through clenched teeth.

"Just what the hell is it with you speed demons anyway? Nobody needs to run that fast, ever," Frank managed to say between breaths.

"Gunny Sherlock and I are setting the pace from now on. He beat me this morning, but I'll get him," Kim continued with a wink at Jim and a beaming smile to everyone else.

"Everybody catch your breath and we'll double time to the mess hall. The smoking lamp is lit." Sherlock pulled his cigarettes and lighter from his pocket.

The unimaginative breakfast was quickly finished and the group double timed back to the barracks clearing. "Okay, you've got forty-five minutes to get squared away and get back out here with your field equipment. Make sure both canteens are full. Move out, you're on your own time," the gunnery sergeant said before he entered the building and walked toward his room. *That Kim is one fine woman. I think she could give me a real hard-on if I let her have the chance.* He opened his locker and pulled out a bottle of vodka, taking a long swallow before putting the cap back on and returning it to it's place on the shelf.

"Tom, if you don't get out of those clothes, I'm going to rip them off," Karen said as she closed the door behind them. "You know what working out does to me."

"Sounds like a winner. Remember we have to be outside and able to move in forty-five minutes," Tom replied with a lascivious grin as they rushed to undo each others buttons.

"Frank, you're going to have to stop smoking," Mi Ling remarked as she started making the bed. "You're going to need all the lung power you can get before we finish here."

"Yeah, I know. I'm starting to think I'm too old for this shit. If this wasn't your mission I'd be happy to stay in Steamboat and vegetate.

"I know, Frank, you could really care less that Doc and Sparks are still buried in that bunker. I know you don't mind that they'll stay MIAs forever. You're just too old and out of shape to want to do anything for your men."

"God damn it, Mi Ling, you know better than that!

Not only is that incorrect, it's unfair!" Frank sat in the folding chair, removed a cigarette from his pocket, stopped, thought, then returned it to the pack.

"What do you think of the people you're going to be working with?" Don asked Segretti as they each sat on the sides of their bunks.

"Well, I'm not worried about Hayes And Bosworth. You and Frank look like you're going to die before we finish. I'm sure Mi Ling can hold up her end of things if the shit hits the fan, but I haven't got the foggiest idea about the rest of the women. Sherlock is a professional, I know I can count on him all the way. Who knows, we've still got a lot of time before we have to worry about it. Maybe things will change."

"David, I hate to say you're wrong, but like you said, there's plenty of time. Don't count us old men out just because we're old and out of shape. We've been there before. Don't discount the experience we've got," Don replied as he laid back on his bed and closed his eyes.

"Did you notice the sparks fly between Kim And Sherlock this morning?" Janet asked while Hayes filled the canteens at the small sink.

"You'd have to be blind not to. I don't think Gunny is the type of guy that'd put the moved on someone during training, though."

"He might not be, but I'll be willing to bet Kim's screwing his brains out before we're halfway through here," Janet replied with her musical laugh and a wave of her long red pigtail.

I wonder if I can get him to make the first move? Kim thought as she adjusted the shoulder strap on her load-bearing equipment. *Someway, somehow, I'm going to get him before it's over. There's no way I'm going to spend all this time without a man. Segretti looks okay, but something about him turns me off. I feel a coldness when he's around. I don't think he feels he needs or wants anybody. I wish we knew what he was up to.* "Well, time to get out there and do or die," she said aloud as she opened the door.

Gunnery Sergeant Sherlock opened his door and yelled, "Time's up! Outside and on the line! Move it!" He walked down the hall, banging on each door he passed. He stepped outside and saw Kim sitting on a log that separated the dusty assembly area from the sparse lawn in front of the barracks. "Well, Kim, I see you can tell time, that's more than the rest can do."

"I'm just trying to be a good soldier, Gunny," she replied with a smile and a sparkle in her eyes. "What's up for today?"

"Wait until everyone gets out here so I don't have to explain it twice. Let's go, we don't have all day," he yelled. "On the line."

Jesus Christ, thought Karen, *and just last night I was thinking he might turn out to be a nice guy.*

"This morning we're going to have our first briefings on this operation. This afternoon we're going to start on our hand-to-hand combat training, and this evening after chow, we're going to make a trip to the PX. After today there will be few easy days. We're going to be busy every day with some kind of training we'll need to pull shit this off. Any time you have free time, I suggest you spend it on self training of some kind. Frank, Don, front and center." The two old men of the group broke rank and stepped forward. "Lead off up the trail to the first building. Double time it. Everybody else stay on their heels and push. Move out."

They moved into the woods, side by side, with Hayes and Janet close behind, whispering encouragement. They reached the clearing with Frank and Don in a heavy sweat, their shirts starting to soak through. The group slowed to a walk as Sherlock passed them, opened the door and turned on the light. H walked to the other side of the room and switched on the two window air conditioners. "There's a coffee pot at the back of the room. Somebody make a pot; the rest of you, find a seat at the table."

Mi Ling moved to the back of the room and started measuring coffee into the filter as everyone else dropped their equipment and pulled the folding chairs away from the long table.

Sherlock walked to the hanging maps beside the

blackboard and pulled down the first one. "This is where we are. This post is a little over thirty miles square, and as you can see it's divided into four areas. This small area here is called REMF Row. That's the headquarters area, hospital, supply, PX and everything else that makes civilization."

"Gunny," Karen asked, "what does REMF mean?"

"Ask your husband."

Tom looked at her and grinned, "Rear echelon mother fuckers," he answered in a whisper.

Sherlock continued. "This is the area we're in. This is the staging area where we get supplied and you start getting into shape. We'll be here approximately two weeks. Then we move to this next quadrant. As you can see from the map, this area has almost everything; forests bordering on fields, cliffs, a river, and swampland with quicksand and hostile inhabitants, reptile and insect. We'll spend about two weeks here. The last area is totally primitive; no buildings, trails or anything else. We're going to have to rely on what we take in with us. One of the things we'll be doing is working with a new Landsat positioner. It'll tell us, within an inch, where we are at any time. We'll be briefed on this item shortly. The information that Mi Ling had is supposed to be fed into the computers to make finding things a lot easier."

"How long will we be in this last area?" Janet asked.

"Only a few days, and then we take off to Panama for a week of real jungle. Then it's back here to regroup and it's off to Vietnam. The coffee's ready. Let's get a cup before we continue."

They all stood and moved toward the rear of the room to the coffee pot. "Sarge, what's the rest of the briefing about?" Segretti asked.

"I've got more to cover on this place and then there's going to be an intelligence man to tell us all he knows about Vietnam."

"What's to know that we don't know already? Mi Ling's from there. You, Don and Frank have been there. We know what we're supposed to do, so what else is there?" Segretti asked again.

"We know what our job is, but we don't know anything about yours," Tom replied sarcastically.

"I'd tell you if I could, Tom. When it's done, maybe I'll give you the whole story."

"Look, David, we're not going to be seeing or talking to anyone outside this group. So why can't you tell us?" Kim asked.

"I'm sorry, I'm just following orders."

"Okay, enough of this, let's get back to work." Sherlock effectively cut off the conversation before a debate could start. He pulled down the next map. "This is a blow-up of this area. As you can see, all the trails radiate from the barracks building. We're here." The gunnery sergeant pointed to a spot on the map and continued. "This afternoon, we're going to the pits. This is a sandy area where we start our hand-to-hand training. This area," he added, moving his finger to another position, "is the armory and the range. As you can see, these two areas are almost directly opposite each other. The distance is about five miles. Tomorrow we start at the range, have lunch, and then it's back to the pits. Depending on the time of day we finish, we'll probably take one of the trapped trails back to the barracks. These simulations are placed by the group in the next area. They're going they need all the practice they can get." Sherlock continued the briefing on each area, and described the problems the group would have to solve in each place.

The door opened and a very nondescript man of medium height and weight, wearing a short-sleeve shirt and striped tie, walked in. He looked to be the type of person who could blend into any crowd – average in all respects. "Please continue," he said as he set down a large attaché case.

"I'm finished sir," Sherlock said, moving away from the maps.

"The coffee smells good. Why don't you people take a break while I get things set up."

"Anybody who wants to smoke, outside. The general doesn't like anyone smoking in his classrooms. The head is through that door, fifteen minutes."

"Good morning, ladies and gentlemen, my name is Cross," the brown-haired man started, much as he would a lecture to a preppy, eastern university class. "I'm one of the many senior analysts the CIA has working on this project. Director Mason has briefed me on your mission, and I must tell you I believe it is commendable. What I have for you this morning is the latest satellite pictures of the area where you're going. Could someone kill the lights and turn on the projector?" Hayes stepped to the light switch as Don switched on the Kodak slide projector. "Thank you. This first slide is a complete overview from Laos to the ocean, the area circled is where you're going to be working. As we magnify the area," he flipped to the next slide, "we can see the reason for the reports of outlaw activity. At this magnification, you will notice the differences in the terrain and vegetation patterns." He moved to the screen and started pointing. "This is high canopy forest and these are rice paddies. This, my friends, is where your trouble will probably begin. These are fields of opium poppies." He advanced to the next slide, showing a higher magnification of one of the fields. "We estimate the production from each of these fields to be somewhere between three and five million dollars at the source, and all the fields are in the area where you're planning to be working. I believe anybody would kill you for the amount of money involved in these fields." He pressed the button on the remote control. "This is the village of Cam An, you can see the remnants of the walls some of you built. It is evident that at the most about a thousand people lived here. Now we guess there's fifty to seventy-five. As you can see," Cross advanced to the next slide, "these people aren't living very well as evidenced by the rice paddies around the area. We believe they are being pressed into servitude to work the poppy fields. Now this is where things start to get sticky." He advanced to the next slide showing people in the field of flowers. "As you can see, three of these men are Caucasian and the other two are Negro. We believe these are American deserters working with the local drug lords. If it is at all possible, and without undue danger to yourselves, we would like to have one of these men to interrogate."

"If these men are Americans, don't you think they might hesitate to cause trouble for us?" Kim asked.

"Miss, these people are deserters and/or mercenaries. They could care less about nationality, and with the amount of money involved, I think Jesus Christ would have trouble with these people. You are going there at harvest time, and I think you're going to be opening a real hornet's nest. This is all we have at this time. I assure you we will have some kind of update before you leave. Now, do any of you have any questions that I might be able to answer?"

"Mr. Cross, this mission is being sanctioned by the Vietnamese government. Think we might get some help or protection from them?" Frank asked, his voice showing worry.

"With an operation this size, we believe some high government or military officials are involved. My gut feeling is to say no."

"We're going there armed with handguns; that's not much help against AK-47s and M-16s. Think we could get away with taking some heavier weapons in?" Tom asked.

"That would have to go through State and the Vietnamese government. Somehow, I doubt it can be done."

"Sir, if we can capture one of these men, what the hell are we supposed to do with him?" Hayes asked.

"Your radio will have a link to our office in Hong Kong. Just give us the word and we'll come get him. Are there any more questions at this time? No? Well, I'm sure you'll think of more later. Thank you for your attention. Sergeant, they're all yours." Cross moved from behind the table and back to the projector, turning on the lights as he passed.

Sherlock moved back to the maps and pulled down an enlarged copy of the map Frank Jr. had shown the senator. "Mi Ling, this is your map. Like to give us a run down on it while we wait for the man who's going to brief us on the global positioning system?"

Mi Ling moved from her seat at the table. Her five-foot frame looked even smaller next to the six-foot-four-inch gunnery sergeant. "Most of you already know this, but for those of you who don't, I'll be as brief and as informative as possible." Mi Ling started with her history lesson of what happened to her, the fall of Cam An, and her coming to work for the state department. She told of the interviews, the cross-checking with witnesses, and how she and Frank Jr. had developed the map coordinates of the probable finds. Next she detailed how the computer program had taken each square mile and broken it down into ten thousand squares, and extrapolated each point to within a few inches. She illustrated by drawing a large square on the blackboard and cross-hatching it. She turned back to the group as another man carrying a large suitcase opened the door. "What we have done is much like putting a square inch of skin under a microscope, then being able to look at one individual cell, then marking it so we can find it again whenever we reexamine that slide. Using what we know, our statistics come to a ninety percent confidence line. In other words, I believe we'll find something or someone ninety percent of the time. That's all I have, and it looks like our next instructor is here, so I'll turn the floor over to him," Mi Ling concluded, taking the seat where Sherlock had started.

"Thank you." The man in the grey, summer-weight suit walked forward and laid the suitcase on the table. "I caught the last part of your presentation, and I must congratulate you on your fine work." He opened the case and removed what looked like four pairs of binoculars. He closed the case and shoved it under the table. "My name is Grant. I work for one of the electronics companies which does a lot of work for the DOD. One of the things we make is an Individual Global Position System, much like these. These are prototypes that have been put together for you and your mission." He started handing the units around. "The on/off button is on the left. As you look through these you will also notice they are fine binoculars. Look up in the right-hand corner. The numbers up and down and across are your present latitude and longitude to two decimal places. Look out the window and focus on something. The number in the upper left is the distance to that focal point. I have taken the liberty of programming in a point outside about fifty yards away. Push the button on the right side, and you'll notice a string of LED's surrounding your field of vision. Turn your bodies and watch them light up. The red one is the direction you need to travel. All you have to do is line up the red light with the top center and away you go. When you get to that spot, the LED will come on in the center of your field of view. The chips in the system can store up to two hundred different coordinates." Reaching into his pocket, he pulled out what looked like a credit-card-sized calculator. "This keypad plugs into the system and you can designate any set of coordinates that have been entered just by punching in the number between one and two hundred. Or you can use this to designate a new co-ordinate you wish to find. Where I work, we are in the process of taking Mrs. Wilson's data and transcribing it into the satellite which will work with this system. We think you will be impressed with the ease with which you can find your way around. The battery has a life of about five hundred hours and a shelf life of about seven years, so you should have no problem with power. The units are completely waterproof; you could take them down to a hundred feet if you wanted to with no ill effects. Let's see, have I covered everything?" He paused. "Do any of you have any questions?"

"You say the company you work for is programming the spots we're looking for in Vietnam. Does that mean that these aren't the units we'll be working with?" Frank asked.

"That is correct. As I said, these are prototypes. There are a few bugs we still want to work out. We'll have the ones you'll be using in your hands within three to four weeks."

"What is the distance from a programmed spot you can start using these?" Tom asked, continuing to examine the rubber-coated piece of equipment..

"At the present time, the range is about five miles; that's one of the things we're working on, to increase the distance."

"We're going to be orienteering for the next few weeks. Will these work as guidance systems for us?" Sherlock asked.

"Yes indeed, you will be given your latitude and longitude anywhere on earth. You have your maps, so all you have to do is to use this card to punch in where you want to go, then follow the blinking lights."

"I noticed the padded case you brought these in," Hayes started. "How much shock can these things take?"

"That's another thing we will have completed in the units you'll get. These units could probably withstand a drop to the floor and still function. The finished product should be able to fall ten feet on to concrete and still function."

"We believe in what you're trying to do – any American would – but we've also got to make a buck now and then. What you're doing is one of the roughest tests we can think of."

"I think we've covered everything about these units. I don't think any of us have any problem with someone making money, I'm just glad we have something to make our lives easier. Thank you, Mr. Grant, and thank your company for us. You can't know how grateful we are."

"Thank you, Mrs. Wilson. I'll relay your kind words to the main office. These units are yours to work with until we get the replacements. The program pads and instruction books are in the case. Give them your best shot, and I'll see you in a few weeks."

Sherlock stood as Grant walked toward the door. "Thank you, Mr. Grant." Grant waved his hand as he closed the door. "Okay, time for chow. Get your equipment back on and leave the new toys here. We'll pick them up on the way back from the pits."

Chapter Nine

"This is a Beretta model 92. It is a sixteen shot, double-action, semi-automatic pistol. After you sign the property cards, I'll give you each one like this. The caliber is 9 millimeters, and the bullet leaves the barrel at somewhere between eleven and thirteen hundred feet per second, depending on the ammo. I have yet to find anybody who can run faster than that." The man in unmarked fatigues continued the lecture in a bored voice. "The stopping power is somewhere between a .38 and a .357 magnum. Like all recoil operated pistols, the kick's straight back. Your arms will absorb the recoil in an up and down motion. This allows you to recover your sight picture quicker. I'm sure all of you are strong enough to hold your sights on target in spite of the recoil. It's all in the practice. I think I can promise you that after a few days on this range you'll all be able to keep ninety percent of your shots in the kill zone. How many of you have not used a handgun before?" he asked, looking from face to face. Karen, Kim, and Janet raised their hands. "That's all right, ladies," the range master continued, "before you finish here you'll be as good as anybody else. You don't have any bad habits I have to break. I'm going to teach you everything there is to know about the care and use of this weapon. I plan to make sure that if you learn nothing else, you'll learn proper sight picture and body position. The ranges we'll be working with go from arm's length to the maximum effective range of the weapon. You will be shooting at a variety of target types, including moving. How many of you are familiar with this particular weapon?" the range master asked.

Bosworth, Hayes, and Segretti raised their hands. Tom asked, "Will there be any modifications from factory specs in these weapons?"

"They're right out of the box," the range master answered with a puzzled look that indicated this was not a normal question.

"I'd like to see the trigger pull cleaned up and the chamber polished a bit more. Everything can be improved."

"What you're talking about needs an armorer and we don't have one handy."

"Considering where we're going and what we know, I think we should have a couple of these barrels threaded for a suppresser," Segretti added, looking to Frank and Sherlock for support.

"That may be possible. I have some barrels that are equipped with high grade silencers. They're the wiper/ bleed off variety," the range master replied. *What the hell is a bunch like this getting mixed up in? I can understand all men, but what the hell are women and old men doing in a place like this?*

"I have to agree with David," Frank said. "We'll take them if we can get them."

"Some of us old farts were weaned on the government .45; what's the chance of getting our hands on some of them?" Don asked with his southern drawl.

"I think you would be better off using these because of ammo weight and availability. Besides the advantage of lighter weight, you have a higher magazine capacity. Any more questions or comments before we start?" The range master handed out the black plastic boxes with the property cards attached to the top with cellophane tape. "Take them over to the table and start filling out the cards. Make sure the numbers on the card match the weapon. After you finish that, we'll get into the care, maintenance, and operation of the 'Burrito' 92." The range master counted heads and disappeared into the room behind the counter.

Tom opened the box, checked the serial number against the number on the card, and then picked up the deep blue pistol. He dropped the magazine and jacked the slide back, checking for a round the chamber. He stood and moved to an empty space behind the seated group. His eyes searched for a suitable target. He saw a thumbtack holding a range poster on the bulletin board across the room. Starting with the weapon at his side, he started raising his right arm, and his left hand made an audible slap as it wrapped around the grip. His index finger locked around the front of the trigger guard. From this ready position, Tom continued to raise the weapon, sliding the safety off inches before he aligned with the target. He pulled the long, double-action trigger a fraction of a second after he lined up the sights on the target. There was the soft clack as the hammer fell, hitting the firing pin.

"Not bad," The range master said as he walked up to the table carrying a large box. "Your stance could improve, but you've got good flow and grip."

"I guess it's just like riding a bicycle. Once you know you never forget," Tom replied, returning to his seat.

"You're right there. Come on, let's go over the specs and maintenance of these weapons," the range master said as Tom sat down. "I have a cleaning kit for each of you." He handed them around. "It contains everything you need to properly take care of your weapons. Remove your weapons from the box and follow along with me." He waited until everyone had removed their pistol from the plastic, foam-lined box. "Okay, jack the slide back and check the chamber. Release the slide and drop the magazine with this button here." He demonstrated, catching the empty magazine in his left hand. "Now hold the weapon in your right hand, press the disassembling latch, and rotate it to a forward position." He held the pistol at eye level and swiveled the slide catch. "Now slide the top half forward and off. Lay the frame aside, lay the slide down on the sights, gently depress the spring and guide forward and lift up." Frank's fingers slipped as he removed the pieces and they flew across the room. "I should have warned you about that. Sorry, my fault," the range master continued. "There's a fair amount of tension on that spring. Now, depress the block plunger and lift the barrel out, like this. That's all there is to field stripping this weapon. Before we finish this week, you'll be able to do this blindfolded. To put it together, you just reverse the procedure. Go ahead and start, I'll be wandering around if you have trouble." The range master walked behind each of his new students and looked over their shoulders. "Miss," he said to Karen, "turn the whole assembly over and slide the frame into the grooves on the slide. That's the way. This weapon weighs a little over two pounds; with a full fifteen-round magazine and one in the pipe you have about another eight ounces." Returning to the large box, he pulled out holsters and magazine pouches and started handing them around. "This is the new military design holster. It's padded and it's also rot proof. We'll get around to some of the other points later. Put these on your belts and let's move outside. Grab yourselves a pair of earmuffs on the way out, we run a hot range here. I'm sure you've heard the expression: 'Treat every gun as if it were loaded.' Well here, all guns are always loaded. In fact, the only time I want to see an unloaded weapon is when the slide is locked open. You're going to be in a dangerous area, or you wouldn't be carrying weapons. You'll be carrying them loaded when you get there, so you might as well get used to having them that way now. Let's do it." The range master walked out the back door into the hot South Carolina sun.

"Hey, Hill," the man in the black cotton work clothes called across the fire, "what do you think of the shit Howard's trying to pull, making us responsible for getting a full harvest out of this field?"

"duPage, you know he's a crazy motherfucker, but this time he's right. There ain't no way in hell we can cut pods and gather that sap by ourselves."

"Yeah, you know damned well if we go up there and ask those folks nicely to come be our field slaves they're just going to tell us to go fuck ourselves," another man replied.

"That may be true, but the general gave orders to leave Cam An alone. Another thing, we may be deserters but I think we still consider ourselves Americans. I know I do, and I'd hate like hell to get into it with another round-eye," duPage continued as he passed the joint to the man on his right.

"The way I see it, we're fucked no matter what we do. If we don't get the shit in, we'll have Howard on our asses. If we use the people in the village, we'll have the general on our asses. We're royally fucked guys. We all know damned well Howard ain't going to be spreading the other help around." Hill opened another bottle of warm Tiger beer and drank deeply to moisten his mouth, dry from the marijuana.

"What do you think our chances are of telling these

people we don't want any trouble but we're taking the people anyway?" another voice asked from the back of the shaded straw hut.

"Christ, what do you think they're going to do? Just say, sure, here, take 'em. Fuck no, they're going to be on the horn to somebody in the government and we'll have them on our collective asses," duPage answered from his position in the dope smoking circle.

"Yeah, well the general is the government in this area, and when it comes to his opium, you know he ain't going to do shit," Hill answered in short words while he tried to retard his exhalation of the potent smoke.

"Well, if he don't do shit, somebody above him will. Let's face it, no matter what we do, we're fucked," duPage replied, taking another drink of warm beer.

They sat quietly for a few minutes, thinking. A black soldier lit another large marijuana joint, inhaling deeply before passing it on. "One thing we haven't talked about is taking Howard out and taking over."

"Washington, are all you niggers crazy? Howard's one crazy nigger, but that idea of yours is even crazier. Shit man, we all saw what he did to Bates a couple a months back. Hell, Bates probably would have died from that beating anyway, but that crazy motherfucker just smiled when he broke his fuckin' neck," duPage replied, taking the offered joint. "Look, we all know Howard's the meanest son of a bitch in the valley and there ain't no way of gettin' close to him with his spook squad around. Sorry, Washington."

"'S all right man, no offense taken. Them niggers is spooky okay, what else can you call 'em," the muscular black man with knives strapped to each arm answered.

"I think we're goin' a get fucked no matter what we do. Too bad we can't just frag that cocksucker," duPage continued, taking another hit off the massive joint.

"Drawing and firing a handgun is as simple as following the numbers." The range master drew his Beretta, dropped the magazine in to his hand and slid it into his pocket. He then pulled back the slide, ejecting the round in the chamber. "Like I said, on this range, all guns are always loaded. Everybody do what I just did. Good. Now watch, by the numbers. One: the hand lifts the weapon from the holster and starts moving it up and forward. Two: the weak hand moves forward, closes around the fingers and the forefinger wraps around the front of the trigger guard. Three: the safety comes off as you continue to raise the weapon to your line of sight. Notice my finger hasn't touched the trigger yet. Four: the finger goes on the trigger and starts taking up the slack. Five: your arms are up, the sights are aligned, and now you continue to squeeze the trigger until the weapon fires. Now you try it; feet apart about shoulder width, one foot slightly in front of the other. By the numbers; one... two... three... four... five." There were ten clicks as the hammers fell on empty chambers. "Looked good to start with. Keep it up, by the numbers, until your arms get tired. This is called dry firing and you should do this ten times for every round you fire." The range master walked behind the group, watching and occasionally making some kind of a correction on each student. "Aim for the center of the mass, no matter what the mass is.

The range master allowed the dry firing to continue for perhaps twenty minutes. "That's enough for now. Let's get some ammo and see how much good it's done."

Jim Sherlock holstered his weapon and said, "Sir, could I borrow a loaded magazine from you before we start?"

"Damn it, don't call me sir. I work for a living," came the reply as the range master handed over a full, fifteen-round magazine.

"I just went through the same speech the other day with this bunch. What are you, E-8?"

"Yeah, how about yourself?"

"Close enough. No good conduct ribbons in my family. Hayes, front and center." Bill ambled up with a smile. "Take off your shirt and button it on that target out there."

"Sure thing," Hayes answered as he did as he was asked.

"Listen up, everybody. I told you these uniforms were made of a special material. Direct your attention to the target Bill is putting his shirt on." Sherlock waited until Hayes got back behind the firing line. He inserted the magazine, jacked a round into the chamber and started firing. The first five shots hit the heart area. With the last ten he drew a happy face on the head of the silhouette target. "Come on down and see what happened to the fabric and the bullets." the group walked over to the target where Sherlock reached down and picked up five copper jacketed bullets from in front of the light brown shirt. He handed them to Kim. "Pass them around," he said, lifting the shirt from the target. "You can see where the bullets impacted on the target, and the shirt doesn't have any holes in it. What we have here is essentially bullet-proof clothing. Don't get the wrong idea; if this had been a person they'd probably be dead from the impact over the heart. And remember, these are pistol bullets. I have my doubts if it would be of much help if you were shot with a rifle."

"Let's bust some caps people," the range master bellowed. "Come on, I'll get you some ammo. When you get it, go to the bench and load your magazines. We'll start shooting from the three yard line," he said as he walked back inside the air conditioned range building.

"Nice shooting, Gunny," Kim said with a smile as she walked beside Sherlock. *What more could a woman ask for? He ain't all that handsome, but he's got a way about him. I want this man.* She walked as close as possible to the big gunnery sergeant.

"Thanks. No big deal, I get plenty of practice," Jim Sherlock replied, increasing his pace to catch the others. *God, even sweaty she still smells good. Watch yourself Sherlock*, he thought, walking through the screen door. *Keep your mind on the job and your dick in your pants. Now's not the time or place.*

"I'm going to issue you each one box of ammo," the range master said loud enough for all to hear. "I want you to continue just like you did dry firing, only now, every time you draw, fire two rounds. Go through it by the numbers. Don't worry about speed, it'll come with practice. Get your sight picture and trigger pull down today. Two shots each time your weapon leaves the holster," he instructed, handing each person a fifty round box of ammunition. "Sarge, you know you don't have to go through this Mickey Mouse bullshit," he said as he handed Sherlock the ammo.

"Yeah I do, I believe in leading by doing. Besides, it's been a long time since I've had anybody spot me."

"Good man, let's get them on line."

The ten members of the team spread out along the three yard line. "Commence firing," the range master yelled as he started walking behind the shooters. He stopped behind Tom. "Don't palm it, wrap those fingers more around the front strap." He continued to Karen. "Open your stance a little more and come more face on with the target." He stopped beside Janet and put one hand on her shoulder and the other on her stomach and straightened her back. "Open your stance more and have one foot behind the other. You're off balance like this. If you keep this up you'll fall on your ass." He stepped between Frank and Don. "More finger on the trigger, more like a revolver. These aren't .45's." He came at last to Jim Sherlock and noticed him drawing a heart inside the X-ring. He continued another two paces, drew his own Beretta and continued cutting where Sherlock left off. The range master calmly changed magazines and started retracing his steps down the firing line, stopping to give directions.

Sherlock inserted his third magazine into the butt of his weapon and pushed the slide release, chambering a round. He started at the right shoulder and continued down to the left hip. He moved to the right hip and continued a line to the left shoulder. With his last round he took careful aim and placed a shot in what would be the center of the forehead on the target. He closed the slide, reholstered the weapon and walked off the firing line to the shade of the building.

"Nice shooting, Sarge," the range master said. "I'm Marty Kuhl," offering his hand.

"Jim Sherlock, and thanks. Well, I guess we'll give them a few more minutes then run them off to chow. What do you want to do with them next?"

"More of the same, just keep moving them back to where they can't keep them on the paper, and then start over. You've got some fair shots in this group, what are they anyway?"

"Civilians, all except for that tall brunette. She's a

spec four from graves registration. I'm supposed to get this bunch in shape to go back to 'Nam. I'm starting to think it might be possible."

"Is this the bunch that wasted Goode on the hand-to-hand course yesterday?"

"Yep, that little blond, and the guy to her right. Since we're going to be bothering you for a while, why don't you come over to the barracks after chow tonight and get better acquainted. Hell, I'll even buy the beer," Sherlock said as they watched slides lock back after the last rounds were fired.

"Might as well, I haven't got anything better to do," the sergeant said before he yelled. "Okay, people, load your magazines before you leave the range area. I want you back here at 0700 hours. More ammo inside. Fill all your clips," he yelled, much in the same manner as Sherlock had the past few days.

Sergeant Martin Kuhl pulled his jeep up beside the olive drab army van as Sherlock opened the door. Before speaking, Sherlock turned and picked up two cases of Pabst Blue Ribbon beer. "Marty, could you grab that last case of beer for me?" Sherlock asked, walking toward the door. He carried the beer into the TV room with the range master close behind. "They got the fridge fixed today, so I recommend you all fill your canteens tonight and cool them down. It's supposed to be another hot one tomorrow. Beer's here," he said as he ripped open the third case and started handing the cans around, keeping one each for himself and Sergeant Kuhl. "Our range master decided he'd like to get to know us better, so he came by for a beer or ten. I'd like you folks to meet Marty Kuhl."

There was a chorus of greetings as Tom, Bill, and David looked up from their work at the table.

"What in the hell are you men doing to my weapons?" Kuhl asked when he saw all the Barettas torn apart with pieces scattered all over the table.

"Well, Sarge, we thought the actions could be cleaned up a bit, so we scrounged all the nail files and some baking soda from the cook, mixed that with toothpaste, and we're doing a bit of fine polishing," Hayes replied as he held a hammer and sear to the light to examine the fit.

"Here you go Sarge, try this one." Segretti handed over an assembled weapon.

The range master checked the chamber and pulled the trigger. "Nice. What could you guys do with a good set of tools?"

"Probably a lot more," Tom replied. "I'm sure we could slick up the trigger pull a lot more."

"Well, you men just became armorers," Sergeant Kuhl said, setting beer in front of the three men. "Don't bother with the rest of them, you can use the shop tomorrow. Now put them back together and let's drink some beers and shoot the shit."

The conversation during the evening covered a wide range of subjects: weapons; personal stories, which is better, the Army or Marines; the USA; Vietnam. The people who had once been "in country" recalled stories and incidents, both good and bad.

"I hate to break up this party," Sherlock said at last, "but it's getting on to ten-thirty, and 0500 is going to come awfully early tomorrow. Marty, time to kick you out and we'll see you tomorrow."

"Thanks for the beer and good conversation. Most of the people we get through here don't speak English. It's a real pleasure to have you around. I'll see you on the range at 0700," Kuhl replied, downing the rest of his beer.

"You all go ahead. Janet and I'll pick this place up," Hayes said as Janet gave him a questioning look. She shrugged her shoulders and started picking up ashtrays. Bill started with the empty cans. When he came to the last one Segretti had, he slipped it into the jacket pocket of his BDU's. With everything picked up, they turned off the lights and returned to their room. As Bill closed the door he asked, "Janet, where's your baby powder?"

"In the locker, why?"

"I picked up one of David's cans. I'm going to lift the fingerprints and send them to Ted Mason. If anybody can find out about him it's Top."

"I'll get it. What else do you need?"

"Just that scotch tape over on the desk and a sheet of paper. With any kind of luck we can have the complete rundown in a week or so."

Chapter Ten

The first four weeks of training seemed to fly by as each member of the group learned to work with, and for the good of, the others. The physical conditioning had honed the group to the best shape any of them had been in, in years. Frank had lost ten pounds, while Don had lost twenty. With the exceptions of David and Kim, everyone had required a new issue of clothing. The four-thirty wake up was now part of their daily routine. Everyone was standing tall on the line when Jim Sherlock made his appearance at 5:00 A.M.

"Well, good morning everyone," Sherlock said when he walked out of the barracks for formation. "I've got some good news and some bad news. The good news is: we're four days ahead of schedule. The bad news is: we're ready to move over to area three. Come on, boys and girls, smile. We're going camping."

"Oh, Jim," Kim said as she raised her right hand for a one finger salute.

"That's not nice, Kim," Sherlock replied with a wry smile. "Let's get warmed up and see what we can do with a two-mile run. This is going to be the last day for all this physical conditioning bullshit. Push yourselves. Let's see how far we've come. Start with windmills." The gunnery sergeant moved to his usual place about fifteen feet in front of the group and raised his arms. "Count off," he said as they started. They moved rapidly through the forty-five minutes of calisthenics. Frank and Don kept up without the usual moaning, groaning and gasping for breath. The count for push-ups stopped at fifty, the older men were only two or three behind the count when Sherlock called a halt. "Okay, take a breather," he said, doing one last push-up and springing to the balls of his feet.

"Damned showoff," Don mumbled, loud enough for all to hear.

"Listen up, people," Jim said. "Two miles down the trail, cut left and head for the mess hall."

"Last time, Jim," Kim spoke up as she stretched like a cat. "This time I'm going to run your ass into the ground."

"Oh, the lady's getting testy this morning," Sherlock replied with what had gotten to be known as his shit-eating grin. "From here to the ladder. Last one there buys the beer. This will be the last beer we get until we get back from area three. Everybody ready?" Jim took the stopwatch from his pocket. "Kim, come here. Ready? Now!" He hit the start button as Kim sprinted off to a good four-pace lead. The rest of the team started in a bunch with Karen, Janet and Mi Ling leading off, and Tom, Bill and David close behind. Don and Frank were in their usual place in the rear, but their pace was faster than before.

Kim slowed as she made the right angle turn in the woods. Jim Sherlock didn't bother as he cut across the corner through the trees and came out a few paces ahead. "You cheatin' son of a bitch," Kim yelled as she lengthened her stride and attempted to catch the big gunnery sergeant. At the mile and a half mark, Sherlock's foot hooked under an exposed root. When he stumbled, Kim took the advantage of the mistake to regain the lead. She maintained the advantage until they reached the mess hall clearing. She poured her last energy reserves into a sprint, widening the distance. Grabbing the ladder of the horizontal bars, she swung around and caught Sherlock in a hug when he slowed up. She reached up and gave the tall Marine a quick kiss. "Damn, that was nice," she whispered through her panting breath, and kissed him again. "Not only beating your ass but the kiss too. I've been waiting weeks for both of them, but you were to damned dumb to notice." Kim wrapped her arms tighter around his neck and pulled his head down to her level. "You know, it would be nicer if two people did the kissing"

Jim Sherlock returned the kiss, and pulled away enough to look at the stopwatch in his hand. "Eleven oh eight. Now turn me loose, the others will be out of the woods in a second. This wouldn't looked good."

"Bullshit," was Kim's only reply.

Bosworth, Hayes and Segretti broke into the clearing with the other women close behind. Their pain-filled faces turned to grins when they saw Kim with her arms wrapped around the gunnery sergeant's neck.

Tom passed the bars and slowed to a stop. He walked back to where Kim was still clinging to their drill sergeant. "Who caught who?" he asked, grinning from ear to ear.

"Not only did I catch him, I beat his ass," Kim replied with the smile of a Cheshire cat.

Jim Sherlock struggled out of Kim's grasp and managed to say, "Twelve oh five and twelve oh nine." He stuttered as his face started to redden with embarrassment.

"Good job, Kim," Janet said as she tried to catch her breath. "It looks like you've got a beaten man."

"Yeah, Kim, it sure took you long enough," Karen added as she and Mi Ling looked on with smiles.

Kim removed her arms from around Jim's neck and slid her hand into his. "Well, I had to do something," she said, returning the smile.

Frank and Don broke out of the treeline with Frank about ten yards ahead. Sprinting the last few yards, Frank passed the ladder and ran well behind the mess hall. The team could hear him start to retch as he vomited the water he drank before the run.

"Fourteen minutes," Jim called out as he hit the stop button. "That's good time for anybody. That's two seven-minute miles back to back. I'm proud of you."

Frank walked around the corner of the building, wiping his pale, sweaty face with his shirt sleeve.

"You okay, Frank?" Don asked as his oldest friend rejoined the group.

"Yeah, I'm okay. Just give me a couple of minutes to collect myself," he replied, removing his canteen and rinsing the bitter taste from his mouth.

"No problem, we've got time for a smoke before we eat," Jim said with a voice and a look showing his concern. "Go ahead, walk around and cool down. All we're doing today is getting ready to move out to area three tomorrow."

"You're going to be carrying the tent, Jim," the tall brunette beside him said with a smile. "Hey, it only makes sense; you and I are the only two who don't have a roommate."

"Are you going to keep Jim up all night with your

snoring?" Janet asked with a slight giggle in her alto voice and a wave of her long red pigtail.

"Well, keep him up. But all night?" came the reply, as Kim slid her arm around Jim's waist. "If he's man enough."

"Just leave him enough strength to do his job," Karen added. "I'll be damned, Jim, you're blushing."

"Enough of this happy horse shit, let's eat," was the only comment Jim Sherlock could make as he removed Kim's arm. As he entered the mess hall he could be heard to mumble, "God damned dirty old ladies. Lord, why me?" *Funny how things have a way of working out. As much as I wanted this to happen, I could have never initiated it. I'm sure glad she made the move.*

God, what a man, Kim thought as she followed through the door. *Now the next question is, how far can we let this go? Jesus, falling in lust with a jar head. What's gotten into me?*

Bill whispered to Mi Ling as he followed her in the chow line. "This could be the attitude adjustment the old Sarge has been needing."

"I believe you may be right. Jim is about all Kim can talk about when we're in the shower together. You men would be surprised at our girl talk," Mi Ling replied with a smile as she watched Jim and Kim take seats across the table from each other.

Chapter Eleven

As they took their seats at the mess hall table, Jim Sherlock looked around the table. "The people who designed the training schedule thought a few days in Panama might help us get accustomed to the climate in 'Nam. I think we would be better off if we spent the time in Da Nang or Quang Tri or someplace getting our shit together and getting over the jet lag."

"I think you have a good idea, Jim," Mi Ling replied. "Since we're ahead of schedule, I believe this would be a better use of our time, and it would give us a chance to take care of any last minute details that come up."

"I doubt if there is anyplace in the world where we could get acclimatized except in country," Don James remarked, taking a sip of the strong, almost undrinkable mess hall coffee.

"That would give us an extra week or so to work before the start of the highland rainy season," Frank said, looking from face to face. "We're going to be pushing it awfully close as it is, so every day will have to count."

"Thankfully, the rainy season starts later in the highlands, but we still have a lot of lowland searching to do. Even with the usual rains the mud is going to be bad enough," Mi Ling continued as she formed a mental picture of her youth, remembering how the thick, heavy clay would stick to her army issue boots while they were on patrol, how the weight of the mud and the incessant drizzle would tire her legs, body and mind.

"Well hell," Tom started, "I mean, what more can we really do? We're in as good a shape as we're going to get. We spend the next few days working our asses off with the new global positioners and we're finished." Tom pushed his almost untouched tray back and lit a cigarette. He looked to the others to acknowledge his suggestion.

"I have to agree with Tom. Let's go for it," Bill said, leaning back in his chair and interlocking his fingers in his brown hair.

"Well, if nobody has any objections, let's get back to

the barracks and see if we can get this show on the road," Sherlock said, standing and looking at Kim. "Anybody feel like running back with me?"

"Yeah, me," Kim replied as she followed close behind and out the door. *I've made my move, I wonder what Jim will do now. He shouldn't feel threatened by an aggressive woman.* Kim's thoughts ran through her mind as fast as she sprinted up the direct path to the barracks building. *I've never had to come on to a man like this before. Not that there have been all that many. If he doesn't do something soon, I'm going to rape him. God, what a nice butt he has.* Kim didn't say anything as she let Sherlock stay a few paces in front of her all the way up the trail.

They walked through the door together without a word. Kim walked into her room Jim continued down the hall to his own. After he closed the door, Jim walked directly to the locker and pulled out the half empty bottle of vodka. After taking his large after-meal swallow, he recapped it and returned it to it's resting place inside the locker. *Things are going to be a real bitch when we get to 'Nam. No class VI stores around. Well, I guess this will be as good a time as any to try to dry out. What the hell is this damned woman trying to do to me? Sherlock, keep your dick in your pants until this whole damned thing is over. Christ, Jimbo, you're as fucked up as a teenager at his first whore house.* His thoughts were interrupted by a soft knock on the door. "Open," he said.

Kim walked into the room. Even though there was a smile on her face, Jim could see the questions in her large brown eyes. "Jim, I hope you don't mind what I said out there?" she said as she walked across the room to stand directly in front of the big gunnery sergeant.

"Look, Kim, I'm supposed to be ramrodding this bunch through training. I'm concerned with appearances and the possible breakdown of the team. We just can't afford to get involved right now."

"Jim, God damn it, you fucking Marines are dumber than hammered cow shit. None of us are your eighteen or nineteen-year-old-grunts. None of us really give a damn about someone's living arrangements. Everybody has known since the first day I've been wanting to jump your bones, and I'm tired of waiting for you to make a move. After we finish our time in area three, your job as ramrod, as you call it, is over." Kim's voice got louder with every word. "If we're going to be a team, it's going to have to be a partnership of men and women. Look, you stupid jar head, if you don't want to sleep with me, I'll carry my own fucking tent," Kim finished with a voice loud enough to be heard by the rest of the team as they walked into the building. Her tirade over, she turned and stomped out the door, slamming it behind her. Everyone was standing in the hall, each waiting with an ear-to-ear grin as she looked up. Kim was at first embarrassed, then she started to laugh. Her infectious laughter was quickly joined by the team as they moved to their respective rooms.

Jim opened his door and saw the team grinning as they looked from him to Kim and then back again. His expression was that of puzzlement, embarrassment and shock. He cleared his throat and tried to sound off like a drill sergeant. "All right, people, start getting your shit laid out, inspected and packed. Make sure you have everything you need. I'll see if I can get our orders changed and the briefings moved up. Kim, I'll carry the tent." He closed the door and walked back to the locker for another stiff drink. *You dipshit! She's right. Nobody gives a damn about our personal lives. I could be fucking a sheep and no one would care as long as I did my job. Yeah, but Kim's a long way from a sheep. More like a wildcat. She started this shit, remember? Face it, stupid, you want her as bad as she wants you. Sherlock, you are royally fucked.*

The women gathered around Kim like a bunch of mother hens, while the men leaned against the walls, chuckling.

The door opened and a PFC walked in and shouted, "Mail Call," handing the stack of letters to Frank who was the closest.

Frank started to hand out the letters, reciting the names as they came off the stack. "Me, Sherlock, Bosworth, Bosworth, Hayes, James, Segretti, Sherlock, Sherlock, Mi Ling, Matthews, Segretti, Sherlock, and Segretti. That's it for today," Frank finished passing out the envelopes after making a mental note of where David's were postmarked. One from Italy, one from Ireland, and the last from Germany. He said nothing, but filed the information away for further consideration. He knocked on Sherlock's door. No words were exchanged as the tall gunnery sergeant took the letters and closed the door.

Hayes closed the door of their room behind himself and Janet before he ripped open the envelope. "This one's from Top Mason, probably found out who our mysterious Mr. Segretti is," he said, starting to read aloud. "Bill: I've run the name and prints through every national computer I can get into. Nothing. Interpol has no record of a David Segretti from NY or anywhere else. Your man does not exist. We have no idea who, what, or how he is. You kids watch your asses on this one. Say hello to the rest of the bunch for me. Ted." Hayes finished reading the terse letter and then raised his eyes to Janet. "Well, if Top can't find anything, I guess he doesn't exist. I had a difficult time accepting him before, but now we have this shit. I'm going to pass it on."

"Well, Don told us not to try to find out anything, now we come up with this. What do you think he's supposed to do?" Janet asked as she took the letter and reread Ted Mason's large, flowing handwriting.

"Honey, your guess is as good as mine. We're going to have to have a conference on this. I'll be right back," he said as he walked out the door.

Sherlock stepped into the hallway at the same moment as Hayes and bellowed, "I'm going to HQ to pick up our rations and a list of the things they're going to be packing for the trip to 'Nam. Have your shit together and in one sack when I get back."

Kim opened her door and walked up beside him. "Mine's all packed and I'm going with you," she said with a smile that almost made the tall, thin woman look radiant.

Bill looked at the two with a knowing grin, and said "Don't get lost, kids." Kim gave him a wink in reply as she followed Jim out the door Bill knocked on Tom and Karen's door and handed the letter to Karen as soon as she answered.

"What's this?" she asked as she took the folded sheet of paper from Hayes' outstretched hand.

"A letter from Top Mason. I sent him a set of David's prints," Bill replied as she started to read. Tom walked across the small room to read over her shoulder. "Our friend and cohort doesn't exist." Tom and Karen both raised eyebrows in disbelief, knowing that the probability of not being on a computer list somewhere was next to impossible.

"Somehow that doesn't surprise me," Tom replied, reaching over her shoulder and taking the letter. "What do we know about him? One: he's sandbagging us on his physical condition. He's in a lot better shape than the rest of us; he's just been pacing us through training." Tom started trying to think of more of the less obvious quirks and characteristics of their mysterious team member. "Two: he knows a lot more about that Beretta than is common knowledge. Hell, he knows it as well as we do." They all thought back to the night they were first issued the weapons; how Segretti knew the modifications needed and how to do them without instruction. "Three: on the range he places his shots so his score wouldn't be more than seventy-five percent. You've got to be good to shoot that bad. Every time he touches the weapon he's fast, smooth, and precise."

"The fucker's good... too good," Bill acknowledged with a nod.

"And everybody else talks about home and family. He's never once mentioned them, never even a slip," Karen said as she and Janet tried to think of David Segretti from a more emotional point of view.

"He said he's from New York. I don't know about you, but I can't place the accent to New York. It's like he doesn't have a regional accent. His language is just too perfect," Janet added.

Tom looked at the sheet of paper as if there were a message hidden deeper in the short paragraph. He shook his head before looking up and returning the letter to his friend.

"Yeah, and I'll bet that bastard's not Italian either. Let's show this to Frank and Mi Ling. It looks like we're back where we started; nowhere. Oh, by the way, Kim just took off with Jim. Let's see how big their smiles are when they get back."

"Frank," Tom said, knocking on the door, "I think we need to have a talk. Hayes and Janet are in my room, could you two drop over for a second?"

"Sure, Tom. What's up?" Frank answered as he set a partially filled pack on the bed.

Tom put his finger to his lips, pointing to the wall adjoining Don and David's room. They nodded in understanding as they followed Tom down the hall to his room. As the door opened, Bill handed Frank the incriminating letter from the CIA.

Frank read. "Something's fishy here," he remarked. "Everybody is on a computer somewhere. And if he's representing someone who can toss a half million dollars into a project and not worry about results, he has to have prints or something on file somewhere." Frank handed the letter to Mi Ling.

"If Ted said this guy doesn't exist, then he doesn't exist," Hayes said, his aggravation showing. "We've been around this guy for over a month now and we don't know any more than we did."

Frank crossed the room and sat on the unmade bed, his brow wrinkled in thought. "What it still boils down to is that the only one who knows anything is Don, and he's not saying anything. Hell, I've tried to get answers out of him. Christ, we've been friends for over thirty years, you'd think he'd trust me by now," Frank mumbled with thoughts of the years, and the letter Mi Ling was reading for the third time.

Mi Ling joined the conversation at last, "We know he has something to do in Vietnam, but not what. What we do know is that he's supposed to be working with us until it's time to do whatever. We know he started this in good physical condition and he drinks in less than moderation. What else do we know?"

"Well," Karen started her analysis, "you would think that after a month he'd at least have some suggestive looks for us women." She sat in the folding chair beside the small writing desk. Interlocking her fingers behind her neck, she stared up at the light green ceiling. "There's got to be something obvious we're missing."

"Yeah, none of us are what you would consider dogs," Janet replied as she took a seat on the bed beside Frank.

"You'd almost think he was gay the way he hangs around with Don."

"He hasn't been looking at the guys either," Bill continued, taking his place beside the tall redhead. "It's like sex doesn't exist for him, like he's totally asexual."

"All we do know is that this guy refuses to interact with the rest of us," Tom replied to the comment as he started to pace the room, stroking his chin in thought. "The only person he really talks to is Don. This guy is spooky. I'm not sure I'd want him watching my ass." Tom looked to the others around the room.

"I'm beginning to think this guy should have some kind of an accident," Bill said, almost in a whisper, as he lit a cigarette from the butt of another.

"I don't believe that would be wise," Mi Ling answered in her calm, quiet voice. "If something happens to him, the backers might pull their support. I believe our guest is important, or he wouldn't be here. There has to be some reason other than to see how the money is spent. We just need to go with the flow for now."

"I guess we'll just have to wait. If he does anything to jeopardize the mission, or any of us, then we take him out," Hayes said, looking around at the rest of the group nodding in agreement.

"What's so important that you must interrupt my afternoon meditation, Vinh?" the general asked sleepily as he rose from the leather couch as fast as his obese body would allow.

"That *amu con de hoang* (black bastard). Howard has given orders the Cam An field has to produce as much opium latex as the other fields. He doesn't care how the men do it. I believe the mercenaries will have no choice but to press the village into service."

"That *domommie* (motherfucker) will destroy everything I've worked for all these years if he does that now. We must find a way to relieve Comrade Howard from his command before the Americans arrive. You are aware of his cadre of *lam cho den* (niggers) he keeps around him. Find a way of disposing of him without killing too many of the others. They may be of use to us in the future." The general waddled to his desk and removed a Kool from an ivory box.

"Yes, my general, I will see what can be arranged," Vinh replied, taking note of the general's every move. "How much time do we have before the American search team arrives?"

"The last I heard, they will be here in about three weeks." The general lit the cigarette and turned his back on the colonel. General Xuan studied the ragged, faded battle flag hanging on the wall behind the desk before he continued." So, my friend, we must have this done as soon as possible."

"Yes, I agree, but I don't believe I should use any of the regular troops. I'm not sure they would understand the poppy fields are for the good of our country. I will see to it that the teeth and claws are removed from this animal."

"See that they are, Colonel," the general replied as he squeezed his body into the leather chair behind the desk and picked up a report. His actions showed his lack of concern for the situation, and for his abrupt dismissal of the colonel at the same time.

One of these days you fat pig, the colonel thought. *One of these days I'm not going to save your fat ass and all this will be mine. I deserve this command; I fought for it. You kept your ass hidden in Hanoi with that whore of yours while the rest of us died. You would shit your pants if someone ever pointed a weapon at you.* Vinh turned to the office door in disgust.

The poppy plants swayed in the light breeze that brought the coughing sound of a jeep to the area. The men in the bush watched and wondered why Howard and his men would choose midday to visit. They watched as the vehicle slid to a stop at the edge of the irrigation dike. The driver leaned on the horn as the four others climbed down and started to spread out in a line across the field.

"duPage, man we got to find a way to waste that nigger's ass 'for he wastes ours," Washington said as they watched Howard's men approach.

"Yeah, I'd frag his ass if I could get close enough."

"Man, you know his asshole buddies would blow your

ass away then hang your nuts on the hooch to dry ifin they even thought you wuz thinkin' that way," the tall muscular black man replied, adjusting the elastic bands holding the K-Bar knives on the outside of his bulging biceps.

"Maybe we could slip some scorpions or some bamboo vipers into his hooch some night. It'd look like they got him," a third man said as they watched the five men walk the rows toward them.

"Yeah, Wood, you go ahead and pick up those crawly little fuckers and we'll pick you up after they nail your crazy ass. Cool it, let's go see what these assholes want," duPage said calmly as they left their concealed position in the jungle.

Chapter Twelve

"Everybody into the TV room for briefing," Sherlock yelled when he and Kim walked through the front door. They turned left towards the day room. Jim made a beeline to the fridge and pulled out two beers, handing one to Kim as the team gathered. They greeted the pair with smiles and grins, each person seemingly saying, we know what you've been doing. Jim became more uncomfortable with each passing glance, while Kim smiled like a cat with a saucer of milk.

"Let's get this shit out of the way before we start playing grab ass," Sherlock growled as he handed the pages of inventory around. "This is what the powers that be think we should take with us. Let's look it over and see how they fucked it up." Jim didn't allow his eyes to make contact with anyone but Kim as the lists went around, and for a few moments after that when the work started.

Karen's eyes ran down the lists and she was the first to speak. "Two things I notice right off:" she said, "toilet paper and Tampax. Must have been men who put this together. It's typical, things they'd never think of."

"Fine, somebody start a list. Kim, you're elected," Jim said without a second thought. A few eyebrows were raised as Kim pulled a pen out of her pocket and started writing on the back of her copy.

"I see no mention of extra ammo," Bill said, looking over the list. Kim added ammo to the sheet without pausing or looking up.

"Extra batteries and parts for the radios. They always go out when you need them," Sherlock noted, remembering past experiences with Murphy's Law in combat.

"How big is a five hundred watt generator?" Karen asked. "Does that mean it will only power five one hundred watt light bulbs?"

"Right, let's get a replacement; at least two thousand watts. Put down a medium command post tent. That will give us a place to get together until we can build something better," Frank said, watching as Kim added it to the list.

"I'm looking at the contents of the first aid kit," Mi Ling said in her normal, quiet voice that was barely loud enough to be heard above the background noise. "We're going to need a lot of broad spectrum antibiotics, fungicide, anti-diarrhea and anti-malaria tablets, something to sew up lacerations with, and a supply of morphine. These people think they're putting together a first aid kit for an office building. By and large we're going to need something more like a combat medic carries, plus a lot more." Mi Ling tried to remember the route and the distance to the small town of Cam Lo, which was the closest place to the village that had any medical facilities when she left Cam An in 1963.

"Right, I've got it down," Kim replied as she wrote.

"We're limited to a two and a half-ton truck and a jeep. The Vietnam government is supposed to have them waiting when we offload at Quang Tri," Don said, lighting a cigarette, his forth for the day.

Jim walked across the room and started handing around more beer. "Well, on this side of the ocean we're limited to a compak container. That's about the size of a small semi truck trailer. We've only got it about half full already, so we have plenty of room."

"We're going to need chainsaws along with the other tools," Frank noted.

The planning of supplies and equipment continued with everybody adding more things to the new list or deleting things from the official one. At last, no one had any more suggestions and Kim proceeded to run down the combination of lists one more time. With the last item named, she looked around the group, wondering if they had everything.

"When we finish with area three, we'll get our equipment cleaned up and packed away," Jim continued. "They plan to give us a new issue of clothing before we leave. We'll keep the boots; they're already broken in. Everything but our civilian clothes will be packed in the compak container for shipment. That includes the weapons, since we're travelling by commercial carrier. We're well ahead of schedule, so we're going to be spending a few days in Hong Kong getting over the jet lag," Sherlock said, reading the orders and translating them from military jargon to English. *Hong Kong! God, that was a long time ago. I wonder if that place is still there? I remember the times I've said there's nothing wrong with me that couldn't be cured by a week in a Hong Kong whorehouse. But now there's Kim. Jesus, my legs are still weak.* He looked up to see Kim smiling at him while the others stared.

"Do you know anything about our final briefings?" Frank asked for the second time.

"I don't know, but I assume that will happen as soon as we get back from our little camping trip," Jim replied, returning his attention to the present.

"Yeah, there's a lot of things around here we don't know anything about." Tom glared at Don and David.

"There's a lot of things we wish we could tell you, but can't," Don returned the stare. "That's all there is to it."

"A team is built on trust," Bill commented as he walked to the fridge for more beer, "and right now I don't think we trust you two very much." He handed the cans around, including Don and David.

"Thanks. I'm sorry you feel that way, Bill. I'd tell you if I could, but I can't. Just trust I'm on your side," Segretti replied, taking the beer and setting it aside unopened.

Frank took a long hard look at the two men and carefully formed his thoughts before he spoke. "Don, I have to agree with Bill and Tom. I'm beginning to wish we had found our own financing and jumped through the hoops to get the clearances without your help. The secrets you and David are holding are having a direct bearing on the moral of the rest of us, and hence the mission. If things weren't so close to the jumping off point, I'd be tempted to scrap the whole damned thing and start over." Frank showed his exasperation in his tone of voice. "We've known each other for over thirty years now Don," he continued, "and we've always trusted each other, even with our lives. After all we've been through, I would believe Mi Ling and I had earned your confidence by now."

"You have, you know that, but this is something I can't even talk about in confession," the senator replied, seeing the hurt and distrust reflected in the eyes of the others.

Sherlock took control after a pregnant silence held the team for at least a minute. "People, we're going to have to get this shit together one way or another. If there are eight against two, this could turn out to be a very miserable and possibly dangerous trip. I can see both sides and I have to agree with the majority, but I also know about security and following orders. There are only two ways to go, scrap the whole damned thing, or go with what we have now. Right now I'm ready to sign the papers and get back to the Marine Corps, who know what the hell is going on most of the time. Let me know what you decide." Jim finished his beer in one long gulp, and slammed the empty can on the table before he stomped out of the room. Kim followed close on his heels, leaving the group a couple of seconds later. The list was forgotten for the time being as tension filled the air.

Jim Sherlock didn't bother to close his door as he stormed into his room and directly to his locker. He opened the half full bottle of vodka, tossed the cap toward the waste basket, missing. Upending the bottle to his mouth, he drank heavily, watching the level of the clear liquid drop below his hand. He didn't notice Kim as she walked up behind him, until she put a hand on his shoulder.

"I hope to hell you can leave that stuff alone while we're in the bush." Her voice showed a combination of anger and concern. "One thing we don't need is you going through the DT's on us when the shit hits the fan. God damn it, Jim, if this is going to be as rough as you think, we're going to have to get you dried out and straight."

"I don't need to dry out," he almost yelled. "What I need is for this fucking bunch to get their shit all in one sack. It's going to boil down to everybody's ass depending on everyone else. If that fucking Segretti doesn't let us in on what's going down, he's going to get his ass blown away. I'm like the rest of these people. I don't trust that slick son of a bitch either." Sherlock lowered his voice, directing his anger away from the tall woman. "If I could, I would have bounced his ass out of here the first week," he said, looking down at the bottle in his hand and noticing there were only about two ounces left in the quart.

Kim reached her arms around the big gunnery sergeant and squeezed, "I know, Jim, something has to change. Even if it doesn't, he's still part of the group. He deserves the best of you, us, just like everyone else in that room. Neither of us is the kind of person to give less, anytime." She released her hug and stepped back as Jim turned. Picking up the screw cap for the bottle, she handed it to him. "Put this back on and put it away. We've got to find some way to pull this together."

"I know of something that's more fun to pull together – us." He replaced the cap on the bottle and returned it to his locker.

"We've got some serious thinking to do," Kim replied as she playfully slapped his outstretched hand and moved to the metal folding chair. "Now, how the hell are we going to pull this bunch together without killing someone?"

There was no talking as the people in the day room left silently in pairs. Each person could only give the two men a cold stare as they passed. David Segretti and Don James were left alone in the room with the empty cans on the tables. David didn't look at Don as he picked up his two unopened cans and returned them to the refrigerator. Don watched the other man's cat-like movements, and for the first time wondered if he had made the right move in accepting the money and the terms.

For the next hour, the tension built between Don and David. David plopped himself in front to the television set and watched men's tennis. Don sulked close to the refrigerator and poured down one beer after another. "They want to kill you. You know that?" Don said as the alcohol started taking its effect. "I don't blame them. I'm not sure I can trust you myself." Don threw the empty can with all his strength into the trash, then opened another. David kept his eyes on the TV and didn't answer. "David, at least tell me everything so I can buy us some time," Don almost begged.

Segretti turned his head away from the television

and stared at Don with his cold grey eyes. "You asked for me when you took the money. Now you're stuck with me. There's not one damned thing any of you can do about it. I'm in for the duration. And you don't need to know any more about me than you do. Now shut the fuck up." David's sentences came out short, strained, and most of all, emphatic. His voice sent a chill up the back of Don's neck and the cold eyes bored through his skull.

Kim sat at the small writing desk in Jim's room drawing circles and arrows on a sheet of paper. She drew a large, bold arrow in front of each idea that she had written down over the last hour. Small loops and circles covered the right margin and she started connecting them with more arrows. Jim sat on his bed with his elbows on his knees, rubbing his eyes and face, trying to think of a solution that would allow the group to function like a team. Kim looked back at the list and underlined two sentences with heavy strokes of the ballpoint.

"I don't see any more options, Jim," she said as she looked at her list for the hundredth time. "I don't believe we can count on Don or David if things get rough. I'm really afraid that Tom or Bill might just put a bullet in him somewhere along the way." Kim drew a crude picture of a nine millimeter round next to David's name on the paper.

Jim stopped massaging his worried face and stood. "Well, we can only give it our best shot. How the hell did we get into this pile of shit anyway?" He mumbled the last sentence.

"We volunteered," Kim answered. "We should have learned our lesson in basic training."

Jim walked to the door and opened it. The hallway was empty. "Frank, Mi Ling, David and Don, get in here," Sherlock yelled at the top of his voice. "We need to talk." Kim closed the locker, hiding the bottle as she heard doors open and close. Frank and Mi Ling were first, followed closely by Don and David as they walked down the light green hall to Jim's room. "Close the door," Jim said to the senator who was the last one in. "Look, people, we've got some real problems going on here. Do any of you realize that we have three separate groups in this 'team'?" Jim raised his hand, making quotation marks in the air as he looked from face to face.

"Now that I think of it, I guess you're right," Mi Ling answered quietly, looking at the floor as if she were a school girl in the principal's office.

"You can bet your sweet ass I'm right. We've got you, Frank, and the others. We've got Kim and me, who are total outsiders, who are here on military orders. Then we've got you and David." Jim looked directly at Don, who tried to look the big gunnery sergeant in the eyes, but wavered. "Kim and I have orders to go, and I don't think we have a hard time fitting in. Frank, you and Mi Ling are the leaders of the rest of the bunch. Don, you and David are the ones who don't fit into any niche. This group is too small for secrets. If you want to be part of the 'team'," once again he made quotes in the air, "the rest of us need to know about what the fuck is going on."

"I'm sorry, Jim," Don answered, "not until this is over and perhaps not even then. All I can say is that David has an important job that is directly involved not only with financing, but also perhaps the safety of this entire mission. If this means you people won't cover our asses if the shit hits the fan, then so be it," Don James said in anger before he turned and walked out of the room, leaving the door open.

"I'm sorry," Segretti shrugged his shoulders and followed, gently closing the door behind.

"Thanks for trying, Jim," Mi Ling said. "I know this is hard, trying to make us a team, but I think things will turn out all right. At least for now they're working for the good of the group."

"They might be working for the good of the group, but they're still not part of the team, and they won't be until they become part of the family," Kim said with a note of disappointment in her voice.

Jim Sherlock glanced at the locker before he said any more. "Do you think Bill or Tom would kill them if they didn't keep up their end in a fight?" Jim asked, remembering various comments he had heard in the past few weeks.

"To protect the rest of us," Frank said with confidence, "in a millisecond."

Colonel Vinh Ngu watched the squad doing close order drill in the afternoon heat. Each of the fourteen men moved as one; they were almost carbon copies of each other. He watched the sergeant's mouth move and the squad respond to the order a second later. *A good-looking squad to be around a headquarters area. I'm glad I never had to put up with this shit when I was an enlisted man. They wanted us to be as rough and independent as possible. Well, it worked. I stayed with the south army for five years before they started to suspect me. Well, I guess it's time to go out and inspect the troops.* He walked out of the air-conditioned building. The heat started him sweating within seconds. Walking up to the assembled squad, he looked around the former American compound at Da Nang. He closely inspected each man, from the toes of his boots to the top of his pith helmet, then to the AK-47 each was holding. He checked the cleanliness and fit of the web gear, giving a belt or a strap a quick tug here and there. Nothing escaped his experienced eye. *My God, they're so young, just like I used to be. They look good, but are they?* "Sergeant! To the best of my knowledge, no combat-ready force has ever passed inspection, in any army in the world. Your men pass inspection. Now, are they worth a damn?"

"Colonel, I will match my men against any in the Socialist Republic of Vietnam. Some of them are veterans of Kampuchea (Cambodia). They are almost as good as we were," the older sergeant said with a hint of a smile toward his commanding officer.

"Very good, Sergeant, we may see one of these days. Dismiss your men and report to my office, immediately," Ngu saluted the sergeant and men, turned on his toes in a proper parade ground about face and walked into the large, white, air-conditioned building.

"Sergeant, come in here immediately." Vinh yelled upon hearing the door open. The sergeant with the dark green, tailored uniform walked into the office and saluted.

"Sergeant, how long have we known each other?"

Vinh asked in a friendly tone, leaning back and putting his feet on the desk.

"Since you came back to wearing our uniform, about twenty-five years now," the short but strongly built man replied, still standing at attention.

A malicious smile appeared on Vinh's face. "Stand easy, sergeant. I'm sure you know of the American mercenaries working in our province. What do you think of them."

"Colonel, I killed Americans when they had their armies here, as I did the French before them. I have been fighting foreigners as long as I can remember. I wish there was some way to fight the foreign businessmen who are now exploiting our country, but there isn't."

"Good, I'm glad to see your patriotism is still holding strong. Some of our younger people have lost the love of our country. How would you like to fight these mercenaries with a gun in your hand again?" The smile moved to the colonel's eyes as he watched the sergeant relax his stiff posture and start opening and closing his fists.

"If there is a way, sir, in a second."

"The leader of this group of mercenaries is a black called Howard. There are ten opium fields starting a few kilometers west of Cam An." Vinh pulled a map from his desk drawer, spread it on the desk, and started pointing to the locations of the various camps. "He has a group of bodyguards around him at all times, so this mission will be dangerous. We know he has his base at the seventh field." Ngu pointed to the spot on the map and continued. "The general and I believe it is in the best interest of our country if this *den domommie* dies. Do you believe you're capable of causing his untimely death?"

"Yes, Colonel. What amount of time do I have for scouting and preparation?" the sergeant asked, carefully studying the map. "And what may I have in the way of men and equipment?"

"You have seven days in which to get the job done. I don't care how you do it, but get it done. The general and I are unsure of exactly who is paying these men. We believe if their leader is dead the rest will scatter, or at least be easy to control. Because we have no idea who their employer is, we believe it would be best if you limited the men you use to only those you trust. If the person is powerful enough, he could seek revenge. I'm sure you know how these things go."

"Yes, I understand, my Colonel. The job will be done immediately," the sergeant replied, trying to maintain a straight face.

"Sergeant, when you complete this mission I'm sure the general will be more than happy to approve the promotion I'm submitting for you."

The sergeant snapped to attention, saluted and replied, "Yes sir, thank you, sir. I'm doing this not for promotion but for the good of my country, sir. I'll have that man's kinky head on your desk in seven days or less."

"Very good, Sergeant. You may start now. Use my name for any authorization you may need." Vinh stood from behind his desk and saluted the sergeant, then offered his outstretched hand.

Chapter Thirteen

The voice of Howard came over the PRC-25 radio loud and clear as duPage and his men sat in the shade of the thatched hut. "duPage, git yo' mutherfuckin', lily white, honkey ass ova here, rat now. I's don'ts give jack shit whut yo's doin'. Jest move yo' fuckin' ass."

Oh shit, duPage thought as he crossed the large, open thatched hut. Picking up the handset, he replied. "Yeah, I hear you. What the fuck you want?" He listened to the black man's ravings for perhaps three minutes before he answered. "Yeah, I hear you. I'll be there in about an hour." Jerry duPage laid the handpiece down and looked at his men; most of them were stoned, drunk, or well on the way to being there. "Any of you assholes straight enough to be my backup man?" No one answered as they continued passing the large marijuana cigarette.

"Man, the way that nigger sounds, you're in deep shit," one of the men with urine-colored teeth said as he inhaled deeply from the passed joint.

"Washington, Chavez, come with me," duPage ordered, motioning with his thumb. He picked up his M-16 and walked into the hot, bright, Vietnam sun. Pulling his hat low on his forehead to protect his dilated pupils, he got behind the wheel of the Chinese made jeep. *I wonder what that son of a bitch has on his mind this time? I've got to figure a way to off that bastard before he does me. If there was just some way to get his porch monkeys out of the way for a while it'd be easy.*

The sergeant steadied his Chinese made Dragunov sniper rifle across a downed tree. He focused the POS-1, 4-power, telescopic sight on the large black man more than three hundred meters away. He took a deep breath, exhaled, and then another, holding it to quiet his shaky hands and body. He started squeezing the trigger. His finger quickly took up the two millimeters of slack as he applied pressure to the finely machined trigger. He felt the sweat covering his body and soaking through his camouflage uniform. A drop rolled into his right eye. He released the trigger and wiped the stinging salt from his eyes and face with the towel around his neck. He took another deep breath and returned his eye to the telescopic sight. He applied gentle, even pressure to the trigger. The hammer and sear parted as he saw movement in front of his intended target. He watched in what seemed like slow motion as the one hundred twenty-three-grain, 7.62 mm bullet knocked a man forward across the table. He cursed himself as he watched Howard dive to the ground, unhurt. The surreal scene was broken when the men in the compound retrieved their weapons and fired in his direction. Small branches and leaves fell around him as he collected himself and crawled back into the protective cover of the jungle. He could hear the ping, whine and crack as bullets broke the sound barrier over his head. He heard the bullets striking the trees and bushes a few meters behind him. He rose to a crouch and started running, unable to believe he missed.

"Somebody git that mutherfucker!" Howard yelled from under the table. "That son of a bitch done kilt Tyrone! I wants that bastard's head." The men in the camp opened fire in the direction of the shot with their AK-47s and M-16s. The area sounded like the fire-fights twenty years ago.

"He's not shooting back! Move out! I'm goin' t' have all yo' asses in a sling ifin yo' don't git dat sum bitch!" The fifteen men fanned out across the large, grassy clearing, firing short bursts of automatic fire. They dropped the empty magazines and inserted fresh ones without breaking stride.

Well into the trees, the sergeant dropped into his prepared spider hole. Pulling the cover over his head, he waited. He could hear the searchers moving through the dense brush overhead. He leaned back against the cool dirt wall. The sergeant opened his canteen and calmly drank. *Damn! A perfect shot and I missed. Mihn, you're getting old. This would never have happened in the old days.* He took another drink of warm water and capped the canteen. Removing his hat, he laid it on his bent knee as he leaned back against the cool, damp earth. Closing his eyes, Sergeant Trang half dozed while he listened to the efforts of the men above.

When duPage drove up he saw Howard's men running across the open ground toward the bush. *Good kill zone. Anybody with a '60 over in that cover could have a field day. Just looked at those dumb fuckers bunch up.* He got out of the jeep and walked over to where Howard and a couple others had gathered around the body beside the table. *I wonder who blasted his asshole buddy,* he thought as he and his two men calmly looked on.

"duPage, if you had any balls I'd think you had somethin' to do wid this!" Howard yelled. The white man could see the look of the Black man's complexion had lightened by at least two shades. Fear or rage, duPage and his men were unsure of which. "Git de fuck out of here you chicken shit son of a bitch. I'll deal with you later. Shit, I ought to waste your honkey ass right now. Now, git de fuck outta my face." Howard's language switched back and forth from English to Street Black as he glared at duPage while holding the body of his friend.

The fat general sat behind the large, carved teak desk. He toyed with a US Government .45 automatic as the door opened. "Ah, Vinh, come in, come in. Fix us a drink. Make mine scotch. I'll have to order a few more cases the next time someone goes to Hong Kong." The general laid the pistol on the edge of his desk, cocked and locked.

Colonel Ngu walked to the well-stocked bar under the large oil painting of Uncle Ho. He removed ice cubes from the General Electric refrigerator and dropped them into the heavy glasses with the gold embossed US Army eagle and two stars. "I should be hearing soon that our dark problem has been taken care of." Vinh handed the general his drink, being careful no drops fell on the highly polished desk. Keeping the lighter drink for himself, he sat in the comfortable chair to the left side of the desk.

"Good, good. Here's to all of our problems being this easy to solve." The general attempted to shift his bulk to a more comfortable position in the large chair. "Speaking of problems, the Americans will be here in less than two weeks. I have been ordered to allow them the use of a jeep and a large truck. You will greet them as my representative on their arrival in Quang Tri. Keep them away from our fields at all costs." The general finished the stiff scotch in one swallow and handed the glass back for a refill. "This is one thing I have to thank the Americans for – the French had fine wines, but it was the Americans who introduced me to scotch," he said, waiting for his glass to be refilled. "I warned our government about the outlaw activity in our more northern areas. I have also informed them I do not have the manpower to give these Americans adequate protection."

"Yes, it would be tragic if they were robbed or even killed. After all, they did receive warnings and chose to ignore them," Vinh replied, saluting with a raise of his glass and a smile that moved only one corner of his mouth. *You drunken pig, you always have your fat ass covered some way. I'll bet if anything goes wrong it will be me and not you that hangs in the square,* the colonel thought while his cold smile never wavered.

"See the big oak that's taller than everything else? It's at about two hundred degrees," Sherlock said, looking over the expanse of South Carolina's forest. "That's where we're going. According to the map we've got about seventeen miles to go, and I want to sleep in a bed tonight." Jim Sherlock could see the fatigue of the last three days in the faces of the team. The last three days in the forests of South Carolina had taken their toll. The gunnery sergeant had been driving them from before daylight until after sundown, each day trying to push the team to the limits of their mental and physical abilities. The hot morning sun had already brought the temperature close to ninety degrees, evaporating the morning dew and increasing the already high humidity.

Tom slid the bundle of olive green climbing rope from his shoulder and walked to the edge of the limestone cliff. Untying the single knot, he tossed the coils of ten millimeter line over the edge, holding the end. "Somebody hand me a hank of para cord," he said, securing the rope to a large sycamore tree. He tied the thin line to his end of the rope before tossing it over the edge as well, well away from the main rope – a distance where no one would tangle in it and release the main. "I'll see you at the bottom," he said as he wrapped himself in the main line and rappelled down the face of the seventy-five foot bluff. The rest of the group followed, with Jim bringing up the rear. Tom walked over to the para cord release line and picked up the loose end. "Rope!" he yelled before he pulled the thin line, releasing the main rope from the tree above. As the lines fell, he and Sherlock began to coil the lines around their arms.

"God it's hot," Janet said to no one in particular as she looked through the trees at the burning, golden disk of the sun.

"You may as well get used to it, this is the way it is in 'Nam. Even more so, as I remember." Don wiped the sweat from his face with his sleeve.

Hayes looked up at the edge of the cliff, moved a little to his left, and raised the global positioner to his eyes. He raised his arm and pointed. "That way," he said, taking the lead. Tom and Jim finished securing the lines and followed a few minutes later.

They caught up with the team beside a small, clear, cold spring-fed stream. Everyone refilled their canteens and dropped in a halazone tablet – not that the pure spring water needed treatment, but just developing a habit which would be needed in the near future.

"What took you two so long?" Karen asked as she replaced her canteens in the covers on her belt, dipped her hat in the water, and poured it over her head.

"We found a couple of wood nymphs to molest along the way," Tom replied, walking into the shallow water and taking out his canteens.

"Yeah, right. You two just can't keep up the pace," Bill answered with a shit-eating grin.

"Break time's over, let's move out. David, you have the point," Sherlock said in a no-bullshit tone. "The course is two zero three degrees, now get moving. I'm ready for the cold beer and hot shower that's waiting."

Segretti and Don James led off across the stream, with Frank and Mi Ling following close behind.

"If I didn't know better, I'd say those two were queer." Kim observed the two men walking close together as she and Jim joined the rest of the team moving through the woods in single file.

Karen pulled herself on to the bank with the help of

a small willow. "They might as well be. They're part of the group, but they're sure as hell not part of the team."

"Frank and Mi Ling don't like it either, but they've been friends with Don for a long time. If it wasn't their mission, I'd say fuck it all," Tom said as he slid on the muddy stream bank.

"No shit. This shit with Don and David is stretching the bonds of friendship awful thin," Sherlock answered from the rear. "And there's not a damned thing we can do about it."

"Well, we're in it for better or worse," Kim answered. "Let's move out. I want to wash my hair and screw someone clean tonight. Anybody got anything more pleasant to talk about?" she asked as she turned and smiled at Sherlock.

"Jesus Christ, you people look like you're beat to shit," Sergeant Marty Kuhl said, walking into the barracks day room with a case of cold beer in each hand. "I heard Jim call in to HQ, so I thought you folks could use a cool one or two."

"Yeah, that son of a bitch humped us twenty-five miles since the sun came up this morning," Bill said, taking the offered can. The women are in the showers. Us being gentlemen, we let them go first. Sherlock and Kim are scrubbing each other down in his room, probably with their tongues."

"Thanks for the beer, Sarge, it sure tastes good after a long day in the boonies," Tom said, popping the top and taking a long drink.

"Yeah, I'm learning all about long days again," the range master replied. "They just gave me bunch out of Central America who don't speak English and can't understand much of my Spanish. They're being shadowed by a couple of Greenie Beanies who think they're God's great gift to the free world. Oh shit, I almost forgot. I'll be right back. I've got something for you boys out in the jeep." Marty set his beer on the table and started to the door as Karen and Janet come out of the shower and walked towards the day room. They had changed from their tan uniforms into shorts and tee shirts. They continued combing their long wet hair as they approached.

"Hi, Marty," Janet said with a smile in her pleasant alto voice.

"Bet you didn't think we'd make it, did you?" Karen asked.

Seeing the two women dressed as they were, the sergeant could only stop and stare. After a second Marty collected himself enough to say, "God must hate me, he never sent me anywhere with women like you. Oh, the things that can be hidden under a set of fatigues," he said in a stage whisper, giving the two women an approving grin. "And you smell good too; not like them!" He motioned with his chin towards Tom and Bill.

"Thanks, Marty, I think," Karen answered. "Okay, you dirty old men, hit the showers and don't come back until you're clean," the tiny blond ordered the two men watching the exchange.

"Excuse me, ladies, I left something in the jeep. I brought beer, so help yourselves. I'll be back in a second." Marty stepped aside and watched the women continue into the day room.

"Come on Tom, you stink." Hayes finished his beer and dropped the can in the trash. "And you smell delicious," he murmured to Janet, starting to nibble on her neck as he passed.

"Well you don't," she replied. "Get the hell out of here, you two are smelling up the room." She pushed Bill and Tom through the door and into the hall.

Sergeant Kuhl returned in a few minutes carrying four plastic boxes, much the same as the ones the Berettas were packed in. "I brought some more toys for you folks. These were supposed to go to Kennedy's Commandos, but somehow they got lost along the way. I'll explain as soon as everyone gets back from cleaning up. Could you hand me a brew, please?" he asked Janet, who was standing closest to the refrigerator.

"You clean up pretty nice for a redneck." Kim rubbed soap from the back of Jim's neck to his heels. "Turn around and let me get the fun parts."

"That's supposed to be leatherneck, and you've got the nicest ass of any grave digger I've ever seen," Sherlock replied, turning in the water of the small, glassed-in shower.

When Kim had him covered with lather from chin to toes, she put her long arms around his waist. Holding him tightly, she rubbed her tall, lithe, muscular body from side to side. "This is the fun way of taking a shower," she said as she felt his growing erection between her legs. "Rinse," Kim commanded as she stepped back a couple of inches, allowing the stream of cool water to cascade down their bodies.

Jim cupped each small, firm breast in his large hands, gently caressing each and giving special attention to the nipples. He bent forward as much as possible in the small space and gently flicked the tip of each peak with his tongue. She reached between his legs and started gently massaging his testicles. "This place is too small to fuck in," she said. "Come on, you're clean enough." Kim reached behind the big man and turned the shower off as Jim opened the shower door and stepped out, passing a towel behind. He made a quick pass over his short hair and face and then turned to Kim and started toweling her shoulders and continuing downward, slowing at the places he found most interesting. Kim's hands automatically moved to his head as she arched her back. "To hell with drying off. Let's fuck," she murmured as she raised him with gentle pressure under his arm and led him toward the bed.

"David, we have to tell those people out there something. They're just tolerating us. If and when the shit hits the fan they're going to be covering each other and we're going to be sucking hind tit," Don said in frustration, pulling on a fresh, civilian, short-sleeved shirt.

"Look, Don, you know the rules. You knew them when you accepted financing for this," Segretti replied in a tone that told Don there would be no negotiation.

"For once, you listen to me, you arrogant son of a bitch," the senator started. "It may come to a point to where the only thing keeping us alive are those people out there. They don't trust us for shit right now, and you can't blame them. So you know they won't go out of their way to save our asses. I know damned well I wouldn't. Right now they're on one side and we're on the other. As they say in South Texas, we're fucked." Don finished pulling on his pants, slipped on a pair of well-used moccasins, and started for the door. "Just think about it. There is a need to know," he said, slamming the door on the way out.

Segretti sat on the edge of his bed with his elbows on his knees. He interlaced his fingers, making a steeple with his index fingers. He continued to stare at the floor after Don stormed out. *He's right. What right do I have to put these people in any more danger than they're going to be in? Christ on the cross! How in the hell can I protect these people, keep them out of the way, and still do my job?*

"I think I feel twenty years younger," Frank said, pulling a tee shirt over his head.

"You're looking and acting younger too, dear," Mi Ling replied. "You've lost twenty pounds, you've been eating right, and you've almost stopped smoking. I'm proud of you."

"Thanks, honey, and just like everything else, I owe it all to you. If you hadn't come back into my life, if you hadn't been so dedicated to your work... If, if, if! There are so many ifs," Frank said, looking into the dark eyes of his wife. "I think I love you more now than I did thirty years ago, and I don't think you've changed a bit since I met you." Frank gently touched Mi Ling's shoulder. "What do you think it's going to be like when we get back to Cam An?" he asked.

Frank's mind was drawn back to the village as he first saw it in 1962 – a collection of small, well-built huts, and people who wanted to be left alone by all sides. He remembered the times; drinking new beer through straws from the buried earthen jars, the smell of *nuc mam*, the fermented fish juices used for seasoning almost everything, the sweet peace of smoking opium after a banquet with her father-in-law. In a second he ran through most of his time in the village as if it were a movie flashing through the recesses of his brain.

"I have no idea how I'll feel," Mi Ling replied as she buttoned her shirt. "It will feel so strange to be home again after all these years. For some reason I feel like something is drawing me back, something more than just our mission, something I can't explain, and if I could, you probably wouldn't believe me."

"I think I understand. I've been having a lot of strange dreams about Cam An lately. It's not the Cam An that we knew, but something different; but I know it's supposed be the village. Come on, let's see what the rest of this bunch is up to." Frank held the door open for his wife, and followed into the hall.

Frank and Mi Ling walked into the day room followed closely by Jim and Kim. Marty Kuhl stood by the refrigerator and pulled out a can of beer for each of them. Jim noticed the black plastic boxes on the table and asked, "What did you bring us, Marty?"

"These are the new silencers I told you about. I'll explain when the rest of the guys get here. The girls have been telling me how you humped their asses off today." The sergeant looked at Karen and Janet with a grin.

"Yeah, we covered almost thirty miles in about nine hours. Hell, I'm proud of these people. My recon boys couldn't do much better. We've come a long way since we started," Sherlock replied. He put his hand in the small of Kim's back and guided her to a seat on the couch.

"That we have," Kim interjected as she sat down and took the first drink from the cold can of Bud.

"That must have been a hot shower you two had! Both of you are still red as beets," Janet said with an sly grin.

"We got clean," was Jim's only reply.

"Yeah, right?" Karen questioned as she looked up to see Tom and Bill coming down the hall.

"Well, we might not look any better, but I'm sure we smell better," Hayes said as they walked into the room.

"Speak for yourself, buddy," Tom replied. "Well, Sarge, what do you have for us?"

"Well, the Greenie Beanies I just got in were supposed to get these, but somehow or other they got lost. Besides that, you folks are better people. This is the AWC Warp Six suppressor," the range master started explaining. "It's a totally new design that uses a lithium grease in the first chamber. The extra weight is only about six and a half ounces, and it'll bring a full-house 9mm load down to thirty-five dB. Flies fart louder than that. It's welded stainless steel, so all you have to do is rinse it out and replace the grease. The problem is you only get about fifteen rounds before you have to replace the lube; a ten cc plastic syringe is the best way to do it." Sergeant Kuhl unscrewed the tube from the barrel and tossed the barrel to Tom. "Put it on," he said as he started injecting a syringe of lubricant into the first chamber of the threaded, black stainless-steel pipe. The few seconds that it had taken to add the grease to the silencer was all it took for Tom to change the barrels on his Beretta. "Screw it on." The sergeant handed Tom the tube. "Now, let's step outside." They walked out to see the sun, a burnished red disk, setting through the pine trees. "That tree over there," the sergeant pointed out for Tom.

Tom took a triangle stance and squeezed off two quick rounds, "Nice," he said. The sounds of the shots were quieter than a whisper. "The recoil is stronger and just a bit different."

"It's got a spring-loaded piston that increases the back pressure, so even with subsonic loads there's no ejection problems that can occur with the old style wiper suppressers. The system only needs to be cleaned every hundred rounds or so. Let the rest of them pop off a few rounds.

Tom handed the weapon to Sherlock, who fired three rounds and passed it on. Each member of the team fired two or three rounds, with Frank firing the last round in the magazine. He exchanged the empty magazine for a full one Marty handed him and passed it on. When the weapon made the full circle to Marty Kuhl, he unscrewed the tube and replaced it with a short, threaded nut. "This is a thread protector for the barrel, leave it on unless you're using the silencer. Your weapons will still fit the holsters with it. Did you notice about half way through the second magazine how the sound started getting louder? Even at the end the noise wasn't bad. I don't know of any situation where you would have to fire more than twenty rounds of silenced ammunition. Anybody got any questions? Good, let's take a look at that tree and then go drink some beer." They walked to the pine tree and examined the knot Tom used for an aiming point, with everyone following on the same target. "If this were a man, I think he'd be dead. If nothing else you would have totally fucked up his day." The sergeant moved his finger around the six-inch area that had been chewed away by the Silver-Tip, hollow-point ammo.

"Nice shooting, everybody," Jim said. "Let's get inside, the mosquitoes are getting bad. Besides, that's where there's cold beer waiting!"

Chapter Fourteen

The next three days seemed to fly by as the team readied for departure. Their uniforms were replaced, field equipment was cleaned, turned in, and replaced by new gear. Everything was packed, repacked and packed again. The compak container was emptied, everything rechecked against the master list, and repacked. The tent was set up and taken down. The new Honda five thousand-watt generator was unpacked, run for an hour, and then put back in the box. The activity around the barracks building was more like a disturbed ant hill than a training camp.

As the last of the personal footlockers were stowed away, David brought out a long, thick, heavy aluminum case. He could feel the eyes of the other team members boring into his back as he grabbed one of the packing blankets and moved to the small grassy area between the company street and the building. He said nothing as he laid out the blanket and set the ominous box at one end. Segretti didn't bother to look up when Jim Sherlock's shadow shaded him from the hot sun.

"Open the box," Sherlock ordered, taking a step onto the blanket. "The time for the shit you've been pulling is over. Now open the fucking box."

Segretti leaned back on his heels and looked up at the tall gunnery sergeant before answering simply, "No."

The team watched as the confrontation built. Jim's ruddy face took on a hard, cold look that matched David's. He repeated the order. "Open that fucking box or I'm going to do it." Sherlock's voice held a menace the team hadn't heard before.

"Did your mother have any more idiot children that lived?" David asked in a menacing voice as he started to stand. "Tin soldier, it's about time that we–" He didn't finish the sentence as he rushed Sherlock and received a glancing blow to the jaw. "Somehow I knew this was going to have to happen," Segretti said, picking himself up and rubbing his jaw. For a moment David stood totally still with his arms at his sides. The next second he was a mass of kicks and punches. Sherlock managed to block most of the punches, and even have a few of his own connect. When Segretti dropped to one knee, Jim executed a reverse round-house kick toward Segretti's head. David leaned forward and started to stand as he threw a left to Sherlock's crotch and a right fist to the temple. Both men fell, but it was only Segretti that stood. He took two steps, kneeled beside Sherlock and lifted his head with his left hand. He placed his right hand on Jim's chin. Segretti's shoulders tensed as he started to give the quick twist that was to be the coup de grace.

The team stood paralyzed during the two or three minutes the fight had lasted. Tom was the first to recover and realize what Segretti's next motion would be. He didn't bother to think as he jumped through the air with a flying side kick that knocked David away from the unconscious Sherlock. "Enough!" he shouted. "It's over!" Tom said, dropping into a martial arts defensive crouch. "You son of a bitch, you were going to kill him, weren't you?" Tom said more quietly, still maintaining a defensive posture.

"Don't fuck with me, Bosworth," Segretti growled as he returned to wrapping the aluminum case, "or I'll kill you a hell of a lot quicker than I would have Sherlock." David's grey eyes and expression were cold enough to send chills up Tom's spine as he backed away.

Kim was the first to reach the unconscious gunnery sergeant. She kneeled and gently cradled his head in her lap while the others attempted to revive him. Tom never let his eyes stray from Segretti as he stood guard.

Segretti calmly continued to roll the case in the blanket. He walked it to the compak box and stowed it away. He could feel the team's hate and fear as he turned away and returned to the barracks.

Sherlock's eyelids fluttered as he started to regain consciousness and tried to focus on Kim's worried face. Don James left the group and followed David into the building, wondering what the next step was going to be.

The final briefing the next morning had none of the usual appearances of a team. Don and David sat at one of the card tables in the day room while everyone else sat around the long table. The battle lines had been drawn and even the men from Washington could feel the tension in the room.

"Your Compak container is on the way," the man from the state department said in a bored voice. "From here it will go directly to Quang Tri and should be waiting on a truck when you get there." The man continued as if he were on the way to the dentist's office. "We have you booked on a commercial flight from here to Hong Kong. From there the Vietnamese government will see to it you get where you're supposed to go. Someone from their side will contact you at the Hong Kong Hilton after you arrive. Anything more you need from us will have to come out of the embassy, since we no longer have an office in Saigon. We've taken the liberty of presetting the frequency on your main radio," the man in the summerweight, grey suit continued to drone. "We believe you may have a little trouble from time to time, so we prepared this for each of you." He continued to ramble as he opened his leather briefcase and held up nylon belts. "Each of these money belts contains five thousand dollars in US currency – bribe money if you will. Use it as you see fit. That's all I have today. If we come up with anything else, we'll catch you in Hong Kong. Have a safe trip and good luck. Now, do you have any questions?"

"What if we don't need all the money?" Hayes asked.

"Then we trust you will return it when you get back," he answered, sounding more bored than before.

"What about our expenses along the way?" Kim asked.

"Go ahead and take them out of your belts. I don't believe anyone will be requiring receipts for this money. Anything else?"

"You mentioned the last time you were here that we would have diplomatic status on this trip. Does that still apply?" Frank asked, looking across the room at Don and David.

"Yes, indeed it does. Your diplomatic passports will be delivered to you after you arrive in Hong Kong. The department thought it would be best if you did this leg on your regular passports. Trust me, we at State have cleared all your diplomatic problems. Now, I'll turn you over to Mr. Greene for the latest on the intelligence scene."

The man in the suit finished and walked to the back of the room.

"Thanks, John," the average, nondescript man from the CIA said. He walked forward, carrying the remote control for the slide projector. "See, I told you I'd have an update for you before you left." There were a few chuckles from the group. "Let me start out with a bit of history. Official records show there are well over two thousand Americans listed as MIA in South East Asia. This includes Mrs. Wilson's list, the ones who were supposedly held prisoner, the actual combat deaths not recovered, and the most frightening of all, the ones who decided it was better to desert. I hate to tell you this, but our friend from State made your trip sound like a vacation. Wrong. We've finely gotten some hard intelligence from the area, and we believe you should abort the trip. Here's why. John, hit the lights please." Greene advanced the first slide. "This is General Lang Sam Xuan." The slide showed a fat man about five and a half feet tall, in uniform, stepping out of a helicopter. The chest of his uniform was covered with medals and he was waving to something or someone behind the camera. "Not only is General Xuan the military control of the area, he controls everything else in that section of the country – including the opium fields. I doubt he's very happy about your coming. His second in command is this man." The slide advanced and there was an audible gasp from Frank, Don and Mi Ling.

"Vinh," Frank said in a voice a bit louder than a whisper. "So that's how the NVA knew everything about us."

"We know him," Don said. "He was the translator for our A-Team back in '62. He's a hell of a lot older, but then so are we."

"I hate to tell you this, but he's supposed to be the liaison between you, the military, and the government. Ready to quit?"

"Wonderful, just fucking wonderful," Frank said through clenched teeth. "That little bastard was theirs all along. Shit, he didn't get us killed off the first time, so now he's got another chance. Son of a bitch!"

"Well, at least he's a known," Tom said. "What else

do you have for us?"

"It only gets worse I'm afraid. We've identified some of the Americans guarding the fields." He advanced the next slide, showing the Army ID of a young, Black male. "This is who we believe to be the leader of this rabble – James Wendell Howard. He was not a nice person before he was drafted. He's from Watts, and the LA cops had an arrest record on him as long as your arm, all of them for violent crimes. He was also charged with murder and rape, but no one could ever prove it. He went over the hill in '73. The military had so many deserters at that time they didn't bother to chase him. Their reasoning was that they'd kill themselves or get killed. We have no idea how many of the people on the MIA list actually went over the hill." Greene advanced the next slide, this time showing a young white man. "Gerald Antonio duPage, Baton Rouge. We believe he is the number two man in this group. He killed his squad leader and company commander. He escaped from Long Binh Jail in '74. We have heard that he and Howard are at each other's throats, so you may only have one to deal with. These two we have positive ID's on, and there are another seventy-five or eighty we're still working on. This is the army you people are going against. From what we've found so far, none of these men qualify as altar boys."

"Mr. Greene," Bill raised his hand, "I have to assume these men are ready to kill us to keep us away. We're only allowed to carry sidearms; sure doesn't sound like a fair match to me. Is there some way we can even the odds?"

"Don't go. Forget the whole damned thing. That's what I'm trying to tell you," Green answered in a worried voice, looking from face to face.

"Mi Ling and I are going," Frank said. "She and our son have too many years wrapped up in this to stop now."

"Tom and I are going. We'll leave Janet and Karen here," Bill Hayes said before anyone else could answer.

"Like hell you will," Karen almost yelled. "You're not leaving us behind. Somebody with some brains has to looked out for you two."

"Anybody can drop out now with no hard feelings," Mi Ling said in her calm, quiet voice. "You have all done your best, and we can't expect you to risk your lives in any way."

"Kim and I are in," Sherlock said.

"I have to go whether anyone else does or not," Segretti commented.

"My constituents have gotten along without me for this long, they can get by another few months. I'm in," Don affirmed with the rest of the group.

"Kim, we haven't heard from you, except through Jim. You don't have to go," Mi Ling said as she stared into Kim's large, dark eyes.

"I have to go and keep this damn dumb jarhead out of trouble. Besides, I'm getting used to him," Kim replied, returning the stare.

"Well, Mr. Greene, looks like we're all in. Can we expect any help from you people along the way?" Frank asked.

"Sorry, no. The Company still wants a prisoner if you can get one. Use the preset frequency to call us in Hong Kong if you get one. We'll send in a something or someone to pick him up. That's all I have. Good luck, and God bless," Greene said, shutting off the projector as the man from the state department turned on the lights.

"Wonderful," Frank muttered. "Just fucking wonderful."

Chapter Fifteen

The thirty-six hours before the plane took off were rough on everyone but Sherlock. Jim seemed to take the beating he received with more than a grain of salt. The tension, stress, and now hate, between the group and David were thicker than a shroud. Sherlock still treated Segretti as a member of the team, the only difference being his constant awareness of David's position in relation to striking distance. The senator was more or less ignored by everyone except David; even he was more cool than he had been the past few weeks.

The team members took their seats in the first class section of the United flight out of LAX and buckled in. They were paired as they had been during the training period, with the exception of Don and David, who were now separated by the aisle.

"Good afternoon, ladies and gentlemen, and welcome to United Airlines flight 3703 to Hong Kong. Our flying time will be approximately fourteen and a half hours. Since this is an international flight, smoking will be permitted after the captain turns off the no-smoking signs. Cocktails will be available from the flight attendants," the happy-sounding voice of the stewardess announced over the P.A. system. She continued the pre-flight safety instructions as the other flight attendants demonstrated to the passengers. Most people, especially the team in the first class compartment, were more concerned with getting comfortable than listening to the safety lecture.

As the big airplane started rolling down the runway, Don said to Segretti, "We're on our way. Now to enjoy the flight for a couple of hours, take a sleeping pill, and arrive refreshed."

"Well at least we're flying west. The jet lag won't be as bad," Frank added to the conversation for all can hear. "Not only that, we arrive before we leave."

"How's that?" Kim asked.

"International dateline," Sherlock responded with a smile to the tall woman beside him.

The team did their best to busy themselves during the daylight hours after takeoff. Most read or talked, but Don was never without a drink in his hand. David started reading an action-adventure novel about two scientists breaking up a corruption ring at a small midwestern university. Everyone else settled in for the long flight.

The cabin lights of the airplane came on as the voice of the first officer came over the PA system. "Good morning, ladies and gentlemen. We're a little over two hours out from the island of Hong Kong. The temperature on the ground when we land will be a pleasant eighty degrees, and the weather will be clear with about twenty miles of visibility. The cabin crew will begin passing out coffee and taking your breakfast orders. I'm sure you've found our food better than the domestic flights. Now you folks just wake up, enjoy the rest of the flight, and we'll keep you updated on any developments."

Karen raised her head from Tom's lap. "This is one advantage of being small; you can lie down in an airplane seat. I feel great," she said as she stretched like a cat.

"Well, you may feel great, but I'm stiff as a board," Tom replied as he stretched his arms out from his shoulders and then above his head.

Karen reached her hand under the blanket that was covering Tom's lap. "That's alright dear, it won't be stiff after you make a trip to the rest room," she replied with a laugh.

"Hey, Kim," Janet asked from across the aisle, "want to explain all that heavy breathing and giggling we heard after the lights went out?"

"Explain it? No, just put it down to young lust."

"So, Jim, what's it like to be a member of the mile high club?" Hayes asked with a grin.

"Damned if I know. I thought we were up about five or six miles," Sherlock answered with a straight face.

"All right, children, enough of who did what to whom when the lights went out. You're making this old man feel inadequate." Frank stood and started toward the rest room.

"Don't worry, Frank can more than make up for sleeping through an international flight," Mi Ling said with her innocent smile. "He just doesn't like crowds."

"You people can talk about sex all you like. I'm going to get in line for the rest room and clean up a bit," Don said, stepping into the aisle behind Frank.

"Me too!" Segretti followed closely behind the senator.

"See, I told you they were queer," Kim whispered.

Howard sat motionless, staring down at the body of his friend and bodyguard. A fly circled and started to land on the dead man's face. Without a thought, Howard's arm reached out and grabbed the insect in mid air. *Get the fuck off him,* he thought. *You ain't even good enough to land on this man's shit.* He squeezed his hand. *God damn it, why did it have to be Tyrone? If somebody had to die, how come it couldn't have been one of the honkey motherfuckers. Tyrone, I'm going to get that son of a bitch. I'm going to cut off his nuts, then kill him real slow.*

"What do you mean you can't find that motherfucker!" Howard yelled at the men as they returned to camp.

"Come on, man, it's just like he was never there. You remember how those VC were," one of the men answered. "We'll never find the little fucker."

"Well somebody sure as shit was there, and he kilt Tyrone. Git everybody out there and find that son of a bitch, or I'll have all your balls hangin' from my hooch." Howard continued yelling. "Git on that fuckin radio and git more people in here. Find that little cocksucker."

One of the men moved to the radio while the others started refilling their ammo pouches from the cans inside the large thatched hut.

"You motherfuckers find that son of a bitch! Cover every God damned inch of that bush. He's in there somewhere. Now you fuckin' find 'im."

"Boss," the man on the radio called, "everybody else will be here within an hour."

"Big fuckin' deal. I want them here now. The rest of you hump your asses back in the bush so that bastard don't get away."

When the sergeant no longer heard movement above

him, he raised the lid on the spider hole. *That was a perfect shot, but I missed. They'll be back. I'll circle around to the other side and try again. I hope there's good cover there. They'll come even quicker next time.* The short, strongly built Vietnamese man moved the thick wood and sod lid out of the way and crawled out of the hole, carefully replacing it. He took time to realign the grass and dropped a few small branches around to match the surrounding area. He slung the heavy rifle over his shoulder, picked up a length of bamboo, and started wiping it back and forth through the grass, hiding all but the tiniest evidence of his footprints. *Time to go.* He looked at his handywork. *With luck I'll get him the next time, but there is a lot of time and distance until I get the next chance.*

"Some motherfucker over in them woods took a shot at me and kilt Tyrone. I want you to waste everything you see. I don't want to see as much as a damned piss ant alive over there., you understand?" Howard yelled at the men assembling from the other camps. "I want that motherfucker dead or alive, and I don't give a shit which. I'll give five big ones to the man who brings me his balls. Now move yo' asses."

One of the men mumbled, "What the fuck we goin' to do with five thousand dollars out here?"

"Shit, I don't know," his companion answered. "The bastard will probably pay us in dongs, and there's no way in hell we could carry that much."

"Fix me a drink, Vinh," the general said as the colonel walked through the door. "Make it a strong one. I have just talked to Hanoi, and the Americans have just left San Francisco. They will delay a few days in Hong Kong, but they will still be here within a week."

"I have my most trusted man out to take care of Comrade Howard. With luck it is already done. If we can eliminate Howard, most of the rest will follow the white man, duPage. He will be much more interested in listening to reason." Vinh handed the general a large glass of scotch with only a couple of ice cubes, while his own has just enough liquor to give color.

"Vinh, my friend, you understand the position we find ourselves in. We have to let the Americans conduct their search. Even though they have been warned, we must take steps to see that they are not harmed. There is no way possible they can fail to stumble onto our opium fields, and I believe they will report them to the rest of the world. The fields are ready to start harvesting, we have a crazy nigger for security, we need more field hands, and the Goddamned Americans are coming. I miss the days when all I had to worry about was a simple war."

"We survived and won the war, my General, I'm sure we can survive and win this peace too. Let's wait for my man to return before we make any rash decisions," Vinh replied in a confident tone. *The asshole is starting to fall apart. If things don't work out, he's the one that gets the blame. I'll just step in and take command after he's destroyed. I can see it now, General Vinh Ngu. I can afford one year of a poor harvest. All I have to do is to wait and start planting doubts.*

It's going to be a long shot but it's the last one I'll get today, the sergeant thought as he crawled the last few meters between the trees. *That's got to be at least six hundred meters, I'll have to put his head at the very bottom of my field of view. At least I'm not looking into the sun now. What can I use for a rest? That tree looks like it's about the right height. Damn, I wish I hadn't told Colonel Ngu I'd have him dead within a week. I wish I had more time to scout and prepare.* The sergeant laid the rifle beside the tree and crawled backward into the cover of the high canopy jungle. When he was well away from the edge of the clearing, he stood, took out his canteen, and drank sparingly. He recapped the canteen, opened his fly, and urinated beside the small game trail. The wet stream made a small puddle in the red dust and started to trickle down the path. *I've got time for a cigarette or two,* he thought, removing the damp, crushed packet from his shirt pocket. *I'm far enough away where they can't smell it.*

After a few puffs of this second cigarette, he dropped the butt beside the first and crushed it out with his boot.

It's time, he thought, taking a couple of steps into the low growing shrubs and vines. He lay down and started to crawl back to his Dragunov rifle.

The sergeant stood beside the tree and rested the front handguard across a limb. He looked at the rangefinder built into the telescopic sight, noting the range was closer to eight hundred meters than six. He surveyed the compound for his target. "There," he whispered to himself. "Elevate to about here." He inhaled, held his breath, and squeezed the trigger. After the first round went off, he fired two more in rapid succession. He watched the large black man fall as the others looked on. He picked his targets as rapidly as he could recover from the recoil. When there were no more targets of opportunity, he turned and ran back to the trail, turning away from the camp and leaving the area as fast as possible.

The old dream weaver stared into the faces that formed in the coals of his fire. In his mind's eye he watched while some faces overpowered and extinguished others. Some flared brightly before turning a dead black. Others just crackled and disintegrated to nothing. The old man watched the actions of the larger, brighter coals and their interactions with the others. He shook his head as one of the larger pieces died as quickly as if it were dropped in a pail of water. He closed his eyes and bowed his head. He dropped a handful of herbs and spices onto the small, low fire. Without opening his eyes, he watched the smoke spiral up to be divided toward the east and to the west. "They are coming now," he said aloud, opening his eyes. "I am not sure we can afford the cost of salvation." His gaze was drawn back to the fire as the smallest bits of fire winked out and died. He stood and looked up at the bright, new moon. *It must be so.* He turned away from the dying fire and walked into the hut.

Chapter Sixteen

After the lights came on, the last few hours of the flight passed quickly as the team readied itself for their first day in the Orient. Frank, Don and Jim regaled the team with their memories of an older, wilder Hong Kong. Sherlock made references, then held back on giving more with the simple answer, "It's a surprise." The younger team members continued to badger him, even through customs. With more questions, Jim's reply was an idiot's grin.

"It's been fifteen years since I was last here," Jim said as the hotel van left the airport. "The place sure has grown. I didn't think it could get any bigger, but it has."

"This is probably the only truly international city in the world," Frank added, looking out the window. "Over the years it seems like everyone has gotten a piece of it. I just wonder what's going to happen when it reverts to the mainland." The thought ran through Frank's brain about the consequences of Hong Kong, probably the most capitalistic city in the world - soon to be turned over to the last large communist nation in the world.

"I've always heard stories about Hong Kong whorehouses. I wonder if they're true." Tom said with a wry grin toward the women.

"They're true," Frank, Don and Jim answered together.

"It doesn't matter if they are or not, you're not going to find out," Karen replied as she lightly punched Tom on the shoulder. "If you do you'll never sleep with me again."

"That goes double for you, Bill. Just remember, you can be replaced by a ten-dollar vibrator, and it doesn't snore."

"Yeah, but you'd go broke buying batteries," came the reply from Hayes.

Sherlock watched the city pass outside the van window. He smiled at the memory of his R&R here back in the seventies, and how he and his men had rented a whorehouse for the few days. "I guess it's time to let you in on the surprise. I need to talk to someone who knows the city anyway." Jim leaned forward and tapped the driver on the shoulder as he continued his tale. "There used to be a wild place around here; definitely different. If it's still around I'll take you there using our discretionary funds. They've got a floorshow like you'll never see anywhere else in the world. The place was called Club Paradise," Jim said with a smile toward the rest of the team.

"Sir," the driver said, never taking his eyes off the traffic, "the Club Paradise has been closed for five years. The name of the club that replaced it is The Jade Lotus. The floorshow is of much the same type, but ever changing. I'm sure you will find a number of enhancements that have been made by the new ownership. If you wish, I could take you there this evening."

"Sounds good to us. What time do things start happening?" Jim inquired, looking around at the team still wearing his idiot grin.

"Most of the time the show starts at midnight. There is limited space, so I would be honored to make the reservations for you. I must warn you that it is very expensive, but there is nothing like it anywhere else," the driver replied, leaning on the horn as he barely missed a pedicab.

"Jim, what kind of show is this you are talking about?" Mi Ling asked, having an idea about what he was talking about but not saying.

"A very artistic sex show. At least at the Club Paradise, they did things you could only imagine. If this is better, I'll have to see it to believe it."

"I believe Frank and I are a bit too old for this. I think we'll stay at the hotel and sleep this evening," Mi Ling said as she squeezed Frank's knee, thinking of their own sexual activities.

"Count us out too," James added. "I don't believe either of us would have much fun going by ourselves." After a second's thought, Don added, "I don't believe you would want us with you anyway."

The team spent the rest of the day getting settled in and waiting for the cool of the evening. There were various comments and assumptions made among the group as to the expectations of what the night could bring.

Sherlock gave no more hints than he had on the ride from the airport – nothing beyond his shit-eating grin.

"Tom, what do you think about going to this Jade Lotus place? It sure sounds like a strange place to me." Karen shook clothes as she unpacked them from the suitcases.

"We may as well go. You never can tell, we might learn something."

"I just can't see spending a hundred bucks a person to watch someone else fuck. A couple of dollars to rent a porn tape is one thing, but a hundred bucks a person?" Karen said, looking into Tom's brown eyes. Even though she was not averse to spending money, most of her adult life had been spent economizing, spending more for needs than wants. Old money habits died hard, even now that she didn't have to worry about such things.

"What the hell, I think we earned it. Besides, it's not our money, it's Segretti's, or whoever is backing him. Come on, get dressed and let's get down to Jim and Kim's room," Tom said as he moved to open the door.

"I can tell when you've got something sneaky planned, Jim. Now what is it?" Kim asked as she slid into her well-worn blue jeans. "It's about this club isn't it?" Jim only grinned more, saying nothing, but pouring a small shot of vodka into a glass. "You're not going to tell me, are you?" Kim continued as she put on a white shirt and tied the long tails around her slim, tanned waist.

"Not on your life! I'll only say you won't regret it and it'll be the perfect cure for jet lag," Sherlock answered, slowly sipping his drink.

"Jim Sherlock, you can be a real asshole when you want to be, you know that?"

"Yes, dear," he replied. There was a knock on the door. Kim continued brushing her short brown hair as Bill and Janet arrived.

"Anybody care for a shot or two of sourmash before we go?" Hayes asked when he and Janet stepped into the room. "With a cover charge of a hundred bucks, I'm going to hate to see their drink prices."

"Hi, guys, I brought some extra glasses. Kim, if I

could fill out my jeans like you do, I sure as hell wouldn't be hanging out with people like us. Hell, I'd be a model somewhere," Janet said, giving Kim an admiring look.

"Well, you know how it is – pearls before swine. And this fucking jarhead is the biggest pig you ever saw. This asshole won't tell me a thing about this place we're going to tonight. You can bet your ass that he's not going to be getting it for a while."

"I can't threaten him that way," Janet replied. "I wish I could."

"Hey, don't look at me. I don't know any more than the rest of you." Bill poured two bourbons as another knock came at the door. "Get the door, will you?"

Janet opened the door on the third knock, allowing Karen and Tom to enter. "Jesus Christ, I'm beginning to feel like the ugly stepsister around here." She whistled as she saw the way Karen was dressed.

Karen walked into the room to the admiring looks of the men and the almost jealous glances of the other women. Her small frame and long, blond hair gave her a look of radiance when matched with her white, see-through blouse, lace bra, and full, pleated white skirt, all accented by Karen's golden tan.

Kim reached over and gently slapped Jim to bring his stare away from Karen. "Jesus, am I glad you're married and have your husband with you. Honey, I knew you were cute, but this is fuckin' ridiculous."

"Give me that drink and get your tongue back in your mouth before I stomp on it," Janet said, taking the glass from Bill but not taking her eyes from Karen.

"Maybe I should change," Karen offered, feeling a bit self-conscious at the reactions she received from all in the room.

"Not on your life," Jim stammered as he regained his composure. "It's just going to be a shame that the most erotic looking woman around is going to be in the audience. At least some people will get to see you."

"Mr. Sherrock," came the call with the quick, incessant knocks at the door.

"Hello, Kao, come on in. I think we're all ready to go. Everyone ready for the adventure of your lives?" Jim asked as he stepped aside, allowing the small Chinese man to enter.

"Hello, Kao," Janet said in her sexy, alto voice. "Can you tell us some more about the Jade Lotus club you're taking us to?"

"Yes, Miss, it is one of the most–" he was quickly cut off.

"Don't say any more, Kao, you'll spoil my surprise," Jim blurted out.

"Yes, sir. Mr. Sherrock say not to tell you any more. I sorry. The van its downstairs. Come, please. Or we walk. Its not very far, only a few blocks."

The streets of Hong Kong appeared to be a bizarre cross between Las Vegas, Disneyland and a circus – from old women cooking and selling their wares of exotic delicacies, to the neon-lighted skyscrapers. Hand-pulled rickshaws competed for street space with Jaguars and Mercedes Benzes. The sounds and smells were an overpowering influence when coupled with what the group saw. Tenth and twentieth century technologies existing side by side, sharing the same place and time without one infringing on the other. The streets and sidewalks were crowded despite the late hour – they could only imagine the masses of humanity during rush hours.

The ride through the streets took only a few minutes as the driver weaved through traffic and down alleys where he had only inches of clearance. When they stopped, the first thing they noticed was the salt air mixed with the sewage of the bay. The building across the street was made of old, weathered wood. The entrance was lit by a small bulb hung above a delicately painted lotus blossom. At first glance, one would believe it was only one of the many warehouses in the area. The doorway was set well into the shadows. They saw and heard nothing that showed signs of occupancy besides the one small light. As they approached, they noticed the cherry glow of a cigarette in the shadows.

"Good evening, Master Chiang." Kao bowed to the portly man standing in the doorway. "This is Mr. Sherrock and his party. I telephoned you about them this afternoon. Mr. Sherrock was once at the Club Paradise, and wanted his friends to experience your unique entertainment."

"Thank you, Kao," the man replied. "I shall take care of our guests from here and make sure they are returned safely to their hotel." He turned to the group. "We have been waiting for you and your party, sir. If we may step inside and dispose of the distasteful matter of money, the entertainment will start soon," he said, holding the weathered door open.

"Thanks, Kao." Jim handed the young man a twenty dollar bill. "After you, Master Chiang." He used the same form of address as did their guide.

"I am sorry, Mr. Sherlock, but I must ask for one hundred dollars U.S. for yourself and each member of your party. In exchange, I promise we will give you the show of a lifetime. There will be no further charges or gratuities this evening. Please, come, and welcome to delights for all your senses."

Jim reached into his front pocket and counted out six one-hundred dollar bills and handed them over with a smile.

"I will provide safe transportation back to your hotel at the end of the entertainment. Please step through these curtains and you will be guided to your respective couches. Refreshment will be provided," Chiang said as he waved his fat arm like a maestro, directing the group through the door draped with many layers of silk and richly colored velvet.

They entered through the curtains and their eyes took a few seconds to adjust to the even darker room. They only saw shadows illuminated by indirect lighting from each of the eight corners. Soft incense from a charcoal brazier was being spread throughout the room by a young girl waving a large palm fan in the smoke. They soon began to feel the euphoria of the place as they were greeted by young boys and girls barely into puberty, wearing only sarongs. Each couple was taken by the hand to a separate enclosed area, its floor only inches above the heads of those in the cubicle below. Their guides motioned for them to be seated. The ornate, well-padded brass couches were covered with large, soft, rabbit-skin throws. For the first time they noticed the soft soothing sound of a bamboo flute, as another youngster appeared with an ice bucket of champagne and two glasses. Her young, oiled, perfumed body seemed to glow in the mysterious, dark surroundings. As quickly as she appeared, she was gone without a sound.

They could barely see Chiang when he stepped through the curtains and dropped more incense onto the charcoal brazier. Tom and Karen quickly began to feel the effects of the sweet odor of burning opium. A silk curtain to their right was opened to expose a small orchestra of wooden drums and bamboo flutes. As they started to play, the amber lights went out, and for a second there was nothing but blackness and the sweet smoke. There was a long, slow, rising note from an ancient bass flute. The low note gave rise to a soft blue light surrounding where the ceiling should be. Even this light wasn't distinct in its brightness; just a warm, soft, erotic blue.

Another flute, a fifth higher than the first, started. With the second flute, small blue spotlights started moving across the lacquered floor in a random pattern. A tenor took up the note and a range of soft turquoise and yellow spotlights joined the soft blues drifting in random patterns around the room. The music and light seemed to swell and swirl with the drifting haze of smoke. There was now enough light to barely make out shapes moving around the floor. An alto flute joined, along with the beat of a single drum, as a white light was directed from above to the center of a black octagon inlaid with a jade lotus. The melody changed as a soft soprano flute joined and spots of reds and orange appeared. Tom and Karen were calmed as their heartbeats matched the drum. Their senses felt heightened to a point higher than either had ever experienced in their lives. They could now see a number of dancers dressed in long, flowing silk robes floating around the floor on the clouds of smoke. Each seemed to move as a separate but joined entity as they flowed from one to the other. Each dancer moved in and out, weaving bodies into the melody and the flowing silk of other dancers. As they passed there was the lightest touch, a gentle caress, or the most fleeting of kisses. Now and then a tongue could be seen to touch a passing performer. The sexual differences were lost in the flowing motion and the veiling smoke from the brazier. The tempo and motions became more sensual and frantic. The drum beats were well over a hundred per minute, taking the heartbeats of the audience with it as a crescendo was reached. All then stopped, except for the single bass flute and the soft indirect blue light. The dancers stood like statues, frozen in time and place when the music stopped. As the melody started again, their gossamer silk robes floated to the floor where they stood. Once again the music started, soft and slow, melodic. The dancers gathered around the octagon in the center to be illuminated by the soft, pale, white light. They touched and caressed each other and themselves. Music seemed to follow each movement. There was still the weaving of bodies. They moved around the green shape, without taking notice of the entranced audience as they separated into twos, threes or fours and moved closer to the edge of their stage.

They kneeled, and from nowhere appeared small bottles of perfumed oil. Their mutual rubbing was in perfect timing to the music. The soft, slow, gentle motions became more intense and sexual while Tom and Karen watched two dancers moving hands across their chests, stomachs and thighs.

The smoke seemed to have become thicker. Tom and Karen could no longer see anything beyond the couple directly in front of their couch. Their eyes were glued to the dancers as they began to recline, still caressing, licking and kissing. As the music swelled, so did the woman's breasts and the man's penis. The music increased, as did the gyrations of the man and woman seen through the haze.

Karen gazed into Tom's glazed eyes as she dug her fingers into his thigh and pulled his head into her lap. She didn't know if she was imagining the woman on the floor smiling only at her as Tom started to slide down her nylon panties. Karen continued to stare as she forced Tom's head tighter between her legs.

The dancers continued to move and change positions and timing along with the music as Karen clenched her teeth to stifle her sounds of pleasure. She could hear others in the auditorium as she continued to watch the woman in front of them. Beads of sweat formed on her brow and upper lip, her heart beating faster than the drum. She held Tom by the hair as she pulled him up and started fighting with his belt and zipper. The woman on the floor continued to smile at Karen as she worked Tom out of his slacks and between her legs. Karen watched almost hypnotized as the woman arched her back and neck. Her long black hair touched the floor and spread like a fan.

After a time that seemed like hours, the music stopped and all was left in darkness. The dancers were replaced by two nude children entering from either side. Each carried a solitary candle. They placed them in the center of the black octagon. They kissed, and bypassed into the darkness. Tom and Karen could still hear the sounds of sexual activity, as well as soft sighs of contentment mixed with the occasional clink of glasses.

"Medic!" one of the men lying beside Howard yelled. "Get your ass over here!"

"It came from that direction! Fan out and find that son of a bitch!" someone else yelled.

A tall, thin white man rushed over to where the injured men lay. He quickly examined Howard and then moved to the other two men lying in the iron oxide dust. Bush had a small hole in the back of his head with little blood around the entrance wound. As the medic carefully turned his patient, he saw the empty space from the bridge of his nose to his chin caused by the .30 caliber bullet. He left the first man and moved quickly to the second. He saw the blood on the man's chest and, without feeling for a pulse, he knew he was dead. Experience told him both men were dead before they fell. He returned to Howard as men moved him to a sitting position before ripping his sleeveless shirt off.

"That son of a bitch shot me," Howard said in disbelief. "I can't believe that son of a bitch shot me!"

"Shut up and let me look at that." The medic kneeled beside the injured leader and started to examine the wound. "Boss, you got to be one of the luckiest motherfuckers alive. Two inches down or two inches to the right and you'd be dead. Shit, man, you got a through and through that didn't hit anything but muscle. It's going to hurt like a bitch but you're going to be all right." The medic opened his bag, removed the nylon-wrapped instrument pack, and set it on the chair. Selecting the five-inch malleable probe, he held it between his thumb and forefinger. He slowly inserted it into the bullet hole as Howard started to scream. The sensitive fingers detected a foreign body. Without moving the probe or looking away, his left hand picked up the fine forceps from the kit. Inserting the long tweezers into the wound, he followed the probe until the ends met. He gently opened and closed the forceps and withdrew a small piece of black cloth that was carried with the projectile. His right hand continued to probe while he wiped the debris on Howard's shirt.

"I wants that motherfucker dead! You hear me!" Howard yelled to the empty camp. "I can't believe that son of a bitch shot me."

"Let me put some magic medicine on that, and a bandage, and you'll be as good as new in a couple of weeks." The medic kept working, not listening or caring to listen to the black man's babble. He gave Howard a shot of morphine from the bag. "Help me move him into the hooch. He needs to stay still for a while," the medic told the bodyguard sitting beside his leader.

"I can't believe that son of a bitch shot me," Howard mumbled as they laid him on the rice straw mattress.

"Here's where he was!" one of the men called out as he picked up the 7.62 X 39 mm shell cases. "He couldn't have gotten far. Fan out and be ready."

"Make sure of your target. We don't want to go shooting each other," someone yelled back.

"Here's his trail!" another searcher called. "The bastard even stopped for a piss and a smoke."

The men gathered on the small game trail looking at the cigarette butts and the damp circle on the ground.

"Franklin, you take your men and go up the trail. I'll take the rest and head down this way. Let's get that fucker." duPage took command as the men jogged down the narrow trail.

"Hey Jerry, wait up, man!" Washington whispered to duPage as they followed the narrow path. "Hey man, we don't need to work real hard to catch dis dude. I mean, shit man, he's doin' us a favor. Maybe with his next shot he's goin' t' waste that mutha."

"Yeah, well, did you ever stop to think that the son of a bitch might be after us next? Jose, you're the tracker, you've got the point. Move out, let's get us a sniper and find out what's going on." The short Puerto Rican man called Jose moved out about twenty yards ahead of the rest of the squad. Even though he was almost running, his eyes never missed a partial footprint in the dust or a broken blade of grass beside the trail.

"Hey Wash, how many of Howard's men do we have with us?" duPage whispered to the black man behind him.

"We got five of Howard's and three of Franklin's. Whut you thinkin', buddy?"

"Waste Howard's men on the next curve. We waste 'em now and that's five we ain't going to have to fuck with later on," duPage said without bothering to look back.

"Hey, look man, that's murder. They ain't got a chance. Man, I ain't sure I can do 'em," the almost purple black man replied, staying close enough to be heard.

"Look, you dumb shit, Howard was planning to waste my ass this afternoon before this shit happened; we both fuckin' know it. You're going to have to ask yourself, who's going to make your life easier, me or Howard?"

"Yeah, I reckon you right. They're hangin' together behind Fritz and ahead of Donovan from Franklin's bunch. You just be fuckin' careful where you're shootin'; I'm goin' t' have my ass right across the trail from ya'," Washington whispered before taking a few more paces and ducking into a stand of bamboo.

duPage's men passed with their standard patrolling separation of two meters. The next five men were bunched with less than a foot separating them. duPage flipped the safety lever on his M-16 to auto, turned the weapon on its side, and held the trigger down. Within a millisecond Washington opened up from across the trail. The recoil of the weapons, instead of forcing the muzzles up, pushed them across to the side. The five men on the trail were hit a number of times from each side. They almost seemed to be held up by the impact of the bullets slamming into their bodies as they did their strange, jerky death dance. The misses flew well above the rifleman across the trail. The men from duPage's and Franklin's squad hit the dirt and waited for a target as Howard's men crumbled to the path. Their blood turned the red dust to red mud, and added nutrients to soil of the high canopy jungle.

duPage and Washington stood from their hiding places beside the trail. They stepped over and examined the bodies of the five men laying at their feet as the rest of the squad collected themselves and gathered around. "Man, what the fuck you doing? Those were our men you just wasted!" Donovan yelled as he looked from the bodies to duPage and Washington.

"They're not our men, they're Howard's. And that bastard is out to waste my ass. Now it's just a matter of who does who first. Come on, we got a sniper to catch."

duPage didn't bother to say more. He turned and led the remaining squad down the path. Within minutes they caught Jose, who recognized the sounds of the weapons and continued his assignment. He squatted beside the trail and signaled a halt with his raised clenched fist. Using hand signals, he pointed out the location of the sniper and indicated a plan to encircle and capture. duPage nodded and returned an okay sign with his thumb and index finger, and then held up five fingers, indicating time. Jose looked at his watch, nodded and slid silently into the brush. duPage followed the second hand on his watch and then dropped one finger. At the three-minute mark he motioned for three men to enter the brush beside the trail and circle toward the position. As the second hand moved toward the last second, duPage and the rest of the men rose to a crouch and charged down the trail, firing in the direction Jose indicated. Washington stayed behind and offered covering fire for the men exposed for a matter of a few seconds.

Jose waited for the firing to stop as he watched the sniper lying behind a small outcropping of limestone. He removed his K-Bar knife from the sheath on his shoulder harness, and like a snake, slid forward. The sergeant concentrated on the threat in front, hearing nothing as Jose rose and took the last couple of steps closing the gap between himself and the sergeant. The blade of the large, sharp knife slid under his chin, nicking the skin. The sergeant removed his hands from his weapon and spread his arms in submission. "Got him!" Jose yelled. "Hold your fire, I got him!" Jose and his prisoner rose and walked toward the squad gathering in the small open space on the trail.

The short sergeant was stopped in front of duPage, who grabbed the front of his shirt and delivered a hard backhand across his face. "Who the hell are you, and who are you trying to kill?" duPage demanded in broken Vietnamese with a Louisiana lilt. He slapped the sergeant again and again, asking, "Who the hell are you trying to kill, and who's paying you? Give me the right answers and I might let you live."

The sergeant could feel the return of the knife blade to his throat and the increased pressure in his bladder. He swallowed hard as the sphincter muscles of his bladder released. He felt the warm wetness covering the front of his pants and running down his leg. He answered, "I'm Sergeant Trahn. My commander is Colonel Ngu. He ordered me to kill the black man Howard because he is the leader. He believes with him dead, the rest of you will scatter to the wind. He doesn't believe foreigners like you are good for our country."

"Bullshit," duPage spat out. "Colonel Ngu knows exactly what's going on around here. Shit, he's part of it! I'm going to let you go, so you can tell Ngu I want to see him at the field by Cam An before three o'clock tomorrow. Tell him you failed, but there are a lot of us who want to see that bastard dead too. You just tell him that duPage – got that, duPage – thought we might be able to work together. You got that? duPage! Now remember it! Jose, let him go."

The short Hispanic man replaced the knife in its sheath and stepped back. The sergeant stood in shock at his freedom, unable to believe he was unhurt and the knife was gone from his throat.

"Get the hell out of here!" duPage yelled at Sergeant Trahn.

Worried he could still be shot in the back, the sergeant took a few slow steps along the path and then broke into a run, putting as much distance between himself and the Americans as possible.

David Segretti had spent the last three hours walking the back streets of Hong Kong. He had tried every technique he knew to still his hyperactive thoughts. Nothing had worked. One side of his brain would pose a problem and the other side gave him conflicting answers of emotion. When he returned to the hotel he saw the van parked at the end of the half-circle drive. *Well, I guess the rest of them are having a good time. I almost wish I could have gone with them. Any diversion is better than this.* David walked across the drive and into the almost empty lobby. The clerk was half dozing at the desk, and didn't even look up as Segretti entered. Walking across to the ornate doors of the elevator, he pushed the up button. The doors opened and closed immediately as he pushed the number ten with Chinese characters below it. As the elevator ascended, David suddenly got a feeling of danger. The small voice inside his head that had given him warnings in the past now screamed for his full attention. Quickly stepping out of the elevator and to the side, his senses went to full alert. His mind was calmed for the first time in days. David's soft-soled shoes made no sound on the thick carpet as he inched his way down the hall to their bank of rooms. He saw Jim and Kim's door open a crack, and the light was on. Reaching under the long sleeve on his left arm, he withdrew the space-age plastic Cross dagger from its sheath. The door swung open noiselessly and he stepped into the room. He saw a tall oriental man searching through Jim's large envelope of documents. The man stopped when he found the orders assigning Jim to the team. As the man read with fascination, David took four steps across the room. Grabbing the man's mouth with his left hand, he slid the sharp triangular blade into the base of the intruder's brain. Slowly he lowered the body to the floor, leaving the dagger in place to prevent bleeding. Taking the few sheets of paper from the dead fingers, he returned them to the envelope, and the envelope to the drawer. *He's not a thief. I wonder who or what he is.* David closed the door, returned to the body, and casually turned him over. He first checked the pockets, but found nothing but a slightly used tissue – Nothing that could give him a hint of the man's identity. He did find a .32 caliber Tokarev in the inside pocket of the expensive suit. His examination of the clothing showed no labels. *Professional. Damn. I should have waited. What the hell, I guess I might as well get rid of the body and get some sleep. Tomorrow is going to be a busy day.* David walked out of the room, leaving the door open a crack, and walked to the bank of elevators. He pushed the button and the door opened. He returned to the room and casually threw the man over his shoulder, leaving his blade in place. Returning to the elevator, he dropped the body on the floor, removed the dagger, and pushed the 'P' for penthouse. *Things are going to get real exciting around here when he's found,* David thought. He walked toward the room he shared with Don, stopping to close Sherlock's door as he passed.

Chapter Seventeen

When Sergeant Trahn was out of sight, duPage, Washington and the others returned to where they had ambushed Howard's men. "Let's drag these bodies back in, it wouldn't be Christian just to leave 'em here, " duPage said as he surveyed the carnage.

"Jerry, just what the hell we goin' t' do with Howard an' his boys when they see us draggin' these dudes into camp?" Washington asked, moving into the pile of bodies.

"To start with, if they give us any shit we blow their fucking asses away. Then we'll take Howard back to Cam An and turn him over to Luke the Gook. Hell, Wash, me and you are running the whole damned show now. Think of it. Shit, man, we'll be back in the world covered with pussy before you know it. We might have three or four of Asshole's men who'll give us trouble, but most of them are like the rest of us and really don't give a fuck as long as they get paid. Grab this fucker's other arm," duPage said, reaching down and picking up the man's AK-47 and slinging it over his shoulder before he grabbed the dead man's arm and started dragging.

"I figure I's got another two years afore I got my million," Washington answered as he grabbed the dangling arm. "Then I go to Hong Kong an git me some new papers and it's back to the world of the round eyes. Sheeeit, with that much money I can even git me a white woman. Hey, Fritz, you got a sister?"

"Fritz, how much you got in the bank, and what the hell you going to do with it?" duPage called to one of the other men.

"Shit, I don't know. Money's just something that's in the bank. Shit, I'll probably never see it. I just know I'm never goin back to the world. Hell, I'm home."

"Me, I'm going to buy me a big rancho in Mexico," Jose proclaimed. "Maybe somewhere in the mountains or maybe down on the Yucatan. Sure will be nice to hear somebody talk like me again."

"Jesus, this bastard's getting heavy. Now I know why they call it dead weight," one of the men from Donovan's squad said. "Let's just leave 'em here for the buzzards, you know damned well they wouldn't bother to carry one of us back."

"We don't leave nobody behind. I never left anybody while I was in the army, and I sure as hell ain't going to start now. I don't give a fuck who they were, they were part of us. I think you're going to find a lot of things changing now that me and Washington have took over. Come on, let's move out," duPage commanded with a voice that showed more comradeship than leadership. He smiled to himself, watching the men following without much complaint. *A bitching trooper is a happy trooper.*

They had to move up the narrow trail in a crab-like motion, almost sideways, half dragging half carrying the bodies of the five men. The heat and humidity rapidly forced the fluid and energy from their bodies. They had to stop, rest and drink about every hundred yards or so. Most of the canteens had been emptied within the first half mile; duPage passed his around before he drank. The men noticed how he seemed to think of them before himself. Each of the men following Jerry duPage noticed a style of leading by doing. They respected the man even before the command was in his grasp. None of the men dragging the bodies had any qualms about being backup for Jerry duPage from then on.

"Ladies and gentlemen, this must conclude this mornings program. You may exit through the curtain below the lighted green lotus at your leisure. There, in the light of morning, you will find tea, cakes, and a small gift to remind you of us when you are far away," the soft voice of Mr. Chiang said from the side of the room where they entered. He almost sounded like he was singing as he repeated the message in Chinese.

The potent smoke of the incense and opium started to dissipate, but the lights were still not bright enough to see across the floor. There were the sounds of whispering in many languages, the rustle of clothing from the audience, the clink of a bottle against a glass, and an occasional sigh or quiet grunt could still be heard. No one sought to break the magic spell that had been woven during the past few hours.

"Jesus, Jim, even if you had told me about this I still wouldn't have been prepared. I've never experienced anything like this. It was almost like you and I were out there on the floor. That has got to be the most erotic thing in the world," Kim whispered as she stood and buttoned her jeans.

"Now you can see why I didn't say anything. You wouldn't have believed me anyway," Sherlock answered with a contented smile and a barely noticeable glint in his brown eyes.

"Sex is nice, but this went so far beyond that. It was almost like making love in another dimension, another plane of existence. God, this is almost like a dream. Can we do it again tonight?" Kim asked as she forced Jim back down on the fur-covered couch with the length of her tall body.

"Janet, I'm not real sure of what we saw or did tonight, but I loved it," Bill whispered, picking up the long tulip-stemmed wine glasses. "Jim Sherlock can be my exotic tour guide anytime."

"I hope you've got more energy left than I do. I'm not sure I can walk out of this place. Not only that, I'm so stoned I don't want to walk out of this place; I think I'll float instead. There's only one way to describe this place – wow!"

The clinking of the wine glasses and the sounds of the champagne bottles being pulled from or replaced in the ice buckets continued to be the loudest sounds in the big room. There was a very soft whirr of an exhaust fan venting the room, and an occasional understood word was whispered. The voice of Mr. Chiang once again broke the stillness. "Ladies and gentlemen, for those of you who have transportation arranged by our humble establishment, the cars are waiting. Please, I only remind you. Stay as long as you wish, enjoy the moment to savor for a lifetime. The hospitality of our outer room can wait."

The air had cleared enough to see across the bare lacquered floor, and the soft lights were increased only a fraction. The guests began to stand and depart through the curtains in pairs – Just as the animals left the ark. There was still no talking above a whisper. Everyone was still afraid of breaking the magic spell before they departed through the curtains.

Pair by pair, they entered a well-lighted foyer with a wall of windows facing the east. Dawn was just starting to illuminate the garden of trees, flowers and a small reflecting pool beyond the glass. Each person was handed a small, ornately wrapped box by a beautiful, tall, older oriental woman. She was dressed from neck to ankles in a jade green, silk dress, almost seeming to be the lotus herself. She said nothing; her smile conveyed her thoughts and feelings to everyone in the room – peace and contentment.

"Good morning, Don," Frank said as the senator walked into the hotel dining room. "Where's David?"

"He's still asleep. He tossed and turned a lot last night; jet lag, I guess. Ah, good! Coffee," Don said, pouring a cup from the pot on the table. "What's all the excitement?" he asked, watching the number of uniformed policemen in the lobby.

"Someone got knifed in the elevator last night," Frank replied. "A real professional job. He put a spike right up through the guy's brain stem. No blood at all. Whoever did it is a real expert. I remember how hard that shot is," Frank answered as he took a sip of his coffee.

Mi Ling looked up from her tea and toast. "Don, we're only a few days from going to Vietnam," she started. "I believe we have a right to know who David really is, and what he's doing with us besides seeing how his money is being spent."

Frank looked into the eyes of his oldest friend, trying to judge his response. "You had best tell us, old buddy. Mi Ling and I have been talking. We're ready to scrub the whole mission right here and find our own financing. So if you want to help your friend, you had best start talking," he said in a matter-of-fact tone before he took another sip of coffee. Don realized Frank meant what he said from the serious expression in his cold grey eyes.

"Okay, I'll tell you what I know, which ain't a whole hell of a lot. You know when I'm trying to bullshit you. Here it is." Don took a sip of coffee and lit a cigarette, trying to stall while he thought. He sighed and began. "You remember three years ago when I was making all that noise on Capitol Hill about the POW-MIA issue? Well, David's people approached me with an offer to finance a half million dollars of the trip if it could be run as a search and not a fact-finding job. They told me, and I believed them, that they're an organization dedicated to the peace, health and stability of the world. Sounds like a bunch of liberal Democrats, doesn't it?" Don paused for another drink, and to collect his thoughts. "They've known for a long time that a large quantity of South East Asian opium is produced in the area around Cam An. It wouldn't have mattered where in Vietnam it was, we just had to get David there as part of the search team. David is supposed to be one of their key people, a troubleshooter I guess you can call him." Again a pause for coffee. "He told me he's supposed to investigate, find the people responsible for the growing, and report back to their main office in Belgium. Honest, that's all I know." Don looked into the faces of Frank and Mi Ling, trying to judge their belief by their expressions.

"Come on, Don, there's got to be more to it than that." Frank said with a note of disbelief.

"I swear that's all I know about it," Don said. "Having spent time as David's roommate, I know he's got the same type of flashbacks we used to have, and he always carries a weapon of some kind."

"What do you think, dear?" Mi Ling asked as she looked deeply into Frank's eyes.

"You did all the work, so it's your decision. Me, I still don't trust the son of a bitch. I think he's liable to do something that could get us killed," Frank answered, giving the final decision to his wife.

"Look, for what it's worth, he's told us that what he's supposed to do could endanger us. We've come this far, let's see it through," Don said, waving his cigarette in the air. "We were the most alive we ever were during the war. I think we need to try and get some of that excitement back, before we die of old age."

"I agree. We will continue," Mi Ling almost whispered as she sipped her tea. "We must watch David and try to keep him from doing something that could harm the rest of us, and we must do all in our power to protect the young people."

"Speaking of young people, here they come," Frank said, looking up and seeing the group walk through the front doors. "Well, are you kids hungry after a long night of debauchery?" he asked as they joined the breakfast table.

The surviving squad members broke out of the bush, dragging the bodies if the five dead men. The men left in the compound ran to help the reluctant pallbearers and to hear an explanation of the two episodes of automatic fire.

"What happened?" one of the men yelled as he got closer.

"They bunched up and got themselves killed. Where's Howard?" duPage yelled back.

"He's in his hooch. He ain't hurt bad, but the doc filled him with morphine. Shit, I've cut myself worse shaving," one of the men replied, taking the limp arm of one of the bodies.

"You men take these stiffs from here. We've had it. We're going to see Howard. Let's go guys," duPage ordered as he and Washington dropped the dead man face down in the grass.

The men with duPage handed over the bloody bodies to the men from camp. Walking toward the compound, they unslung their rifles as they ambled through the field of poppy buds.

duPage walked confidently into the compound. As he neared the huts, his thumb slid the safety on his M-16 from safe to semi-auto. He saw two of Howard's bodyguards leaning against the door posts of Howard's thatched hut. duPage could tell by their careless, lazy posture they expected no demands on their time. Jerry duPage closed the distance and casually laid his rifle across his shoulder, holding it by the plastic pistol grip with his finger on the trigger. "We got the little bastard," he said calmly. "Unfortunately, five of your boys bought it too."

"So Mr. Charles got five of our dudes. How many of yours did he get?" the larger of the two black men asked.

"I didn't say the gook got 'em," duPage answered, swinging his rifle from his shoulder into firing position on his hip and pulling the trigger twice. "I did. You dumb fuckers always got to bunch up, don't you," he said to the two dead men on the ground.

Men came running from all directions in the compound when they heard the shots ring out. duPage slid the safety to auto and stepped back against the wall of the hut as Washington, Chavez and the others took positions to offer covering fire if needed. The medic ran up and kneeled between the two men on the ground, feeling for a carotid pulse on each. Looking up at duPage, he shook his head.

"Doc, what's the story on Howard?" he asked, his eyes never leaving the troops in front of him, his finger not leaving the trigger.

"Shit, he's just got a flesh wound. He'll be okay in a week or so. He's more pissed off that someone would have the audacity to take a shot at him," the medic said as he stood to face the gathering men.

"Well, that don't matter none," duPage said quietly to the medic. "All right, you yahoos, listen up. As of right now, Howard don't have command of shit around here. I do. If any of you have a problem with that, speak up and we'll discuss it – just you, me, and Mr. Colt." He returned the rifle to his shoulder, but leaving the safety off, he glanced at Washington, Chavez and the others standing ready in the street. No one in the group made an aggressive move or said anything. They just stared. "Everything is going to continued like it was, only it's going to get better if I have anything to say about it. There's a hell of a lot more we can get done if we work together, and that's what we're going to do. It wasn't me or any of my men that shot Howard. It was that fucking bastard Colonel Ngu. Howard's just an asshole who thought he's a god. Ngu wants him. So we're going to give him to him, tomorrow at the Cam An field. I want all group leaders there tomorrow by noon. We're going to have to do some re - negotiating. Wash, this is your vill now. If you have any problems, let me know." duPage finished his speech and looked over at the medic. "Doc, get Howard ready to move and in my jeep. I'm ready to go home," he said with a heavy sigh.

The old man looked out from the shade of his hut to the tall kapok tree at the edge of the jungle. His look was returned by a flock of ravens staring back at him and the village. They made no sound, they just watched. *Yes, I know,* he thought. *Not today, but soon. Who are you waiting for? I know it is not me, but who?* Bending down, he picked up a handful of the finely powdered red dust. He turned his grey, wrinkled face in all directions, searching for a breeze in the hot, stagnant air. Trickling the dust through his hand, it fell, to be caught by an air current flowing from the southeast to the northwest – the direction of the mercenaries and the opium fields. *They will be coming now. Which of them is going to die? Who among us will find the eternal peace?* The last few grains of dust fell through his gnarled, skeleton-like hand as he turned and walked in the direction of the cemetery behind the village. *So many more graves have to be dug. Why, Buddha?* He asked the statue guarding the rows of wooden and stone markers.

Chapter Eighteen

After a day of rest, and spending the morning touring, Frank, Don, and Mi Ling settled down for lunch in the Hilton restaurant. Since the conversation at breakfast about David, the subject of their mysterious member had been put on hold. Any discussion of the trip, Vietnam, or the mission had been shelved in favor of friendship and tourism. Now the subject of lunch conversation was the same as everyone else's in the hotel – the body in the elevator.

"Dr. Wilson?"

"Yes, we're the Wilson's," Frank answered the cleancut man of about thirty wearing a tropical-weight white suit. *Jesus, if this guy doesn't reek of imperialism, no one does,* Frank thought, looking up from his plate.

"My name is Anthony Reed, I'm from the U.S. embassy here in Hong Kong. Do you mind if I sit down?" Not waiting for an answer, he pulled out the chair next to Don.

"What can we do for you, young man?" Mi Ling asked, obviously perturbed by the lack of manners. Her first thought was to dislike this brash young man. *You can always tell the ones born with a silver spoon.*

"I have your new passports and the rest of your travel documents," he replied, moving the glasses and silverware and replacing them with his expensive leather briefcase.

"For once you fellows at State are on the ball," Don said, momentarily halting his fork in mid-bite. "We just got in yesterday."

"Ah, uh, yes," Reed answered, noticing the light insult delivered by the senator. "I'm to collect your other passports and return them to Washington. Where's the rest of your group? I had hoped to catch you all together. It looks like now I'll have to make another trip." His irritation and disappointment made it clear that he believed this part of his job was beneath his dignity.

"Don't worry, Mr. Reed. All of the passports are together in the hotel safe. When I finish eating I'll get them," Frank said, taking another bite of lunch, indicating they did not wish to be bothered during their meal.

"Well, I had hoped we could get this taken care of as quickly as possible. I have a great many other things to do this afternoon," Reed sputtered at his dismissal.

"Look, boy," Don started, "when we want something out of you people we have to make an appointment and then cool our heels for at least an hour after we get there. You didn't have the courtesy to call ahead to see if we were even out of bed yet. Now you're going to have to wait until we finish eating, and then, maybe, we can get this taken care of."

"Well, I'm sorry you feel you must be so rude about this," Reed answered, unsure of what else to say.

"Young man," Mi Ling said, "you are the one who joined us without being asked. If you will please wait in the lobby, we will join you when we finish."

Reed closed his briefcase, stood, and without another word, attempted to make a dignified exit from the dining room. The three ignored him and continued with lunch, now taking their time much more than before. The conversation turned to Reed and his arrogance, and how he couldn't handle rejection.

The sergeant slid the Chinese-made jeep to a halt in front of the large, white, air-conditioned building. He jumped out almost before it came to a stop. Trahn rushed into the building, through the office area, and into Colonel Ngu's office without knocking.

Vinh looked up to see the tired, sweaty, filthy sergeant stranding three feet in front of his desk, saluting and starting to talk at the same time. "Sergeant!" Vinh almost yelled as he stood and walked over to close the door. "Now, please sit," he continued in a softer voice. "Relax, I'll get you a glass of ice water."

Trahn started his report with his pupils dilated, and in a machine gun-like staccato. "Sir. I failed, but, I didn't. The American is not dead, only wounded. The other American, duPage, has taken command. He ordered me to tell you if you want the black man Howard, come to the field near Cam An tomorrow afternoon." The sergeant barely paused to breathe before he delivered the message.

"Very good, Sergeant. How badly injured is the man?" The colonel continued to probe in a soft, calming voice.

"I don't know, sir. I saw him fall when I fired, then I shot two men standing next to him."

"Fine, Sergeant, fine," Colonel Ngu said as he tried to calm and reassure the sergeant. "This little mutiny might be the best in the long run. Perhaps we can deal with this other American. If not, then we will have to find one we can deal with. Let me refill that for you. Would you like for me to add a bit of whiskey to it this time?" *God, I'm going to have to air this room out tonight. He should feel disgraced, the way he stinks of sweat and piss.*

"Thank you, sir," the sergeant replied, looking up from the floor for the first time since he sat down. "I did accomplish my mission, then?" he asked, looking the clean, neat colonel in the eyes.

"You did very well, my friend. How does it feel to be killing the enemy again?" Vinh asked, handing the sergeant a glass about half full of whiskey.

"It was wonderful, better than being in bed with my wife or mistress. It was almost like I was alive again," the sergeant replied, savoring the burning, amber liquid.

"I must pass on your report to the general. Rest here a while where it is cool, and enjoy whatever you would care to drink. I have no idea how long it will take, but enjoy yourself, then go rest. I will talk more with you in the morning." Vinh picked up his hat from the table beside the door. Walking out with a smile, he left the sergeant and his liquor stores to his own vices.

Vinh's crisp uniform was soaked with sweat by the time he covered the hundred yards to the general's office building. As he entered, he was immediately halted by the general's Amerasian secretary as she politely but efficiently blocked his way when he started toward the office door.

"Colonel, the general has left strict word that he is not to be disturbed. This is his time for daily prayer and meditation."

"I believe Buddha can wait until after my report. Now, wake him up. I don't have all day, and for this I'm sure the general won't mind.

"Colonel Ngu, I hope you enjoyed your rank while you had it," she said as she tapped lightly on the door before entering.

Vinh paced back and forth in the office; he shivered a bit as the air conditioning evaporated the sweat from his uniform. He thought about lighting a cigarette, but stopped as the woman walked out, leaving the door open.

"You got lucky," she whispered, then louder, "You may go in now."

"This had better be good," the general growled as Vinh closed the door.

The general's eyes brightened as Vinh finished relaying the sergeant's report. The colonel could sense the general's mind working as he paced back and forth while listening, stopping at the liquor cabinet.

"We have Howard, and at least two more dead, and this white man is the new commander. The American group will be here in a few days to search for their MIAs. Let's give them fresh bodies and maybe they will go back where they belong." The general continued to outline his plans. "Get all the bodies prepared and have them waiting at the Quang Tri airport. Talk with this new commander and emphasize leaving the village of Cam An out of this harvest if the Americans decide to continued their search. If the Americans are satisfied and return home, we can continue. If not, then we will have to make other arrangements. Things may work out to where we may yet get a full harvest. You're doing a good job, my friend, and believe me, you will be rewarded for your efforts. Now, go and take care of your sergeant, he's a very valuable man," the general said in dismissal.

"Jerry, just what the hell you going to do when that hot shot colonel shows up this afternoon?" Washington asked.

"He wanted Howard, so I'm going to give him to him. Beyond that, I'm going to let him know we're going to be using the people in Cam An come hell or high water," duPage said, looking out over the poppy field. "These pods have to be cut this week or we're going to lose a hell of a lot of sap. The rest of you have already gotten started on your fields and some of the guys have even gotten two or three collections. I sent some of the guys to get the people at An Luk and Dak Ung, but we still need Cam An."

The big black man replied, "Man, you know he ain't going to go along wid that idea. Hell, he's just as likely to send that gook after yo' ass too!" He put a hand on the white man's shoulder.

"All I've got to do is to make it through this year's harvest and I'm outta' here. Getting rid of Howard and his bodyguards is going to mean a lot more for the rest of us. One of the first things I'm going to do as the new honcho of this bunch of misfits is to spread some wealth." duPage looked around the camp and field, while thinking of the bijou country of Louisiana.

"You got any idea how much he squirreled away over the years?"

"Well, he offered me ten million to let him go. That only goes to show you how much that son of a bitch has been skimming over the last couple of years. That should give the men about a hundred thou apiece, the team leaders about a hundred and twenty-five, and you and me about a hundred and fifty. If I can get a full harvest out of all the fields, we should be able to match that much or more."

"Man, I'm wid you," Washington answered, already imagining himself spending the money. "Sheeeit, I can go back to the world with a million bucks in m' pocket and be the biggest dude on the block. Yep, last harvest fo' dis nigger. Damn, it's been a long time."

duPage turned away before he replied, "Yeah, but we ain't got it yet. We'll just have to see what happens next."

"Morning is a much better time to talk business, don't you think, Vinh?" the general said, sipping his morning tea behind the massive carved desk.

"Any time is a good time as long as one can profit," Vinh replied as the corner of his mouth pulled up in what barely passed for a smile. "What are we going to tell the Americans about the bodies?"

"They were outlaws who tried to assault an armed

village. This will also confirm our claims about the bandit activity in this country being caused by American deserters. Perhaps this is a way we can convince them to go home where they belong." General Xuan stroked three of his four chins in thought.

"If we don't get that field in, we stand to lose millions in hard currency. These people have been warned about the danger of coming, so let's let them come. If some or all of them get killed, well then it's very sad, but they were warned. Just remember, it isn't us in charge out there, it's the American outlaws. We just send the bodies back to the U.S. with our condolences and a promise we will attempt to deal with the ones who did it," Vinh responded after pausing to think.

"Yes, that could work. Go tell this new American commander to use the people of Cam An. If anyone gets in the way, kill them. I will call Hanoi and tell them about the American bodies, and inform them about the dangers we believe these people to be in. We receive the profits and none of the blame," the general said with a short belly laugh as he set his tea on a stack of papers and reached for the telephone.

"Tell them we do not have sufficient troops to offer the Americans sufficient protection in their quest," Vinh added as his sneer became larger.

Chapter Nineteen

"Thank you for having us for lunch, Mr. Phoung," Frank said to the Vietnamese ambassador in the dining room of the Vietnamese embassy. "I'm glad you will be accompanying us at least as far as Quang Tri. I'm sure I speak for all of us in commenting on how wonderful the food is. But I think it's time we get down to business, since, I believe, we're finished."

"Yes, I'm sorry, I forgot, most of you Americans have yet to develop the patience for meals that we in this part of the world have." The distinguished gentleman at the head of the table stood, took a sip of water, and began. "Dr. Wilson has told me that you are ready to leave on your mission to my country. First, I must commend you all on what you are setting out to do. Not only will it help the families of both sides who lost someone in the conflict, but it may help our countries to once again become friends. Yes, we were friends during the war with the Japanese. Needless to say, I wish you all the good luck in the world." He paused for another sip of water.

"As you Americans say, I have some good news and I have some bad news. The good news is, your search for missing Americans has been decreased by eight. There are the bodies of eight men at the Quang Tri airport awaiting your authorization to ship back to the U.S. They were killed when they attempted to raid one of our armed villages. My government believes they were employed by some outlaw drug lord that we have not been able to bring to justice, yet." Son Phoung took another sip of water, appearing to be nervous. He started twirling the bottom of the wet glass on the white tablecloth before he continued.

"Now I must give you the bad news. The area where you are planning to go is under the control of one or more of these drug lords. They are also the ones who pay these American mercenaries. I, we, do not believe they would hesitate to harm or even kill you to protect their crops. I have been in contact with the military commander for this area, and I am afraid they can not give you protection in the areas in which you wish to travel.

The time of opium harvest is started. Therefore, the mercenaries will do everything in their power to keep strangers away. The commander of the area recommends, and I must agree, that you should take the eight bodies and return home. Perhaps you can return at a later time, when we may offer you greater protection." The emissary took another sip from the glass he had been using to occupy his hand.

"We were advised of the problems and dangers before we left the States," Mi Ling said as she patiently sipped her tea. "One of the things your ambassador promised us was military help and protection. It looks like the situation has now changed. We... all of us, have prepared long and hard for this trip, and we believe the value is worth the risk. Frank and I also have personal reasons to wish to return to Cam An."

"Anybody want to back out?" Frank asked, glancing into the eyes of each person around the table. "Last chance." No one answered while everyone looked to everyone else.

"It looks like we will be continuing our trip, Mr. Ambassador," Mi Ling said after the few moments of silence.

"Very well," Phoung answered. "I have some papers that you must all read and sign before we go. Dr. Wilson has told me you can be ready to leave tomorrow; do you believe early in the morning would be possible?" The team nodded their heads, but it was obvious each one was thinking about the weeks ahead. "Fine, we will pick you up at your hotel at eight o'clock tomorrow morning. South China Airlines leaves at nine. Please have these papers filled out for me at that time. When we get to my country, I will turn you over to your military liaison, Colonel Ngu. He will take care of you from there. Until tomorrow, then," Phoung said, looking at the group. "Transportation is waiting to take you back to your hotel." With this, he turned and left the room as a white-jacketed man escorted the team to the front door.

They refrained from making serious conversation until they arrived at the Hilton. Don was first out of the cars and into the hotel lobby. "I need a drink." He left Segretti, Jim, Kim, and Karen waiting for the others as he hurried through the automatic doors.

The group walked in as Don took his large scotch to what now had become their regular table. Frank and the others took their seats and signaled for a waiter. Frank started. "Any or all of you can still back out. It doesn't look like it's going to be a fun trip."

"Yeah, if our intelligence is right, we've got the fox guarding the fucking henhouse," Don added, taking a stiff drink. "With a line of bullshit like that guy's got, he could be a U.S. senator the first time out.

"Well, we knew we could back out anytime since this started," Karen said as she looked around the table. "If Tom's going, so am I."

"I'm following my little sister, and if Bill knows what's good for him, he'll follow me," Janet added.

"I'm in." Kim said.

"Jesus Christ, if you people are crazy enough to go on with this, you're going to need the Marines. Count me in. Hell, get me a drink too, Don," Sherlock said, not sounding enthusiastic.

"I have to go regardless. I'd be honored if you'd let me go with you," Segretti said with the affirmatives, attempting to sound humble.

Frank looked around the table before answering. "Looks like we're all going. Let's drink up; today is our last day and night in Hong Kong."

"Jim, can we go back to the Jade Lotus?" Kim asked with a wry smile and a twinkle in her eyes.

"No!" came a resounding chorus from the men who were involved.

"Yes, General, I understand," Vinh said into the telephone. "Well, we did try to stop them. Yes, it would be terrible if something happened to them, but, after all, it will be done by the American mercenaries. I will arrange for Sergeant Trahn to be their guide. I wish his English were better, though. Oh, they have their own translator? That may or may not be good. Yes, sir, I will meet them at the airport and introduce them to Sergeant Trahn. Yes, I will caution him not to be over-protective. Rest assured, my friend, things will turn out for the best. Yes sir, Trahn knows of our involvement with the opium.

He believes that it is being grown for the good of the country. Look, trust me, it will be taken care of. Wasn't I right to give them the bodies of Howard and his men? I don't believe they will search quite as hard now. I know Americans – they have to come, just to say they have been here if nothing else. One way or another, we will see they cause us no trouble. Yes, General, I will most definitely keep you informed. Yes. Good-bye." Vinh hung up the telephone, shaking his head. *This man is full of indecision. As the Americans used to say, no guts, no glory, and no money. I'm almost ready to do what the white American did. That weak bastard.* Vinh pushed the button on the intercom, "Find me Sergeant Trahn and have him report to me immediately. Then get my helicopter ready to leave for Quang Tri at two o'clock." *Now to get hold of duPage and let him know he's going to have guests in Cam An tomorrow.*

Chapter Twenty

The South China Airlines jet rolled to a stop outside the single-story terminal beside the grey and white Air Vietnam prop plane. The steward opened the door as the steps were being pushed into place. In less than a second the cool air inside was replaced by the hot, humid, sticky air from outside. It felt to the few Americans as if they had left an Arctic winter and walked into a steam room. Along with the heat and humidity, their noses were assaulted. It was like they'd landed in a sewer. The combination of elements were almost enough to make them want to vomit. Karen, Kim, and Janet turned noticeably pale under their tans as they learned to mouth breath.

"Welcome to Quang Tri, Vietnam." The voice came over the loudspeaker in Vietnamese, Chinese, French and English as the passengers struggled toward the door.

"That's us," Frank said as they stood. "Mr. Phoung, after you, since you know what we're supposed to do next."

"Thank you," the distinguished man answered as he stood and stepped into the aisle.

"This place smells like shit," Tom whispered to Don. "What is it?"

"Shit. That's what they use for fertilizer over here. Any kind – pig, chicken, buffalo or human – it's all the same. Don't worry about it! You'll get used to it soon enough. Try breathing through your mouth for a while," the senator advised.

Mr. Phoung picked up his briefcase and followed the crowd to the door. He stopped, looked around and smiled. "It's good to be home," he said in Vietnamese to no one in particular. "I believe I see our welcoming committee," he said, turning to Frank when he noticed the uniforms of Colonel Ngu and Sergeant Trahn coming toward the plane.

Frank clenched his teeth and his right hand balled into a tight fist as Vinh stopped at the foot of the stairs. Vinh's eyes showed a light of recognition at the three people behind the ambassador. "Lieutenant Frank, Mi

Ling, Sergeant James. I thought you were all dead. My God, it's wonderful to see you."

Phoung stepped to the side as his feet touched the hot cement. Frank took two steps closer to the colonel. "You traitorous son of a bitch!" were the first words Frank said as his arm came up and out from the shoulder in a powerful, martial arts punch. When it connected, Vinh fell back. His body was ramrod straight as he hit the concrete. Frank took another step off the ramp, and drew back his right foot to deliver a kick. He stopped when he heard the bolt of the AK-47 slam closed, loading the sergeant's weapon.

Vinh started to rise, shaking his head, trying to clear the effects of the punch. "Sergeant! Stop!" he yelled. "Lieutenant Frank, I guess you can be allowed that one, I was only doing my job – as were you. I want you to know the entire time we were together I never compromised you." Vinh raised to a sitting position and rubbed his jaw. The sergeant moved to help with a hand on Vinh's elbow. "Yes, I was a spy, but the only information I gave was what I heard from you and the rest of the men. I tried to keep my army away from the village." Vinh regained his feet with help. "If you had not been as efficient with the ambushes and working with the locals, the village would probably have been left alone. I could have been killed just as easily as anyone else. Frank, you must believe me, I did my best for my country and the village."

"Vinh, as far as I'm concerned you're still a traitorous son of a bitch," Don said. "We trusted you then, but I'll be damned if we trust you now."

The rest of the team came down the steps and joined the group, unaware of what had just transpired.

"We can discuss personal matters later," Vinh said, trying to get to the business at hand. "Now we must get to the reason you came. Let us walk to that building." He pointed. "That is where your supplies are, and also American bodies for which you must authorize shipment. Sergeant, you may relax," Vinh said in Vietnamese. "These are old friends of mine." Switching back to English, he continued, "This is Sergeant Trahn, he's going to be your guide and protection while you are here.

The sergeant nodded his head as he examined the

assembled group of men and women. *The colonel is worried about these people? The big one looks like he could make trouble, but not the rest. The old man can hit hard for his age and size, but I don't believe he would have been effective if it had not been for surprise. I wonder how much protection I am really supposed to give these people.* The sergeant slung his weapon and followed them into the warehouse beside the terminal.

The hot, stale air almost knocked them over as the colonel raised the tin overhead door. The first thing they saw were eight, red painted wooden coffins sitting on sawhorses. Each box had an envelope tacked to the top.

"These are your people, all black men. Their personal effects are inside with them. This," Vinh pulled a sheet of paper out of one of the envelopes, "is a summary of who they were and the personal effects they had with them when they were killed. There is also a copy inside the box with the body. We have embalmed them so they will not decay, and they are packed in plastic body bags. All you have to do is to sign the release and they will be sent to your base in Hawaii. Men like these," he motioned with his palm up, "are why you should abandon your mission and return home. These men were animals; they raped and killed for pleasure. We were lucky they picked the wrong village."

"This may be so, Vinh," Mi Ling said, "but there are a lot of dead on both sides who will never return home without help. Remember how we always buried the people after ambushes? I doubt if you or your government ever went back for them. That was then; now all the dead should be laid to rest as the heroes they were.

A very honorable lady, Trahn thought, understanding most of the conversation. *This will be a most interesting mission.*

"The dead are dead, it doesn't matter to them where they are. The dead you don't have to worry about, you have to worry about the living. Men like these," he motioned again towards the boxes, "will kill you on sight, just to keep their secrets. There are hundreds of men like this left in my country."

Sherlock asked, "What about the ones who are still being held as POW's?" staring down on the arrogant colonel.

"I'm sorry, to the best of my knowledge my country is holding no American against their will. I will not say there are no prisoners, it is that I do not know of them."

"So the dead don't matter to you." Kim spoke up for the first time. "There are a lot of people in the States who need the body of their loved one to put this war behind them. That's why we're here, and by God we're going to do our best to help them."

"Let's talk no more of the dead for now. Sign this, Frank, then we can look to your equipment." Vinh handed Frank a paper and a ballpoint pen. "After we check your transportation and equipment, we can clear you through passport control and customs and get you to your hotel." Vinh continued to smile, while thinking, *Damn, if it had been anyone but these people they would have taken the bodies and gone home. Frank and Mi Ling are the kind of people the rest will follow to the gates of hell to accomplish their mission. I hope they go home before they get killed.* Vinh opened the door on the far side of the building and everyone was temporarily blinded by the bright, hot sun. When their eyes adjusted, they could see two U.S. Army jeeps and a two and a half-ton truck. "As you can see, your equipment container has been loaded and it is still sealed. You may check it if you wish."

Hayes jumped to the truck bed and finished pulling himself up by the canvas top. "The locks look good and the seals are still intact. Doesn't looked like anyone's bothered it."

"I don't believe your friend trusts me," Vinh mentioned offhandedly.

"He doesn't, and I'm not sure the rest of us trust you either," Frank replied, his voice sounding cold and hard.

"Ease up, Frank." Tom reached out a hand to stabilize Bill as he jumped. "He's just doing his job. Everything's cool. We've got a job to do, so let's make life as easy as possible for ourselves."

Vinh tried to redirect the conversation. "Come, I'll get your immigration taken care of and we can load up and go to your hotel. You can get a fresh start in the morning."

"Since you're so intent on us staying, I think we should go today." Don looked around at the rest of the team. "There's plenty of light left, and it ain't all that far."

"What the hell, let's do it," Frank replied with a grin to match Vinh's frown. "The sooner we get moving, the sooner we start to work."

"Whatever you say, Frank," Vinh replied, turning his hands palm up in a sign of submission.

With the colonel leading the way through customs, it was little more than a formality of stamping passports. The checked baggage was waiting as the group walked out the side entrance and back to the jeeps and truck. The colonel reached beside the seat in one jeep and pulled out a plastic envelope.

"These are the newest road maps for this northern area. From now on, Sergeant Trahn will be your guide and the only protection I can give you. Frank, Don, be sensible. Mi Ling, try to convince them you should return to the States. This country is still very dangerous. Go home. You were lucky to have survived the war; don't tempt the fates now."

"Vinh, we never gave up before; would you expect us to start now?" Mi Ling answered as she looked the colonel straight in the eyes.

"No, I guess not. Sergeant Trahn knows the way to Cam An, he should be able to get you there in about an hour and a half. I wish you would reconsider."

"No can do, Vinh. You should know better than that. We're wasting daylight, let's move out," Don said, loud enough for all to hear. "Sergeant, I guess you're driving the lead jeep. We'll go with you."

The traffic on Highway One was heavy with pedestrians, ox carts, bicycles, motorcycles, and the occasional automobile. To either side of the smooth concrete road were rice paddies as far as the eye could see. An occasional dike had a few willows or a bamboo thicket growing on it to hold the soil in place during heavy rains. Almost every small square had people working at the various stages of rice production, from planting to harvesting. The peasants' backs were permanently bowed. Their long years of bending over trying to produce enough to stay alive and feed their people had turned the old people into cripples.

Sergeant Trahn spoke for the first time since they left the airport. "What is the real reason you came to Vietnam?" he asked Frank. "Do you work for someone who will exploit my country even more? I have a hard time believing you are here for the reasons you gave my colonel."

"We're here to take our dead home," Mi Ling answered in Vietnamese. "Cam An was my home, and these two men lived there for a while and helped protect us from the soldiers and the Viet Cong. We killed and buried many of your soldiers before the village fell. We also have friends who are still buried there. We just want to give the dead a place to rest with honor. People from both sides fought and died bravely. They deserve more than to be left lying in the jungle, or to be buried in a mass grave. We are here only to take people home."

"That sounds honorable, but I remain to be convinced. My colonel was correct in saying the area around Cam An is a dangerous place for strangers. If there is trouble, I have my doubts about how effective I would be in protecting you."

"Don't worry, Sergeant, I'm sure you will find we are more than the old people you see. Time may have blunted our bodies and skills, but not our determination."

They turned west off the main road onto a secondary highway covered with asphalt. The marks from the tanks and armored personnel carriers were still evident, causing the jeep to bounce like it was on a washboard. The cultivated land dwindled, except for the occasional stand of banana trees or the remains of a French rubber plantation. The traffic was now exclusively pedestrians, carrying baskets balanced on long poles across their shoulders. Mi Ling noticed the faces had no more than the blank stares of people barely surviving. She had expected at least a few smiles – even during the worst of the war, the peasants could still smile at having land, food and at least some margin of shelter.

"Sergeant, are things really so bad here that even the peasants see no hope?" Mi Ling asked in Vietnamese.

"Yes, I am afraid so. After the war we were short on everything except people." Trahn started to explain in detail what had happened since the war ended. "The Americans stopped sending food and medicine to the south and the Russians and Chinese did the same to the north. After all these years we still have people starving. We have gone from being one of the richest countries in the world to perhaps the poorest. Now most people in our country are lucky to make the equivalent of a hundred of your dollars a year. The years of war have taken their toll, not only on the people, but on the land."

"I am sorry for all of us, Sergeant. I feel uncomfortable calling you by your rank – we are not formal people. I am Mi Ling, this is Don, and this is Frank," she said, putting her hand on their shoulders. "How do your friends call you?"

"The few friends I have call me Mihn," he answered, his eyes not leaving the road."

"I hope that soon you will consider us your friends, Mihn," Mi Ling replied. Then, switching to English she said, "Gentlemen, this is Mihn."

Mihn guided the jeep around and through the pedestrians and the occasional water buffalo, making every attempt to stay out of the tread tracks that caused the tooth-chattering bounce.

Frank and Don had said almost nothing during the trip. Each had turned his mind's eye back to the time when the road was packed clay and the trails had to be constantly reclaimed from the jungle. They remembered how they watched the birds, animals and insects as an indication that there was something or someone around besides themselves. They tensed their muscles each time they passed a farmer in black pajama-like clothing, each waiting for the shot that didn't come.

Mi Ling had been talking constantly to their guide and driver since they left Quang Tri. The constant talking was unlike her, but she felt excitement at returning to her country and experienceing the feel of the land near her village after all these years. Mi Ling almost felt like a school girl again.

Tom, Karen, Bill, Janet and David followed closely in the second jeep. Their noses slowly became accustomed to the smell of human and animal waste used as fertilizer to enrich the clay soil. Their senses of hearing and vision became more acute as they moved farther away from the city. Each person seemed to pick up different things. Karen and Janet saw mainly the flowers, especially the parasitic orchids. Bill took more notice of the bushes and trees, noticing the animal trails and the other things he was trained to notice when he went through survival school many years ago. Tom kept his eyes on the road; his peripheral vision noticed the explosion of birds as they took off from the ditches. David Segretti sat facing straight ahead in an almost catatonic state saying nothing. Only his eyes moved – back and forth, up and down, like a video camera, constantly recording and storing the images of everything they passed. Even the small green-yellow snake beside the road or the gecko lizard on the tree failed to escape his notice.

Jim hadn't said but a few words during the drive, he too was remembering the way things were when he was here before. "I'm glad to see the land is healing itself," he whispered to himself as he shifted gears. "I'm anxious to see what the defoliated areas look like after all these years," he said, turning to Kim.

"This is a beautiful country if you can ever get used to the smell and the heat," Kim replied as she tried to see everything, almost like a child in a toy store.

"The smell doesn't take long, but you never get used to the heat. Just wait until this evening when the mosquitoes come and carry you off," Jim replied with a grin.

Sergeant Trahn turned off the scarred asphalt onto a dusty, dirt road barely wide enough for the jeep. Branches and grasses brushed against the jeep and its occupants. The dust kicked up by the tires hung in the hot, humid air, blinding Tom and the others following in the second jeep. Tom downshifted and slowed the jeep to a crawl, allowing time for the dust to settle.

After following the track about fifteen miles into the bush, they crossed one of the many streams leading from the highlands. Now Mi Ling, Frank, and Don knew exactly where they were: less than a mile from the village of Cam An. The road started to widen as the village came into view beyond a bend in the road. The veterans were shocked at what they saw. Now there was only a mound where the five-foot-high protective wall once stood. The rice paddies that were capable of supporting a thousand people had now turned to grass, weeds and swamp. There were only a handful of huts, where there had been almost two hundred. The huts, made of lashed bamboo with thatched straw or palm roofs, stood in general disrepair. Here and there a piece of salvaged lumber was used, and in some places a trace of olive green paint was still visible. Two of the huts had ancient, rusting, corrugated tin for roofs, with woven bamboo covering the doors and windows for protection from the elements. Years after the war, the signs of the American occupation was still evident in the bits and pieces of refuse used in the buildings. Sergeant Trahn stopped the lead jeep between the two long-dead palm trees that were the western gate. They noticed a few people milling around the village, the very old or the very young. When the people saw the Caucasian faces, they quickly disappeared inside. The second jeep pulled up and they could hear the truck close behind.

"Time to go see what's going on," Frank said in a quiet voice as he stepped over the low bamboo fence made to keep the long departed pigs and chickens in. "Sergeant, did anyone tell these people we were coming?"

"I would have to say no. Colonel Ngu was hoping you would return to the U.S. This is a very dangerous area. I know of one opium field only a few kilometers from here. I would guess the people have been put to work by the growers, a common practice in this part of the country. The military has too much trouble with the populated areas to worry about what goes on in hamlets."

As the truck rolled to a halt and Jim and Kim joined the rest, Frank said, "Time to go gain friends and influence people." He started walking forward into the village. The memories rushed back. *The last time I was here it was to win the hearts and minds. Was Vinh right? Were we the cause of this destruction?*

As they walk into the hamlet, Frank, Don, Mi Ling and Jim spread out, and their old training took hold.

Their short, cat-like steps and the occasional breeze kicked up enough dust to make mud on their sweat-soaked clothing. Their eyes missed nothing as they moved. They saw the mound that was the defensive wall, the depressions caused by high explosives. They stopped for a second when they reached a slight depression with a few pieces of rusting metal protruding through the dirt. It was the grave of a medic and a radio man – their brothers under fire. The rusted concertina wire had been unrolled and was now a pen for a few hogs and three half-starved water buffalo. *Jesus Christ,* Frank thought, *this place is worse off than the first time I saw it. At least then they had some pride and hope. Looks like they've even lost that now.*

What has happened to my home? Is there anyone left I once knew? Mi Ling thought as she surveyed the squalor. *I can feel the pain and despair that's here.*

Don't worry guys, we came to get you and take you home, Don thought, looking at the collapsed bunker. *Your war is finely going to be over. You can rest now.*

What the fuck is going on here? Jim thought, looking around. *It feels like some kind of shit's ready to hit the fan, and me without a weapon! Watch your back and be ready to hit the deck. How the hell can I protect these people when I can't even protect myself?* He felt Kim's hand slip into his and he relaxed, for a second.

Mihn walked ahead and disappeared into the hut where he had seen one of the villagers go. Loud voices broke the stillness as an old man fell through the woven grass door. When he hit the ground he curled into a fetal position with his arms protecting his head. The sergeant followed, still yelling. He drew back a foot to deliver a kick to the old man's ribs.

"Trahn! No!" Frank yelled as he and the others ran closer. "We don't need to scare these people any more than we already have."

"Back off, Sergeant." Don motioned for Jim to get Mihn out of sight.

"We're not here to cause you harm," Mi Ling said in her soft calming voice. "We came here to collect the bodies of our friends, so they can be laid with their ancestors. Two of them are still here, over there." She pointed to the depression. "This used to be our village many years ago." Mi Ling switched to English. "Hand me some water," she said as she gently pulled the old man's arms from his head and helped him to a sitting position. Karen handed over a plastic canteen she carried from the jeep. "We will not hurt you. We need your help, and perhaps you can use ours," Mi Ling continued as she held the canteen to his mouth. "We will not harm you. Do you think you can get up now? Let us move to the shade where it is not so hot." Mi Ling nodded to Frank and they each took an arm and gently assisted the old man into the shade of the hut. "Can you tell us where everyone is?" she asked, as if talking to a small frightened child.

The old man looked up at Mi Ling and the others with sad, tired eyes. They held a spark of something none of the team had ever seen before. They seemed to look through them and into the team's souls. Answering in Vietnamese, he said, "Other Americans came and took them to work in the field upriver. Only those of us who are too old or too young to work are left. This is the way it has been for years. We plant, we weed, we harvest – this is the way it is. We are paid in rice – not much but some, enough to keep us alive. There is not time for us to grow our own. We must do as they say or they beat us. Some of us have been shot for refusing to work. We tried to resist, at first, but we are too few. We tried to leave, but the other villages within day's travel are also controlled by these Americans. We have been waiting for you. What took you so long?"

Mi Ling handed him the canteen and turned to explain the conversation in English.

Frank looked around the empty village. "Tell him we are going to stop this slavery, and find out how long the rest of the people are going to be gone, and if they're guarded at night. Tom, Trahn, take one of the jeeps and find enough good food to last a full village a couple of days. Jim, move the truck around back, and start unloading the stuff we'll need immediately. Get the clothes and guns out and pass them around. Then hide the truck and jeep in the bush. Mi Ling, tell him what I just said, and tell him we made this village safe and prosperous once, a long time ago, and we'll do it again."

Mi Ling translated the conversation and saw a look of disbelief and then hope on the old man's face. "I know, my father-in-law didn't believe it could happen either," she said, speaking as calmly as she could. *I recognize him, he was with me at the wall,* she thought. *How did he know we were coming? What does he mean when he said he has been waiting for us.*

"Don, come with me," Frank said. "Let's have a look around. Mi Ling, stay with him." He motioned to the old man. "Tom, you and Trahn get moving and get back as soon as you can, and the rest of you get moving on the truck. Looks like we've got a job to do before we can do our job."

duPage stood beside the empty irrigation ditch with his hands on his hips as the short Puerto Rican walked up and handed him a rusting, .30 caliber ammo can. "Washington sent this down. Jesus, Jerry, you've got these people working like ten thousand mother fuckers. How the hell did you do it?" Chavez asked.

"Oh, not much. I just told them if they do a good job I'll give 'em more rice. If they fuck off, I'd kill 'em." duPage flipped the latch on the box and looked inside. "Yeah, this is what we need. Let's head back to the hooch and see what Howard left us in his will." They turned back to the group of huts a few yards away from the field.

"Wash heard, Ngu say that there were going to be a bunch of people showing up around here tomorrow. What we going to do about them?"

"We finish cutting tomorrow, so we'll have a couple of days to make plans. As I see it, there's only two choices – they can co-operate or die. Right now I don't give a rat's ass which. This harvest is going to be my ticket back to the world," duPage said as they entered his hut and he dumped the contents of the box on the table.

Chapter Twenty-one

Within minutes after the team left Quang Tri for Cam An, Colonel Ngu was well on his way back to Da Nang. The flight by helicopter took less than an hour. Minutes after he landed he was in the general's office with his report.

The general tried hard to show his disappointment in the team's decision to stay. What he did manage to convey was his worry about his cash crop. "So the Americans were not smart enough to take what we offered and return home," the general said as he sipped the drink with his feet propped on his massive desk. "You did warn them they could be killed?"

"They were warned," Vinh replied. "They decided to go in spite of the warnings. Three of these people I worked with years ago during the war. For the first time I wonder about duPage's chances for success. I watched these people, and a few more, turn Cam An from a hamlet to a fortified city in a matter of weeks. They were able to beat some of the best troops our government had to offer. These are not people who will give in without a fight."

"What do you think your Sergeant Trahn will do? Will he be loyal to us or the Americans you assigned him to help?"

"He'll be of little help to them. He's a nationalist; he still hates all Americans for what they did to our country. He'd be happy to see both sides kill each other. His loyalty is with us," Vinh replied confidently as he made himself a drink from the general's well-stocked bar.

"If and when the fighting starts, which side will win?"

"It doesn't matter which side wins, as long as we win. Mr. duPage has the men and the guns, Lieutenant Wilson has six men and four women; I don't believe we have a thing to worry about. We will win just as we always have. The opium will be ours," Vinh replied as he sat back in his chair. *How did someone like this get to be a general?* he asked himself as he sipped the glass of American whiskey.

"What do you think, Don, can we pull it off again?"

Frank asked as they walk around the area that used to be the village.

Don stopped and was silent for a moment. "That's where Marsh got it. I'll never forget him standing there, killing everything in sight. Shit, I can see it as clear as if it were happening now. Over there's where you and I got it." He pointed. "Jesus, Frank, why did we come back here? It hurts too fucking much."

"We came back for Doc, Sparks, and the others. Now, God damn it, snap out of it. Can we make this place defensible?"

"Shit, no we can't. We don't have the guns, we don't have the people, we don't have support, we don't have the time. Wake up, Frank, we don't have shit. It'd be like you or me taking on a heavyweight champ. I don't think we've got a prayer." Don looked around the area that was the village of Cam An and shook his head in defeat.

They walked across the area. Memories of the people and events flashed through their minds with a clarity undiminished by time. Just beyond the mound that was the wall, they saw the cemetery, taking up more space than the current hamlet. Each grave was well cared for, and had a stone or wood marker. A three-foot stone statue of a standing Buddha protected the dead and offered hope to the living. Frank and Don stopped, bowed their heads, and then offered a silent prayer, not just to Buddha, but to gods everywhere.

When they returned to the group, most of the personal equipment had been unloaded from the compak container. The women moved them from the truck to a spot next to one of the huts, protected by the overhanging thatch. The last piece handed down was Segretti's long aluminum box, the source of most of the hostility.

Mi Ling stopped shoving boxes under the eves of the roof and walked over to meet Frank and Don. "He knows us," she said. "The crazy American who was always whistling, the mean sergeant who used to slap him awake when he was on guard duty. He barely remembers me, but he does remember my father-in-law. He said he had been sending for us for years. He wanted to know if there will be fighting this time. I told him I didn't know."

Don looked at his toes and then into Frank's and Mi

Ling's eyes. Rage started to boil deep in his chest as he spoke. "This was our village once, and as far as I'm concerned it still is. We've got basically the same problems we had before, and we need to correct them." Don's mind started to work like it did as a Special Forces NCO thirty years ago. Everything started to click as his ideas meshed.

"Let's go talk to the old man," Frank said as he led off. "We need all the intelligence we can get."

The old man waited, sitting on his heels in the shade of the hut. A bit of red drool drips down the corner of his mouth from the betel nuts he chewed. As he watched the group unpack the boxes he shook his head slowly from side to side and mumbled, "Dinkey dau, dinkey dau." It was the bastardized Vietnamese term for *dien cai dau*, meaning crazy.

They watched the villagers enter the clearing from the trail on the north side. Some were barely moving, and some of the weaker ones were being supported by the strong. Most staggered from exhaustion. They were dressed in the pajama-like cotton clothes associated with the peasant class, in T-shirts and cast-off pants, or in cheap cotton dresses. At first, Frank was reminded of the B-grade zombie movies of the fifties. The walking dead – not living, but not dead either – just moving by putting one foot in front of the other. The team watched in silence as the people staggered in, most going directly to huts. Women stopped beside the fire rings and started to build fires. For them, the day was far from over.

Jim broke the silence as he whispered more to himself than anyone else, "Jesus Christ, these people are being worked to death." Then louder, "Think these people would eat some freeze dried food?"

"These people will eat anything right now," Mi Ling answered. "Let's go see what we can do to help." She walked to where a woman about her own age was starting a fire. Without saying a word, Mi Ling squatted and covered the woman's gnarled hand with her own. Smiling, she started laying the small bits of wood to form a base. Then she reached for the larger pieces, building the fire the way they had always done it in the village.

Other members of the team followed her example. Jim opened a case of the freeze-dried rations and handed the packages to Kim to open and pass around.

Everyone looked up when they heard the jeep coming down the road. The team showed signs of relief, and the villagers apprehension, when Tom and Trahn drove through the dead palms. "We got rice, beans, and about a hundred pounds of pork. There's a bit of fresh fruit, but not much. We had to go all the way to Cam Lo to find anything," Tom said as he climbed out and walked toward the others.

"Where is everyone?" Trahn asked Mi Ling. "I don't see many more people than we saw when we came in."

"Most of them have collapsed from exhaustion," she answered in Vietnamese.

"Let's see what we can do to get these people fed, and then maybe we can find out what we're up against," Frank said as he picked up a sack from the jeep and started toward the *dinh*, the central meeting house.

"Hey, Fritz!" duPage yelled across the field, motioning with his arm.

"Jack, finish out these rows and send 'em home. Tell 'em we'll get them about sun up. I'm going to see what the boss wants."

"Good enough, buddy," the one addressed as Jack responded. "You want me to cut out some sweet, young, tender meat to warm your hooch tonight?"

"No, and you're not getting any either. Jerry's about as nervous as a whore in church about this bunch that's coming in. So you leave the fucking women alone."

"Jesus, man, lighten up. Since you got promoted to field boss, you're almost as bad as Jerry."

"Look, asshole," the shorter of the two replied, "if you're that horny, go jerk off. But I told you to leave the fucking women alone, understand?" Fritzpatrick said as he turned and walked between the rows of plants. Stopping every once in a while, he checked the small cuts across the buds. When he reached the end of the field he climbed out of the irrigation ditch and walked the few feet to where duPage stood. "They're doing a good job, but I've got a problem with Jack. I've got an idea he's going to be causing trouble with the women. He just can't keep his dick in his pants. So what's up? You got any new ideas on what we're going to be doing with this bunch of people that're supposed to be coming to the ville?"

"Yeah, Chavez and I were just talking about that. If they leave us alone, we leave them alone. If they try to fuck with us, well, there's going to be more Americans here that don't go home." Jerry duPage looked across the field with what used to be called the thousand-yard stare. He remembered the adrenaline rush from killing Howard and his men a few days ago. A strange smile came to his face as he said, "I hope they do try to fuck with us, but it'd be a shame to shoot somebody who don't shoot back."

After an evening meal that turned out to be a feast, the five younger members of the team spread out in the village, each doing whatever they could to help. They carried water from the river, washed dishes, and helped slice what was left of the pork for storage. No task was beneath them, they just did it. The communication was done by sign language, smiles, or tone of voice.

With the help of a full meal, the villagers regained some of their energy. There was even a spontaneous smile now and then. Some of the younger and more aggressive villagers met with the old man and the foreigners while they discussed the opium operation. They answered the team's questions as Mihn and Mi Ling translated. Don and Jim made notes and drawings of the mercenary camp. Occasionally they would ask a question for clarification, but they allowed the others the honor. The team gathered every possible scrap of intelligence without a personal trip to the enemy camp. That would come in the morning.

As the sun dipped down below the tall pines and kapok trees, the village and the team got squared away for the night. All stomachs were full for the first time in months as they prepared for bed and the long day ahead. By the time it was dark, only a couple of candles burned in the village, and the team bedded down in the large, open community hut.

By moonrise, everyone except the old dream weaver was sound asleep. He stared into the fire and watched the coals. He dropped a handful of herbs into the fire and watched the smoke rise into the still night air. The ghosts of the fire directed the smoke toward the opium fields, but it dissipated to nothing before it left the village clearing. The old man smiled as he concentrated on following the smoke as it rose and boiled. His attention was drawn back to the fire. He froze with horror while he watched the coals blink out of existence. *No!* his mind screamed as he dumped a bucket of water on the fire. *No! No! No! It can't be! It's not worth it!* As the steam rose, he bowed his head and closed his eyes. An unseen tear ran down his leathery cheek.

The team remained hidden behind the huts as the villagers went about their morning routine. The smoke and the smell of cooking rice and barbecuing fish and pork filled the still morning air. The people of the village were doing as they always had. Everything was normal, with the exception of an occasional covert glance in the direction of a team member.

Three shots rang out from the north trail, breaking the morning quiet. People started packing away food and covering the pots to keep flies away during the long hot day. As each finished their morning chores, they walked across the dusty compound in the direction of the trail. The team members watched helplessly as the man with the rifle roughly pulled or shoved the villagers into a ragged line. "*Chuyen dong*" (move out)" he yelled as he fired his AK-47 into the air to emphasize his order.

When the line had moved into the rich, green jungle, Frank motioned for the group to gather. "Jim, you and Tom take the flanks. Bill, you run drag. See if you can find out what else we're up against. Be careful." He slapped each of the three men on the shoulder as they moved toward the still dark trail.

"Let's get some coffee going and see if we can figure a way the hell out of this mess," Don said as he moved toward the Coleman stove sitting on one of the boxes.

"Okay, pass out the blades and get 'em started where

they left off yesterday. I'm going to Da Nang and I want to see this field done when I get back. Jack, you leave the women the fuck alone, you hear?" duPage said, briefing his men while the villagers filed by. They stopped at the table and picked up the large rings with fine blades that fit the palms of their hands. Slowly they started down the long rows of poppies as the sun started to evaporate the haze. "Fritz, get the books and meet me at the jeep. Time to go move some money."

Jim Sherlock watched and listened from his hiding place a few feet away. His light brown clothing blended well with the vines, grasses and other undergrowth, hiding his massive frame. He didn't move a muscle when duPage walked over, unbuttoned his fly, and started to urinate inches from his face. duPage shook off the last few drops and looked directly into Jim's eyes. He turned and buttoned his fly as he walked toward the driver's side of the jeep and waited.

Tom watched the field from the cover of a large tree. As the sun climbed higher, he noticed a guard stop and fondle the breasts of one of the young women with each pass he made. The woman attempted to ignore him while she continued to touch each large bud with the palm of her hand.

Hayes made a mental map of the compound. His eyes and training told him the use of each hut. Watching, he attempted to place each of the men in the hierarchy of command. He counted the men and the weapons and then started looking for any security systems – there were none but the guards in the field and the tower. *Okay, that's about all I can see,* he thought as he slid quietly backward toward the trail.

Gunnery Sergeant Sherlock watched each man carefully, giving each a close inspection, the kind he would his own troops – dirty weapons, torn clothing, how they walked and moved, how they interacted with the other men in the compound. He looked for anything that could distinguish these men as soldiers and not a mob. In this case, he saw that the mob ruled. With his recon complete, he snaked back into the jungle, leaving no trace of where he had lain for the past two and a half hours.

Tom picked up a small rock and tossed it, hitting the girl on the back. Nonplussed, she straightened, stretched and looked around. With gestures, Tom communicated to the girl to lure the guard into the bush. The woman nodded twice in understanding and continued her task. When the guard stepped into her row the young woman looked up. She removed her cutting ring and laid it on the ground, then started walking across the rows toward the cover of the bush. The guard noticed and started to follow, smiling ear to ear as he set an intercept course. Tom moved silently to the position where the woman would be entering the jungle and stationed himself behind a large tree. As she passed, she looked to the side and nodded without stopping. The guard crashed through the brush, not caring that the woman knew she was being followed. He looked straight ahead, his thoughts on the pleasure that would happen when he caught her.

Tom stepped from behind the tree as the man passed. "Freeze, motherfucker," he said as he stepped behind the man. The guard stopped in his tracks and slowly started raising his arms, still holding the AK-47 in both hands. When his arms reached just above shoulder height, he turned with the speed of a cobra, striking Tom above the right eye. As Tom fell, the man brought the weapon down, slid the safety off with his thumb, and fired.

"What the hell was that?" one of the guards in the field asked another.

The guards turned toward the woods as the second answered, "Ah hell, that was just Jack firing a warning shot to stop that little piece of fluff he's been feeling up all morning. You can bet your left nut Jerry's going to have his ass when he gets back. He told Jack specifically to leave the women alone."

"I didn't hear anything, did you?"

"Hear what?" replied the second guard as they continued walking down the rows of poppies.

The 7.62mm bullet hit Tom in the chest as he hit the ground. Before the trigger could be pulled a second time, the guard fell, hit from behind. The woman stood, looking down at both men as she dropped the rock and picked up the rifle.

Sherlock heard the shot seconds after he reached the trail. Moving as quickly as possible, he ran toward the sound. Hearing someone moving through the brush, the woman aimed into the undergrowth. "No!" Tom whispered loudly when he caught a glimpse of the tan uniform before he fell back. Hesitating for a second, Jim stepped out of the cover, exposing himself to the possible fire. She laid the rifle down and turned her attention to Tom while Jim moved in the last few feet. She looked first at the head wound and then started unbuttoning Tom's shirt. They saw a large red welt just to the right of Tom's nipple. They knew all the blood was coming from the gash above Tom's right eye.

"I'm okay," Tom managed to say as he coughed.

Jim heard the guard groan, and turned his attention from Tom for the first time. Picking up the rifle, he handed it to the young woman and pointed to the guard. Then he turned back to Tom. "You got lucky, boy."

"Yeah, I know, thanks to these fancy clothes of yours. It still feels like something's broken inside," Tom managed to say, coughing up a bit of pink tinged mucus.

"We'll get you back," Jim replied, helping Tom to his feet and leaning him against a tree. "Hands behind your head and get up real slow," Sherlock told the guard. "I believe this lady just wants an excuse to blow your ass away." Jim reached down, picked up Tom's Beretta and slid it back in the holster. Nodding to the girl, he took Tom's left arm over his shoulder and held him by the belt with his right hand. Moving through the woods, they made a diagonal course toward the trail and the village, being careful to watch behind them.

Jerry duPage watched the sway of the general's Amerasian secretary's hips as he was led into the ornate arsenal the general called an office. "Welcome, Mr. duPage, welcome," the general said with the smile of a tiger. "How are things going for the new commander of my irregular troops?"

"Fine, sir," duPage answered in a worried voice. "We'll finish cutting in the Cam An field today and start harvesting the latex day after tomorrow. I decided to use the people of the village," he blurted out. "I know you gave orders not to, but you also gave orders to get the field harvested. I decided the harvest was more important."

"That is fine, Commander. You used your initiative," the fat general replied as he put his highly polished boots on the corner of his desk. "On rethinking the problem I came to the same conclusion – the harvest is most important. Have you seen anything of the people who were coming from the States to look for bodies? They should have arrived in Cam An yesterday afternoon."

"We didn't see any sign of them this morning when we got the people. They could have stopped somewhere along the way. I plan to have a little meeting with them when they get here, just to welcome them to the neighborhood, so to speak. I'll tell them flat out, if they mind their own business they won't get hurt," duPage said, rubbing his right fist into his left palm.

"I believe that will be a fair way of handling your countrymen. Colonel Ngu tried to persuade them to take the fresh bodies and leave. They have less intelligence than he gave them credit for. Now, to what do I owe this visit?"

"I, we, need to contact our bank in Hong Kong and transfer the money from Howard's and his men's accounts to ours. The bank is aware of what happens if someone has an untimely death."

"If you would leave the information, I would be happy to have my secretary do it for you," the general replied as he reached and brushed a mote of dust from the toe of his boot.

"I'd rather do it myself, sir. Nothing against your secretary, but if it got screwed up then I'm to blame and no one else. I'm sure you understand."

"Fine, fine, I understand." The general moved his feet off the desk and pushed the button on the intercom. "What is the name of your bank? I'll have her put the call through."

"Banco de la Royale," duPage answered, standing to leave.

The young Vietnamese woman roughly shoved the

guard ahead of her as they broke into the sunlight of the village. Tom was more able to support himself, but was still being supported by Jim's hand on his belt. The bleeding from his right eye had slowed since the swelling had almost closed the eye.

Jim steered them to the rest of the team squatting beside the open hut where Hayes was making his report with the aid of a map drawn in the dirt. Karen was the first to look up and see the blood covering Tom's clothing.

"Tom!" she screamed. "Tom, what happened? You're hurt. You're bleeding," she managed to say through tears and sobs as she ran to his side and put her arm around him for extra support.

Tom coughed twice and spat blood at his feet, leaving some of the pink-tinged spittle hanging from his lip. "Don't," he managed to whisper slowly, painfully moving his arm to try to disengage Karen.

"Jim, what happened? Here let me take him." Karen moved to Tom's left side and put his arm over her shoulder.

"Somebody get the medical kit!" Don yelled as the rest of the team started to rush the few yards to the injured Tom.

Trahn stopped the woman and the prisoner. "I'll take care of the prisoner," he said gently in Vietnamese, removing the woman's locked fingers from the rifle. "Go make ready a bed. *Chuyen dong*" he said to the prisoner as he sadistically jabbed the muzzle of the AK-47 hard into the prisoner's kidney area.

"*Dien cai dau,*" the prisoner replied, an obscene comment about what the sergeant should do with his sister. Trahn slammed the rifle butt into the man's back, knocking him to the ground as his reply.

Karen assisted Tom to a stool in the shade of the open thatched-roof hut. Kim laid out the first aid kit and Mi Ling started unbuttoning and removing Tom's shirt while the rest of the team stood aside, giving the women room to work.

"What happened?" Frank asked.

"I got stupid and tried to get a prisoner, and he got me," Tom replied with a short breath. "If it hadn't been for her," he said looking to the young woman, "you'd be taking me home in a bag."

"You've got a broken rib," Mi Ling said, her fingers probing around the welt. "Take a deep breath." Tom did as he was told, grimacing with pain. "Let it out slowly." She put her fingertips around the injury, "I think your lung is just bruised. Keep coughing the blood out so it can't collect."

"I've never sewn anyone alive before," Kim said, pushing the edges of the laceration together, "but I think I can do an okay job on this. Looks like you're going to live after all."

"We'll leave you in the capable hands of the women while we go see what we can find out from your prisoner," Frank said as they turned toward where Trahn was securely tying the man to one of the hut supports.

The old man walked over and placed his right hand over the injury on Tom's chest. He didn't say anything, but the women stood aside and gave him room. He placed his left hand on Tom's back, mirroring his right. He looked to the sky then bowed his head and concentrated.

Tom could feel an intense, warm feeling flow through the old man's hands. The pain in his chest was gone in seconds, and he could feel the healing taking place as the old man held him. Tom's mind was clear and calm. His only thought was, *Magic.*

"What's your name, fellow?" Frank asked in a normal conversational tone as he pulled a cigarette from his pocket and lit it with his aging Zippo.

"Fuck you!" came the reply.

"All right, Fuck You, I hope that's the name you want on your tombstone," Frank continued with a smile. "Now, Fuck You, we want to know more about what's going on up the road."

"Fuck off and die, you motherfucker! I ain't telling you shit."

"A man of few words. I don't believe he's ready to talk to us yet," Frank continued in his normal conversational tone.

Sherlock delivered a swift, hard punch to the prisoner's lower back. When he stopped screaming in pain he answered, "You don't know who you're fuckin' with! The boss'll take care of all of you good for this."

"Yeah, but you won't be alive to see it," Don said. "Now tell us what we want to know."

"Fuck you, old man. Jerry'll have me out of here and you'll be dead before sundown."

"Jerry, is that your boss or your girlfriend?" Hayes asked before he punched the man in the back again.

The Vietnamese sergeant watched from behind as the Americans attempted to extract information by punching the prisoner. "You Americans are crude. You want him to talk, I make him talk. You just hurting your hands."

"All right, Mihn, your turn," Frank said as he calmly smoked his cigarette and looked for signs of fear in the prisoner's eyes.

"I learned from the Montengnards while we were all fighting the Khmer Rouge. Please untie one hand and hold it flat on table," Mihn asked, picking up a chop stick from the table and tapping it into the palm of his hand.

"Fuck you, gook, the general'll have your ass for this."

"I not hairy like the monkey. You the gook. What general have my ass?" Trahn asked while Jim held the man's hand flat on the table with the fingers spread. Gently, Mihn started tapping on the first joint of the man's index finger. "Soon you start telling everything, as bones in hand become like cooked rice."

The old man removed his hand and started talking to Mi Ling while he looked at Tom. He handed Tom a large, wooden pipe and smiled through his missing, blackened, betel nut-stained teeth, nodding for him to take it.

"It's opium, marijuana, and some other herbs," Mi Ling translated. "It will help you to breathe and heal more. He says it's not magic, but it's close."

"Thank him for me," Tom replied as Karen took his lighter out of his left shirt pocket and held the flame to the pipe.

"I'll sew that cut after you get loaded," Kim said, continuing to swab the deep gash above his eye.

"I think I'm going to need some of that, too," Janet said. "What they're doing over there really bothers me."

"Yeah, I know," Karen replied, looking at the men standing around the screaming prisoner. "I think I'm going to be sick."

Mi Ling left Tom and the rest of the women and walked to where Mihn Trahn was tapping on the prisoner's fingers with the slim bamboo utensil. The man's first and second fingers were blue, swollen, and about half the length of the others. As Mihn had said, the bones had become like cooked rice.

Sherlock had trouble holding the man's hand on the table. His sweaty palms continued to slide down the arm and his grip loosened. Beads of sweat fall from his forehead to the table, and his mouth was drawn into a macabre grin from the effort and the stress.

Segretti's normally tanned face was a number of shades lighter as he watched, as much in fascination as disgust, while Trahn tapped each phalange. He vowed to himself he would never again tap a pencil on a desk as he felt the bile building in his stomach.

Frank touched Mihn on the shoulder and the tapping stopped, the first bone in the man's ring finger had just exploded, driving small chips of bone into the bruised and battered flesh while the muscles contracted. The man's scream was replaced with crying his chin fell to rest on his chest. "Well, Jack," Frank said, "I think I'll just continue to call you Fuck You." The prisoner tried to raise his head but was unable to. Gasping, he breathed between sobs. "Now, Fuck You, how many men in this mob of yours?" The man didn't answer. Frank reached over, pushed on one of the destroyed fingers, and the man screamed again. "How many?" Frank asked again when the prisoner's head fell back to his chest.

"Twelve here," came the whispered reply. "Twelve here and more or less the same number at the rest of the fields."

Frank pushed on the finger again. As the man screamed in pain, Segretti put his hand over his mouth and ran behind the hut. The sounds of his retching could be heard above the man's sobs. Bill Hayes turned away, shaking his head, and started walking to where the women were taking Tom to the waiting straw mattress. *God, what's happened to Frank? I never thought he was capable of being a part of something like this. And the others helping and standing by, Jesus. I never signed on for shit like this.*

"Give me a hit from that pipe," Hayes said as soon as he walked into the hut. "I don't give a shit what it is but it must be good." Janet inhaled deeply and passed the pipe to Bill. "I knew I might have to kill somebody but I sure as hell didn't expect anything like this." He inhaled deeply, feeling the narcotic from the smoke enter his bloodstream. He held his breath as he passed the pipe back to Janet, who passed it to Karen.

"I'm not prepared for any of this," Karen said, sitting beside Tom and taking the pipe. "They told us, but I really didn't believe them."

Kim finished putting the last stitch in Tom's forehead and cut the thread. "There were a hell of a lot of things they didn't tell us when we signed on with this outfit," she said, taking the pipe from Karen.

Mihn laid his instrument of torture on the table as Jim let the unconscious man slide to a squatting position by the bamboo pole. Sherlock held the prisoner's beaten hand up for all to see, the fingers were a deep purple and contracted to almost nothing; but what was there, flopped like a wet rubber glove.

"Mihn, how much of what he said did you understand?" Mi Ling asked.

"Most of what he said. I knew about Colonel Ngu being involved, but I did not know about General Xuan. I knew about this field and one other, but not the rest. I work for Colonel Ngu and he assigned me to help and protect you while you are here. If this man's commander brings reinforcements, I would not be much help. I do not believe there is anyplace in this province where I can get help. It would be better if you left this place and returned to the United States."

Mi Ling translated the conversation for the others and then turned back to Mihn. "In the day you have known us, can see why we can't go home?"

"I understand it is a matter of old promises and

honor. I respect you for these. If we live, I may be forced to call some Americans friends," Mihn replied with a hint of a smile as he put his hand on Mi Ling's arm.

"What can we do now?" Mi Ling asked in English.

"Right now I think we had best combine our intelligence and decide what our options are. Let's start with Tom before he passes out," Frank said, looking toward the hut where Tom was taken. "Jim, make sure our prisoner is secure and then come on over, we've got a lot to do."

Chapter Twenty-two

The villagers finished cutting the long rows of poppy pods and stood at the camp end of the irrigation ditch. Last night's meal had left them in better shape than the day before, but their faces were still drawn with exhaustion. None of the mercenaries noticed the hate and rage that filled their eyes, or the faint glimmer of hope.

"Okay, that's it," shouted Chavez from the shade of the open hut. "Send 'em back to the ville and tell 'em they got tomorrow off. Where the hell is Jack?"

"The last time I saw him he was chasing his dick into the woods," replied one of the guards. "That was about four hours ago."

"Well that dumb son of a bitch better get back here before Jerry does, or Jerry's going to have his ass. When he gets back, have him see me first."

"Right," came the reply from one of the men standing in the dry, shallow irrigation ditch. "Man, I sure as hell wouldn't want to be Jack when Jerry finds out, he'll rip off his dick and shove it up his ass."

"No shit," the other man responded.

Jim caught up with the rest of the team before they reached the hut where Tom had been taken. "As small as the local group is, I'm sure they've missed their man by now."

"I agree. We better stay on our toes and put out guards from here on." Frank replied.

"One at each end, just like the old days," Don said as they walked up to the hut.

Frank entered first and stepped aside for the rest. The first things he noticed were the mindless smiles and glassy eyes of the occupants. "Well, we can't count on any of these people for about twelve hours: they're stoned out of their fucking gourds. Jesus Christ, just what we need at a time like this."

"Lighten up, Frank," Don said, almost smiling. "How did you feel the first time you watched a field interrogation? Let them get straight then we'll chew their asses. It won't do any good now. Sort of makes me remember the first time I saw you loaded on opium." Don looked at Mi Ling with a grin and she smiled back.

"That was a most interesting evening. If we weren't in danger, I might like to try that again," she said, slipping her hand in Frank's and giving it a comforting squeeze. "What are we going to do now?"

"Let's break out the radio and see if we can get any help from those bastards in Hong Kong. When these people can't find their man, they're going to come looking for us," Jim said with a look at Kim, remembering the Jade Lotus.

The villagers started returning as the team unpacked the powerful radio. Mi Ling and Mihn left the preparations and walked to meet the incoming villagers as they left the shade of the jungle. The few scrawny, foraging chickens scattered as the pair walked through the flock toward the head of the line. They started questioning the people at random. Most were too tired to answer with much more than a shake of their heads as they placed one foot in front of the other, walking toward their waiting huts and a short rest.

"Well, I guess that's it then," Frank said, switching the radio to standby. "Give them a chance to surrender, the man said."

"There's the outside chance that some of them might go for six months and a DD, but not all," Jim said as he started to sit on the primitive table, and then thought better of it. "Even if they want to get out, how the hell are they going to get by Xuan and Ngu?"

"If there's a plane on the ground, if nobody tells about what's going on, if their own men don't shoot them first – 'if'," Don said, his voice sounding more cynical with each if. "There are just to damned many ifs."

"The real wild card is what the people in Hanoi are going to do. As hard as they've worked at getting on America's good side, they might help us," Frank commented, removing a cigarette from his pocket and accepting a light from Sherlock. "No matter what anybody says or does, I'm afraid we're still in deep shit."

Mi Ling and Trahn returned to the group after questioning the returning villagers. "The soldiers are laughing and joking about this one called Jack. The villagers don't believe his disappearance is being taken seriously, and the two men who left this morning still have not returned." Mi Ling related what she and Trahn had found. "What have you learned?"

"They're going to talk to Hanoi and send in one of their indig people to pick up our prisoner," Frank replied, inhaling deeply on his cigarette.

"Some desk jockey suggested we tell them to surrender," Don added. "Ain't that a kick in the ass? Better than ten to one odds and *we* tell *them* to surrender!"

"I think the best thing we can do is to hang loose and start digging out that bunker," Jim suggested. This would make us look like what we are, a search and recovery group. They won't see any real threat when they make first contact. We can tell them about the terms of surrender, but for all intents and purposes, we're exactly what we seem to be."

"Who said the Marines never come up with a good idea," Segretti said as he took a step to the wall and grabbed a pick.

"Come on, Don, let's get these vehicles out in the open; we have arrived." Frank dropped the cigarette on the dirt floor and crushing it out with his heel.

The team split and Jim and David started towards the remains of the bunker. Frank, Don and Mi Ling moved the truck close to the hut and finished unloading the large tent and other supplies. The exhausted villagers soon joined the efforts and the tent went up quickly and the folding tables were soon in place. Don strung the light bulbs and plugged the line into the small gas generator. The freeze-dried food and cooking utensils soon followed with the help of the village people. The search camp in the village of Cam An, Vietnam was officially established.

Chapter Twenty-three

Chavez heard the jeep coming down the well-used dirt road shortly before he saw it and its occupants. He looked towards the large open hooch where the rest of the men were drinking beer and getting stoned on the potent, local marijuana. His pulse increased as he tried to think of a way to tell duPage about the missing man without him flying into his usual rage. *No way in hell,* he thought as the jeep sped into the clearing, and slid to a stop in a cloud of dust.

Jerry duPage slowly and carefully poured himself from the driver's seat, and almost fell as his foot hit the ground. He waved his arm and the almost empty bottle and gushed, "What you say, Jose?" He laughed at his own joke, his speech so slurred that Chavez could barely make out what he was trying to say.

No fucking way, Chavez thought as he answered, "we got the field finished and sent the people home. Everything's cool and the guys are mellowing out a bit."

"That's good," duPage slurred as he wove back and forth. "There's a case of booze in the back to help 'em out. Be a good boy and get it while I go help 'em relax." Fritzpatrick and duPage wrapped their arms around each other's shoulders for support, as they staggered towards the thatched roof shelter.

Some fucking commander! I sure as hell hope Jack gets back before he finds out he's gone, Chavez thought as he followed with the cardboard box.

"Here, man, try a hit of this shit," one of the men said as he handed duPage a large, well-rolled joint. "I mixed in a little bit of this year's crop and it's some good shit, better than last year."

duPage took the offered joint and inhaled deeply. "Nice and smooth," he replied through his controlled exhalation. "Brought back some booze for you guys; you owe us," he said, passing the joint to one of the black men. "Hey, Jefferson, I got a question! How come so many of you black guys got names of presidents?"

"Shit, man, I don' know," he replied in a slow drawl. "I reckon it's all depends on who knocked up our grandmamas. You know them presidents'll fuck anything."

"Yeah, we know, Nixon sure fucked us," one of the other men replied.

"Speaking of fucking, that bunch from the States got to Cam An yesterday or today, and tomorrow we're going to pay them a little visit. Tell them to get lost or get fucked."

"Right on, Jerry," Jefferson replied, thrusting his clenched fist in the air in a power salute.

"I'm going to take a little nap before supper. Don't you men get too fucked up now, y' hear."

"No more than you, boss, no more than you," one of the men replied as they watched duPage stagger toward the largest living hut.

"All right, everybody, up and out – now!" Sherlock yelled as he walked into the hut where the younger members of the team had passed out the night before. Jim nudged Bill with his toe while he shook Kim and Janet by the arms. "Up and out, time's a wasting," he said as they started opening their eyes.

"What time is it?" Janet asked, reaching over and shaking Karen.

"0530, and we've got a lot of work to do today. Get everybody up and be in the tent in five minutes," Sherlock growled like the gunnery sergeant he was. "Come on, Kim," he said, pulling the tall brunette to her feet. "Five minutes," he repeated as he pulled Kim out the woven bamboo doorway after him. "I want you to know that what you people did yesterday," he started as soon as they reached the dusty street, "was damned irresponsible. If those bastards had come looking for their man last night we would have all been in deep shit, just because you and the others decided you wanted to get loaded."

"But, Jim," Kim started to defend her actions, "none of us were ready to watch what was going on."

"Then you had damned well better get ready to watch. There's going to be a hell of a lot rougher things to see before this is all over, and you won't be able to rush out and get stoned when things start to bother you."

"Look, I know, okay? I'm sorry. Now just leave me the hell alone. We can discuss it later," Kim replied as they reached the large canvas tent.

"Good morning, Kim," Frank said in a stern voice. "I'll wait until the rest of the bunch get here before I say anything. The coffee's ready."

"Somehow I get the idea we fucked up big time," Hayes said as he stood, rubbings his eyes and running his fingers through his short hair.

"Somehow I think you're right," Tom replied, rising to a sitting position. He groaned. "Jesus, it hurts to move this arm, but at least I'm breathing a lot better."

"Well if it wasn't for kevlar you wouldn't be moving at all," Karen said, helping Tom to his feet. "Come on, let's go face the music." She and Tom led the way out of the hut.

"Looks like a lot got done without us yesterday," Tom said when they noticed the tent and the beginnings of the excavation. "One more thing we're going to catch shit for."

"I can't say we don't deserve it," Hayes said as they walked along. "If anything had happened last night we would have been totally worthless."

The rest of the team looked up from their cups when the last four members ducked under the open tent side. "I've only got one thing to say," Frank began the chewing. "You endangered all of us with what you did yesterday. Now if you can't handle the brutality that's probably going to happen, you're free to leave. There will be no more hiding behind a cloud of smoke, is that understood?" The four members looked at their feet and nodded their heads in the affirmative.

"While you people were stoned, it was business as usual for the rest of us," Frank continued. "We're going to go about our mission of digging up bodies while we wait to see what happens. The people are going to be working with us and not going back to the fields, so be prepared at all times."

"Friends and neighbors," Don said quietly. "I do believe the feces is about to hit the flinger."

The rising sun hit Jerry duPage full in the face as he

opened his eyes. *Oh shit,* he thought, *what a fucking hangover.* He looked at the floor beside his metal bunk and saw the almost empty, open bottle of Canadian whiskey. "Hair of the dog," he said to the empty hut, picking up the bottle and finishing the last couple of ounces. He stumbled across the room to the shelf holding a galvanized bucket and a large clay basin. As he poured the water, he looked at himself in the broken piece of mirror hanging on the straw wall. *Man, you look as bad as you feel.* He started splashing water on his face and hair. He dried with an old, threadbare, olive green towel. *Man, you look like shit. Time to get a hair cut and a shave; you're looking like the rest of the mob.* He laid down the towel, picked up a comb with his shaky hand, and started running it through his greasy, shoulder-length hair. "Time to get some coffee and go terrorize the neighborhood," he said aloud as he slipped on a sweat band and walked through the open door into the hot morning sun.

"Morning, boss," Chavez said as duPage walked into the mess hall, and to the large coffee pot sitting on the wood-burning stove. "What's the plan for today?"

"We're going to see what the hell that bunch of people are doing in the ville, and let 'em know we'll kill 'em if they fuck with the program," duPage replied tersely.

"I hate like hell to tell you this, Jerry, but we got one man AWOL. Jack followed some tasty young thing into the bush yesterday and he didn't come back. I've had some guys out looking for him since daylight. I think something might have happened to him."

"He better have had something happen to him! I told that dumb son of a bitch to leave the women alone. He best give his heart to Jesus, cause his ass is going to belong to me when I find him." duPage took a chair as the cook placed a plate of eggs, bacon, beans and rice in front of him. "Thanks, Phan, get me some more coffee." duPage was silent as he shoveled the food into his mouth with a large spoon. He finished the last bite, wiped his mouth with the back of his hand, then wiped his hand on his pants. "Round up three or four of the guys; we're going to make a visit to Cam An."

Frank and Don stood looking into the pit of hard-packed, dark red clay. The first of the rotting two-by-four beams and flaking plywood boards had been exposed for the first time in thirty years. Jim, Hayes and the villagers increased the depth and width with each pick swing and every basket of dirt. "We should have the radio room completely cleared in an hour or so," Don said, looking to Frank as they remembered each minute detail of the command bunker. "Sparks should be the only body there."

"Yeah, I know," Frank replied. "After we get down to the floor we can just go straight across into the hospital area. That's where we'll probably have trouble separating bodies. There's no telling how many patients Doc had when this place was hit."

Hayes scraped the last of the red dirt from around the border of a spongy, flaky, four-by-eight piece of plywood as Jim sunk his pick into a joint and lifted. The sheet started peeling away from the rotting rafters when four pairs of hands grasped the edge and started to pull. The rusting nails started popping loose as the first section came off. It exposed a jumble of wire, electronics equipment, and a piece of olive green cloth partially covering a long bone.

"I wonder if he got the message off?" Frank asked in a whisper. "Okay, use the hand tools to get the rest of the dirt off him. Be sure to look for dog tags; there should be one around his neck, and one was in his right boot. We always carried one in our right boot," he again whispered, remembering.

Hayes continued to expose the next area as he filled baskets to be emptied. "Okay, I've got this piece cleaned off. Somebody give me a hand." The Viets did't understand a word he said, but moved to help raise the second piece of roof and rafters. "All together now! Lift," he grunted as the piece came up and was pushed against the wall to be removed.

Frank and Don pulled the heavy piece up and let it fall between them. "Listen," Frank said. "Sounds like we're going to have company." They caught the sound of a very noisy vehicle coming down the rutted road toward the village.

"Well, let's go meet our neighbors," Don quipped as they turned and looked.

"Bill, Jim, come with us! Mihn, find someplace where you can give us cover," Frank said as the men climbed out of the hole and started walking across the village, pulling the release on their holsters as they went. Mihn took a position in the last hut on the left beside an open window where he could watch and not be seen. He saw the four Americans spread about a meter apart walk toward the two palms that marked the entrance. Mihn was fascinated at how much the four men looked like gunfighters in American western movies he had seen. He slid the safety on his AK-47 off and watched an ancient jeep slide to a stop in front of the four tall Americans.

duPage stepped out of the jeep, leaving his M-16 laying beside the seat. The other three men dismounted, took their weapons, and stood back to back where they not only had a full view but also full fire coverage. The four team members stood relaxed, their bodies poised for immediate movement if the situation warranted.

duPage walked the few feet separating the groups. He wiped the sweat from his forehead with his hand and then on his dirty, black cotton pants. "Sure is hot today," he said. "It's hot every day. We heard we had new neighbors and we just wanted to drop by and let you folks know some of the rules around here."

"We're listening," Don retorted.

"It's good you're listening," duPage replied. "You see, me and my friends have a little agricultural project going on a few klicks down the road and we're not about to let anybody fuck it up for us. I'm sure you've heard by now that we hire these people to do the work for us. We don't want you interfering." duPage stared at the team and then threw a quick glance back to his own men.

"Slavery is more like it," Frank growled. "We're paying these people a good wage to work with us, so I guess they'll quit your opium field."

"Yeah, but I let them live," duPage growled. "Around here I make the rules and you just broke the first one. That's don't fuck with Jerry duPage. If you fuckers want to survive, you had best remember that."

Frank didn't answer, instead he slowly reached into the left breast pocket of his tan shirt and removed his cigarettes and lighter. He took one and lit it before returning them to his pocket as he exhaled in the man's direction. Then he said, loud enough for the guards to hear, "The government has a message for any American we come across – they want you home. Every case will be considered, but in most cases the worst that will happen is a dishonorable discharge. Now as far as the villagers go, I've got two words – fuck you."

"I'll have people here in the morning to make sure these people get to the field, and they damned well better be ready to go or somebody's ass is going to be grass. Let's go, guys."

"Boss, what about Jack?" one of the guards asked.

"Fuck Jack!" duPage yelled. "Mount up."

The guards climbed back into the jeep as the driver grinded the gears. "Remember what I said!" duPage shouted as they roared off in a cloud of dust.

"I don't think we'll have any trouble until at least morning," Sherlock said, fastening his holster.

"We might get lucky and not have to fight all of them if the word of amnesty gets around," Frank said. "Let's get back to work and we can talk it over when everyone gets back."

"I'd really hate to bet on that," Hayes answered, waving at Mihn coming out of the hut slinging his rifle.

When the five returned to the excavation, they were greeted by the sight of two piles of loose bones. The iron oxide and other chemicals that make the clay red had invaded the structure of each bone, turning it to an almost mahogany color. Frank reached down and picked up the beaded chain with the dog tag. Slowly, he wiped the dirt off enough to read, "Pfieffer, Norville A., Sparks. If I had a first name like Norville I'd change it too," he said as he handed the dog tag with a kick notch to Don.

"You do Francis," Don replied.

"A pocket knife, a plastic comb, a silver dollar, the engagement ring he never got to send home, and his Zippo. Not a hell of a lot to die with, is it?" Frank asked the air in a whisper. "We're taking you home, buddy. It's taken us long enough, but we're taking you home," Frank said to the skeletal remains. "Bill, get some bags. I'm sure we'll need more than two before the day is out." Frank stood, turned away from the group, and walked toward the cemetery and the standing Buddha.

Don started to follow, but was stopped by Jim's hand on his arm. "Not now, Don," Jim said. Taking the chain, he draped it reverently across the intact, brown ribcage. "Let's get to work, there's more people here who need a proper burial." Jim jumped into the pit and took up his pick, and with all his strength, bit deeper into the hard-packed red clay.

Don slid down the wall, took a shovel from one of the Viets, and started matching Jim's efforts as he kept the men busy moving and dumping baskets.

Hayes returned with his arms full of large, black, zippered plastic bags. Laying them down, he carefully, and gently, started packing the bones of the unknown Vietnamese.

Mihn knelt and helped hold the bag open while he picked up pieces of the skeleton and placed them in the black plastic with the others. He seemed surprised at the reverence with which these Americans treated the dead of almost thirty years.

"It's good to have you here, Kim," Mi Ling said as they continued to uncover the mass grave. "At least we'll stand a better chance of having the bodies complete. Except for the NVA identity disks, there is no way to identify the rest of these."

"We'll do the best we can to get the right bones together. I haven't any idea how they can ever be identified. I'm sure they don't have dental records," Kim replied as she used a stiff paint brush to finish the exhumation of a body.

"They will be buried with a grave marker that says... Vi *anh hung*," Mi Ling replied, zipping closed a bag of bones.

"What does that mean?" Tom asked, stacking the filled bags.

"Hero," Mi Ling replied as she picked up another empty bag and began filling it from the individual piles. "This was our first ambush, and these people didn't stand a chance. I can't believe anyone can be filled with as much hate as I was the day this happened."

"This is the last one," Kim said. "Hand me a bag and I'll get him."

The jeep bounced from the rutted dirt road onto the tank-grooved asphalt without slowing down. duPage was still too angry to speak, and the other three men were afraid to.

Imagine those crazy bastards telling me to surrender. Surrender, my ass! Bullshit! A dishonorable discharge? Shit, those fuckers would stick me so far under Levenworth I'd never see daylight. Fuck, the way the people in Hanoi are kissing Uncle Sam's ass, they'll probably come after me themselves. Fucking gooks would sell their mother if they could. No choice, we're going to have to waste that bunch. At least the odds are in my favor. Yeah, we'll start tonight.

I could stand a DD and a free trip home, Chavez thought as he attempted to drive between the tread marks. *Hell, the only thing they had on me was dope charges. I beg for mercy and tell 'em how bad things were for us PRs in LBJ, they might even make that a BCD. I could live the rest of my life in Puerto Rico on what I've got in the bank – most of us could. I wonder what Jerry's thinking? Shit, they had him cold on murder one. You can bet your sweet ass he's not going to say anything about this amnesty thing. Word'll get out somehow. I wonder how many of the men would be interested in going home. Most of them, I'll bet.*

Fuck it, one of the two men in the back thought. *First chance I get I'm going to diddy bop back down the trail and give up. I wonder if my folks are still alive? Mom always worried that I wouldn't come home, and I didn't. Fuck it, I'm outta of here.*

I wonder what things are like in the States now? the forth man thought. *I'll bet it's a whole new world. There's nothing waiting for me there that I can't find somewhere else. Fuck 'em. I wonder what Jerry's going to do.*

"All right, you assholes," duPage started, "we're going to hit Cam An tonight and we're going to hit it hard. I don't want even a hint of surrender to get around to the rest of the men, is that clear? If I find out any of you started a rumor, I'll blow your ass away on the spot."

"Right, boss," Jose answered as he turned the jeep and slowed down from the paved road to the well-used dirt trail toward the opium field and the camp.

"Fuck you, fuck you," came the cry of a disturbed gecko lizard from a tree beside the road.

"Fuck you too," duPage said, lifting his M-16 and dumping half a clip of ammo, splattering the four-inch lizard with a 5.56mm bullet. "That'll teach that little bastard to talk to me like that!" duPage slid the safety on and returned his rifle to between his legs.

He's lost it, Chavez thought. *I always heard it was over when you shot a 'fuck you' lizard. Jesus, and I thought Howard was crazy!* "We're home," he said when they broke from the claustrophobic, shaded jungle road into the bright sun of the compound.

The jeep slid to a stop in a cloud of red dust, almost hitting the short man running from the hooch with the tall radio antenna.

"Boss, we got big trouble," the man yelled. "A couple of MIGs dumped a load of napalm on fields seven and nine. Everybody's dead at seven and five are dead at nine. The guys from eight and ten are picking up the pieces."

"First get the rest of the camps alerted and have the men spread out and get under cover. Even with small arms we can make it hot for the bastards. Next, get me a complete report on seven and nine. Find out what we've got left, and then get me the general on the horn; he should be able to find out who's behind this. Move, damn it!" *If it's not one damned thing it's another,* duPage thought. "Jose, position the men for an air attack.

"Right, boss," Chavez replied. "Come on, everybody move your asses. Willard, take half the men and set up along the sides of the field. I'll take the rest and set up over here." *He shouldn't have shot that fucking lizard,* he thought. *It's bad luck to kill a 'fuck you' lizard.* "Come on, let's go!"

"General, this is duPage," he yelled into the microphone. "A couple of MIGs just fried fields seven and nine with napalm. I've got a lot of KIA's and WIA's. What the fuck is going on? I thought these fields were protected?"

"They are, commander," came the general's voice over the radio. "I'll send helicopters for the wounded. As for the dead...bag 'em and tag 'em, we'll give them back to the Americans like we did Howard."

"Look, General, we can't do shit until we know some fucker's not going to fly in and toast our asses."

"Calm down, Mr. duPage. I will get in contact with the air force and see why this happened. Believe me when I say I am as upset as you are. I promise you, those pilots will never fly again. Now see to your defenses and I will get help on the way. Rest assured, I will find out how and why this happened and I will contact you as soon as I do." The general switched the radio off before duPage could say more.

"You heard the general, they're sending choppers for the wounded. Make sure the guys know it. When he calls back, find me. I'll be out seeing what I can do around here."

The general pushed the button on the intercom and said, "My dear, please get me General Trong at air force headquarters in Hanoi, on a secure line. Then have Colonel Ngu report to me as soon as possible. Thank you." The general's voice sounded calm and collected as he released the button. He could only stand by pushing himself up from the massive desk as he walked over to the bar across the room where he filled a glass with scotch, his hands shaking. *Who and why,* he wondered as he returned to the desk. *There is no one who would do this to me. After all, I've had this command for ten years now. Why now?*

The telephone rang and he picked up the receiver. "General Trong, sir."

"Linh," the general said. "Sam Xuan. What the hell is going on with the air force dropping napalm in my province?"

"Your fields, I guess," came the reply. "Look, Sam, we got orders this morning to burn every opium field we see. The orders came out of the prime minister's office, so there's nothing I can do about it."

"But why now?" Xuan asked.

"I don't know, I just follow orders and the orders are to hit every field from Saigon to Hanoi. If you've got any more fields, I suggest you get them under camo netting until this thing dies down. I'm supposed to put a dozen planes a day in the air and continue until we can't find any more. If we can't see them, we can't hit them. I may be able to hold off on your section a day or so, but no longer than that if you have any more fields."

"Hell yes, I've got more fields! Is there anybody else I can talk to about this?"

"Just the prime minister," came the reply.

"Okay, I'll do what I can to cover them. A day or so, you say? Well, if that's the best you can do. I owe you, Linh."

"Yes, you do – In gold," replied Trong, hanging up the phone.

The general slammed down the receiver as Colonel Vihn Ngu walked in. The general looked up with glassy eyes, "The government has ordered all poppy fields between Hanoi and Saigon destroyed. Fields seven and nine have already been hit. I told duPage I would send helicopters for the wounded. See to it. Find all the camouflage netting in the province and cover the largest fields. We have maybe a day."

"Does duPage know yet?" Vihn asked in surprise.

"Only about the two fields that have been hit already. He contacted me, or I would not have known. I'll tell him the rest as soon as I get you on your way. See what you can do, and stop at Cam An and tell the Americans we have more of their bodies waiting for them in Quang Tri."

"Yes, sir," the colonel replied, "I'm on my way." He crossed the room, and in four steps he was out the door.

The general turned to the radio and turned up the squelch until he could hear the static crackle. "Camp one, come in. Camp one... camp one... come in."

Chapter Twenty-four

No air was moving in the tent as they made a mock up of duPage's camp with bits of straw, bark, wood, cigarette packs and a coffee cup. "Here's the compound," Jim Sherlock said, putting the last piece in place. "Now we know there are twelve or thirteen men there. Will they be a real danger to us? From what I saw, most of them are a bunch of stumble bums who are more of a danger to themselves than us. Anybody who treats their weapons, clothes and bodies the way these guys do can't be worth much. What do you think, Bill?"

"I think they're big men against unarmed peasants, but most of them would fall apart if someone was shooting back. duPage basically gave us until morning to get the fuck out of Dodge, but I'll bet he tries something tonight just to be sure."

Frank made circles on the table with the bottom of his coffee cup as he spoke. "I have to agree with you both. I wasn't impressed by the three men he had with him this morning, and I'm sure word of an amnesty is going to get around whether he wants it or not. But, even if half the total manpower gave up, that's still five to one odds, and we'll have to have someone to guard them."

The old man squatted on the floor beside Mi Ling smoking an American cigarette held with his thumb and forefinger. Mi Ling quietly translated the majority of the conversation. The old man just nodded in understanding.

"To my knowledge there's no rules that say we have to wait for them to hit us first," Don said. "The smart thing to do would be for us to get in the first shot. From the way you guys describe it, they don't have a large field of fire anywhere except the poppy field. We could go in there with these super-duper silencers and it'd be all over with."

Tom held his bruised chest muscles with his left hand and moved his right arm and shoulder, grimacing at the pain. He pulled his hand up from his side and straight out as though he were drawing his pistol. "The way I see it, we've only got two choices: hit them or let them hit us. If we can take this guy out, it might soften up the rest of them some. I say we go after them before they can get a shot at us."

Frank listened to the babble of everyone talking at once. He took a swallow of his cold coffee, lit a Winston, and looked at the Special Forces crest on his lighter – De Oppresso Liber. "All right, everybody shut up. This is not a democracy yet, but we need to get a consensus on whether to hit or wait."

"Frank," Mi Ling said, "he said if we get guns, his people will fight."

""There's only one place to get guns around here and we're going to have to take them," Segretti said at last. "And may God help us."

The conference was halted by the increasing sound of helicopter rotors. The team left the table to watch as a Huey UH-1 landed in one of the long, unused rice paddies. The blades went to neutral, and the door opened. Colonel Ngu jumped down and ran in a crouch in their direction.

Trahn tugged on Frank's sleeve. "Colonel Ngu is in command of the opium growers. Be careful."

"I know. Thanks, Mihn," Frank replied as they walked to meet the colonel.

They stop far enough away from the helicopter to be able to carry on a conversation, but close enough to feel the breeze from the prop in the hot, humid, still air. Ngu offered his hand but it was ignored by everyone except Sergeant Trahn, who saluted.

"Frank, Don," Vinh started with a nod of greeting. "I dropped by to tell you we have had more contact with the American mercenaries, a few kilometers to the west of here. There will be more bodies for you when you depart Quang Tri.

"The dead ones don't worry us none," Don said with a growl in his voice. "What about some help with the ones a couple of klicks up the trail?"

"Don, I warned you before you came here the only help I had to give was Sergeant Trahn. This is still all I have to give you. Pack up and go home."

"Vinh, you know we can't do that," Mi Ling replied.

"Mi Ling, listen to reason. These men are animals. They don't care that you are their countrymen, they kill for enjoyment. General Xuan and I have discussed forcing you to leave, but you have the blessings of Hanoi. All we can do is advise you to get out before you all get killed."

"How about giving us some weapons that we can defend ourselves with?" Tom asked. "We would be lucky to be able to hit your chopper from here with these pistols."

Vinh noticed Tom's bandaged forehead and shook his head. "I will ask the general. He doesn't want guns in the hands of the peasants. That is what would happen if something were to happen to you."

"You've got all the answers, don't you, Vinh?" Don replied. "Well, here's one for you. If anything happens to any one of us, I'm going to kill you personally."

Ngu went rigid with rage as he drew himself up to full height and stepped closer to the senator. From a step away, Vinh looked almost straight up to stare into Don's eyes. "Don, our old friendship is very thin. This time I will overlooked this threat as the heat of the moment, but never again. Is that clear?"

"Fuck you, you traitorous son of a bitch," came the reply.

Before any more could be said, Mi Ling put her hand on Vinh's arm. "Vinh, remember the first ambush we had in this village? We recovered all the bodies from where we buried them," she said, trying to extinguish the already incendiary conversation.

"Keep them," Vinh growled through clenched teeth. "I will send someone after them and to retrieve your bodies as well," he spat. Turning on his heels, he walked back to the waiting chopper, holding his arm before his face to protect from flying dust and debris.

"Fuck him," Don said as they watched the chopper lift off.

"I'm afraid we're the ones who are going to get fucked," Sherlock said as they turned back to the open tent. "I think we need to go in."

Mihn was deep in thought, trying to formulate what he wanted to say in English. "From what Colonel Ngu has said, and as mad as he was, I believe something has happened in some of the other fields. If this is so, there is great confusion, and now is the time to strike. I believe a can of hornets has been opened."

"That's a nest of hornets or a can of worms," Janet corrected, "but we get the picture."

"That's it then. We leave after dark. We'll use the four silenced Berettas and a rifle for backup. The rest of us will stay here," Frank said, looking from face to face.

"Ngu only has enough netting to cover fields five and six," duPage briefed the men standing in the shade of the thatched mess hall. "The rest of us are going to have to protect what we have with what we've got. The general believes all this trouble is a result of those fucking people in Cam An. If we can get rid of them, things'll go back to normal. I'm going to check out the other fields and try to bring back some men. You bastards had damned well better stay alert or you're going to have to deal with me, is that clear?" duPage's voice and face showed signs of worry, stress and anger as he looked into the faces of the men in the hooch.

"Boss, what about this amnesty offer I've heard talk about?" one of the men asked.

"There ain't no fuckin' amnesty program, and if I find out who started that rumor, I'll kill 'im. Now get the fuck out of here and to your posts!" duPage yelled as the men stood and milled about hesitantly before going into the bright sunshine. "Jose, let's move."

The short Puerto Rican started the aging jeep while duPage watched the men conceal themselves around the camp and field. As the commander took his seat, Chavez grinded the transmission into gear and peeled out toward the jungle road.

"Man, I don't know about you, but I'm thinking real strong about this amnesty shit those dudes were talking about," a man whispered to his partner as they slipped into the bushes.

"No shit," came the reply. "After what happened to those guys today, I want the fuck out of this mess."

"We wait until everybody gets settled in and then we beat feet down the trail. We sure as shit ain't got nothin' to lose," the first man commented.

"What do you have to report, Vinh?" the general asked when the colonel walked into the office without knocking.

Before he answered, Vinh walked over to the bar and poured himself a full glass of the general's private scotch. He added two ice cubes, and began. "I came up with enough netting to cover the largest two fields, and I have feelers out for more. The two fields hit this morning are a total loss, as were the men who were guarding them. Those *troi day ai* (god damned) Americans in Cam An are staying. One of the *con de hoang* had the nerve to threaten me. Commander duPage will take care of them just as soon as he takes care of the fields." The colonel stopped speaking and swallowed half the glass of whiskey.

"Yes, that is what I told him to do," the general replied, lowering himself into the tooled leather chair. *Even with two fields gone I can still make a profit. I'll have to cut Ngu out, but I was going to do that anyway. He's gotten to where he believes he is the one in command around here. I'm sure the Americans would be happy to do it for me.*

Jose Chavez kept the accelerator on the floor as they traveled down the washboard-like Highway Nine, following the burnished red sun which was which was starting to set over Laos. He caught sight of a lone MIG flying north at about five thousand feet. Removing his right hand from the wheel, he slapped duPage on the arm and pointed as the jet started pulling up and into a loop. They watched helplessly as the plane leveled out about a mile in front of them at tree top level and released a long egg shaped object from its belly. They saw the flash and the oily smoke rising before the sounds of the explosion reached them in the still air.

"There goes five," duPage said dejectedly. "Let's go see what's left."

Chavez didn't bother to answer as he downshifted to regain the speed lost as they watched the destruction of another field.

"Hold it right there," came a voice from beside the trail. "Where the fuck do you two think you're going?"

"Same place you are, Wayne, the fuckin' ville to see about getting out of this shit."

"Yeah, that's what we thought," answered another voice as three men stepped on the trail.

"Then let's get the fuck out of here before some gung ho son of a bitch like Jefferson catches us," the one called Wayne said as they jogged down the well-worn trail.

A hint of a breeze moved the cigarette smoke above the table in the canvas tent. The argument on tactics was over, but the argument continued about who was going and who was staying. Points were made and just as quickly negated. Frank listened patiently to all sides.

"That's enough," Frank yelled when he got tired of the bickering. "Don, you're out. Even with that improved leg you still can't run fast if need be. Tom, with that broken rib and bruised chest, you're out. You're better, but you still aren't a hundred percent; not to mention that you can barely see through that black eye. Karen, you're out because of your size, and along with Janet and Kim, all three of you women lack the experience. David, we still don't know a damned thing about you or your experience, so you're staying." The arguments started again, but Frank quickly regained control. "Stop it, now!" he yelled. "This is how it's going to be. Leaving part of you here is just as important as the mission. You all know they could come in here and gun us down when we got back if we didn't leave a rear guard."

"Frank's right and we all know it," Sherlock said, "I propose we get as much rest now as we can, because it's going to be a long night."

"Dear," Mi Ling said, "I think we should move the people into the jungle, at least at night. I know, this is their fight too, but they have nothing to fight with."

"Good point," Don replied. "Sure would be nice if we had the time to get this place ready like we did in the old days," he commented out of the corner of his mouth as he lit another cigarette from the butt of the one before.

"Yes, but this—" Mi Ling started to say.

"Hello in the ville," a voice yelled from the trail. "Can you hear me?"

The team members removed their Berettas from their holsters and Tom and Mihn slid the safeties forward on the AK-47s. "We hear you," Jim replied. "What do you want?"

"What's this deal on giving ourselves up?" the voice called back.

"A free trip back to the States and a military court. So far they've been easy on deserters," Don answered, trying to find the source of the voice in the woods.

"How do we know you're not trying to feed us a line of bullshit?" the voice called back.

"You don't," Frank answered, "but your buddy Jack is in Hong Kong right now. This is your only offer, think it over."

There was silence from the area of the trail for about two minutes. "Okay, we're coming in. Don't shoot," the voice called back as five men walked into the clearing, holding their rifles above their heads.

The jellied gasoline started burning only a few meters into the camp clearing. The thatched huts had been knocked aside and flattened by the force of the explosion. Everything was totally consumed in flames by the time Chavez and duPage drove up. High flames and thick, black, oily smoke were all that was left of the camp. duPage could see three burning, blackened forms, probably bodies, lying curled close to where the first hut had been. Chavez leaned on the horn button, hoping any survivors would be able to hear it above the roaring inferno. Jerry duPage walked toward the right side of the field, staying as close to the flames as he could tolerate. Only the last three rows of flowers survived the initial blaze, and they started to burn as the nylon camo netting melted and burned. Three burned, blackened men managed to walk out of the bush as duPage watched his dream go up in flames. The men's blank stare and blistered, peeling flesh made duPage want to vomit as they staggered closer.

"Dead, all dead," one of the walking corpses managed to mumble as they approached.

"Can you make it back to the jeep?" duPage asked, just loud enough to be heard above the roaring flames. "Come on, this way." He took the man by the sleeve and walked back the way he came. The other two men followed like sheep to the slaughter. "Jose, get these guys over to six! I'm going around the field to see if there's anyone else. Get 'em out of here and bring someone back to give me a hand. You boys are going to be okay," he said to the men before he turned and walked away. *I'm going to kill every fucking one of those sons of bitches,* he thought, threading his way through the underbrush. *My last fucking crop. Christ, I was on my way out of here. Every fucking one of them.*

He found the first body just at the edge of the field. The front was burned away to the bone, the back seemed to be untouched as the man's clothing smoldered along the unburned edges. *I just wonder who the hell you were,* duPage thought. *One more home in a bag.*

"Here are some of our guns," the old man said to Mi Ling, smiling his blackened, toothless grin.

The team walked cautiously closer toward the five men coming into the clearing. Each had their finger on the long, double-action trigger of their Beretta, and the safeties were off. The men in black moved forward and lowered their rifles in front of them with outstretched arms.

"How many men are left in your camp?" Frank asked, removing the AK-47's from the offering hands.

"Six or seven," came the reply. "Jose and the boss went to check on the other fields. Everybody else is hiding around the field, watching for planes."

"What about planes?" Segretti asked.

"Somebody napalmed two of the fields late this morning and Jerry's trying to get the others squared away."

"The boss said he'd bring back some more men to take care of you, but the word's getting around about this amnesty thing," the man called Wayne replied.

"I guess you men know you're going to be treated like prisoners until this is over," Frank said as he took an M-16, looked it over, then handed it to Tom.

"Yeah, we thought as much," one of the other men

responded, "but it's better than getting fried."

"Mi Ling, tell our friend to take these men into the jungle with him, tie them up, and guard them," Frank said as Mi Ling translated. "Tell him if they give him any trouble to shoot them."

"Don't worry, man, we ain't going to give nobody no trouble. We already been here too damned long and we're ready to go home."

The old man called out, and two of the younger men rushed forward with lengths of homemade hemp rope. They tied the men's hands behind their backs and roughly shoved them toward the center of the village.

Frank took the rifles from Hayes and Segretti and handed them to the elder. "Tell him to guard these men well and we'll see him in the morning." The old man smiled and nodded as Mi Ling translates the instructions.

"*Quan say vien chien truong duc cao*," the old man said quietly as he turned and followed the younger men and the prisoners.

"He said the body count is getting high before we have to fight," Mi Ling translated with a half smile.

Don followed the old man with his eyes. "Yeah, well, I wonder what the count from the napalm is, and whose ass we need to kiss for giving it to us," he said almost sarcastically.

"I'll second that," Sherlock said as they walked back to the tent.

Frank put both hands on the table, palm down, and waited for the team to assemble before he started. "Well, looks like we're going to have to change our plans until we find out more about what's going on. I hate like hell to do it, but it looks like we play defense again," he said, looking at the table with the mock up of the enemy camp.

"We need a rotating guard," Jim announced. "Two for the first shift then three after that. With what these guys said, I don't expect anything to happen tonight, but you can't be sure."

"What do we do if more give up?" Janet asked.

"Same as this time; we'll tie them up and put them with the others," Frank replied, not bothering to look up from the table.

Don sat on one of the folding campstools and started examining the surrendered AK-47. The phosphate black was almost gone and was replaced with a thin coat of rust. He rubbed a film of it off with the palm of his hand. He released the magazine and looked at the two exposed rounds. Each one showed bits of green from copper oxidation. Next, he tried to pull the bolt open with his finger, but it was stuck shut. He started slamming the operating handle with the heel of his hand until a corroded round fell out. "Folks, the first thing we'd better do is to take care of these weapons. They might function the way they are, but I doubt it. Just look at this shit," Don said, stripping the ammo from the thirty-round magazine.

"Karen," Tom said, "get some cooking oil and steel wool out of the kitchen supplies, and find something we can use as rags. David, check the butts of those '16s for cleaning rods."

Segretti picked up a spoon that had been used for coffee and tried forcing the handle under the rusted trapdoor in the plastic butt of a rifle – nothing. He moved to the next one. "Got one," he said as he dumped the rusting sections into his hand before moving on.

Mihn removed a brass weight, string, patches, and a small bottle of gun oil from one of the pouches on his belt and laid them on the table. He picked up one of the abused AK-47s and had it completely stripped and laid out on the table within seconds. He picked up each piece and examined it with a critical eye. "*Nquoi khong cu dong*," he said, looking down the barrel.

"What?" asked Kim looking up.

"He said this man is dead," Mi Ling translated.

"If you lovely young ladies would like to take the steel wool and start polishing the brass, we'll see what we can do with these rifles," Bill remarked, starting to field strip an M-16. "I hope I remember how to do this."

"Put a pot of water on to boil so we can clean out these magazines," Segretti added to the orders.

"Where did you learn about boiling out magazines?" Tom asked, giving David a curious look.

"Just one of the things I was taught in school," he replied, as if everyone was taught about firearms as part of a public education.

"Some school," Bill answered, removing a firing pin from a bolt.

"Come on buddy, I'll get you out of here," duPage said to the burned man. "You're lucky, I already passed ten bodies on this side of the field." duPage scooped the man up into his arms and carried him like a baby back to the small unburned clearing beside the road. The man didn't move or speak; the only sign of life was the movement of his blank, staring eyes on his blistered, blackened face. "Easy now, I'll get you taken care of." The man slowly closed and opened his blackened eyelids. duPage didn't know whether it was understanding or just a muscle reaction. He didn't care; it showed the man was alive. "I'm going to kill the people responsible for this," duPage continued, talking in a soft calm voice, "and you're going to be around to see it happen. Just hang in." The man slowly closed and opened his eyes again as duPage stumbled into the clearing that was once the start of the compound.

Chavez eased the jeep to a stop when he saw duPage stagger under the weight of the man. The medic jumped from the front seat before the Chinese-made jeep stopped. He started running toward the two, holding his aid bag high to protect his face from the searing heat of the still-burning napalm. Two other men climbed off the back with one of the many stretchers made from shirts with poles running through the neck openings.

Jerry duPage laid the man on the ground as the medic started to look him over. The burned man closed his eyes and opened them again, and tried to turn his head as the light went out of his deep blue eyes – forever.

"He never had a chance," the medic said. "He's dead."

duPage slowly reached over and closed the blackened lids over the clouding blue eyes. "You men spread out and check the left side of the field as far as the end for survivors. Then start bringing in the dead. I found at least ten on this side, and I'm sure I missed some. We'll recover the rest when the fire dies down." He barked the orders then turned away to the waiting jeep. He walked purposefully, seeing nothing, but the dead man's deep, clear blue eyes surrounded by blackness.

"The general is sending a chopper," Chavez said quietly as his friend and commander collapsed in the front seat. "Let's get on up to six. These guys will handle things here."

"I'm going to kill all of them," duPage said in a disembodied voice. "I'm going to kill every fuckin' one of them and hang 'em up for the buzzards."

"Right, Jerry," Jose responded, "but first there are a lot of other things that need to be taken care of," he said as he ground the transmission into gear and turned away from the half-mile-long funeral pyre.

The red sun was setting on the distant mountains of Laos as Chavez swerved back onto the asphalt of Highway Nine. Birds were starting to flock to roost and the mosquitoes rose in clouds from the thick, damp elephant grass. Jose looked over at the slack-jawed figure of his friend. *Nothing, no one home, just a blank stare.* Jose eased off the gas, slid into neutral and let the jeep glide to a stop. Jerry duPage didn't notice. He still looked straight ahead, catatonic. Jose walked around the side and put his hand on his friend's shoulder – no reaction. He pulled his arm back, slapped duPage with his open hand. His arm came across his chest and returned with a hard backhand. Jose swung again, duPage's hand came up and caught Chavez's wrist like a vice, causing Chavez to wince in pain.

"Enough, buddy. I'm back," duPage said, turning to face his friend. "I guess I lost it for a while, huh?"

"Yeah, man, you lost it. I got you out of there before anybody noticed. We're on the way to six to see what we can salvage out of this mess."

"You're a good friend, Jose. I sure as hell won't forget this," he said, looking into the Hispanic's almost black eyes. "That guy had the bluest eyes I've ever seen. Ya know, almost like the sky after a hard rain."

"Let's go, boss, we've got a long night ahead of us," Chavez said as he returned to the driver's seat. He took a quick look behind, and with the exception of the red glow and the smoke, the twilight was normal.

"I'm going to kill every fuckin' one of those bastards

for this," duPage said as Chavez slipped into first gear.

The former US military base at Da Nang was calm. The barracks buildings were lit, as were a few others such as the mess halls and the clubs. The massive complex had stopped work for the day. Guards stood or walked their posts, while other soldiers were on their own time until the next duty day. The base was much the same as any other military base in the world. There was one window lit in the long white headquarters building. The general sat at his large ornate desk with the heavy brass ashtray full of Marlboro butts, along with another just lit. He rolled the tall, iced glass of scotch across his forehead in an attempt to ease the increasing pounding behind his eyes. He looked up as Ngu walked into the office without knocking. Their eyes met for a second before Vinh turned to the bar and started pouring.

"Five was bombed about four hours ago," the general started to explain. "Nothing survived. The men were putting up the camo netting when they were hit. I've ordered duPage to concentrate on field six for now." General Xuan stared at the blotter on the desk. "If we lose any more fields, we're not going to be able to cover the expenses for this year."

Vinh finished pouring his drink before he bothered to answer. "The first thing we do is protect what we have, then we take care of the Americans in Cam An. The fields are in danger during the day, and if we get six covered it should be safe. The men can cover the others with small arms fire, just like we did with the American planes during the war. We should be able to go after those bastards in Cam An in a day or so." Ngu swallowed a large portion of the drink before he sat in the chair in front of the huge teak desk. He leaned back and put his highly polished boots on the edge in front of the general's face. *How has this man maintained command as long as he has?* Vinh wondered. *Kahn before him wasn't that smart either. It must have been the Americans doing all the work – and the thinking.*

"Don't shoot, I'm coming in," a voice called out from

the darkness.

"Come in easy, with your hands above your head," Kim yelled back.

"You're a woman," the surprised voice answered before the man stepped into the moon-lit clearing.

"That's a woman with a weapon to you," Kim replied. "Jim, we got another one," she yelled into the night.

Sherlock was almost invisible as he moved, cat-like, around the patches of moonlight. His tan clothing blended into the surroundings so well Kim barely saw him until he was behind the new prisoner, wrenching the AK-47 from the upraised arms. "Nice job, Kim. Stay sharp. Let's go, fellow," he said as he prodded the man in the back with his own rifle. "That tent, over there," he barked like an NCO, directing the man toward the blacked-out command post tent.

Frank raised his head from his folded arms on the table and blinked a couple of times to clear the sleep from his eyes. "One more, huh?" he asked. "Okay buddy, you want to tell us what's going on in that camp of yours?" he asked the small man wearing a Vietnamese battle dress uniform.

"Nothing, sir," the man replied immediately. "There ain't nothin' going on. Jerry's not coming back tonight; he called in a couple of hours ago. He's making sure the rest of the other fields are taken care of."

Jim looked at Frank and then the radio. "Jesus Christ, I should have thought of that. We could have had a handle on this bunch all along."

"Don't worry about it, we all should have thought of it. You want to tell us what frequency you boys use?" Frank asked the cooperative prisoner.

"One forty-seven point niner for the camps, Colonel Ngu is one fifty-five and General Xuan is one fifty-eight. The general told the boss to secure the fields before he did anything about you folks. My guess is you all got a couple of days to get your asses out of here. Is this shit I hear about not going to jail really true?" the small, balding white man asked.

"All depends on what you did before you went over the hill," Frank answered, pouring a cup of strong, black, almost corrosive coffee from the pot simmering on the

Coleman stove. "Most people get a DD and the time served while processing."

Sherlock stuck his head out the tent flap and whistled through his fingers.

"I ought to be okay then. I just did some dope and wanted to get off the line. I sure as hell never figured I'd be in 'Nam this long," the prisoner said as two villagers came to escort him to the holding area.

"What the fuck is that?" Jim asked as they heard a vehicle bouncing down the dirt road with its horn blaring.

"Damned if I know," Frank replied as they stepped into the moonlight, "but they sure as hell want us to know they're coming." Even before their eyes adapt to the gloom they saw the lights bouncing down the rutted road. The rest of the team awakened and rushed to the clearing, weapons at the ready, as the Chinese-made three-quarter-ton truck broke into the clearing and rolled to a stop just inside the two dead palm trees. The occupants of the truck climbed down and out in slow motion, making no overt hostile movements.

"If we get a trip out of here, we give up," the driver announced, handing his M-16 to Frank.

"That's the deal," Frank replied, grinning through the darkness at Sherlock. "Now lay all your weapons in a pile over there and you'll be taken to join the others. You, come with us," Frank ordered the speaker.

"There's others here?" the man asked in surprise.

"Yeah, there's others," Don replied sarcastically. "Now move out," he said, directing the bunch with his rifle barrel.

A young Viet boy walked over to the pile of surrendered weapons and picked up a battered, rusty AK-47 from the top of the heap. He released the magazine, looked at the rounds, reinserted it and pulled back the bolt, ejecting one round and inserting another. He motioned with the business end of the weapon and said, "*Cuhyen dong, domommie.*"

The lights strung in the tent made everyone squint when they walked in. Frank blinked a couple of times before he sat on the stool at the head of the folding table. "All right, tell us about it. Who are you and how many men do you have with you?"

"I'm Bauer," the man in black cotton replied. "We're all from field two. Somebody out there is napalming the shit out of the fields and everything else around. Hell, they've got three fields already today. Somebody on the radio said you were takin' prisoners, so here we are. We quit."

"How many men does duPage have left?" Sherlock asked, standing behind the man.

"After everybody got wasted at five, and us here, I'd have to say fifty or sixty. I ain't got no idea how many of them want a fight, though. I'd guess less than half."

"What makes you think so?" Frank asked as he took a drink of his now cold coffee. He frowned.

"Well, sir, most of us really don't give a shit anymore," came the reply from the prisoner.

"Put him with the rest of them," Frank said, nodding to the young villager standing inside the tent flap. As soon as the prisoner was outside, Frank looked at Don and Jim. "Well, that brings us down to about three to one odds. Hell, we might even survive this thing yet," he said with a half-assed grin as he got up and poured a fresh cup of the mud-thick coffee. "Now, what the hell do we do with the prisoners?"

Sherlock didn't bother to reply. He took a seat in front of the radio and flipped the preset frequency to the CIA in Hong Kong. "Chickens to Henhouse," he said into the built-in microphone.

"This is Henhouse," came the reply, "go, Chick."

"Mother Hen, we've got twenty-five or so foxes without teeth here," Jim said. "What do you want us to do with them?"

"Chick, do you have a place to keep them out of trouble for a few days?"

"Negative," Jim replied, "the hawks are starting to circle."

"Stand by, Chick," the voice said. "We'll get back to you in five." The transmission ended and the carrier wave returned.

"At least we can arm some of the villagers now," Don said as he examined the dirty weapon he brought in. "Thankfully these were made to take a lot of abuse. They didn't have toy guns like this when we were in. Tom, can you show a couple of old men how to tear this thing apart?"

"Sure, no problem. Hand it here." Don handed the black plastic rifle over to Tom, who first dropped the thirty-round magazine and pulled the charging handle to the rear, ejecting the round in the chamber. "These were designed to use a round to tear them apart," Tom said picking the 5.56mm round from the ground. "Take the point of the bullet and push out this pin by the stock; it opens like this. Next, all you have to do is to pull the bolt out, like this. Now you're ready to run a cleaning rod through it. Use a toothbrush for the bolt and you're all set to rock and roll." Tom quickly examined the major components of the weapon and quickly assembled it as Frank and Don look on. "Now you do it," he said as he handed it to Don.

"Mother Hen to Chicks," another voice came over the radio.

"Chicks. Go ahead," Jim replied.

"We have a PBY on the island of Hainan that can be at Point Lay in three hours. That's about forty miles from your position. Can you get the foxes there?" the voice asked.

"Stand by, Mother, we have to check. Tom, go get that guy that was just in here. Let's see how bad they want to leave."

"Right," Tom replied as he left the lighted tent.

"Boss, I can't reach field two," the radio man replied to duPage. "They musta got hit too."

"Shit, that's four down," duPage replied. "Wash, how we doing out there?"

The tall black man looked into the moon-lit night before answering. "Sounds like they be most of the way done. Course, we goin' a have to check it in the mornin'."

"Get hold of the rest of the fields and see what they're doing to cover the crop. Tell 'em to do the best they can. Then get hold of Jefferson and call me. Time to start doing something about this shit."

"Right, Jerry," the radio man replied as he started flipping switches and turning knobs.

"Mother Hen, Chicks. The foxes are ready to come home," Jim said into the radio. "They can be on the beach at your ETA."

"Roger Chicks. PBY will be at Point Lay exactly three hours from mark. Have them give us some kind of a beacon, we'll be coming in at fifty feet or less. This is a one run deal; if they're not there we're gone."

"We roger that one, Mother. 0400 hours. They'll be there," Sherlock replied to the radio. "Out."

"Baur, do you know where Point Lay is?" Frank asked.

"Yeah, up the highway about fifty klicks."

"You heard the radio, if you and your people aren't there by 0400, forget it. Jim, Tom, get them loaded on that three-quarter and get them out of here," Frank said with contempt.

"Thanks, sir," Baur answered as he saluted, "we'll make it. Good luck to you all now," he said before he followed into the night.

Chapter Twenty-five

The night in Cam An had been a busy one. The team members had been able to snatch little sleep between guard duty and prisoner debriefings. The adrenalin rush was about over, leaving everyone in a state of near exhaustion. The night was far from over. There were still three hours until sunrise. Now was the time of the physiological and psychological ebb for anyone attempting to stay awake or work.

Mi Ling and Kim left their post at the last hut near the east end of the village. The last two hours of guard duty had been exhausting – two hours of chasing shadows, staring into the darkness, and coming to full alert with every sound.

Mi Ling's face was drawn tight as she and Kim walked behind the blackout flap in the tent. For the first time she showed every one of her fifty-four years. The last few hours of stress had taken their toll. She could now see how Kim had fared, her hands were shaking so much she could barely hold the M-16. Even in the light Kim's pupils refused to constrict. Her eyes still continued to dart from side to front to side again.

Don and Frank looked up as the women entered. Both men remembered the first time they were on guard duty in a combat zone. They had an instant picture of themselves thirty years ago, doing the same duty, in the same place, but with a different enemy.

Mi Ling was first to speak. "Bill is in the command bunker pit," she said, picking up a coffee cup and pouring the thick black liquid from the pot. "Everything has been quiet out there for the last hour or so. There's nothing unusual about the night once you can identify the sounds. I think we've made it through."

Kim didn't say a word. She laid her rifle on the folding table and sat on one of the canvas stools. She placed both hands palm down on the flat surface and watched her arms continue to shake. She breathed a heavy sigh and then began to sob quietly. Kim had found her release.

Don glanced at his expensive gold wristwatch, then

picked up his AK-47 from the table. He stopped for a second beside Kim as she sobbed in her arms. Gently he rubbed his hand on her back in concern before speaking. "Don't worry, Kim," he said, "it's like this for everyone the first time in a hot zone. You'll do fine." Don looked from Mi Ling to Frank, and then down at Kim. Giving them a weak smile, he said, "I'll find Karen and Janet and get out there. We'll see you all in a couple of hours." Don walked out of the tent and into the warm, shadowy night.

Maybe things will stay quiet the rest of the night, Frank thought, laying his head on his arms and trying to doze as the flap closed behind Don. Mi Ling looked at the tent flap while she attempted to drink the coffee. She stepped over and gave Kim a small hug before she, too, sat down and pillowed her head on her arms.

Don looked into the night sky from his position beside the first hooch in the village. His ears could detect nothing but night birds and the incessant chirping crickets. The bright gibbous moon touched the treetops to the west, and the village was turning to blackness in the shadow of the tall jungle. He looked to the sky. *There are more stars in Vietnam than in any place in the world,* he thought, trying to pick out familiar constellations. "Thank you, God, for this night. Keep us safe and let us get out of here alive again. Amen," he said quietly to the stars as he crossed himself.

"Scared?" Karen whispered, looking out of the hut towards the main trail leading west toward the poppy field.

"Uh... a... yeah. I'm so scared I could pee my pants," Janet replied from the other side of the open doorway.

"Do you really think they'll come after us?" Karen whispered. "I mean, after all, most of them have given up and left."

"I think the guys are worried, and if they're worried I think we should be too," Janet whispered back. "I sure wish I could have a cigarette, but they said not outside the tent at night."

The only things they heard for the next few minutes were the normal night sounds, their breathing, and loudest of all, their hearts pounding like kettle drums in an empty auditorium. "I'm starting to wonder why I ever came on this thing," Janet whispered again.

"Because you wouldn't let Bill or me come without you. Quiet now," Karen whispered back as she stuck her head and the muzzle of her M-16 out the doorway and looked around.

"Three-thirty; another hour and a half to go," Janet whispered, pushing and releasing the light button on her Casio watch. "I've really got to pee; I'm not sure my bladder will last until daylight."

"Go ahead and go, but shoot anything that moves, 'cause nothing else is supposed to be out there."

"Thanks, hon," Janet replied, rising from a crouch. "I'll be back in a couple of minutes. Just don't shoot me when I come back," she whispered, moving alertly out of the round hut and toward the primitive community toilet.

Karen moved to the center of the doorway where she had almost a 180-degree field of view into the nothingness of the night. She shifted the weight of her hundred-pound frame from foot to foot. Spots appeared and disappeared in front of her eyes as she kept shifting them back and forth. *Shadows on the mind,* she thought, blinking a couple of times.

A silent shadow reached down, grabbed the plastic forend of the M-16 and pulled. Karen would have fallen forward if not for the fist that slammed into the side of her head. The shadow scooped the unconscious woman into his arms and made a beeline towards the north trail. He threw Karen over his shoulder like a sack of rice as he moved across the twenty or so yards of village clearing to the well-worn trail to the poppy field. He stopped at the wide spot in the trail less than a hundred meters away from the village. Throwing Karen to the ground, he pulled the K-bar knife strapped to the outside of his upper arm. Slicing through her shirt and bra took only a second. Her belt and pants took even less time. He pulled the pants down around her ankles and returned the knife to its sheath as Karen began to groan. He spread her flaccid legs as he loosened the drawstring on his pants and let them fall. *It's been a long time since*

I fucked a round eye, he thought, *especially a white one.* Karen groaned louder as he squeezed between her legs and kissed her roughly while his large, rough hands started to fondle her small breasts. The shadow felt and heard Karen start to regain some measure of consciousness and stiffen under him. He placed one hand over her mouth as she started to struggle. Her blows had no effect on the big man as he pressed harder. "Quiet, bitch, and I might let you live," he whispered loudly as he plunged into his unwilling sex partner.

Karen continued to hit and claw as the big man continued his rape. His strokes became longer, harder, and deeper with each movement. Karen continued to flail her arms ineffectively, until her hand came in contact with the inverted knife. He pulled back for another lunge as Karen's hand pulled the weapon and placed the butt on her tiny chest. With his next lunge he buried the blade under his ribs and into his heart while Karen twisted the handle with her remaining strength. He paused for a second in mid-stroke, then collapsed on his tiny victim. The butt of the knife pushed into Karen's soft breast. She could feel the blood dripping onto her chest. I started to pool on her flat stomach, then run down between her legs.

Karen started screaming and didn't stop until her voice was nothing more than a whisper mixed with a louder sob. She turned her head and vomited to the side. The contents of her stomach stuck to her long blond hair in the darkness. With her strength gone, she stopped trying to move the massive, dead weight. She whimpered quietly as she felt the dead man's penis soften and contract.

"Karen," Janet whispered, seeing the rifle lying on the ground. "Karen," she whispered louder – no answer. She could see shadows moving at the edge of the jungle as she aimed her rifle and pulled the trigger – nothing. She remembered, fumbled with the safety, then pointed and emptied the thirty-round magazine into the darkness. The first round hit a few feet in front of her feet and the last sailed over the trees when she lost control of the automatic fire in her panic.

Within a second, Frank and Mi Ling were out of the

command tent and running in Janet's direction. They stopped cold as they found the prone body of Don James laying beside the hooch. Frank knew instantly from the pool of blood that his oldest friend was dead. *He can wait,* Frank thought. *Time to take care of the living.* He rushed to where Janet was standing.

Janet was still pointing the rifle towards the trail and pulling the trigger on the empty weapon. Frank removed the useless piece of plastic and metal from her hands as the others arrived. "They took Karen," Janet managed to get out in her panic. "I think they went up the trail."

"Tom, Jim, Bill and David, move out and be careful; they killed Don," Frank ordered as he put an arm around Janet. "We'll get her back, don't worry," he said, trying to sound comforting. "Mi Ling, take care of her."

The four men moved across the clearing at a jog but slowed to a snail's pace once they entered the trees. Sherlock led while the others followed single file, thumbs on safeties and fingers the trigger guards – ready.

Frank, Kim and Trahn examined Don's body while Mi Ling took Janet inside the tent and attempted to control her panic. "Very professional job of throat cutting," Frank said in a cold, clinical tone as they gently rolled the body over. "Knife straight through the neck, and then he used the spine as a fulcrum and just pushed. Got both cartoids and both jugulars; Don was dead before he hit the ground."

"Let's get him out of this mess," Kim said. "I'll clean him up as much as I can. We'll have to take him to the city to be embalmed."

"I know a man in Quang Tri who embalms the rich," Mihn said, starting to lift the body. "We can take him there."

"It's not your fault," Mi Ling said as she pushed Janet's long, red braid from her shoulder to behind her back. "It was just as possible that it could have been you, or even both of you. Dear, it's not your fault." Mi Ling continued to gently rub the tall redhead's back, then turned Janet and gave her a long motherly hug. "The men will get her back."

Sherlock stopped in his tracks and held up a

clenched fist as he heard the whimpering sobs a few meters ahead. "Tom," he whispered and pointed, "careful now, this is a good place for an ambush. We've got you covered."

Tom took the lead as they eased up the trail. The pale moonlight was barely bright enough to guide the way. He saw the large shape of a man lying face down on Karen. Her pale, bare, bent knees stuck up on either side. "Karen," he yelled, forgetting caution as he ran to the body and rolled it off. "Karen," he said more gently when he saw her chest, stomach and crotch covered with blood. "Where are you hurt?" he asked urgently. His wife continued to whimper like a kicked puppy. She looked straight ahead, her eyes fixed in the distance, seeing nothing. Tom gently slid his arms under Karen's tiny frame and picked her up like a baby. "It's all right, everything's okay. I'm going to take care of you," he continued in a soft, soothing voice as he kissed her gently.

"Let's go," Sherlock said, picking up Tom's AK-47 and sliding the sling on his shoulder. "I've got point," he added, leading off down the path back to the village. Tom continued to whisper loving encouragement as he tenderly carried his precious bundle, trying not to stumble. "We've found her," Sherlock yelled before they entered the village clearing.

Tom brought Karen into the well-lighted tent and laid her on the table as Mi Ling raked the cups, ashtrays and other junk to the floor. Kim responded instantly as she soaked a towel in the large pot of water sitting beside the stove. She started to wipe the drying blood from Karen's body as they examined her for injuries. Karen continued to lie limp as a wet rag, her eyes still staring straight ahead, glassy and unseeing. She didn't make a sound as Kim wiped her with the warm, wet towel.

"There is a missionary hospital in Dong Ha," Trahn said. He put a comforting hand on Tom's shoulder and looked at him with concern. "There is a French doctor there. It is only about twenty kilometers from here. We can get there in a few minutes," Mihn said in halting English.

"Get the jeep," Frank ordered as Janet walked in

carrying a blanket, closely followed by the old dream weaver.

The old man gently moved Kim and Mi Ling aside as he took a position next to Karen's head. He stood close, looking down at the small, still, pale woman. He put his palms together and touched her forehead with the tips of his index fingers as he closed his eyes and took four deep breaths. When he opened them, he gently placed his right hand on Karen's face, covering her blue eyes. With the other he cupped her cheek and chin. *"Su buon ngu,"* he said, *"nhung cai khak, song lai tai sinh."* Karen's eyes were closed in peaceful sleep when he removed his rough, wrinkled hand.

"He told her to sleep and recover," Mi Ling translated as the old man looked at Tom. "He said she will sleep now and be better when she wakes, like you were. He doesn't know how long she will sleep. It may take days for the power of *Chi*, but she will be better."

"Thanks," Tom replied, looking into the black eyes of the frail looking old man. "Thank you."

"I'm going with you," Janet said as she pulled up Karen's pants and started to wrap the blanket around her still limp body.

"Fine, let's go," Tom replied, picking up his unconscious wife and rushing to the waiting jeep.

The old man was first to break the silence as the sounds of the jeep faded away. "We would be honored if we could bury the earth that is covered with Sergeant Don's lifeblood. He will be in the cemetery with the rest of our honored dead," Mi Ling translated. "We know you must take the body back to his home, but his blood and some of his spirit will stay here to strengthen and protect us. He died helping protect us and we wish to do honor to his spirit."

"I believe he would want that," Frank whispered through his tear-glazed eyes. "Well, I guess we had better let the State Department know about this." Frank crossed to the radio.

"Could a couple of you guys give me a hand with Don?" Kim asked. "There's not much we can do but clean him up and wrap him in a sheet, but it's the least we can do."

David Segretti laid his M-16 beside the tent flap and replied, "I'll help. He was the only friend I had in this group. Not that I expected more, but we've been together this whole time. I would like to—" His sentence was stopped by Frank and the radio.

"Mother Hen, Mother Hen, this is Chicks, over," Frank said into the microphone.

"This is Mother Hen, over to you, Chicks."

"Mother Hen, get me a GS-12 or above on the horn."

"Man, do you have any idea what time it is?" came the reply through the speaker.

"This is a priority message," Frank said, his agitation showing. "Now get some son of a bitch out of bed and get him on the horn or I'll personally come kick your ass all over that radio room."

"Yes, sir," the radio man in Hong Kong replied. "Stand by."

"I would like to conduct a short funeral mass for Don before he leaves us," Segretti said. "It's the least I can do."

"You're a priest?" Sherlock asked in dismay. "What the hell are you doing on this trip anyway?"

"It's a long story," Segretti replied as he sat on one of the canvas stools, took one of Frank's cigarettes and lit it. "Yes, I'm a priest. I belong to the Brotherhood of The Sword. I guess you could call us assassins of God. There are, and have been for the last three hundred years, fifty of us. Our mission is to deliver the wrath of God to those man's laws can't touch. This place supplies a lot of the world's heroin, and I was assigned to eliminate General Xuan, and others I find to be the head of the snake. Don didn't know. No one was supposed to know. All he knew was that I was along because I had a part in paying for the trip. We had no idea trouble would start this quickly, or that someone in the group would die."

The radio broke the astonished silence of the team. "Chicks, Chicks, this is Mother Hen. Is a GS-14 good enough for you? Here he is."

"This is Dallas Mart. What can I do for you?" a new voice asked.

"We've had some trouble here," Frank spoke calmly into the built-in microphone. "Please inform the necessary people that Senator Don James of Texas was killed in action on this date. We are going to have him embalmed in Quang Tri, but we request a quick pickup flight so he can be taken home."

"I believe we can have a private jet at Quang Tri this morning. We can take care of the embalming ourselves. There are channels we have to go through, but I'm sure we can expedite the process and be there in a few hours. Stand by on this frequency and we'll keep you informed."

"Thanks. Out," Frank replied.

"Let's do what we can for Don; we won't know anything about Karen for a while," Kim said as she stood and looked at David, her eyebrows raised by the new information.

"What the fuck you mean, Jefferson didn't make it back?" duPage yelled as the radio man reported shortly after dawn. "Those bastards were just supposed to look and report back. Now what the fuck happened?"

The small RTO took off his glasses and looked at the ground before he answered, "Spears came back and said the last he saw of Jefferson, he had a white woman over his shoulder and was running for the bush. He ain't come back yet, and that was three hours ago." The radio man nervously wiped his glasses on his dirty shirt, afraid of duPage's reaction to the bad news.

"Jesus fuckin' Christ, do all God damned spooks think with their dicks?" duPage yelled. "I'm going to kill that son of a bitch when I catch up with him. The rest of those bastards were supposed to check out field two, did they get it done?" duPage continued his tirade at the radio man.

The slight RTO returned his glasses to his mousy face. "They did, boss. There ain't nobody there, and most of the guys at one are gone, too."

"Son of a fuckin' bitch! Get the word out to everybody, and I mean every swingin' dick, that there ain't shit to this surrender bullshit. Anybody that tries to leave is goin' t' be shot on the spot." duPage splattered the man's face with droplets of saliva as he emphasized each word.

"Right, boss," the short, balding RTO said the instant before he turned and ran back to the radio shack.

"Hold it," duPage called out. "Tell everybody that after we get these fields secured we're gonna waste every fuckin' one of those fuckers in Cam An. Make sure they all know those bastards are responsible for all this shit comin' down."

"Right, boss."

"The rest of you," he yelled, "get that netting in place and quit fuckin' off! Those MIGs can be here anytime. Now move your lazy asses."

Chapter Twenty-six

Colonel Ngu was sitting behind the general's ornate desk in the hand-tooled leather chair when the general arrived promptly at 0800. The short Viet had had no sleep during the night. His hair was disheveled, his uniform jacket unbuttoned, and his eyes showed more red than white. Ngu looked up without moving and said, "General, at least half of duPage's command is gone; part through the air strikes and the rest through desertion. Two of his men went into Cam An last night but only one made it back. They did manage to kill at least two of the Americans in the village though. duPage has barely enough men left to provide marginal protection for any of the fields. I believe we must do something to hold what we have. After I get cleaned up and have some rest, I will go out and evaluate the situation myself."

"Very good, Vinh," the general replied. He took no notice of where the colonel was sitting but he did notice how Vinh's breath smelled – like old sweat and alcohol. *I'm going to have to air the room after he leaves. This man is a disgrace.* "Do you believe this incident will be enough to force the Americans out of the village?"

Vinh stood, allowing the general to have his chair while he returned to the bar across the room. The fat general slumped into the vacated seat, leaned back, and started stroking his chins with his pudgy fingers. "Years ago this would have made the Americans fight harder," Vinh replied, picking a bottle at random and filling a glass. "Now I don't know."

"Find out what you can. We can't afford to lose any more men or fields. If need be we can take control of the situation ourselves," the fat man ordered.

The small colonel didn't bother to answer. He looked down at the general and swallowed half the glass of burning amber liquid. *Right – we can take control of the situation. You fat pig. You mean I can take control of the situation. You don't know how to control shit. You never have. I will show you about control, you lazy ineffectual son of a bitch.* Vinh stared at the general as he brought the glass away from his lips. He didn't notice the liquid that ran down the corner of his mouth and onto the chest of his dirty uniform. His face reddened and his tired eyes shone like black diamonds – just as hard, just as cold. The general didn't notice the rage in Vinh's face or in his stiff posture. He did notice the power of the colonel's whispered answer. "The situation will be brought under control. I will get everything under control." Vinh set his wet glass on the highly polished desk and bent forward, close enough to make the general turn away from his stench.

"Karen's going to be all right physically," Tom began his report. "The doctor said she had some vaginal lacerations and abrasions, but she's going to be okay, and there is no danger to the baby."

"Baby?" the group responded at once.

"Yeah, she's about seven weeks pregnant, the doctor said, and she didn't even tell me." Tom took a sip of the hot, black coffee. He paused a second to savor the nutty taste and the powerful aroma of the coffee beans that had been grown and processed by the villagers. "He said he can't make any judgements as to her mental status until she wakes up. God only knows when that will be. He said she is clinically asleep, but he can't get any reaction out of her – just like she was under anesthesia. Her reflexes and everything are fine, she just won't wake up."

"She's a tough lady," Kim replied. "She'll make it through this. Especially with you supporting her."

"Yeah, I hope so," Tom replied. "Whatever we're going to do, let's do it. This shit's personal now," he said with a voice that would freeze boiling water.

"We'll wait until Mihn gets back from Quang Tri," Frank replied, watching David walk under the tent flap with the aluminum case that had caused so many problems.

"We understand," Segretti said. Laying the large, long box on the table, then starting to dial the first of the four built-in combination locks.

"Holy shit!" Hayes exclaimed when David finally opened the lid. "What the fuck is that thing? Oops, sorry, Father."

"It's still David, and don't worry about the language, I use it myself. This is a custom-made .50 caliber sniper rifle. Israeli Technologies made it for us. The accurately range is over two miles, with a mile and a half being dead on. The scope is a twenty to sixty-power zoom and is self-correcting for range." Segretti started getting into the explanation and description, almost like a proud parent. "The ammo is also custom made. All loads are corrected to a seven hundred and fifty-grain bullet, no matter what the weight. As you can see, they're color-coded to the type of round they are." He pointed to the rows of exposed, color-tipped bullets under the layer of neoprene.

"Must kick like a Missouri mule," Sherlock said as Mihn walked into the tent and silently looked on.

"Not bad at all," Segretti continued his explanation. "There is a mercury cylinder in the stock that reacts to the recoil, something with a gyroscope, and the muzzle has a compensator that forces most of the gasses upward so target recovery time is almost nil," David said as he started loading the massive rounds into the five-round box magazines.

Trahn reached out and touched the slightly rough, non-reflective, stainless steel finish on the bolt of the massive weapon.

"Go ahead and pick it up," David said, noticing Mihn's interest.

"Heavy," was his only reply as he passed the twenty-pound weapon to Sherlock after his examination.

"I'll take a position in that tall teak tree about a quarter of a mile from the camp. I'll be able to cover you from there." Segretti laid aside the four loaded magazines and started to assemble the complicated sling system. "These bullets may be slow, but they always get there. A different way of touching the heart."

Frank looked at the seven team members gathered around the table. "I think we can consider the place an Anglo free-fire zone. They're all fair game now."

"I should be able to see the road from my vantage point, and this," he added, pointing to the rifle Bill held, "can stop anything short of a tank."

Mi Ling had been translating for the old man as the

conversation continued, and he spoke for the first time since they started. "We can protect the village with the weapons we now have when they come here," Mi Ling translated. "You taught me well many years ago. I will remember, we will be safe."

"Good," Frank replied. "If we're ready, let's do it," he said tersely, with an air of determination.

The sun was well up as they moved into the shadows of the triple-canopy jungle. The shade was cool and the morning dampness had yet to burn away as they moved almost silently up the trail. They stopped beside the tall teak as David uncoiled a climbing rope and tossed it over a lower limb. "Give me a half hour to get into position," he said. "I should be ready by the time you get there, but give me a full thirty minutes just in case. I can watch the whole camp on low power, so don't worry, I'll cover your asses. Good luck. See you when it's over," he said, starting to climb with the massive weapon strapped to his back.

"We've still got five minutes, and I saw three bad guys," Sherlock said after he returned from a quick recon of the camp. "Spread out and pick your targets. Kim, you and Mi Ling cover us from here, the rest of us go in."

"Right," Kim replied in a whisper. "Jim, be careful," she said, and gave the tall gunnery sergeant a quick kiss before she moved into deeper cover off the trail.

"Two," Frank whispered as he held up two fingers. Jim, Tom and Bill drew their Berettas and screwed on the silencers. "One." There was the clicks of safeties being removed. "Now," he whispered loudly.

There was a 'poof' as the three weapons fired at once. The clack of the slides cycling was much louder than the combined shots. The three men inside the camp collapsed without a sound. They slid the long-barreled pistols into their belts and moved cautiously into the clearing, rifles held ready with the safeties off.

Frank unleashed a short burst of fire at a Hispanic-looking man who made the mistake of walking around one of the closer hooches. "That's four," Frank said quietly. There was another burst of fire behind them and they turned to see another body falling from the makeshift tower beside the poppy field. "Make that five. Six," he said as a man fell through the thatch of the mess hall building, with no sound of a shot being fired.

A rifle fired from one of the huts. Sherlock could see the dust kicked up by the muzzle blast and the ugly snout of a M-16 sticking through the thatch. He returned fire, and saw Trahn go down in his peripheral vision. The stand-off continued while the team hugged the ground and returned concentrated fire on the hooch. There was a single scream when the grass hut started to burn. The firing stopped. Frank rolled to where Mihn lay and saw shattered bone sticking through the left pants leg and two holes through the cloth covering his right thigh. There was very little bleeding from the wounds. Frank nodded, patted Mihn on the shoulder, and continued the sweep through camp.

"Looks like that's all," Sherlock said as he came out of the last hut. "How bad did Mihn get it?"

"Broke one leg and holes in the other," Frank answered in a calm voice, still keeping a close eye on the area. "He'll be okay. No major damage."

"Good," Jim acknowledged as he changed the magazine in his AK-47.

"Let's burn this fucking place to the ground," Tom said, removing his Winstons and disposable lighter from his pocket. He lit his cigarette and then touched the yellow flame to the thatched roof next to him.

"We better check 'em out before we burn 'em," Hayes suggested as he stepped inside one of the larger huts. The inside was clean and the dirt floor was covered with woven rice straw mats. The bunks were the same kind the U.S. Army has been using since time began. Both were made, with clean towels lying across the foot of each. Everything looked and smelled clean. Bill was surprised as he surveyed the interior. He saw a small brown foot sticking out of a rolled mat in the corner. He released the hand guard and allowed the weapon to fall to waist level, holding the plastic pistol grip in his right hand, with his finger on the trigger. He took up the few millimeters of slack in the trigger an instant before he grabbed the top of the mat and pulled. Hayes was surprised when he exposed a girl of about fifteen, naked from the waist up. "Out," he commanded, motioning with his left hand while he kept his weapon ready. Bill finished his inspection and found nothing. He removed his lighter and set fire to the inside back wall.

"Looks like you caught yourself a hooch mouse," Sherlock called from across the street as Hayes walked out of the burning hut. "Quiet! Listen!" Jim yelled, holding up a clenched fist for silence. "Chopper coming! Scatter!"

Each man moved in a different direction as the ominous sound of the rotors got louder.

The two women were concentrating on Mihn's wounds and refused to run when they heard the approaching 'whump whump' of the blades. Machine gun fire from the helicopter door started chewing the dirt around them. One of the first salvo of bullets went through Kim's right arm just below the elbow. The kevlar clothing had no stopping effect as the 7.62mm bullet ripped through cloth, flesh and bone. Mi Ling and Trahn recovered quickly and grabbed their rifles. An instant later they saw the door gunner knocked backward in his safety harness. They watched, almost in slow motion, as the contents of the man's chest cavity exploded out of his back. The red stain of blood and tissue painted the interior of the cabin. The whirling blades of the chopper seemed to stop, and the fuselage started spinning out of control toward the ground. The four men ran across the compound as the helicopter slammed to earth. They saw Colonel Vinh Ngu in his full dress uniform, ribbons and all, start to struggle with the seatbelts. His eyes were wide with panic. He knew what would probably happen within the next few seconds. As Vinh accepted his death, he stopped struggling. His face was a mask of blood as he laid his hands in his lap. Vinh was calm. He stared out at the Americans, his coal-black eyes filled with hate. He attempted to project his rage and hate beyond the Plexiglass windshield. He stopped and stared into Frank's eyes for a full second before the burning gasoline reached the cockpit. The men were knocked to the ground by the force of the blinding fireball when the fuel tank went up.

Recovering quickly, they ran to their teammates on the other side of the burning Huey. Mi Ling struggled to get Kim to her feet as Sherlock scooped the wounded Viet into his arms like a baby. "Move!" he yelled as a secondary explosion showered the area with flying shrapnel. Mihn didn't stop screaming in pain until Jim set him down well away from the flaming wreckage.

"I'll get the truck," Hayes yelled above the roaring blaze. Laying his M-16 on the ground and removing his web gear, he dropped it on top of the black rifle. "I'll be back as soon as I can!" He took off at a mile-eating pace down the jungle trail.

"Jim, take care of Kim," Tom said, noticing the big Marine's concern for Kim's injured arm. "Frank, let's go see what else we can destroy."

"Go ahead, Frank," Mi Ling answered. "We'll take care of these two. Tom needs back-up. Look for something we can use for splints while you're at it." She didn't bother looking up at her husband as she expertly applied a field dressing to Mihn's thigh. "We'll need to splint these breaks before we move them."

"Let's go, Tom," Frank said, walking back toward the flaming helicopter.

The fire and explosion had ignited two of the huts closest to the crash. Tom walked into the first hut that wasn't burning and was surprised at the neatness considering the soldiers who occupied it. Everything was in its place, the mat-covered, dirt floor was clean and the bunks were made. Tom saw a gold Buddha sitting on a small table next to one of the bunks. A souvenir, he thought, picking it up and slipping it into his side pocket. He was surprised at the weight of the four-inch statue as he continued his search. He noticed a squat green box in the corner with three packaged Claymore mines lying on top. He twisted the latch and raised the lid. The yellow markings on the cardboard tubes of the M-67 fragmentation grenades seemed to leap out. Laying his rifle on the bunk, Tom carried his find to the door.

"And you told me to be careful," Sherlock chided as he gently cut the sleeve from Kim's shirt. "You should have stayed hidden in the bush like we told you."

"We did what you would have done, Jim," Mi Ling said as she cut off Trahn's boot.

"Yeah, I know, but I'm supposed to do things like

this," he replied, pulling the sleeve away. "It's a bad break, doll. There's a lot of nerves and things in this area, so all we can do is to splint it and get you some help. At least it's only one bone." He saw the pain and fear in Kim's eyes. Sherlock realized for the first time that Kim had become much more than a soft member of the team.

Frank noticed the nylon pack with the U.S. Medical Corps caduceus hanging on a wall peg. Crossing the hooch in three steps, he unzipped the largest pocket and found rolled wire splints and bandages. Without further searching, he left the hooch and dashed back to the injured.

Tom continued his inspection of the first hooch and found nothing more of interest. Picking up his rifle, he moved to the next hut in line. The shaded interior looked more like a trash heap than living quarters – the bed was unmade, clothing and trash covered the floor mats, and cigarette burns covered every flat surface. He started his inspection in the far corner by kicking the debris away from the wall while his hands checked the shelves. Moving along, he found an unopened bottle of Johnnie Walker scotch sitting on the shelf. This immediately went into his other side pocket. Kicking clothing on the floor, he uncovered a wooden ammo case of cloth bandoleers loaded with 5.56mm ammo already in M-16 magazines. He continued to kick the surrounding trash, and disturbed a large rat which ran to a safer place across the room. *Big mother,* Tom thought when his heart came back into his chest. He picked up the ammo box, carried it to the door, and returned to kicking through the mess. His next discovery was a locked footlocker. Sliding the safety forward on his weapon, he fired one round, breaking the lock. Lifting the lid, he uncovered antique figures and vases made of gold, porcelain and stone. *Spoils of war,* he thought as he carried it to the door and laid the ammo on top. *To hell with the rest of this mess,* he thought as he picked up the load and started back toward the team.

As Tom walked through the center of the camp, a shot rang out. He felt the impact of the bullet on his side, just above his left hip, and staggered under the force as Frank loosed a three-round burst into the bare

chest of the young woman Bill had found and released.
"Thanks," Tom yelled.

"You okay?" Frank called back.

"Yeah, thanks to modern fabric," Tom replied, continuing on toward the group. "Ammo and antiques," Tom said as he walked up to the injured and their caregivers. "Here's some pain medicine." he said, removing the bottle of scotch from his right pocket and handing it to Sherlock as he was finishing splinting Kim's arm.

"Frank found a medic's bag that had everything we need in it, even morphine," Mi Ling said without looking up from her work on Mihn's broken leg.

"Yeah, but there ain't nothing to dull the senses like alcohol," Sherlock added, opening the bottle and passing it to Kim. She drank heavily and passed the bottle to Trahn. "What else did you find?" Jim asked, still holding Kim lightly in his arms.

"Some frags and Claymores. I'm going back after them now," Tom answered as he stood to leave.

"What was the shooting we heard?" Kim asked, her voice taking on a faraway tone from the morphine.

"The gal Bill found took a shot at me. Frank nailed her ass before she could get off another round," Tom replied. "I'll be back with the next load. We should recover the weapons laying around, the villagers might be able to use them." He turned back to the burning camp. Tom walked toward the unburned huts, pausing to look through the smoke-stained windshield of the downed helicopter. The blackened, burned face that was Vinh Ngu stared back from empty eye sockets as the flesh fell away. *Burn in hell, you son of a bitch! You and the rest of your mob aren't worth a pimple on the ass of either Don or Karen. Burn, baby, burn.* Tom spat pink-tinged, smoky dust from his throat in the direction of the wreckage and continued.

"Tom," Frank called from a hooch that was better constructed than the rest, "give me a hand with this."

Tom looked in the direction of the hut he was going to check, shrugged his shoulders, and walked across to where the older man waited. Following Frank into the shaded dimness, Tom's first words were, "Holy shit! Jackpot." One long wall was covered with food supplies, while the short wall was filled with green boxes of munitions. Boxes labeled in Chinese, Vietnamese and English were stacked to the crude rafters. "Christ, there's enough stuff to equip a small army, and feed 'em too."

"My thoughts exactly," Frank replied, picking up a box with '7.65 mm' stenciled on it. "Let's get what we can back to the ville when Hayes gets here with the truck. Grab a case. I hate to delay getting Mihn and Kim to the hospital, but it won't take much more time."

Jesus, Bosworth, you're getting old, Tom thought, attempting to pick up two cases of ammo. *All you need is a hernia about now.* He grabbed one case and followed Frank to where the group waited.

"Sorry about that chopper," Segretti said, walking off the trail and up to the team. "I was starting down the tree when I heard it. How much damage did it do?"

"Kim got it in the arm, but it could have been a lot worse," Sherlock answered, looking up from his work on Kim's arm. "Buddy, you can be my back-up anytime. Damn fine shooting. Oh, by the way, Colonel Ngu is sitting in the right hand seat of that bird you brought down, so at least part of your job is finished."

"Yeah, I know," David replied coldly as he looked down at Mihn and Kim. He laid the massive .50 caliber on the footlocker, "The cost of doing business is too high. None of you were supposed to get involved in this. If I hadn't come, maybe you would have been safe."

Mi Ling stood, reached up, and put a hand on each of the priest's shoulders. Bending her head back, she looked into Segretti's troubled eyes. "David, you didn't start this. It would probably have happened even if you hadn't been here. Because your people financed this, a lot of men are going to go home at last. You're a big part of that. Some people have died, yes, but there are also a number of people who gave up and are going home alive."

"She's right, David," Kim added, pressing the bottle of scotch into his limp hand. "If it hadn't been for you, probably none of the good parts would have happened, and the bad things could have been a hell of a lot worse. That helicopter would have made mincemeat out of us if you hadn't stopped it. Now have a drink. The morphine and the booze make me feel so good I don't need any more."

"Welcome back, David," Frank said, setting a crate down. "Nice shooting. We found their storeroom. It's got plenty of food and ammo. We should get as much as we can and drop it off at Cam An on the way to the hospital. Mi Ling, stay with Kim and Mihn. We'll get the rest of it."

"Do we leave what we can't take, or burn it?" Sherlock asked after the third trip. "If we leave it, maybe we can retrieve it later."

"Yeah, or they can," Tom said in a cynical tone as they started back for another trip.

"Ready, lift," Frank said as he and Segretti lifted Mihn up to Tom and Bill on the truck bed. They carried the injured sergeant to a spot as close as possible to the cab while the team members on the ground loaded boxes. Tom took the footlocker of artifacts and slid it gently under the bunk, treating it with care and respect. Mi Ling tossed up the recovered rifles. They were stacked along with various boxes along the sides. The only weapon that got special attention was an M-60 light machine gun found in the last hut they searched – the first and only weapon they had come across that had been properly cared for. There were signs of wear on the black phosphate coating, but the weapon was clean, oiled, and loaded with a two-hundred and fifty-round belt. Sherlock handed it to Hayes, who laid it on top of one of the boxes to be hand-held on the trip back to the village.

"That's the last of it," Sherlock said, reaching his hand up for assistance. Mi Ling gently assisted the stoned and grinning Kim into the front seat. David handed his sniper rifle to Tom and climbed in last.

"Let's roll," Frank commanded, climbing into the driver's seat.

With the surrendered and captured weapons, every adult in Cam An was armed. Their eyes lit up as the cases of ammo were quickly unloaded and sorted.

"Bill," Sherlock yelled above the chatter of voices, "make sure everyone has plenty of the proper ammo."

Tom slid the last box to the end of the truck – the footlocker filled with the religious artifacts. He looked for the old man as he jumped down, pulled it after him, and started walking toward the crowd. "Mi Ling," he yelled above the noise of the excited villagers, and motioned with his head. Tom set the footlocker at the old man's feet, stepped back a pace, and bowed low from the waist. "Tell him these belong to his people," Tom said to Mi Ling as the old man opened the box.

Mi Ling translated as the frail old man opened the box and gently examined the pieces on the top of the pile. "He said some of these are hundreds of years old. He said he knows the temple where they will do the most good, but he wants you to take your pick of these before we leave."

"Tell him thanks, but they belong to his people," Tom replied. "One more thing." He reached into his side pocket and brought out the gold statue. For the first time he noticed the 7.65 mm bullet half buried in its chest. "It wasn't the clothes that stopped the bullet that woman fired, it was the statue," Tom said, looking at the piece with a new respect and reverence.

"*Cai nay Phat ben vuc su song tu khi vien dan,*" the old man said. "*Phat lu ken chon ahn. Ahn duy tri thoat chet no bao ve ahn.*" He reached out and covered Tom's hand and the statue with his own.

"He said the Buddha now protects only you and your family and keeps you safe. This Buddha has selected you, and now it is yours, forever. Keep him safe and he will always protect you," Mi Ling translated.

"How do you say thank you?" Tom asked quietly.

"*Su cam on ahn,*" she replied.

"*Su cam on ahn,*" Tom said to the old man. "Tell him I'm honored and will do as he said. You and Frank better get Kim and Mihn on down to the hospital now. We can handle things here with sign language. *Su cam on ahn,*" he said again before he turned to join the men passing out ammo.

"We'll set two Claymores on the road and one on the trail," Sherlock said. "I wish to hell we had more than a dozen frags," he continued, making a defense plan. "We'll put the M-60 in the pit and use the bone bags as sandbags. Bill, you set up on the trail. Tom, you've got the road. I'll take the pit. David, what do you think?"

"I think I'm going to take my ammo and little toy

and get my butt up that big kapok tree over there. That's the highest point around. I should be able to stop any vehicle on the road and still give you cover fire in here. Let me have a couple of those grenades, just in case someone gets too close," Segretti said as he took two of the cardboard tubes and dumped the grenades in his pockets. "See you later, and may God help us all."

"Yeah," Tom replied, "or at least let's hope he doesn't help the other guys."

"Boss, look over there," Chavez said, pointing to the east. "Looks like they got our place."

"Shit," duPage replied, "there's not a damned thing we can do about it now. If it's like the rest of the fields, there's not a damned thing we could do anyway. I'd better call Ngu and let him know we lost another one. We'll pick up the pieces later." duPage was silent for a moment. "Ya know, Jose, with all the dead and the way we split things up, we can probably retire now. Fuck it. Get a head count on who's alive, dead or AWOL."

"Right, boss, I'll get on it," the short Puerto Rican replied. "Jerry, does this really mean we're going home now?"

"Yeah, buddy," duPage responded, looking at the smoke coming from the direction of his camp. "Just as soon as we waste every fuckin' round eye in Cam An. Make that list and we'll get the money transferred. Jesus, I'm tired," the lanky commander said as he held his hands in front of his chest and watched his fingers shake with exhaustion.

"We're all tired, Jerry," Chavez said with a note of sympathy. "What's it been, four days since you had any rest?"

"Hell, I don't know. Seems like a year. Find out who we've got left and tell 'em to get into the bush and get some sack time. We're going to Cam An as soon as I get an hour or so on the rack." Turning, he shuffled toward the radio shack.

"Yes, General," duPage said dejectedly into the microphone. "We have the western fields as well hidden as we possibly can."

"Commander, you must protect these fields at all costs," the disembodied voice answered. "If you can't do the job, I will replace you with someone who can. There should have been enough men left at field one to give adequate cover fire. You failed. Colonel Ngu is flying out to assess the situation. He should have been there by now!" The general's voice rose with rage as he released the mike button.

"General, I've tried to raise the colonel on his frequency, with no response. I will confer with him when he arrives. But, sir, my men need rest. Most of them haven't stopped for the last three days."

"Mister duPage, your men can rest after they're dead. Right now I want every one of them on the alert for aircraft. This includes you. If Colonel Ngu isn't there within one hour, I want to hear about it. Remember, you can be replaced," the general continued ranting. "Here is my secretary, make it quick and get on with your duties."

The general's angry voice was replaced with a soft, melodic, feminine one, speaking almost faultless English. "How may I help you, commander?"

"Yes, could you contact Mister Kao at our bank in Hong Kong and give him the code 76K854? Ask him to transfer these accounts to the others evenly." duPage started reading off the list of names Chavez had prepared, picturing the face of each man, starting with Anderson – Anderson, the man with the deepest blue eyes in the world, surrounded by the burned, blackened face. duPage shuddered as he remembered the man looking up at him as he carried him away from the burning field his calmness when he died. The list continued through Zularicia, the short, skinny Mexican from Laredo who was so proud of his Aztec heritage. "Mister Kao will give you a series of letters and numbers when you finish. Please call me back with them," duPage said politely as he finished the transmission.

"Yes, Commander, let me read this back to ensure my accuracy." As she read, each face came more quickly to his troubled mind.

"That is correct," duPage replied. "Thank you, I will be standing by." He flipped the switch to standby and walked across the room to collapse on the RTO's bunk.

Jerry duPage was asleep before his feet left the floor, but he got no rest; the ghosts of the dead men haunted his dreams.

"Jerry, off and on, old buddy," Chavez said, tapping the sleeping duPage on the sole of his boot. "Jerry, come on, wake up. We got to get moving."

"Huh, uh, what?" duPage mumbled as he forced his tired eyes open.

"That sweetie pie from the general's office called back and she got the accounts taken care of. We've got another fifteen men AWOL, and the general wants us to hit Cam An at fifteen hundred hours. The bastard said he'd be there to watch and give us support fire if we need it. The bastard!" Jose continued as duPage sat up.

"How long did I sleep?"

"A little over two hours. It's one-thirty. I've got everybody ready to move out. I thought we'd stop off at home and see what's left, then send part of the men down the trail. That son of a bitch Ngu still hasn't been heard from. It wouldn't surprise me much if he turned tail too. Here, have a drink." Chavez handed his friend a bottle of Russian made vodka.

"Here's to the end of it all," duPage said, tipping the bottle of clear liquid to his lips. "With any kind of luck, by this time tomorrow we should be in Laos on our way to Thailand. It's time to go home."

"Jerry, I've got a real bad feeling about this one," Jose said, watching his friend try to stand. "If it were up to me, I'd say fuck it and head west now."

"Yeah, but you know we can't do that," duPage replied, taking another drink, swirling it around in his mouth, then spitting it on the floor. "Those assholes are responsible for too many of our friends dying. It's payback time." He took another drink and handed the bottle back. "Let's get mounted up and move out. Now it's us offering surrender terms, and there ain't none. We got 'em outnumbered and outgunned. There ain't a damned thing for them to do but die." duPage sounded confident as he walked out of the radio shack and into the blazing afternoon sun. "Okay, listen up," he yelled to the men wandering around the camp. He lit a Vietnamese cigarette and waited for the mob to gather. "I reckon Jose told you the general wants us to waste those bastards in Cam An. That's what we're going to do at three o'clock. Any round eye there is fair game. After all, they're the ones responsible for this shit in the first place. Every fuckin' one of us lost brothers in the last couple a days. Well, now it's time for payback. This is not for Ngu or Xuan, this is for us. When this shit's over, Jose and me are on our way to Thailand and home. You can come or stay, it's up to you. Now, let's mount up and go kick some ass."

duPage stood, staring at the burned wreckage of the Huey. "Well at least we've found out what became of the good Colonel Ngu. I never liked that sanctimonious son of a bitch anyway." He turned to survey the rest of the burned out camp.

"Hey, Boss," yelled one of the men. "Come here and take a look at this." He knelt beside one of the bodies. "Looked like he was hit with a fuckin' cannon," the man added, rolling the body over, showing the spine and back missing from the shoulder blades to the belt. "Man, I ain't afraid of dyin', but I sure don't want to get fucked up like this."

"Yeah, he is that," duPage replied, swallowing hard to keep the vodka in his stomach.

"Jerry," a choked voice said from behind, "they killed Lin."

He turned to see a big bearded man holding the stiffening body of the young woman in his arms. "I'm sorry, Willis, I really am. Put her down beside Tony and we'll take care of her when we get back. Like I said, it's personal now. Right?" duPage said, putting a sympathetic hand on the man's shuddering shoulder.

"Yeah, it's personal. Kill every fucking one of them," Willis replied. "The bastard that did this is going to die."

"How we going to do this, Jerry?" Chavez asked, looking down at his commander and the bodies.

"We're going to hit 'em from all sides at once. Let's get the men together so every swingin' dick knows what he's supposed to do. Killin' women! The bastards."

"All right," Chavez yelled, loud enough for everyone to hear, "gather 'round over here."

duPage waited as the men filtered back from what

used to be home for some. "Okay, everybody, here's the plan: Jose, take a dozen men and go down the trail. When you get there split up. Part of you hit from the east and the rest of you hit from the north. Me and everybody else will take the trucks down and spread out on the west and south. Once we get them surrounded, there's not a damned thing they can do but kiss their asses good-bye. Anybody got a problem with that?"

The men shook their heads, and one shaggy looking black man asked, "How many people do you figure we're up against, boss?"

"The initial word was ten, but Washington took care of two of 'em. That leaves eight. Some of the gooks might have guns by now, but I ain't worried about them none. Hell, first shot they'll probably drop 'em and take off runnin'. Anybody with a weapon is fair game, understand? Fuck, even if they don't have a weapon they're fair game," duPage yelled with an evil grin. "It don't make a fuckin' bit of difference. When we finish, we're on our way to Thailand."

"You heard the man," Chavez yelled. "Who's coming with me, and don't all you fuckers volunteer at once." The Puerto Rican started counting as the men started stepping over to join him. "Ten, eleven, twelve, that's it. The rest of you go with Jerry."

"Everybody check your watch if you've got one. We're going to hit at exactly three o'clock," duPage yelled as he stuck out his hand to his friend. "I'll see you when it's over, buddy," he said as they clasped forearms.

"Yeah, good luck," Jose replied in a worried voice, looking his friend in the eyes.

"The general's supposed to give us air cover starting at three, but don't count on it. Remember, this is a free-fire zone, just like the old days. Waste everything. Now let's move out; we've got forty-five minutes to get there and get set up. Can you make it, Jose?"

"Hell, man, we can crawl that far in forty-five minutes. Be careful now," Chavez said as he led his men to the well-worn dirt path to the village.

"I'm afraid both of your friends will require surgery to repair their injuries," the French physician replied in heavily accented English. "There are European trained orthopedists at the hospital in Quang Tri who can do a very good job on them. Their injuries are much too complicated for me to handle here."

"Is there any way you can contact them to let them know we are on our way?" Mi Ling asked.

"Yes, I have a radio here, and would be happy to do it," the doctor replied. "Your other friend, the woman, has not regained consciousness yet, but her friend is with her at all times. Do you wish to take her also?"

"No, Doctor, I'm sure you are doing as much for her as can be done. We'll take these two," Frank answered, indicating Kim and Mihn, both sleeping a morphine-induced sleep on the stretchers in the primitive emergency room. "We'd appreciate it if you could give us a hand getting them back in the truck."

"But of course," the physician replied as he spoke to his orderlies in Vietnamese.

"When this is over," Frank started, "we'll make sure your hospital is much better stocked and equipped. We may need it later."

"Thank you for everything, Doctor," Mi Ling added, following the stretchers into the hot sun.

Chapter Twenty-seven

The three remaining team members took their squads of villagers and set up around the area. Every possible way into the village was covered with an ambush. Nothing moved, not even a breeze to disturb the mosquitoes hanging in the hot, stagnant air. The silence was deafening. Eyes, ears and noses were alert for any signs of the ex-GIs from the west. Mouths were dry, and almost everyone could taste the green-brown copper taste of fear. No one was immune, not even Gunnery Sergeant James Sherlock as he waited in the excavated command bunker with the M-60.

The first warning of attack was the thundering boom of Segretti's .50 caliber. His first shot was followed in a measured cadence by five more. *Make them walk for their fun,* David thought with a grin that would have shown his stress if anyone were around to see it. He removed the magazine and replaced it with a full one before he yelled down to the village, "Looks like twenty or thirty of them coming down the road." He lifted the heavy weapon up, rested it on a limb, refilled the empty clip. David brought the weapon up to his shoulder, twisted the magnification ring on the optical sight, and started picking his targets. Each time he caressed the light, crisp trigger, he watched a man fall a fraction of a second later. When he emptied the second magazine, he pulled a loose round from his shirt pocket, laid it on the magazine follower, and closed the bolt. Letting the rifle rest on a large limb, he slid the safety on and replaced the spent magazine with a fresh one. He didn't bother to look at the color coded bullet tips as he reloaded; he knew they would all kill. He slid the fresh magazine in his pocket and returned the weapon to his shoulder, looking for more men willing to die. His breathing was slow and easy, one breath about every seven or eight seconds. The cross-hairs of the scope never wavered after they locked on a man almost a mile away. One shot, one kill. Even with the recoil-reducing features of the custom rifle, his right shoulder started to ache after the second clip. *I'm going to have to get some more modifica-*

tions made in this thing when I get home, he thought, squeezing off another round and ejecting the case to hear it fall through the branches below.

Jim Sherlock looked through the sandbags toward the main trail leading to the opium field. Pulling the stock of the M-60 to his shoulder, he checked his field of fire for the fifth time in as many minutes. He pounded his fist into one of the rubberized body bags to add another couple of degrees to his kill zone. *Damn. I wish I had let one of the younger guys have this so I could be out in the boonies where I belong. I can't let these guys buy the farm like I did the first time I was here. Jesus, Sherlock, what the fuck you thinking like this for? You were out cold. There wasn't a damned thing you could have done about it. You just can't let it go, can you?* Sherlock scanned his field of fire again, almost with tunnel vision. He removed his sweaty right hand from the MG and wiped it on his shirt, then did the same with his left. He glanced at his old analogue Timex. *Ten till three, and it looks like the shit has hit the fan. Wonder how Kim's getting along? Dumb shit, get your mind on what's happening here. Kim's out of it now. These people here need your attention. God, I wish I had a drink.* No sooner did he finish the thought than one of his assistants tapped him on the back and handed him a bottle of clear liquid, making motion to drink. The two Viets smiled as he lifted the bottle and took a small cautious sip. He was surprised at the almost sickly sweet taste that was followed instantly by the burning of high proof alcohol. Jim returned the smile, saluted with the raised bottle, and took another long drink. He could feel the burn go all the way to his empty stomach. One last long drink and he handed the bottle back as a warm glow started to spread through his body. He returned to looking over the M-60 sights through the slit in the sandbags. Thank God, he thought, checking the 7.62 mm ammo fan folded in the ammo box. *All right you bastards, anytime you're ready.*

Bill Hayes and his squad of villagers were spread out on the trail north of the village, within visual distance of the man Karen had killed the night before. *It's been a long time since I killed anyone. I wonder if I can do it anymore. If anyone deserves to die it's these cocksuckers. Especially after what they did to Don and Karen. I'm glad Janet's gone. At least she's safe. I'm just sorry I didn't tell her I love her. If we get out of this alive I'm going to ask her to marry me. We could even have David do it here.* Hayes looked to his left and to his right, making sure all his people were well under cover. Even though they were yards away from the body of the black man they could still smell the sweet, putrid odor of decaying flesh. *Sure don't take them long to start rotting over here. I'm glad we got Don taken care of, he deserves a lot better than this. I'm sure glad Janet's with Karen and out of here.*

His thoughts stopped when he heard activity on the trail. Rising to a crouch beside a tree, he could see the body of Karen's assailant, his K-Bar knife still buried in his chest. Hayes watched the muscular Hispanic, and his men start to gather around the bloating body. *After all these years you fuckers still haven't learned the basic rules of combat. Never bunch up, and the easy way is always mined.* Bill pressed the firing lever for the Claymore hidden on a tree a few feet from the body. Hayes and his companions watched the shaped charge send a beehive of ball bearings into the group of mercenaries. The one closest to the blast was cut in two and four others caught the majority of the rest of it. Their blood mixed with that of Karen's attacker and formed a small pool in the path. The Puerto Rican and the rest of his men hit the dirt and emptied their weapons blindly in all directions, having no idea where the attack came from. The villagers held their fire and stayed low. *Bunch of real dumb sons of bitches,* Hayes thought from the cover of his tree.

Tom and his people waited patiently on both sides of the rutted asphalt highway. *Come on you bastards, it's payback time,* he thought, looking down the road. *You're all responsible for Karen and Don and I'm going to enjoy killing you.* Tom looked at the faces of the villagers on his left and right. Their faces were frozen into masks of fear, determination and hate. He could smell fear as each did what they could to control it. All watched as three white men crept closer up the ditch on the village side of the road. *Get closer, you bastards. I'm going to nail your asses. You fuckers should have gotten out when you had the chance. Now you're going to fucking die.* Tom continued to wait with the igniter for the Claymore in his left hand and his M-16 in his right. The ones close to him could see his face, red with rage under his tan boonie hat. He heard the boom of David's rifle and the distant explosion of Hayes' Claymore. *Shit, it looks like I'm in the wrong place at the right time. Everybody else is getting the honor of blowing these bastards to hell. God damn it, it's not fair. I'm the one who's owed the payback. I wonder how Karen's doing. The old man said she would sleep and be well. But how long? Bosworth, you dumb son of a bitch, get your mind on here and now, and give some thought to staying alive. She's going to need you. The baby's going to need you. Get your head out of your ass and stay alive.* Tom forced himself to pull his mind back and concentrate his thoughts on the three men moving in the ditch.

Tom could almost hear the safeties of the villagers' rifles being slipped off as they watched the first of the men move into the range of the mine. The leader motioned to the tight jungle and started to step out of the ditch. "Shit," Tom whispered, pressing the lever on the clacker. "Too far away." The first and second men fell, while the third dove to the ground and tried to make himself as small as possible. Not that it helped when the villagers started raking the area with automatic fire. *Yeah, payback time,* he thought, holding up his hand to signal a cease fire.

The tall white man with long greasy hair pulled back in a headband looked down the ditch at the string of bodies. He yelled, "Somebody get that son of a bitch with the cannon." duPage barely got the words out when Washington's head exploded like a melon dropped from a skyscraper. *Shit!* he thought as he wiped the combination of brain, blood and bone from his face. *This shit wasn't supposed to go down like this.* duPage dove for cover into the low brush and tried to get a better idea of the village defenses.

Tom's people started to fire across the rutted highway. Their fire was a long way from being accurate; not that it mattered as the mercenaries were driven into the bush towards the village.

Eight fucking people caused all this. duPage crawled through the vines. *You should have listened to Jose. The fucker was right when he said he had a bad feeling about this place. Jerry, old son, you could have been in Laos by this time. Now you've got half your men gone and the rest being chewed to pieces. Jesus fucking Christ, I can't even call them back now. Why did I have to do it? Shit, I've got enough money to last the rest of my life. You did it for Anderson, didn't you? Those dead blue eyes reaching out got to you, didn't they? Now you've gotten everybody else killed.* duPage looked at his watch. *Ten after three. Where the fuck is that fucking Xuan with the support fire? That fat son of a bitch was supposed to be here by now.* duPage fired a three-round burst into the back of a villager who didn't hear him coming. *Man, you done fucked yourself. Boy, you best start going to church again if you get your ass out of here alive, 'cause God's going to own your ass.* He looked around to see some of his men close but scattered in a ragged line behind him. He used hand signals to spread them even more before they started to advance through the bush. Jerry duPage led off, taking point. *duPage, you're one dumb son of a bitch.*

Within a couple of minutes after Bill's Claymore went off, Sherlock caught a flash of movement on the left side of the trail. He brought his shoulder to the butt of the SAW and fired a short burst. His efforts were rewarded by a scream of pain and a cry for help. He lifted the M-60 off the ground and raked the treeline until the belt ran through. He pulled the weapon back into the pit and popped the chamber cover as his two assistants slapped in a fresh belt and poured water over the hot barrel. It took only a few seconds before he had the cooled, loaded black weapon pointed at the jungle again.

Chavez kneeled beside one of the two men cut down by Sherlock's murderous fire. "Sorry, Dansk, there's not a damned thing we can do for you right now." One of the men started putting field dressings on Dansk's front and back and tying them in place. "We'll get you and Striker out of here as soon as we can. How's Striker?" he asked, looking toward the other injured man. The man attending the wounded Caucasian looked back and shook his head. *God damn it. I told Jerry not to try this shit,* Jose thought, looking at the two men dying at his feet. *I wonder how many of the rest of us are going to end up like these poor bastards. If we survive this, I'm going to kick the living shit out of that son of a bitch. Fuck, we could have been miles away from here by now.* "Spread out and take cover," he yelled to the survivors standing around. "We've got to nail that son of a bitch with the '60. Aimed, concentrated fire. Don't just go blasting away. We ain't got the ammo to spare. The fucking general ought to be here with cover fire by now, so just stay alive and do your best." *Where the fuck is that fat fucking gook?* he thought, looking at his watch and then toward the clear blue sky through the hole in the canopy of leaves.

The bright, hot sun seemed to have stopped its western migration. No breeze stirred the acrid smell of smokeless powder, or the sharp ketone smell of fear from either side.

David was first to see and hear the small, black, fast, two-man observation helicopter with the machine gun mounted on its belly. From his perch high atop the tall kapok tree, he watched the muzzle flash and puffs of smoke as the chopper swayed from side to side, raking fire into the village. Segretti changed his position and started to bring the twenty pounds of precision rifle around. He aimed, compensating for the fast forward movement of his target. Before the sear released the firing pin, he was lifted by a bullet slamming into his pelvis from below. He shot went wild and he almost dropped the fifty caliber when he was hit. Letting the weapon dangle in its sling, he pulled the two fragmentation grenades from his pocket and pulled the pins. He dropped one on either side of the tree and listened to them bounce from limb to limb before exploding on the ground. David tried to regain a stable position as he ejected the spent case and chambered the last round in the magazine. He dropped the empty magazine and let it fall as he pulled out a loaded one and slapped it home in the belly of the weapon. He returned his attention to the small, deadly helicopter and the two occupants.

The old man didn't flinch as he picked his targets and fired well-aimed shots the way he was taught by

Don James thirty years ago. *This is for all the years of slavery,* he thought as a black man fell, never to rise again. *This is for my wife.* He caught a glimpse of another mercenary and fired. He watched and waited, knowing the mercenaries could only come close to entering the village. The one small trail leading through the heavy brush was where the old man had set the last Claymore with a trip wire. *Die, you bastard sons of whores,* he thought as he fired a 7.62 mm round into the back of one of the long-haired white mercenaries.

Segretti stabilized his position as best he could and drew a bead on the fast-approaching helicopter. He squeezed the trigger and watched the pilot as he was knocked backward and then bounced forward in the seat. He watched the fat man take the collective with his left hand and continue firing while the chopper started to buck and dive. David cycled the bolt and tried to bring the sights to bear on the erratic helicopter. He wavered when he lifted the heavy instrument of death. Taking a deep breath, he held it and raised the stock to his shoulder. Before he could squeeze the trigger, he saw the black bird of prey fly into the treetops with the belly gun still firing.

Tom motioned for his people to spread out more and stay put as he slipped back to a narrow trail paralleling the dirt road. He arrived in time to see the four men trip the old man's booby trap. The C-4 propelled balls tore the men to pieces and the old dream weaver stood and riddled the bodies with the rest of the clip in his AK-47. Tom smiled at the grinning, toothless old man and flashed him a thumbs up before he dove across the road. When he landed he saw one of duPage's men in the chest-high undergrowth. He didn't think – he fired and rolled, and came up ready to fire again if need be.

The men and women with Hayes moved through the jungle with the stealth of cats. With the few of the enemy they had found, they saw their poor aim has been more than compensated for by the automatic weapons. They caught sight of a man firing toward Sherlock and the M-60. The four villagers fired at once, killing the long-haired, Hispanic instantly. They failed to see the next man in line, who turned and emptied a full magazine from his M-16 into their chests. The two men and two women collapsed like wet rags in the rain of 5.56mm bullets. Bill Hayes stepped around from behind a tree when the man started to change magazines. "Hey you!" he yelled. The startled man looked up as Hayes fired. A surprised looked crossed his face as a small hole appeared in the center of his forehead before he fell back into the mess that had been the contents of his skull. Bill looked back and watched his remaining troops pause over the bodies only long enough to relieve them of extra ammo before moving on.

Sherlock continued to rake the area where the last incoming small arms fire originated. He now used only short bursts at probable target. The M-60 was hot enough for him to see the waves of heat shimmering in the air above the barrel. The big Marine pulled the weapon back from the firing slit, burning his hand in the process. He didn't have to tell his assistant to pour more of the tepid water over the weapon, he did it automatically. Jim listened to the brown water sizzle on the metal and turned his grim, powder-streaked face to his assistants, motioning them to the empty buckets. He wondered how long it would be before the heat softened the metal or the chamber was hot, enough to cook the rounds off prematurely. The hot still air held the smell of burnt powder in the pit. His throat was brick dry as he looked up through the haze of smoke to the clear blue sky. His first thought was that the sun had stopped moving, and he hazarded a quick glance at his watch. Three-twenty – the fight had been going on only a little more than a half hour. He wiped his face on his sleeve, pulled the muzzle of the MG from the bucket of water, shook it once, and returned to the sandbagged firing slit. *Damn, I wish there was some other way to cool this mother down,* he thought, sighting above the heat waves. *There's only one bucket of water left until that kid gets back, and it's almost boiling.* Jim looked at his remaining assistant and tried to give him a confident grin. The boy tried to return the smile, only to have his face drawn into a death mask, his eyes wide with fear. Sherlock looked back at the green curtain and fired another short burst at a puff of smoke.

With the ringing in his ears and the chatter of the

M-60, Jim Sherlock didn't hear or see the oncoming black helicopter. He had no idea which round hit first, the one in the M-60, the one in his shoulder blade, the one in his lower back, or the one that went into his assistant; not that it mattered to him as he rolled over to watch the helicopter fly into the trees before he passed out.

Tom staggered from the force of the barrage of .223 caliber bullets that stitched him across the right side of his chest around his previous injury. He stumbled back and emptied his M-16 into his assailant. "Jesus Christ," he coughed, "same fucking spot I got hit before." Tom rolled over in the weeds and vines and sat up. His left hand started to explore the injuries under his tan kevlar shirt. The first thing he felt was the slug puncturing his chest that was being held in place by a magazine in his bandoleer. The second was a gash in his pectoral muscle through his nipple. The third he found was the hole through the meat under his right shoulder next to his arm-pit, just missing the bone. *Not bad, it's just going to hurt like a bitch in a few minutes,* he thought as he pulled his bloody left hand from his shirt. *This shit ain't over by a long shot. Not enough of you bastards have died yet.* Tom dropped the empty magazine from his M-16 and then looked at the damaged one with the bullet sticking out from the pocket of his bandoleer. He dropped it on the ground beside the empty one. "Thanks, Buddha," he whispered, slamming a loaded clip home in his weapon. "Glad you were on the ball." Next, Tom walked over to the dead man and relieved him of the ammo he never had a chance to use. He continued his trek through the bush in the direction of more small arms fire. He had no idea who was doing the shooting; everyone was using the same mix of weapons, and he had no idea which side he would find first.

"Son of a fucking bitch!" duPage yelled, finding himself alone for the first time. He listened to the scattered firing in the direction of the village. *Son of a bitch. Ten fucking civilians caused all this shit. Un-fucking-believable.* Jerry duPage took advantage of as much cover as possible as he moved in the direction of the heaviest firing. The dirty, long-haired white man made about fifty steps before he felt the hot muzzle of a rifle touch the base of his skull.

The firing was as scattered as the combatants. There was no way a person could tell by the shots where the heaviest combat was. Now everything had been reduced to random firing by the unseen warriors. A voice yelled out of the jungle, "*Dung lai ben sung. Dung lai ben sung.*" The command was followed quickly in English by another voice. "Cease fire! Everybody, cease fire! It's over! Hold your fire and come out!"

Tom, like everyone else, was cautious making his way to the village clearing. He kept his rifle ready while he waited to see who had yelled. He watched duPage walk into the open, followed by the old man with an AK-47. Tom grinned through the pain in his chest and shoulder at the sight. The tall, long-haired, scraggly mercenary was being forced to march into the open. The bent, withered old man was walking almost on his tiptoes trying to keep the rifle touching duPage's brain stem.

"It's over!" duPage yelled again. "It's finished! Throw out your guns and come out!" The frail old man rammed the rifle barrel into duPage's head, hard enough to make him stagger forward. "God damn it! Everyone get the fuck out here before this old bastard blows my head off!"

duPage's men started to step into the clearing in ones and twos from almost every compass point. Tom stayed ready when he stepped from the cover of the thick curtain of leaves. He watched around the village as the surviving mercenaries stepped into the open with their hands on top of their heads. He, raised his rifle with his left hand when he saw the powerful Puerto Rican step out, still holding his weapon. Chavez slowly laid the M-16 on the ground and placed his hands on his head, one at a time. He walked toward duPage and the old man, while the rest of the surviving mercenaries did likewise. The mercenary force was quickly surrounded by the now victorious Viets. They were shoved, kicked, and rifle-butted into a bunch and forced to sit cross-legged while duPage, Chavez and the old man stood apart and watched.

Bill Hayes was half dragged, half carried out of the thick forest. From almost sixty yards away, Tom could see that the belly of his shirt was saturated with blood. Tom started across the village, then thought better of the idea when he saw people rushing forward with a bed. *Better go check on David while I'm over here,* Tom thought, turning away from the scene and walking toward the big kapok tree that had been David's nest.

The wounded, dead and dying from both sides were now being carried or dragged to the center of the village. The dead defenders were being laid in a neat row, as opposed to the growing pile of mercenary bodies being dumped inches from duPage's feet. Jerry duPage hung his head and whispered a name for each man added to the growing heap.

Tom stopped under the tall tree and yelled up, "David, you okay up there?"

"If I was, I'd be down by now," came the reply.

"I'll get some rope and some help, just hang in there," Tom yelled back as he and was hit with another fit of coughing. He spat out the blood and held his chest until the coughing stopped. Pulling his hand away, he looked at the fresh blood covering his fingers. *There's always some kind of trade off when you get lucky... or when someone's watching over you.* He added the afterthought walking towards the supplies. *Hell, by all rights I should be dead.* Tom laid his black rifle aside and picked up two coils of their 10 mm climbing rope. Walking back to the tree, he recruited three of the young villagers by holding up the line and pointing to David's tree. The young men nodded enthusiastically, took the ropes, and ran to the tree. By the time Tom arrived they were already up the tree, securing the lines around the injured man.

David laughed at the man who had taken his big .50 caliber and slung it across his back. The weapon was almost as long as the man was tall, and at least one fifth his weight. The kid got a puzzled looked on his face until one of his companions laughed and said something in Vietnamese that David didn't understand. The young man with the rifle grinned, shrugged his shoulders, and started scampering down the tree, threading the lines as he went.

Tom watched the men almost dance through the limbs as they climbed down like monkeys. Their hands and bare feet hardly touched any branch, and when they did it was only for a fraction of a second. The man without the rifle dropped the last ten feet. When he landed he slipped in a small pool of blood and his feet slid out from under him. He gave a quick laugh when he looked at his bloody hands and pants. He continued to smile, wiping his hands on his cotton shirt and handing Tom one of the lines, motioning him back. Tom could feel the line in his hand go taunt with David's weight. He slowly let the rope slip through his hand at the same rate as did the men across from him. The third man guided Segretti down through the branches, being careful of the bloody, injured hip. Tom could see the blood dripping down David's pant leg as he got closer. He moved to the side of the tree to help support Segretti when he touched down.

"I'm going to have to tell Sherlock his bulletproof clothing doesn't work worth a damn," David said almost nonchalantly when his feet touched the ground.

"He already knows if he's still alive. I saw them lifting him out of the pit a few minutes ago; he didn't look good. Now, let's get you untied and over with the rest of the wounded."

The pile of bodies in front of duPage continued to grow. So did the lines of wounded, and the lines of dead villagers. The Viets laid David on a cot next to Sherlock and Hayes while an old woman applied bandages as best she could. Tom was quickly stripped of his shirt and a pungent, yellow salve was plastered over his wounds. Next came a covering of some sort of aromatic lancealate leaves, followed by makeshift cotton bandages

While Tom's wounds were being tended, he watched the old man guarding duPage and Chavez. He kept the rifle barrel only inches from the back of the tall man's head. Tom could see the old man stiffen as two young women were carried out of the bush and laid in the line of the dead. The old man's eyes glassed over and tears started to roll down his leathery cheeks as he watched the women's arms being crossed gently across their bloody chests.

Chavez stood to the left of the growing pile of his dead men. *I knew we shouldn't have done this. I had that feeling that we were going to get our asses kicked, but Jerry wouldn't listen. Jesus, Jerry, what's going to happen now?* Jose watched as the two women were laid in the line, then his gaze shifted back to the old man. He watched the jaw tremble and the tears start rolling down and dropping into the dust from his brown, wrinkled cheeks. He watched as the old man started to slump from his shoulders down. The old dream weaver's eyes kept shifting from the two women back to duPage, his prisoner. Chavez watched the old man relax everything from his old, wisdom-filled eyes down – every muscle except one. The finger on the trigger moved a fraction of an inch, taking up the slack. Jose started to remove his hands from his head as the old man continued to apply pressure to the trigger. "No!" he yelled, diving for his friend as the hammer and sear parted.

duPage's head exploded in fireworks of bone, blood and brain. A large portion of the mess caught Chavez in the face as he grabbed the body of his friend before he could fall. He gently lowered Jerry duPage to the ground, not allowing him to become just one more body on the pile. Carefully, he moved his hand over the dead face and closed the empty brown eyes. "You didn't have to do that," he whispered in English, looking up at the old man with hate. "You didn't have to shoot him. It was all over. You didn't have to do that." Jose moved to where he could cradle the head of his friend in his lap. Looking up at the tired old man, tears filled his eyes and dripped on the body. "You didn't have to shoot him," Chavez said again as he started to cry.

The old man let the AK fall from his limp, bony hands. His eyes were blank as he walked around duPage and the pile of bodies. Slowly, putting one foot in front of the other, he moved to the young women who had been laid side by side – twins in death as well as in life. The old dream weaver collapsed to his knees and placed one hand on each girl's forehead. He bowed his head for a second, then brought it up to looked into the face of the blood-red sun. His wail of grief echoed for miles through the still air.

General Xuan used a limb as a makeshift crutch to

struggle through the dense underbrush to the river. Most of his cuts had stopped bleeding by the time he reached the river and found one of the long, thin, open-ended canoes. *Gone, all gone.* He dragged his fat body in and managing to release the hand-braided hemp rope. The cigar-shaped boat started to drift down the ten-yard-wide, clean river. *Nothing left for me here, or anywhere else in Vietnam.* Xuan's mind drifted in and out of consciousness the way the canoe drifted in and out of the shadows of the dying sun. *They can't know about me yet. I'm still the general. Air base... Air base on this river about twenty miles east of here. I can order them to fly me to Hong Kong.* The lengthening shadows closed over the river and the man whose fat hung over the gunwales. The river got wider and slower, and the clear highland water mixed with the brown runoff from lower streams. The overloaded canoe continued to drift.

It was dark when the general woke again. There was no light but the stars, and no sounds except for the loud buzzing of insects. He could smell the runoff sewage in the warm, brown water that soaked his torn shirt. *All these years wasted if I don't make it to Hong Kong. Where can I go now? Where's the air base? I should have been there by now. The river patrol station at the mouth of the river. If I can only get there. If I can only make it to the ocean.* He passed out again.

The tigress led her two cubs to drink from one of the tributaries of the Ben Hai river. She lifted her large, magnificent head and sniffed the air before nosing the kittens down to the water's edge. Something in the air caught her attention and she raised her head again. Her long pink tongue flicked out and licked her nose and whiskers. Her ears perked up when she heard something bouncing into the limbs overhanging the water. She smelled the intruder and licked her lips at the smell of blood in the air. The magnificent cat nosed her cubs away from the water before she ambled downstream alone, following the scent.

The fat general raised his head enough to see the lights of the air base illuminating the night a few hundred yards down river. *I've made it!* He threw both arms over the sides and started to paddle. *By dawn I'll be away from here and a rich man. I'm safe. I can be there in less than an hour, and in Hong Kong in time for breakfast.* He continued to flail his fat arms in the water, opening a number of his cuts. The blood flowed freely and the smell was carried on the light breeze.

Xuan didn't see the black shadow moving across the downed tree in the water ahead. He did hear the worried cries of the two cubs and the loud purring of their mother as the canoe slid under the long-dead tree in the water.

Chapter Twenty-eight

Tom was the first to hear the two-and-a-half-ton truck through the din of the cries of pain and pleas for help in the village triage. He swung his legs over the side of the rope and bamboo cot and forced himself to stand. The adrenaline of the firefight was long gone, and he had to make a conscious effort to place one unsteady foot in front of the other. Every footfall sent bolts of pain through his right side as he half ran, half staggered toward the two dead palms thirty yards away. He reached out his left arm and caught the old palm before he fell. The sun-warmed, rough growth rings scratched his bare chest but he still hugged it for support.

"I wonder how many have survived?" Frank commented, steering the deuce and a half around the body of one of duPage's men lying in the road. "It must be over. I don't hear any shooting." Downshifting to second, the transmission grinded into gear and the motor roared through the muffler. *I wonder if the boys made it. At least they had a better chance than the rest of the village. They definitely had a better chance than Don. None of them would hesitate to go in harm's...* Frank's thoughts were interrupted by Mi Ling, and he missed her first sentence.

"I believe most of the people would believe it was worthwhile to die for freedom. At least the dead are free now, asleep with Buddha. I wonder if we won?" Mi Ling's thoughts flew back through the years to the last time she, Frank and Don had fought together for the freedom of Cam An. *At least this time my husband is safe. I couldn't bear to lose him again. What about the others? How can I tell any of the women that their men are dead. No cause is worth losing your mate. I should have insisted on cancelling the trip when we found out about the danger. I'll never forgive myself if any of them are dead. First Don and now the others. Was getting revenge against Vinh worth all this?* "There's Tom!" she shouted when they drove into the clearing. "He's hurt but at least he's alive!"

Frank slowed the truck to a crawl before they passed through the gateposts. Tom stepped onto the running board and held on with his left hand. He was covered with the sweat of exhaustion and the dust that now filled the air from the moving people.

He yelled into the cab, his voice excited, but sounding very tired and old. "Go back and get that French doctor and all the help he's got!" Mi Ling winced as he yelled in her ear, "We've got a hell of a lot of wounded and we're going to need all the help we can get!"

Frank shifted to neutral and allowed the truck to roll to a stop beside their command tent. Turning off the engine, he replied in a stern, calm, clear voice – the voice of command. "Give me a report, Tom. We've got plenty of time. We can get medevac out of Quang Tri."

Tom stepped off the truck as Mi Ling got out, followed by Frank. He sat on the running board and leaned his head back against the olive green door. Mi Ling placed her soft hand on his good shoulder and Tom took a deep breath before starting. "We've got a lot of the villagers killed or wounded, along with a bunch of duPage's men. Jim and Bill are hit real bad. David caught one in the ass and I've got a couple of flesh wounds. They're still bringing people out of the bush." Tom had calmed down enough so he could report the damage in a calm, quiet, clear voice. "What's this about medevac?" he asked, his voice barely audible this time.

"Mi Ling, get on the radio and get some medical support in here while I explain what's gone on." Mi Ling moved toward the tent as Frank sat beside Tom, lit a cigarette, and placed it between Tom's lips. He lit another for himself and started to explain the events of the past few hours. The French doctor had alerted the hospital in Quang Tri, the hospital had alerted the local government, the government had alerted the ambassador, and the ambassador had alerted the military. Frank went on to explain the reports he gave to the military and the ambassador about General Xuan and Colonel Ngu, and duPage and his men.

It had taken only a few minutes for Mi Ling to get the message off to the military command in Quang Tri. She returned to Frank and the barely conscious Tom. "It's done, they're on their way. They'll be here in less than an hour. Now, let's get you lying down and see what we can do to help."

Frank helped Tom stand and supported him back to the center of the village, back to the lines and pile of dead. The wounded were being cared for the best the people could. One of the first things Mi Ling noticed was the old man. He was on his knees between two bodies with an arm stretched across each. His forehead rested in the dust while his back and shoulders showed his sobs. While Frank helped Tom back to the makeshift bed, Mi Ling walked over, knelt beside the old dream weaver, wrapped her arm around his shuddering shoulders.

The smell of carnage and the sound of the medevac helicopters lifting off into the clear blue sky and propelled Mi Ling back to the time when she watched Frank and Don leave. She looked at Frank, put her arm around his waist, and held him tightly to her side. *At least not this time,* she thought, trying to squeeze closer under Frank's arm. She and Frank stood together, watching the formation of choppers disappear from view beyond the treetops.

Quang Tri Hospital, five days later.
"I'm very glad you all survived," Ambassador Phoung said, looking from one face to another. "My government owes you a debt of gratitude for doing what we were unable to – damage the opium trade. You see, the military is still very much in control of the countryside, while we politicians have little power outside the cities. About all we can give you is our undying thanks and a handful of medals, and believe me we have plenty of both."

"What about the mercenary survivors from the battle?" Sherlock asked, scratching under the edge of his upper body cast. "What will happen to them?"

"That will be up to the courts in this country," Phoung replied. "It is my understanding your government wants them back, but it's up to my government whether they arrive alive or dead. I'm not sure either side cares one way or the other." The ambassador in the light silk suit clasped his hands behind his back and started pacing the small ward area. He seemed unsure of what and how he should continue. "Both the military and civilian authorities want to interrogate these people to see if they know of more units like themselves, and who is in charge."

"What about the people of Cam An and the other villages around the opium fields?" Bill asked while Janet fluffed his pillows, then sat on the bed beside him.

"The other hamlets are to be relocated to Cam An and the opium fields destroyed, all except for the first two. I believe I will let Mr. Mason explain about those."

"The people in the State department found a German pharmaceutical company to buy the raw opium. The villagers sell it to the government, and the government sells it to the Germans for hard currency. Everybody makes out," the assistant director of the CIA answered, smiling at the group.

"What about our original mission to bring out the remains of MIAs?" Kim asked as she attempted to snuggle closer on Sherlock's bed. "None of us will be able to do anything for a number of weeks, and this was what we were supposed to do in the first place. Are we going to stay around here until we can go back to work?"

"Frank and I are going to be staying," Mi Ling answered quietly. "We will continue with what we started. Don't worry dear, we'll be home in a few months. There will be plenty of people to help in the new Cam An. Your jobs are over now and you deserve some rest. We'll get it done. What about the rest of you? Are you starting to make any plans for when you're well?"

"I think we'll have plenty of time to decide something before we get up and moving again," Segretti replied. "For one thing, I plan to make sure that French mission hospital gets well-stocked and funded. You never know when we're going to need it again. After all, they are Catholic. You know something, I've always heard of people having their ass in a sling," he said with a grin, "but I never thought it could happen to me. You know, it's damned uncomfortable!" His comment brought a laugh to the rest of the team.

"Yeah, but if it hadn't been for you and that big gun of yours we'd be in worse shape." Tom said as he sat on Bill's bed beside Janet. "It's packed up and waiting until we go home. It's even cleaned and oiled."

"Captain Trahn, you haven't said much about your promotion and new assignment," the ambassador addressed Mihn, who was sitting in a wheel chair.

"I have been trying to follow the conversation in English," Mihn said. He then switched to Vietnamese while Mi Ling translated. "I did my job the best I could; I am but a soldier. I have learned a lot about honor from all of you, and now call you friends. Cam An will now be my home, and I am sure they wish all of you to think of it as your home also. You risked your lives to help when you knew you would receive nothing in return. Cam An will never forget you."

"I haven't heard him say that much at one time in the three weeks we've been here," Hayes said with a smile at the new captain. "Thank you."

A white-uniformed nurse eased through one of the swinging doors of the ward, and with her forefinger motioned for Tom to follow into the hall.

Tom crossed the hall and walked into the bright, sun-lit, private hospital room that was filled with the soft scent of local flowers. He found Karen awake and sitting up. Her deep blue eyes were clear, but her tanned skin now had a pallor a few shades darker than her long blond hair.

"Tom," she almost yelled, stretching her arms straight and almost disconnecting her I.V. tubes in the process. "Tell me what happened!" She looked down at herself in the hospital bed. "What happened to me? How long have I been here?"

"Easy, little mother," Tom replied, slipping between her outstretched arms. "It's all over and we're going home soon."

"Mother? Over? Home? Where are we? The last thing I remember is Janet having to go the bathroom."

"We'll explain everything later," Tom crooned as he held his wife tightly. "It's all over. We took a beating but won. The only one of us who was killed was Don – he got it the night you were raped."

"Raped? So that's what happened and what those dreams were all about? Tom, they were terrible. Am I all right? I mean, will you ever want to..."

"Yes, dear, you're all right, and just a bit over two months pregnant is all. It must have happened on one of those wild nights in South Carolina. And yes, I will, just as soon as the doctor gives the okay and we get out of here." Tom kissed his wife gently then reached to the bedside table. He picked up the small, heavy, gold statue of Buddha, with the 7.62 mm bullet still half buried in its stomach. The metal felt warm to his touch. "Thank you," he whispered as he caressed the chest of the god with a new reverence, then laid it on the pillow beside Karen. "Honey, you rest now. I'm going to tell the others. I'll be back in a few minutes and we can all explain what's gone on."

"Tom," Karen whispered as he reached the door and turned back, "I love you."

"I love you too. Now rest," he replied, letting the door close softly behind him.

Tom returned to the ward where the rest of the team was listening to Ted Mason explain what had gone on behind the scenes the past few days. "As soon as you are all healthy enough, the President's going to have you over for dinner," Ted Mason said with the booming voice of a senior NCO, the voice that remained after over ten years of civilian life. "I'm sure you are aware that the particulars of what has gone on on this trip are classified, and that you can't say anything to anybody, except maybe your grandchildren. But you do get a lot of credit for bringing home seventy-five Americans that weren't on the MIA lists. It's a real shame Frank and Mi Ling can't be there for the honors you folks are going to get," the assistant director of the CIA said, waving his cigar for emphasis.

"What about Don?" Karen asked.

"He was buried with full military honors in San Antonio. The Senate has elected to have Caroline fill out his term. I think she'll do a good job."

"How about the rest of us?" Kim asked. "What happens now?"

"Well, as far as I'm concerned, you still belong to the CIA and me. The Army and Marine Corps are going to have to fight like hell to get you two back, but that's up to you. Mr. Segretti. Well, son, you're free to do as you please, but you all make a good team. Think about it. I'm sure we can find a use for your talents again sometime."

"I'm going to have to get back to my people, but needless to say, I'll stay in touch with this bunch," David replied from his wheelchair.

"Hey, look, I've got to go. The ambassador wants to meet with me and some others about this hornet's nest you folks stirred up. Don't worry, I'll be back soon to visit," Mason said as he walked to the door.

"Sorry, sir, you're wrong," David said. "That's a nest of worms or a can of hornets, a friend of ours once told us," Segretti said, grinning from ear to ear toward Mihn.

The director of the CIA looked puzzled as the team started laughing for the first time since they got together in the hospital. Mason shook his head and walked out, letting the door swing closed behind him.

THE END

About The Author

Ray Davies is a Vietnam veteran who lives in Iowa City, Iowa, and has been a part of the University of Iowa medical research staff for twenty years. His first book, A SONG FOR MARTY was started after the death of his son in 1989. Mr. Davies has written numerous magazine pieces dealing with grief, along with scientific articles in peer review journals. His hobbies include reading, scuba diving, target shooting, and many other outdoor interests.

WATCH FOR THESE NEW COMMONWEALTH BOOKS

JUNE 1995	ISBN #	U.S.	Can.
☐ **POWER DEFICIT,** Frank Kelly	1-896329-09-8	$5.95	$7.95
☐ **THE BLOODY RENEGADE OF A'RADI,** Betty B. Simmons	1-896329-60-8	$6.95	$8.95
☐ **THE LONG WAY HOME,** Ray Davies	1-896329-20-9	$5.95	$7.95
☐ **FINGERS OF THE BLACK HAND,** F. Joseph Rosati	1-896329-46-2	$5.95	$7.95
☐ **P.O.W.,** Gil Hash	1-896329-01-2	$4.95	$6.95
JULY 1995			
☐ **THE WIRE FENCE,** Henry A. Craig	1-896329-18-7	$4.95	$6.95
☐ **BLACK ALERT,** Julian Hudson	1-896329-03-9	$6.95	$8.95
☐ **SACRIFICING INDEPENDENCE,** Adrian Golding	1-896329-36-6	$5.95	$7.95
☐ **THE COUNTESS,** Harry H. Sullivan	1-896329-68-3	$5.95	$7.95
☐ **GOODBYE TOMORROW,** Gryzelda Niziol-Lachocki	1-896329-36-6	$4.95	$6.95
☐ **FIONA,** Jacqueline Baity	1-896329-04-7	$4.95	$6.95
☐ **MEDICAL DOMAIN,** Michelle Burmeister	1-896329-14-4	$4.95	$6.95
☐ **THE RAINBOW,** Herbert A. Gold	1-896329-34-9	$4.95	$6.95
☐ **THE BLACK CHAMBER,** William G. Hyland, Jr.	1-896329-07-1	$4.95	$6.95

Available at your local bookstore or use this page to order.

Send to: COMMONWEALTH PUBLICATIONS
9764 - 45 Avenue
Edmonton, Alberta, CANADA T6E 5C5

Please send me the items I have checked above. I am enclosing $_____ (please add $2.50 per book to cover postage and handling). Send check or money order, no cash or C.O.D.'s, please.

Mr./Mrs./Ms._____
Address_____
City/State_____ Zip_____

Please allow four to six weeks for delivery.
Prices and availability subject to change without notice.

Not all the 2261 servicemen listed as missing in action are missing. Some are deserters, now working as mercenaries for the drug lords of some of the best opium plantations in the world. What happens when a group of people invade their domain looking for the bodies of men known to be left behind? You can bet these men have no intention of letting their presence be known to the world. Frank Wilson and the others must not only battle the mercenaries, but also members of the Vietnamese army high command. What happens to the expatriated Americans who decide they've been away long enough? There is a battle for more than life, some must take...

The Long Way Home

by
Ray Davies

Available at your local bookstore or use this page to order.

❑ 1-896329-20-9 – THE LONG WAY HOME –
$5.95 U.S./$7.95 in Canada

Send to: COMMONWEALTH PUBLICATIONS
9764 - 45th Avenue
Edmonton, Alberta, CANADA T6E 5C5

Please send me the items I have checked above. I am enclosing $_____ (please add $2.50 to cover postage and handling). Send check or money order, no cash or C.O.D.'s, please.

Mr./Mrs./Ms._____

Address_____

City/State_____ Zip_____

Please allow four to six weeks for delivery.
Prices and availability subject to change without notice.